3—

MADAME BOVARY

Madame Bovary

by Gustave Flaubert

IN A NEW TRANSLATION
by JOAN CHARLES

ILLUSTRATED BY BEN STAHL

HOLT, RINEHART & WINSTON

New York · Chicago · San Francisco

To

MARIE-ANTOINE-JULES SÉNARD

MEMBER OF THE BAR OF PARIS
EX-PRESIDENT OF THE NATIONAL ASSEMBLY
AND FORMER MINISTER OF THE INTERIOR

Dear and illustrious friend:
Permit me to inscribe your name at the beginning of this book and above its dedication; for it is to you, above all, that I owe its publication. Accept here, then, the respectful acknowledgement of my gratitude which, great though it may be, will never attain to the height of your eloquence and your devotion.

GUSTAVE FLAUBERT

Paris, April 12th, 1857

Robert W. Arnold '16

Gustave Flaubert 1821-1880

PART ONE

𝒲ᴇ were in study hall when the
Headmaster entered, followed by a "new boy"
dressed in ordinary clothes and by a classmate who was
carrying a large desk. Those who were asleep woke up, and everyone stood up as if taken unawares while at work.

The Headmaster made us a sign to be seated; then, turning toward the master in charge of study hall:

"Monsieur Roger," he said in a low tone, "here is a student whom
I am putting in your charge. He is entering the fifth form. If his
work and his conduct warrant it, he will be promoted to the upper
forms, as befits his age."

Standing in the corner behind the door, so far back that one could
scarcely see him, the new boy was a country lad of about fifteen,
and taller than any one of us. His hair was cut straight across his
forehead like a village chorister's, his manner ingenuous and highly
embarrassed. Although he was not broad in the shoulders, his suit
coat of green cloth with black buttons must have been uncomfortable for him around the armholes, and exposed, below the edges of
the cuffs, reddened wrists accustomed to being bare. His legs, in blue
stockings, emerged from yellowish breeches pulled up very tight by
his braces. He wore heavy shoes, badly polished and ornamented
with nails.

Recitations began. He listened to them with all his ears, attentive
as if to a sermon, not even venturing to cross his legs or to lean on
his elbow; and when the bell rang at two o'clock the study master
was obliged to call his attention to it, to get him to take his place
with us in line.

It was our habit, upon entering a classroom, to throw down our
caps in order to leave our hands more free; the thing to do was,
from the doorsill, to hurl them under the bench in such a way that

3

they struck the wall, stirring up a great quantity of dust; that was the *fashion*.

But, whether because he did not notice this maneuver or because he did not dare perform it, after the prayer was finished the new boy still held his cap upon his knees. It was one of those head coverings of a composite nature in which may be found elements of the woolen cap, the chapska, the round hat, the otter-fur cap and the cotton bonnet, one of those sorry objects, in short, whose mute ugliness has a certain depth of expression, like the face of an imbecile. Ovoid and stiffened with whalebones, it began with three circular sausage-rolls; then, separated by a red band, alternate lozenges of velvet and rabbit fur; there followed a kind of sack which ended in a pasteboard polygon covered with a complicated design in braid, from which hung, at the end of a long and inadequate cord, a small gold thread ornament like a tassel. It was new; the visor gleamed.

"Stand up," the professor said.

He stood; his cap fell. The whole class burst out laughing.

He stooped to pick it up. The boy next to him pushed him with his elbow, causing him to drop it again; he picked it up once more.

"You had better extricate yourself from your cap," said the professor, who was a man of wit.

There was a shout of laughter from the students which so abashed the poor boy that he did not know whether he should hold his cap in his hand, leave it on the floor or put it on his head. He sat down again and placed it upon his knees.

"Stand up," the professor said, "and tell me your name."

The new boy, in a faltering voice, pronounced an unintelligible name. "Repeat it!"

The same faltering syllables were heard, overridden by hoots from the class.

"Louder!" the master shouted. "Louder!"

The new boy, achieving a supreme resolution, then opened an inordinately large mouth and bawled at the top of his lungs, as if calling someone, the word *"Charbovari."*

There was an uproar which broke out upon the instant, rose in crescendo, with piercing shrieks (we were shouting, howling, stamping, repeating: *Charbovari! Charbovari!*), then sank away into isolated notes, quieting with great difficulty, and suddenly swelling out again from time to time along the line of a bench where some stifled

4

giggle still spurted up here and there like a carelessly extinguished firecracker.

However, under the rain of threatened extra tasks, order was gradually restored to the classroom, and the professor, having succeeded in grasping the name of Charles Bovary, having had it dictated, spelled and reread, abruptly ordered the poor devil to go and sit on the dunce stool at the foot of the rostrum. He started to move, but hesitated.

"What are you looking for?" the professor asked.

"My cap . . ." the new boy said timidly, casting uneasy glances about him.

"Five hundred lines for the whole class!" exclaimed in a furious voice, put a stop, like the *Quos Ego,* to a fresh outbreak. "Be still, now!" the professor added and, patting his forehead with the handkerchief he had just taken from his mortarboard: "As for you, new boy, you're to write the verb *ridiculus sum* for me, twenty times."

Then, in a gentler tone:

"There, you'll find your cap. It hasn't been stolen."

Everyone was restored to calm. Heads bent above books, and the new boy remained for two hours in an exemplary position, although from time to time a random spitball, launched from a pen nib, came to splatter his face. He wiped it away with his hand and continued to sit motionless, his eyes lowered.

That evening in study hall he took his sleeve guards from his desk, put his small effects in order and carefully ruled his paper. We saw him working conscientiously, looking up every word in the dictionary and taking infinite pains. Thanks, no doubt, to the good will he evidenced, he was not forced to go back to a lower form; for although he had a passable knowledge of the rules, he had not the least elegance of style. It was the parish priest in his village who had started him in Latin, his parents having put off sending him away to school as long as possible, for financial reasons.

His father, Monsieur Charles-Denis-Bartholomé Bovary, a former assistant surgeon-major compromised in 1812, in a matter of conscription, and forced to leave the service, had then profited by his personal attributes to the extent of grasping on the fly a sixty-thousand-franc dowry offered in the form of a hosier's daughter who had fallen in love with his appearance. A handsome man, a braggart, jingling his spurs loudly, wearing sideburns which grew down to join his mustache, his fingers always laden with rings, and dressed in gaudy colors, he had the look of a gallant with the easy friendliness of a traveling salesman. Once married, he lived for two or three years on his wife's fortune, dining well, rising late, smoking great porcelain pipes, never coming home in the evening until after the theater, and frequenting cafés. The father-in-law died and left very little; he was outraged by this, set himself up as a textile manufacturer, lost some money at it, then retired to the country where he tried to making a living farming. But as he knew no more about cultivation than about fabrics, as he rode his horses rather than putting them to the plow, drank his cider by the bottle rather than selling it, ate the finest fowls from his poultry yard and greased his hunting boots with the bacon from his hogs, he was not slow to realize that it would be better to give up all speculation.

Having an average income of two hundred francs a year, therefore, he found for rent in the borderland between Caux and Picardy a sort of dwelling, half farm, half country seat; and, disillusioned, consumed with regrets, accusing heaven, jealous of all men, he went into retirement at the age of forty-five, disgusted with humanity, or so he said, and determined to live in peace.

His wife had once been mad about him; she had loved him with a thousand servile gestures which had alienated him from her even further. Formerly a gay woman, expansive and wholly affectionate, she had become, in growing older (like a wine gone flat and turned to vinegar), difficult in temper, irritable, nervous. She had suffered so much, at first without complaint, when she saw him chasing after all the village wenches, and coming home to her every evening from a score of low haunts, surfeited and stinking of drink! Then pride had rebelled. She had become silent, swallowing her rage in a mute stoicism which she preserved to her death. She was constantly in action, attending to his affairs. She went to lawyers, to the president, remembered the expiration dates of notes, secured extensions; and, at home, ironed, sewed, washed, supervised the laborers, settled their accounts while Monsieur, without troubling himself over anything, forever immersed in a sullen drowsiness from which he emerged only to make disagreeable remarks to her, remained in the chimney corner, smoking and spitting into the ashes.

When she had a child, he had to be put out to nurse. Returned home, the youngster was spoiled like a prince. The mother fed him on sweets; his father let him run about without shoes and, as a philosophical gesture, even said that he could just as well go naked, like

6

animal children. In opposition to maternal tendencies, he had formed a certain virile ideal of childhood to which he tried to shape his son, wanting him to be brought up ruggedly, in the Spartan manner, to develop a strong constitution. He sent him to sleep in an unheated room, taught him to swallow great drafts of rum and to insult processions. But, peaceful by nature, the boy responded poorly to his father's efforts. His mother had him always at her heels; she cut out cardboard figures for him, told him stories, indulged in endless monologues with him, full of a melancholy gaiety and playful chatter. In the solitary life she led, she transferred to the child all her lost frustrated ambitions. She dreamed of high positions, she saw him already grown, handsome, intelligent, established in the Department of Highways and Bridges or in the magistracy. She taught him to read, and even to sing two or three little ballads, accompanied by an old piano she had. But to all this Monsieur Bovary, little interested in literary matters, said that it was *not worth the trouble!* Would they ever have the money to put him through government school, buy him an office or a business? Besides, with *cheek, a man always gets along in the world.* Madame Bovary bit her lips, and the boy roamed the village at will.

He followed the laborers about and chased crows, flinging clods of earth at them as they flew away. He ate mulberries along the ditches and drove turkeys with a switch, pitched hay at harvest time, wandered about the woods, played hopscotch in the church porch on rainy days and, on holy days, begged the beadle to let him ring the bells in order to hang all the weight of his body on the great rope and feel himself carried off the ground by it.

So he grew like an oak tree. He developed strong hands, a fine color.

When he was twelve his mother contrived to have his schooling started. The parish priest was put in charge of it. But the lessons were so short and so ill conducted that they could be of but little use. They were given in spare moments, hastily, standing in the sacristy between a baptism and a funeral; the rain would come to interrupt them, or a passing acquaintance. Besides, he was always pleased with him, even saying that the "young man" had an excellent memory.

Charles could not leave it at that: Madame was vehement. Ashamed, or, rather, wearied, Monsieur yielded without resistance, and they waited another year for the boy to have made his first Communion.

A further six months passed; and, the following year, Charles was finally sent to the boys' school in Rouen, where his father himself took him, toward the end of October, at the time of the Saint-Romain fair.

Through application he kept always about the middle of the class; once he even took first prize in natural history. But at the end of his third year his parents took him out of school to have him study medicine, convinced that he would be able to go on alone to his bachelor's degree.

His mother chose a room for him, on the fourth floor in the Eau-de-Robec, in the home of a dyer she knew. She made arrangements for his board, bought furniture—a table and two chairs—had an old cherry-wood bed sent on from home, and bought besides a small iron stove with a supply of wood to keep her poor child warm. Then she left, at the end of a week, with a thousand injunctions to behave himself properly, now that he was about to be abandoned to his own devices.

The list of courses, which he read on the bulletin board, had a stupefying effect upon him; courses in anatomy, pathology, physiology, pharmacy, chemistry, botany, and clinical medicine, and therapeutics, not to mention hygiene and materia medica, all names whose etymology was unfamiliar to him and which were like so many doors opening into sanctuaries full of an august gloom.

He understood nothing; it was in vain that he listened, he did not grasp anything. Still, he worked, he had bound notebooks. He attended every course, he did not miss a single class. He accomplished his small daily chore in the manner of a riding-school horse which goes through its paces with bandaged eyes, ignorant of the labor it grinds out.

To spare him expense, his mother sent him each week, by post, a piece of roast veal upon which he lunched when he had returned from his morning at the hospital, tramping all the way on foot. Afterwards he had to hurry to lessons, to the amphitheater, to the clinic, and back to his room through all those streets. In the evening, after a meager dinner with his landlord, he returned to his room and set to work again in his damp clothes which steamed on his body before the glowing stove.

On fine summer evenings, at the hour when the warm streets are

8

deserted, when servants play at shuttlecock on the doorsteps, he would open his window and lean on his elbows there. The river, which makes a sort of small ignoble Venice of this quarter of Rouen, flowed past beneath him, yellow, violet or blue between its bridges and gratings. Laborers, kneeling on the bank, washed their arms in the water. On poles rising above warehouse roofs, hanks of cotton were drying in the breeze. Opposite, beyond the roofs, the wide pure sky stretched, with a red sun setting. How good it must be at home! What coolness under the beech trees! And he widened his nostrils to breathe in the good country fragrance that could not reach this far.

He grew thin, his body lengthened, and his face took on a sort of melancholy expression that made him almost interesting.

Naturally, out of indifference, he came to the point of ridding himself of all the resolutions he had made. Once he missed a clinic, the next day his class, and little by little, savoring his idleness, gave up his courses altogether.

He fell into the habit of going to the tavern, and developed a passion for dominos. To shut himself up every evening in a dirty bar room, there to play on marble-topped tables with small bits of sheep-bone decorated with black spots, seemed a marvelous gesture of freedom to him, one which raised him in his own estimation. It was like an initiation into the world, the introduction to forbidden pleasures; and, entering, he laid his hand upon the doorknob with an almost sensual delight. Then many things repressed within him expanded; he memorized couplets which he sang to the company, became enthusiastic over Béranger, learned to make punch and at last experienced love.

Thanks to these preparatory exercises he made a complete failure of his medical examinations. They were waiting for him at home, that very evening, to celebrate his success!

He set out on foot and stopped on the outskirts of the village, where he sent word to his mother to come, and told her everything. She made excuses for him, throwing the blame for his failure upon the injustice of the examiners, and fortified him somewhat by taking it upon herself to arrange matters.

It was only five years later that Monsieur Bovary learned the truth; it was an old story, he accepted it, being unable, in any case, to imagine that any son of his could be a fool.

So Charles returned to work and studied uninterruptedly the subjects for his examination, all the questions of which he learned by heart in advance. He passed with a reasonably good grade. What a splendid day for his mother! She gave a great dinner party.

Where should he go to practice? To Tostes. There was only one elderly physician there. Madame Bovary had been awaiting his death for a long time, and the poor fellow had not yet taken this final step when Charles was installed across the street as his successor.

But having brought up her son, having made him study medicine and discovered Tostes for his practice was not all; he must have a wife. She found him one: the widow of a bailiff from Dieppe, who was forty-five years old and had an income of twelve hundred livres.

Although she was ugly, thin as a lath and pimpled like an adolescent, Madame Dubuc certainly did not lack suitors among whom to choose. To achieve her aim, Bovary's mother was obliged to vanquish them all, and she very skilfully foiled even the machinations of a butcher who had the support of the priests.

Charles had thought of marriage as an avenue to a better position, imagining that he would be freer and would have the disposition of his person and his money. But his wife was the master; in public he must say this, not say that, fast every Friday, dress as she saw fit, harass patients who failed to pay, at her order. She opened his letters, spied upon his activities, and listened through the wall to the consultations he gave in his office, when there were women there.

She had to have her chocolate every morning, and endless attentions. She complained incessantly of her nerves, her chest, her various ailments. The sound of footsteps was painful to her; if he went away, solitude became intolerable to her; if he came back, it was undoubtedly to watch her die. In the evening when Charles came home she would thrust her long thin arms out from under the sheets, wind them around his neck and, having made him sit down on the edge of the bed, begin to tell him her troubles: he was neglecting her, he loved someone else! She had been told very plainly that she would be unhappy; and she would end by asking him for a tonic and a little more love.

2

ONE night at eleven o'clock they
were aroused by the sound of a horse stopping
just in front of the door. The maid opened the attic
window and had a lengthy discussion with a man who stood below
in the street. He had come in search of the doctor; he had a letter.
Nastasie went shivering down the stairs and opened the lock and
the bolts, one by one. The man left his horse and, following the maid,
entered the room abruptly just behind her. He took from inside his
gray-tufted woolen cap a letter wrapped in a scrap of cloth and
handed it delicately to Charles, who propped himself up on his elbow
to read it. Nastasie, standing near the bed, held the lamp. Madame,
out of modesty, remained with her face to the wall and presented
her back.

This letter, sealed with a bit of blue wax, begged Monsieur Bovary
to come at once to the Les Bertaux farm to set a broken leg. It is
eighteen miles across country from Tostes to Les Bertaux, by way
of Longueville and Saint-Victor. The night was black. Madame
Bovary feared some accident to her husband. So it was decided that
the groom would go on ahead. Charles would set out three hours
later, at moonrise. A boy would be sent to meet him, to show him
the way to the farm and open the gates before him.

At four o'clock in the morning Charles, well muffled in his coat,
started for Les Bertaux. Still drowsy with the warmth of sleep, he
let himself be lulled by his mount's placid trot. When it stopped of
its own accord at one of those holes surrounded by thorn bushes
which are dug at the sides of trails, Charles, waking with a start,
would speedily recall the broken leg and try to recollect all that he
knew about fractures. The rain was no longer falling: day was beginning to break and, on the branches of leafless apple trees, birds
perched motionless, ruffling their little feathers against the cold

11

morning wind. The flat countryside stretched out as far as the eye could reach, and, at rare intervals, clumps of trees about farmhouses made dark purple stains on that vast gray surface which blended at the horizon into the bleak tones of the sky. Charles opened his eyes from time to time; then, his spirit wearying and sleep returning of itself, he soon lapsed into a sort of half-consciousness in which, his recent sensations intermingling with memory, he saw himself double, at once a student and a married man, lying in his bed as he had been doing shortly before and crossing an operating room as in the past. The warm odor of poultices blended in his mind with the fresh scent of dew; he heard the iron bed-curtain rings slide on their rods and the sound of his wife sleeping . . . As he was passing through Vassonville he caught sight of a young boy sitting on the grass at the edge of a ditch.

"Are you the doctor?" the child asked. And, at Charles' reply, he took his wooden shoes in his hands and began to run ahead of him.

The physician, riding along, came to the conclusion from his guide's chatter that Monsieur Rouault must be a farmer in very easy circumstances. He had broken his leg the previous evening, returning from a Twelfth-night celebration at a neighbor's. His wife had died two years before. He had only his daughter with him to help him keep house.

The ruts were becoming deeper. They were nearing Les Bertaux. The youngster, slipping through a gap in the hedge, disappeared, then reappeared at the end of a barnyard to open the gate. The horse slipped on the wet grass; Charles lowered his head to pass beneath the branches. The watchdogs in the kennel barked and pulled at their chains. As he entered Les Bertaux his horse took fright and shied violently.

It was a well-kept farm. In the stables, through open doors, one could see sturdy work horses eating placidly from new mangers. Along the side of the buildings stretched a large dung-heap with steam rising from it, and upon it, among the hens and turkeys, five or six peacocks, a luxury in the farmyards of Caux, were foraging. The sheepfold was long, the barn high, with walls smooth as the palm of a hand. Under the shed were two great wagons and four plows, with their whips, their collars, their whole harness, its blue wool linings filmed over with the fine dust that sifted down from the grain lofts. The yard sloped up, planted with symmetrically placed trees, and the cheerful cackling of a flock of geese echoed up from the side of the pond.

A young woman in a blue merino dress ornamented with three flounces came to the threshold of the house to receive Monsieur Bovary, whom she ushered into the kitchen where a great fire was roaring. The farmhands' breakfast was bubbling over it in small pots of various sizes. Some damp clothes were drying inside the hearth. The poker, the tongs and the nose of the bellows, all of immense proportions, shone as if made of polished steel, while along the walls hung a plentiful array of cooking utensils in which were unevenly reflected the bright flame from the hearth and the first rays of the sun coming in at the window.

Charles went up to the first floor to see the patient. He found him in bed, sweating under his covers and having thrown off his nightcap. He was a small stout man of fifty, with white skin and blue eyes, bald on the top of his head and wearing earrings. At his side, on a chair, he had a large decanter of brandy, from which he poured from time to time to hearten his stomach; but the moment he saw the doctor his spirits fell and, instead of cursing as he had been doing for the past twelve hours, he began to moan feebly.

It was a simple fracture without any sort of complication. Charles could not have dared hope for anything easier. Then, recalling his teachers' manners at the bedside of the injured, he comforted the patient with all sorts of soothing words, surgical caresses which are like the oil used for lubricating scalpels. For splints, a servant went and brought a bundle of laths from under the carriage house. Charles chose one, cut it into pieces and smoothed it with a fragment of broken glass, while the servant tore a sheet into binding strips and Mademoiselle Emma tried to sew pads. As it took her a great while to find her sewing basket, her father lost patience; she made no answer; but, while sewing, she pricked her fingers and raised them to her mouth to suck them.

Charles was surprised by the whiteness of her fingernails. They were shiny, thin at the tips, more carefully cleaned than the Dieppe ivories, and almond-shaped. Her hand, however, was not beautiful, not white enough, perhaps, and somewhat rough at the knuckles, it was also too long, and lacking in the soft variations of line in its contours. The thing about her that was beautiful was her eyes; although they were blue, they looked black because of their lashes, and her glance met yours frankly with a candid assurance.

The treatment accomplished, the doctor was invited by Monsieur Rouault himself to "have a bite" before leaving.

Charles went down to the ground-floor room. Two places, with silver cups, had been laid on a small table at the foot of a great tester bed hung with printed material representing Turkish scenes. One caught the scent of orris root and damp sheets that drifted from the tall oak wardrobe facing the window. On the floor, in the corners, up-ended sacks of wheat were lined. This was the overflow from the near-by storeroom which was reached by three stone steps. As decoration for the room there hung on a nail, in the center of a wall from which the green paint was flaking away beneath the saltpeter, a head of Minerva in black pencil, framed in gilt and having below it, inscribed in Gothic letters: "For my dear Papa."

They spoke first of the patient, then of the weather, the extreme cold, the wolves that prowled the fields at night. Mademoiselle Rouault found life in the country anything but entertaining, particularly now that she had almost the entire responsibility of managing the farm. As the room was cool, she shivered as she ate, which revealed her full lips that she was in the habit of nibbling in moments of silence.

Her throat rose out of a low white collar. Her hair, in two black bands, each of which looked like a single piece, they were so smooth, was parted in the middle in a fine line which deepened slightly, following the curve of the skull; and, barely revealing the tips of the ears, was drawn back into a loose knot at the back, with a wavy effect at the temples which the country doctor saw for the first time in his life. Her cheeks were pink. She wore a shell-rimmed eyeglass, in a man's fashion, inserted between two buttons on her bodice.

When Charles, after having gone back upstairs to say good-by to Monsieur Rouault, returned to the downstairs room before leaving, he found her standing with her forehead against the windowpane, staring into the garden where the bean-poles had been blown down by the wind. She turned.

"Are you looking for something?" she asked.

"My riding crop, please," he answered.

And he began to hunt about, on the bed, behind the doors, under chairs; it had fallen down between the grain sacks and the wall. Mademoiselle Emma saw it; she leaned over the sacks of wheat. Charles, out of gallantry, hastened to her and, as he too stretched out his arm in the same gesture, he felt his chest brush against the girl's back, curved beneath him. She straightened, deeply flushed, and glanced at him over her shoulder, handing him his whip.

Instead of returning to Les Bertaux three days later, as he had promised, he went back the very next day, then regularly twice a week, not counting the unexpected visits he paid from time to time as if fortuitously.

For the rest, all went well; healing progressed normally, and when, at the end of forty-six days, old Rouault was seen trying to walk alone, Monsieur Bovary began to be considered a man of great ability. Old Rouault said that he could not have been better treated by the foremost doctors of Yvetot or even of Rouen.

As for Charles, he made no effort to ask himself why he took such pleasure in going to Les Bertaux. Had he thought about it, he would no doubt have attributed his zeal to the gravity of the case, or perhaps to the profit he hoped to make from it. Still, was it for this that his visits to the farm made a delightful exception among the poor activities of his life? On those days he arose early, set off at the gallop, spurred his mount along, then dismounted to wipe his feet on the grass and pull on his black gloves before entering the house. He loved arriving at the farmyard, feeling the barred gate turn against his shoulder, with the rooster crowing on the wall, the boys coming to meet him. He loved the barn and the stables; he loved old Rouault, who clasped him by the hand, calling him his savior; he loved Mademoiselle Emma's small wooden shoes on the scrubbed flagstones of the kitchen; their high heels made her a little taller and, when she walked in front of him, the wooden soles, briskly raised, slapped with a sharp sound against the leather sole of her slippers.

She always accompanied him to the doorstep. When his horse had not yet been brought up, she waited there. They had said good-by, they said nothing further; the fresh breeze played about her, lifting random curls of soft hair at the back of her neck, or teasing the apron strings that flapped like pennants behind her. Once, during the spring thaws, the trees were dripping in the yard, the snow was melting on the roofs of the buildings. She was standing on the doorsill; she went to fetch her umbrella, she opened it. The umbrella, of iridescent silk, with the sun shining through it, cast mobile reflections over the white skin of her face. Beneath it, she smiled at the mild warmth; and drops of water could be heard falling one by one on the stretched silk.

In the early days of Charles' visits to Les Bertaux, young Madame

Bovary did not fail to investigate the patient, and she had even set aside a fine clean page for Monsieur Rouault in the double-entry account book she kept. But when she learned that he had a daughter she investigated further; and she was informed that Mademoiselle Rouault, brought up in the Ursuline convent, had received a fine education, as they say, and in consequence knew dancing, geography, drawing, embroidery and piano. This was the last straw!

"So that's the reason," she said to herself, "for his having so cheerful an expression when he goes to see her, and for his putting on his new waistcoat at the risk of ruining it in the rain? Oh, that woman, that woman! . . ."

And she detested her, instinctively. At first she relieved her feelings by making allusions. Charles did not understand them; then she took to making direct references which he let pass for fear of a storm; at length came point-blank tirades to which he did not know what to answer. How was it that he kept returning to Les Bertaux, since Monsieur Rouault was healed and those people had not yet paid? Ah, it was because there was a *person* there, a somebody who knew how to make conversation, an artist with the needle, a fine mind. That was what he liked: he had to have town-bred girls! And she went on:

"Old man Rouault's daughter, a town-bred girl! Go along with you! Their grandfather was a shepherd, and they have a cousin who almost had to go to trial for a wicked blow he struck during an argument. She needn't put on all those airs, nor show up in church on Sunday in a silk dress, like a countess. Besides, the poor old fellow, if it hadn't been for last year's colza-seed crop, he'd have been hard put to it to pay up his back taxes."

Out of lassitude, Charles ceased returning to Les Bertaux. Héloïse had made him swear, with his hand on the Missal, that he would not go there again, after many sobs and tears and kisses, in a great explosion of love. So he obeyed; but the potency of his desire protested against the servility of his behavior and, through a sort of ingenuous hypocrisy, he came to the conclusion that being forbidden to see her gave him, in a way, the right to love her. Besides, the widow was thin, she had long teeth; at all seasons she wore a small black shawl whose point came down between her shoulder blades; her bony figure was encased in gowns made like sheaths, too short, so that they exposed her ankles with the ties of her ample shoes crossed over gray stockings.

Charles' mother came occasionally to visit them, but after the first few days the daughter-in-law seemed to rouse her to irritation against her son; and then, like a pair of knives, they devoted themselves to slashing him with their criticisms and observations. It was wrong of him to eat so much. Why always offer a drop to drink to everyone who came along? What stubbornness, refusing to wear flannel!

It happened that early in the spring an attorney of Ingouville, responsible for the widow Dubuc's investments, set sail one fine high tide, taking with him all the money in his keeping. Héloïse, it is true, still possessed her house in the Rue Saint-François in addition to her share in a ship valued at six thousand francs; and yet, of all that fortune which had been so loudly vaunted, nothing, with the exception of a little furniture and a few clothes, had found its way into the household. The matter had to be investigated. The house in Dieppe was found to be riddled with mortgages down to its foundations; God alone knew how much she had invested with the notary, and her share in the ship amounted to no more than a thousand écus. So she had lied, the virtuous creature! In his exasperation, Monsieur Bovary senior smashed a chair on the stone floor, accused his wife of having contrived their son's misery by yoking him with a jade like that, whose hide wasn't worth the harness. They went to Tostes. There were explanations. There were scenes. Héloïse, in tears, flinging herself into her husband's arms, implored him to defend her against his parents. Charles tried to speak up for her. The parents became angry and departed.

But the blow had fallen. A week later, as she was hanging out linens in the yard, she was taken with a coughing spell and spat blood, and the following day, while Charles had his back turned, closing the window blind, she said, "Oh, my God!" sighed and lost consciousness. She was dead! It was a frightful shock.

When all was over at the cemetery, Charles returned home. He found no one downstairs; he went up to the first floor, into the bedroom, saw her dress still hanging on the wall at the foot of the alcove; then, leaning against the secretary, he remained until evening, lost in a sorrowful reverie. After all, she had loved him.

3

$\mathcal{O}$NE morning Rouault came to
bring Charles the payment for setting his leg:
sixty-five francs in forty-sou pieces, and a hen turkey.
He had heard of his sorrow, and offered what consolation he could.

"I know how it is," he said, patting Charles on the shoulder. "I was like you, too. When I lost my poor late wife, I went into the fields to be alone; I dropped down at the foot of a tree, I cried, I called out to God, I talked nonsense to him; I wanted to be like one of those swellings I saw on the branches, with worms crawling about inside them: dead. And when I thought that other men, at that moment, were with their good little wives, holding them close in their arms, I beat on the ground with my stick; I was so nearly mad that I didn't eat any more; the bare idea of going to the café disgusted me, you wouldn't believe it. Well, gradually, one day following another, a spring after a winter and an autumn on top of a summer, bit by bit, crumb by crumb, that passed; for it's gone, it has left me, it has sunk down, I should say—for something still stays with you, deep down, like what you might call . . . a weight, here, on the chest. But since we all come to that in the end, we shouldn't despair and wish to die because others are dead . . . You must shake it off, Monsieur Bovary; it will pass! Come to see us; my daughter thinks of you every now and then, you know, and she says in so many words that you're forgetting her. Spring will soon be here; we'll have one of the rabbits in the warren shot to distract you a little."

Charles followed his advice. He returned to Les Bertaux. He found everything as it had been the previous day, that is to say five months before. The pear trees were already in blossom, and old Rouault, on his feet now, came and went, which added animation to the farm.

Believing that it was his duty to lavish every possible courtesy upon the doctor, because of his grief-stricken condition, he begged him not to take off his hat, spoke to him in a low voice as if he were ill, and even pretended to fly into a rage because special light dishes such as chocolate pudding or stewed pears had not been prepared for him. He told stories. Charles caught himself laughing; but the memory of his wife, suddenly returning, sobered him. Coffee was brought in; he thought of her no longer.

He thought of her less and less, in proportion as he became accustomed to living alone. The novel pleasure of independence speedily made solitude more endurable. Now he could change his meal times, come in or go out without giving reasons and, when he was thoroughly weary, stretch all four of his limbs out over his whole bed. So he pampered himself, indulged himself and accepted the consolations offered him. On the other hand, his wife's death had done him no harm professionally, for people had been repeating for a month: "The poor young man! What a tragedy!" His name had circulated, his practice had grown; and, in addition, he could go to Les Bertaux with a clear conscience. He was possessed of an aimless optimism, a vague well-being; brushing his sideburns before the mirror, he found his face more attractive.

One day he arrived at three o'clock; everyone was out in the fields; he entered the kitchen but at first did not see Emma; the shutters were closed. Through the wooden slats, the sunlight fell upon the stone floor in long thin stripes which broke upon the corners of furniture and went glancing up to the ceiling. On the table, flies crawled up the sides of glasses which had been used, and hummed as they drowned themselves in the cider left at the bottom. Daylight, coming down the chimney, turning the soot on the hearth-floor to velvet, gave a blue tone to the cold ashes. Between the window and the hearth, Emma was sewing; she was not wearing anything at her neck, small drops of perspiration stood on her bare shoulders.

As in the country custom, she invited him to drink something. He declined, she insisted, and at length offered, laughing, to take a glass of liqueur with him. She went then to fetch a bottle of curaçao from the cupboard, took out two small glasses, filled one to the rim, poured almost nothing into the other and, having touched it to his, raised it to her lips. As it was almost empty, she leaned back to drink; and, her head thrown back, her lips parted, her throat elongated, she laughed at being unable to taste anything, while the tip of her tongue, thrust out between her delicate teeth, licked tiny drops from the bottom of the glass.

She sat down again and took up her work, a cotton stocking that she was darning: she worked with her head lowered; she did not speak. Neither did Charles. The breeze, coming in under the door, pushed at a dust-curl on the flagstones; he watched it creep along, and heard only the inner throbbing of his head and the distant cackle of a hen laying eggs in the barnyard. From time to time Emma cooled her cheeks by laying the palms of her hands against them, and afterwards cooled her palms on the iron knobs of the great andirons.

She complained of being troubled, since the beginning of the season, by dizzy spells; she asked whether sea-bathing would be beneficial; she began to talk about the convent, Charles about his school, their tongues loosened. They went up to her room. She showed him her old music books, the little volumes that had been given to her as prizes and the oak-leaf wreaths abandoned in the bottom drawer of a chest. She spoke of her mother, too, of the cemetery, and even showed him the border in the garden from which she cut flowers, on the first Friday of every month, to put on her grave. But the gardener they had was very inefficient; they were so poorly served! She would really have liked to live in town, even if it were just during the winter, although the length of the summer days perhaps made the country still more boring at that season—and, according to what she was saying, her voice was clear, bitter or, suddenly lapsing into listlessness, trailing off in modulations that sank almost to a murmur, as if she were speaking to herself—now joyous, opening innocent eyes, now with eyelids half closed, her glance drowning in boredom, her thoughts wandering.

That evening, returning home, Charles recalled one by one the phrases she had used, trying to remember, to complete the meaning of them, so that he might make himself a picture of that portion of life which she had led in the times when he had not yet known her. But he could never imagine her other than as he had seen her for the first time or as he had just left her. Then he began to wonder what would become of her, whether she would marry, and whom. Alas, old Rouault was very rich, and she . . . so lovely! But Emma's face kept returning to linger before his eyes, and a monotonous rhythm like the humming of a top kept droning in his ears: "Still, if you were to marry! If you were to marry!" That night he did not sleep, his throat was tight, he was thirsty; he arose to go and drink from his carafe and he opened the window; the sky was covered with stars, a hot wind was blowing; in the distance dogs howled. He turned his head toward Les Bertaux.

Thinking that after all he had nothing to lose, Charles resolved to ask when an opportunity offered; but each time it offered, fear of not finding suitable words glued his lips together.

Old Rouault would not have been sorry to have someone relieve him of his daughter who was of practically no use to him in his house. Inwardly he made excuses for her, assuring himself that she had too much spirit for farming, an occupation cursed by heaven, since one never saw a farmer become a millionaire. Far from having made a fortune at it, the old fellow took a further loss every year: for while he excelled in the markets, where he took pleasure in all the tricks of the trade, farming itself, on the other hand, and the management of the farm proper, suited him less than anyone. He never willingly put his hand into his pocket, and yet spared no expense for anything to do with his manner of living, insisting upon being well fed, well warmed, well bedded. He loved strong cider, underdone roasts, coffee with brandy well whipped into it. He took his meals in the kitchen, alone, facing the fire, at a small table which was brought in all set, as at the theater.

When he noticed that Charles showed a tendency to grow red in his daughter's presence, which indicated that one of these days he would ask for her hand, he ruminated over the whole matter in advance. He considered him somewhat puny, to be sure, and that was not the sort of son-in-law he would have wished for; but he was said to be well behaved, economical, very learned, and he would undoubtedly not haggle too much over the dowry. Therefore, since old Rouault was about to be forced to sell twenty-two acres of his property, as he owed a good deal to the mason, a good deal to the harness maker, as the shaft of the winepress needed repairing:

"If he asks me for her," he thought, "I'll give her to him."

At Michaelmas, Charles came to spend three days at Les Bertaux. The last day had slipped past like the ones before, dwindling quarter hour by quarter hour. Old Rouault went with him to the end of the property; they were walking along a sunken road, they were about to part; this was the moment. Charles gave himself until the end of the hedgerow and at last, when they had passed it:

"Monsieur Rouault," he murmured, "I'd like to tell you something."

They stopped. Charles was silent.

"Well, tell your story! Don't I know all about it!" Monsieur Rouault said, laughing gently.

"Monsieur Rouault . . . Monsieur Rouault . . ." Charles stammered.

"As far as I'm concerned, I'd like nothing better," the farmer continued. "Although I'm sure the girl agrees with me, still I'll have to ask her how she feels about it. Go along; I'm going back to the house. If it's yes—listen, now—you needn't come back, because there will be people there, and besides it would be too exciting for her. But so that you won't eat your heart out, I'll push the window shutter wide open: you can see it back there if you lean over the hedge."

And he walked away.

Charles tethered his horse to a tree. He hastened to take up a position on the footpath; he waited. A half hour passed, then he counted nineteen minutes by his watch. Suddenly there was the sound of something striking the wall; the shutter had been flung back, the latch was still swinging.

The next day at nine o'clock he was at the farm. Emma blushed when he came in, while forcing herself to laugh a little, to keep in countenance. Old Rouault embraced his future son-in-law. They began to talk over the financial arrangements; there was plenty of time, however, since the marriage could not decently take place before the end of Charles' year of mourning, or early the following spring.

The winter passed in anticipation. Mademoiselle Rouault attended to her trousseau. Part of it was ordered from Rouen, and she designed shifts and nightcaps for herself from patterns that she borrowed. During the visits Charles paid to the farm, they talked over preparations for the wedding, they deliberated over which room the dinner should be given in; they pondered the number of plates that would be needed, and what dishes should be served.

Emma, for her part, would have liked to be married at midnight, by torchlight; but old Rouault would have nothing to do with this idea. So there was a wedding dinner to which forty-three persons came, at which they remained sixteen hours at table, which began again the following day and lingered on over the next few days.

4

THE guests arrived early in carriages, one-horse carts, two-wheeled wagon-
ettes, ancient gigs without tops, leather-curtained vans,
and the young folk from the nearest villages in wagons in which
they stood upright in line, their hands clinging to the sides to keep
from falling, going at a stiff trot and badly shaken about. Some came
from ten leagues away, from Goderville, from Normanville and from
Cany. All the relatives on both sides had been invited; estranged
friends had been reconciled; acquaintances long lost to sight had
been informed.

From time to time the crack of a whip was heard beyond the
hedge; then the barred gate would be opened: it was a cart arriving.
Galloping to the doorstep, it would pull up short and discharge its
occupants, who sprang out on all sides, rubbing their knees and
stretching their arms. The ladies, wearing bonnets, had on dresses
styled after the city fashions, gold watch chains, tippets with the
ends crossed and tucked in at the belt, or little colored fichus attached in back with a pin, which revealed the backs of their necks.
The boys, dressed in imitation of their fathers, seemed uncomfortable in their new suits (many of them even had on the first pair of
boots in their lives); one saw beside them, not uttering a word, in the
white dress from her first Communion, lengthened for the occasion,
some great girl of fourteen or sixteen, their cousin or older sister no
doubt, flushed, bewildered, her hair sleek with rose-scented pomade,
and in awful dread of soiling her gloves.

As there were nowhere near enough grooms to unhitch all the carriages, the gentlemen turned back their cuffs and set about it themselves. According to their various social positions, they wore suits,
frock coats, dress coats, jackets; good suits, surrounded by all the
respect of a family, which issued from the wardrobes only on state

occasions; frock coats with great skirts floating in the breeze, with cylindrical neck-bands and pockets as roomy as sacks; jackets of coarse cloth which ordinarily were worn with some sort of round cap, its visor stiffened with wire; short jackets with two buttons close together in back, like a pair of eyes, and tails that looked as if they had been cut out of a single block of wood, by a carpenter's ax. Some (but those, you may be sure, were to be seated at the extreme lower end of the table) even wore ceremonial blouses; that is: with the collar turned back over the shoulders, the back gathered in small pleats and the waist caught in very low by a stitched belt.

And the shirts bulged like breast-plates on their chests. Everyone had a new haircut, the ears started from their heads, all were closely shaved; some, even, who had arisen before dawn, not having been able to see clearly to shave, had diagonal gashes under their noses or, along their jaws, spots as large as three-franc pieces where the skin had been scraped away and which the brisk air along the way had inflamed so that all those great white beaming faces were some-what mottled with red patches.

The town hall being no more than a mile from the farm, the party went there on foot and returned in the same manner after the cere-mony had been performed at the church. The procession, compact at first like a single streamer of color winding through the country-side along the narrow path between green wheat fields, presently lengthened out and broke up into different groups which lingered, talking. The village fiddler walked at the head, his violin adorned with a cascade of ribbons; next came the bride and groom, the rela-tives, the friends all jumbled together, and the children brought up the rear, amusing themselves by snatching the beards from stalks of oats, or by playing among themselves unnoticed. Emma's gown, being too long, dragged a little in back; from time to time she paused to lift it up, and then delicately, with her gloved fingers, she picked off the rough grass and little thistle burs, while Charles, empty-handed, waited for her to finish. Old Rouault, a new silk hat on his head and the cuffs of his black coat covering his hands down to the fingernails, had Madame Bovary senior on his arm. As for Monsieur Bovary who, inwardly despising all these people, had come simply dressed in a frock coat with a row of military-style buttons, he was doling out barroom gallantries to a young fair-haired peasant girl. She nodded, blushed, did not know what to answer. The other wed-ding guests chatted about their own affairs or played tricks on one another, stimulating themselves to gaiety in advance; and, listening closely, one could still hear the whining of the fiddle which continued to play out into the country. When the fiddler noticed that everyone was far behind him, he paused for breath, rubbed his bow with rosin for some time so that the strings would squeal more loudly, and then began to walk again, lowering and raising the neck of his violin by turns, to mark the rhythm for himself.

The table was set up under the wagon shed. On it were four rib roasts of beef, six chicken stews, veal in casserole, three legs of lamb and, in the middle, a fine roast suckling pig flanked by four spiced sausages. At the corners stood brandy, in decanters. Sweet cider in bottles pushed its thick froth up around the corks and all the glasses had been filled to the brim with wine in advance. Great plates of yellow cream, which quivered with a motion of their own at the slightest jar to the table, had messages to the newlyweds designed in nonpareil drawn on their smooth surfaces. A pastry cook had been sent for from Yvetot for the tarts and almond-cakes. As he was new in the country, he had taken great pains; and he himself brought in, at dessert, a masterpiece of construction which called forth cries of admiration. At the base, there was first a square of blue cardboard representing a temple with porticoes, colonnades and plaster statuettes placed all around in niches sprinkled with gold paper stars; then came the second layer, a dungeon made of cake, surrounded by tiny fortifications of angelica, almonds, raisins, orange sections; and at last, on the highest layer, which represented a green meadow with rocks and lakes made of jelly, and nut-shell boats, one saw a small Cupid, swinging in a chocolate swing, the two supports of which were topped off with two real rosebuds to represent balls.

They ate until evening. When anyone was tired of sitting down, he rose to stroll about the yard or play a game of quoits in the barn, then he returned to the table. Some, toward the end, fell asleep and snored. But over coffee everyone came to life again; then they embarked upon songs, they executed feats of strength, they lifted weights, they played games, they tried to lift the wagons on their shoulders, they told broad jokes, they embraced the ladies. That evening, when it was time to go, the horses, crammed to the nostrils with oats, rebelled at being put between the shafts; they kicked, they reared, their harness broke, their masters swore or laughed; and all night long in the moonlight, along the country roads, there were runaway carriages dashing at full gallop, bouncing in the ruts, leaping over the graveled stretches, hanging off embankments, with women leaning out over the window ledges to snatch at the reins.

Those who stayed at Les Bertaux spent the night drinking in the kitchen. The children had fallen asleep on the benches.

The bride had begged her father to see to it that she was spared the customary practical jokes. Nevertheless, one of their cousins, a fishmonger (who had even brought a pair of soles as a wedding present), was about to squirt water with his mouth through the key-hole when old Rouault arrived just in time to prevent him, and explained to him that his son-in-law's important position did not permit taking such liberties. The cousin, however, yielded only with difficulty to these arguments. Inwardly he accused old Rouault of being haughty, and he went to a corner to join four or five other guests who, having been served by accident with the less desirable pieces of meat several times in a row at table, were also convinced that they had been ill-treated, whispered about their host and covertly exchanged wishes for his ruin.

Madame Bovary senior had not opened her mouth all day. She had not been consulted about the bride's costume nor about the dinner arrangements; she retired early. Her husband, rather than following her, sent to Saint-Victor for cigars and smoked until daybreak, drinking kirsch punch, a mixture unfamiliar to the rest of the company, which was a source of even greater respect for him.

Charles was not of a facetious nature; he had not shone during the reception. He responded ineptly to jokes, puns, double meanings, compliments and broad remarks which people had felt it their duty to address to him from the soup course on.

The next day, on the other hand, he seemed another man. It was he whom one would have taken for the virgin of the day before, while the bride let nothing be seen from which any conclusions might be drawn. The most waggish of the guests could only comply, and they considered her, when she passed them, with immense concentration. But Charles made no pretense whatsoever. He called her "my wife," spoke to her with endearments, asked everyone for his opinion of her, wanted to be with her every moment and frequently drew her away into the yard where he could be seen at a distance, among the trees, slipping his arm around her waist and continuing to walk half bent over her, brushing the sheer top of her bodice with his cheek.

Two days after the wedding the bride and groom left: Charles, because of his patients, was unable to stay away longer. Old Rouault sent them back in his own carriage, and accompanied them himself as far as Vassonville. There he embraced his daughter one last time, got down and returned on foot.

Monsieur and Madame Charles arrived in Tostes at six o'clock. Neighbors posted themselves in windows to see their doctor's new wife.

The elderly maid came forward, greeted them, apologized because dinner was not ready and urged Madame, while waiting, to make the acquaintance of her home.

5

𝒯ʜᴇ brick front was precisely on
the line of the street, or rather of the road.

Behind the door were hung a cape with a small round
collar, a bridle, a black leather cap and, on the floor in a corner, a
pair of leggings still covered with dried mud. At the right was the
combination dining and sitting room. A canary-yellow paper, set off
by a garland of pale flowers at the upper border, rippled all over on
its carelessly hung backing; white calico curtains edged in red galoon
were crossed at the windows, and on the narrow mantelpiece above
the hearth a clock in the shape of Hippocrates' head stood in all its
splendor between two silverplate candlesticks under oval-shaped
globes.

On the other side of the hall was Charles' consulting room, a small
room about six feet wide, with a table, three chairs and an office
armchair. Volumes of the *Dictionnaire des Sciences Médicales*, un-
cut, but with their bindings worn by all the successive sales through
which they had passed, had the six shelves of a pine bookcase almost
to themselves. During consultations, the odors of cooking penetrated
through the wall, just as in the kitchen one could hear the patients
coughing and retailing their whole case histories in the office. Next,
opening directly into the back yard where the stable was, came a
vast shabby room with a stove in it, which was now serving as wood-
shed, cellar, storeroom, crowded with ancient pieces of scrap iron,
empty casks, disused farming implements, with a quantity of other
dusty objects whose purpose it would have been impossible to guess.

The garden, longer than it was wide, ran between two masonry
walls masked by espaliered apricots down to a thorn hedge which
divided it from the fields. In the center there was a sundial made
of slates, on a masonry pedestal; four borders planted with scrawny
sweetbriars symmetrically inclosed the more useful square of the

kitchen garden. At the far end, under the small fir trees, a plaster curé read his breviary.

Emma went up to the bedrooms. The first was unfurnished; but the second, which was the master bedroom, had a mahogany bed in a red-curtained alcove. A shell-studded box decorated the chest of drawers; and, on the secretary near the window, there was a bouquet of orange blossoms tied in white satin ribbons, standing in a pitcher. It was a bridal bouquet, the other wife's bouquet! She looked at it. Charles noticed it, he picked it up and took it to the attic while, seated in an armchair, Emma thought of her own bridal bouquet, which was put away in a cardboard box, and wondered dreamily what would be done with it if perchance she happened to die.

The first days she amused herself with planning changes in her house. She removed the globes from the candlesticks, had new wallpaper hung, the staircase repainted and garden seats built all around the sundial; and even asked how to go about having a pool put in, with a fountain and goldfish. Presently her husband, knowing that she liked to go for drives, found a secondhand carriage which, having been equipped with new lanterns and quilted leather mudguards, looked almost like a dogcart.

So he was happy and had not a care in the world. A meal alone with her, an evening stroll along the highroad, a touch of his hand on her hair, the sight of her straw hat hung on a window fastening and many other things that Charles had never suspected to be sources of pleasure, now composed the continuity of his happiness. In bed in the morning, side by side on the pillow, he watched the sunlight shine on the golden down of her cheeks, half covered by the scalloped border of her cap. Seen so close, her eyes seemed larger to him, particularly when she blinked her eyelids, waking; black in shadow and dark blue in full light, they seemed to have successive layers which, heavier in the depths, became lighter as they rose to the surface of the cornea. His own eye lost itself in their depths, and he saw himself there, in miniature, down to his shoulders, with the silk handkerchief covering his head and the top of his nightshirt open. He would get up. She would come to the window to see him go; and she would remain there, leaning on her elbows on the sill, between two potted geraniums, in her dressing-gown which hung loose about her. Mounted, Charles would throw her a kiss; with the sun on his shoulders and the morning breeze in his nostrils, his heart full of the night's felicities, his spirit serene, his flesh content, he rode along ruminating over his happiness.

Up to the present, what had been good in his life? His school days, when he had been shut up between those high walls, solitary in the midst of classmates richer or better in class than himself, who laughed at his accent, who ridiculed his clothes and whose mothers came to visit them in the parlor with pastries in their muffs? Or later, when he had been studying medicine and had never had enough in his purse to pay for a dance with some little working girl who might have become his mistress? After that he had lived for fourteen months with the widow, whose feet, in bed, had been cold as icicles. But now he possessed for life that lovely woman whom he adored. The universe, for him, was no more than the silky ripple of her petticoat; and he would reproach himself for not being with her, he would be filled with desire to see her again; he would hurry back, run up the stairs with a beating heart. Emma would be dressing, in her room; he would come on silent feet, he would kiss the back of her neck, she would cry out.

He could not refrain from continually handling her comb, her rings, her scarf; sometimes he gave her great hearty kisses on the cheek, or it might be a row of little kisses all up her bare arm from finger tip to shoulder; and she would push him away, indulgent and wearied, as one does with an importunate child.

Before she had married, she had thought herself in love; but the happiness which ought to have resulted from that love having failed to materialize, she thought that she must have been mistaken. And Emma wondered just what was meant, in real life, by the words felicity, passion and intoxication, which had seemed so beautiful to her in books.

6

$\mathcal{S}$HE had read *Paul and Virginia,*
and she had dreamed of the bamboo hut, the
Negro Domingo, Fidèle the dog, but most of all of the
gentle friendship of some good little brother who climbs trees higher
than church towers to pick you red fruits, or runs barefoot over the
sand, bringing you a bird's nest.

When she had been thirteen years old, her father himself had
taken her to the city to put her into the convent. They had stopped
at an inn in the Saint-Gervais quarter, where they were served supper on painted china plates representing the story of Mademoiselle
de La Vallière. The explanatory legends, obliterated in spots by
knife scratches, had glorified religion, spiritual delicacy and the
pomp of the Court.

Far from being bored at the convent in her early days there, she
had taken pleasure in the society of the good sisters who, to amuse
her, took her into a chapel which was reached through a long corridor leading from the refectory. She had played very little during
recreation hours, had understood her catechism thoroughly, and had
always been the one to answer the vicar's difficult questions. Living
thus, without ever emerging from the temperate atmosphere of the
classroom, and among those pale-faced women wearing chaplets
with brass crosses, she had drowsed gently in the mystical languor
exhaled by the scents of the altar, the coolness of the fonts, the radiance of the tapers. Rather than following the ritual, she looked at the
blue-bordered religious vignettes in her book, and she loved the sick
ewe, the Sacred Heart pierced by sharp arrows or the poor Jesus
stumbling as he walked with his Cross. In her mind she searched for
some vow to fulfil.

When she went to confession she invented little sins, in order to
stay there longer, kneeling in the shadows, her hands clasped, her

face pressed to the grille, with the priest's whisper flowing over her. The references to promised husband, bride, celestial lover and eternal marriage which keep recurring in sermons roused unexpected harmonies deep in her soul.

In the evening, before prayers, they studied some religious book. During the week it might be a summary of the Gospels or the Abbé Frayssinous' *Conférences*, and, on Sunday, passages from the *Génie du Christianisme*, by way of relaxation. How she had listened, the first few times, to the sonorous lamentation of romantic melancholy, reiterated to all the echoes of earth and of eternity! If her childhood had been spent in the back-shop of some market quarter, she would then perhaps have been vulnerable to the lyrical invasion of nature which ordinarily comes to us only through writers' interpretations. But she knew the country too well; she knew the bleating of the flocks, fresh milk, plows. Accustomed to tranquil scenes, she turned away to the more rugged. She loved the sea only for its tempests, and green meadows only when they were scattered with ruins. It was necessary for her to draw a sort of personal gain from things; and she rejected as useless all that did not contribute to the immediate response of her heart—being of a sentimental rather than artistic temperament, in search of emotions, not landscapes.

There was an elderly spinster who came every month to the convent to do sewing. Befriended by the archbishopric as belonging to an old family of gentlefolk ruined during the Revolution, she took her meals at the good sisters' table in the refectory and, after meals, had a few minutes' chat with them before returning to her work. Frequently the students slipped away from study hall to go and visit her. She knew by heart the love songs of the century before, and sang them softly as she plied her needle. She told stories, brought news, ran errands for them in the town and, secretly, lent the older girls one of the novels she always carried in her apron pockets, and which the good woman herself lapped up a chapter at a time in the intervals of her work. They concerned nothing but love, lovers, mistresses, persecuted ladies wasting away in solitary pavilions, posthorses killed at every relay, steeds slaughtered on every page, gloomy forests, troubled hearts, vows, sobs, tears and kisses, moonlight sails, nightingales in thickets, gentlemen brave as lions, gentle as lambs, virtuous as nobody is, always well dressed, who wept like urns. For six months, at the age of fifteen, Emma soiled her hands with that dust from old circulating libraries. Later, with

Walter Scott, she conceived a fondness for things historical, dreamed of chests, guardrooms and minstrels. She would have liked to live in some ancient manor house, like those long-waisted chatelaines who, beneath the trefoil of a pointed arch, spent their days, elbow on parapet and chin in hand, watching a horseman ride up at the gallop from the background on a black horse, a white plume in his hat. At that time she had a passion for Mary Stuart, and enthusiastic veneration for all illustrious or unfortunate women. Joan of Arc, Héloïse, Agnès Sorel, la belle Ferronnière and Clémence Isaure stood out, for her, like comets against the twilight immensity of history, in which still glittered here and there, but more lost in shadow and with no relation to one another, Saint Louis with his oak, Bayard dying, certain of Louis XI's ferocities, a little of Saint Bartholomew, Bearnais' plume, and always the memory of the painted plates on which Louis XIV had been extolled.

In music class, in the ballads she sang, the only subjects were gold-winged angels, madonnas, lagoons, gondoliers: pacific compositions which gave her glimpses, across the vapidness of style and the ill-advised harmonies, of the alluring phantasmagoria of emotional realities. Certain of her classmates had brought to the convent keepsakes which they had received as tokens of affection. They had to be kept hidden, it was a serious matter; they read them in the dormitory. Delicately fingering their exquisite satin coverings, Emma would fix her fascinated eyes on the names of the authors, usually counts or viscounts, who had signed at the foot of their compositions.

She would shiver, her breath raising the tissue paper over the engravings which rose half folded and fell back gently against the page. There was a young man in a short cape, standing below the railing of a balcony, clasping in his arms a young girl in a white dress with an alms purse at her girdle; or it might be anonymous portraits of English ladies with golden curls, who looked out at one with great clear eyes under their round straw hats. Some of them were displayed in carriages, slipping through parks where a greyhound bounded ahead of a carriage driven by two small postilions in white breeches. Others, dreaming on sofas, with an opened note at hand, gazed at the moon through a partly open window half covered by a black drapery. Innocents with tears on their cheeks fed turtledoves from their lips through the bars of Gothic cages, or, smiling with their heads on one side, pulled the petals from a daisy with their pointed fingers turned up at the tips like Turkish slippers. And you were there, too, you sultans with hookas, lolling in the arms of dancing girls under leafy bowers, you Turkish sabers, Grecian headdresses, and you, especially, lurid landscapes of dithyrambic countries who often show us palms and pines at once, tigers at the right, a lion at the left, Tartar minarets on the horizon, Roman ruins in the foreground, then kneeling camels—the whole framed in a very tidy virgin forest, with a great perpendicular ray of sunlight trembling in the water upon which floating swans stand out, at great intervals, in white splotches on a steel-gray background.

And the shade of the oil lamp hanging on the wall above Emma's head would reflect its light upon all these pictures of the world which passed before her one after the other, in the silence of the dormitory, to the distant clatter of some belated cab that still rolled the boulevards.

When her mother died she wept a great deal in the first few days. She had a funeral picture made for her out of the dead woman's hair, and in a letter which she wrote to Les Bertaux, full of gloomy reflections upon life, she asked to be buried in the same grave, later. The good man thought she was ill and went to see her. Emma was inwardly gratified at feeling that she had arrived in one step at that rare ideal of pallid existences to which mediocre spirits never attain. So she let herself slip into meanderings in the Lamartine manner, listened to harps over the lakes, all the songs of dying swans, all the falling leaves, the pure virgins who rise to heaven and the voice of the Eternal descanting in the valleys. She wearied of it, was unwilling to admit it, continued first out of habit, then out of vanity and was at length surprised to find herself comforted, and with no more grief in her heart than wrinkles on her brow.

The good nuns, who had been so convinced of her vocation, became aware with great astonishment that Mademoiselle Rouault seemed to be escaping their guidance. Actually, they had so burdened her with offices, solitary meditation, novenas and sermons, so thoroughly preached the respect owed to saints and martyrs and given so much good advice regarding physical modesty and spiritual health that she behaved like a horse whom one pulls by the bridle: she stopped short and the bit slipped out of her teeth. That spirit, positive in the midst of its enthusiasms, which had loved the church for its flowers, music for the words of its romantic ballads and literature for its appeal to the passions, rebelled when faced with the mysteries of faith, just as she became even more irritated by discipline which was something antipathetic to her temperament. When her father took her out of the convent, no one was sorry to see her go. The mother superior even felt that she had become, during the last weeks, somewhat irreverent toward the Order.

Returned home, Emma at first took pleasure in ordering the servants about, then developed a repugnance for the country and regretted her convent. When Charles came to Les Bertaux for the first time, she was at the point of considering herself completely disillusioned, having nothing more to learn, destined to feel nothing further.

But eagerness for a change of conditions, or perhaps the irritation caused by that man's presence, had been enough to convince her that she at last possessed that great passion which until then had hovered like a great pink-plumaged bird soaring in the splendor of poetic skies—and now she was unable to believe that the tranquillity in which she was living was the happiness of which she had dreamed.

7

NEVERTHELESS, she sometimes thought that these were the most beautiful days of her life, the honeymoon, as they say. To savor the sweetness of them, she would doubtless have had to go to those countries of sonorous names where there is more languorous idleness in the days after marriage! There, in post chaises, shaded by blue silk curtains, one climbs at a foot-pace up precipitous paths, listening to the song of the postilion which echoes in the mountains with the sheep bells and the muted sound of a waterfall. At sunset one breathes the fragrance of lemon trees along the shores of the bays; then, in the evening, on the terrace of the villa, alone and with fingers intertwined, one gazes at the stars while making plans. It seemed to her that certain places on earth must produce happiness, like a plant which requires sun and grows poorly any place else. If only she could lean on the balcony of some Swiss chalet or seclude her melancholy in some Scottish cottage, with a husband dressed in a long-skirted black velvet coat, and wearing boots of supple leather, a pointed hat and ruffles!

Perhaps she might have wished to confide all these things in someone. But how to express an unanalyzable disquiet which changed aspect as clouds do, tormented by the wind? She lacked words, opportunity, courage.

Yet if Charles had been receptive, if he had suspected her trouble, if his glance had even once coincided with her impulse, it seemed to her that a sudden overflow would have poured from her heart as the ripe fruit falls from a tree when one lays hand to it. But, in proportion to the growing intimacy of their life, an inner indifference developed, setting her apart from him.

Charles' conversation was flat as the sidewalk of the street, and the ideas of everyone he spoke to passed through it without excit-

36

ing emotion, laughter or contemplation. He had never been interested, he said, in going to the theater to see the actors from Paris, when he lived in Rouen. He did not know how to swim, nor to fence, nor to shoot a pistol, and he was unable to explain to her a horseback riding term she came across one day in a novel.

But on the other hand, shouldn't a man know everything, excel in divers activities, initiate you into the forces of passion, the refinements of life, all the mysteries? But he taught nothing, this one, knew nothing, desired nothing. He believed her to be happy; and she resented his calm, so firmly rooted, that placid dullness, even the happiness she gave him.

Sometimes she would make sketches; and it was a great source of amusement to Charles to stand there, watching her bend over her drawing-block, squinting in order to see her work better, or rolling balls of bread crumbs on her thumb. As for the piano, the faster her fingers flew, the more he marveled. She struck the keys with assurance and ran from top to bottom of the keyboard without pause. Thus shaken, the old instrument, whose strings were fraying, could be heard to the end of the village if the window was open, and often the sheriff's clerk, passing on the highroad, bareheaded and in slippers, paused to listen, his paper in his hand.

Emma, besides, knew how to run the house. She sent out the patients' statements of accounts in well-turned letters that did not smack of invoice. On Sundays when they had some neighbor to dinner, she contrived to serve attractive dishes, skilfully arranged pyramids of greengages upon vine leaves, served pots of jelly turned out into dishes and even spoke of buying finger bowls for the dessert course. A great deal of respect reflected from all this upon Bovary.

The end result was that Charles set a higher value upon himself for having such a wife. He pointed with pride, in the sitting room, to two pencil sketches of hers which she had had framed in very large frames and hung against the paper on long green ropes. After Mass he could be seen on his doorstep with handsome tapestry slippers on his feet.

He came home late, at ten o'clock, sometimes midnight. Then he would ask for something to eat, and as the maid had gone to bed, it was Emma who served him. He would take off his coat to dine more comfortably. One after the other he would tell of all the people he had met, the villages to which he had been, the prescriptions he had written and, pleased with himself, he would eat the leftover beef, finish off his cheese, crunch an apple, empty his decanter, then go to bed, lie on his back and snore.

As he had long been used to a nightcap, his silk handkerchief would not stay over his ears; so his hair, in the morning, was tumbled about every which way and white with down from his pillow, the string of which came untied during the night. He always wore heavy boots which had at the instep two deep wrinkles extending obliquely up to the ankles, while the rest of the upper continued in a straight line, stretched as if by a shoe-tree. He said that they were *"plenty good enough for the country."*

His mother upheld him in this economy; for she came to see him as before, when there had been some fairly violent squall in her own home; and yet the elder Madame Bovary seemed prejudiced against her daughter-in-law. She found her "too refined in her airs for their financial position"; wood, sugar and candles "disappeared the way they do in a big mansion," and the quantity of coal that was burned in the kitchen range would have been enough for twenty-five meals! She arranged the younger woman's linens in the cupboards and taught her to keep a close watch on the butcher when he delivered the meat. Emma accepted these lessons; Madame Bovary bestowed them profusely; and all day long the words "Daughter" and "Mother" were exchanged, accompanied by a slight quivering of the lips, each uttering pleasant words in a voice shaken with anger.

In Madame Dubuc's time, the old lady had felt herself still to be the favorite; but now Charles' love for Emma seemed to her a forsaking of her own tenderness, an encroachment upon what belonged to her; and she observed her son's happiness in gloomy silence, like some poverty-stricken soul who peers through a window at people seated around the dinner table in his own former home. She kept reminding him, in the guise of recollections, of her struggles and sacrifices and, comparing them to Emma's negligence, came to the conclusion that he was most unreasonable to adore Emma in so exclusive a manner.

Charles did not know what to answer; he respected his mother, and he was infinitely in love with his wife; he considered the judgment of the one infallible, and yet he found the other irreproachable. When Madame Bovary had left he would try timidly, and in the same terms, to suggest one or two of the more painless observations he had heard his mother make; Emma, proving to him with one word that he was in error, would send him back to his patients.

Nevertheless, according to the theories in which she believed, she tried to inspire herself with love. By moonlight, in the garden, she would recite all the impassioned verses she knew by heart and, sighing, would sing him melancholy adagios; but afterwards she found herself as calm as before, and Charles seemed neither more loving nor more stirred by it.

When she had thus struck her heart a few times with the steel without eliciting a spark, and, further, being incapable of understanding what she did not experience, as of believing in anything which was not manifested in conventional forms, she had no difficulty in persuading herself that there was nothing exorbitant about Charles' passion. His ardors had become regular; he embraced her at certain times. It was a habit among others, and like a dessert predictable in advance after the monotony of dinner.

A gamekeeper, cured of a congested lung by Monsieur, had given Madame a small Italian greyhound; she took it for walks—for she did go out sometimes, in order to be alone for a moment and to escape briefly from the eternal sight of the garden and the dusty road.

She would go as far as the Banneville beech grove, near the abandoned pavilion formed by an angle of the wall on the meadow side. In the ditch, among the grasses, there were reeds with long sharp-edged leaves.

She would begin by glancing all about to see if anything had changed since the last time she had come. She rediscovered in the same places foxgloves and wall-flowers, clusters of nettles surrounding large stones, and patches of lichen along the three windows whose shutters, forever closed, were rotting away on their rusty iron bars. Her thoughts, aimless at first, wandered idly as her greyhound ran in circles about the meadow, went yapping after yellow butter-flies, hunted shrew-mice nibbling wild poppies at the edge of a wheat field. Then little by little her ideas focused and, sitting on the grass which she ruffled with little strokes of the tip of her parasol, Emma would reiterate to herself:

"Why, dear God, did I get married?"

She wondered if there might not have been some means, given other combinations of chance, of meeting another man; and she tried to imagine those events which had not occurred, that different life, that husband whom she did not know. No one, as a matter of fact,

39

bore any resemblance to that man. He would have been handsome, witty, distinguished, attractive, as those men undoubtedly were whom her former classmates at the convent had married. What were they doing now? In the city, with the sounds of the streets, the confused murmuring of theaters, and the highlights of balls, they led the sort of existence in which the heart dilates, the senses expand. But life for her was cold as an attic whose window faces north, and boredom, a silent spider, spun its webs in the shadow of every corner of her heart. She recalled the days when prizes had been distributed, when she had gone up to the platform to receive her small crowns. With her braided hair, her white dress and her soft woolen slippers showing beneath, she had had a charming look, and the gentlemen, when she returned to her place, had leaned forward to pay her compliments; the courtyard had been crowded with carriages, people had called their good-bys to her through the windows, the music master had greeted her in passing, with his violin case in his hand. How far away all that was! How far away!

She would call Djali, take him between her knees, stroke his long delicate head and say:

"Come, kiss your mistress, you who have no troubles."

Then, contemplating the melancholy expression of the slender animal as he yawned languidly, she would become tender and, comparing him to herself, would talk to him aloud, as to some afflicted soul whom one comforts.

But toward the end of September something extraordinary occurred in her life; she was invited to La Vaubyessard, to the home of the Marquis d'Andervilliers.

Secretary of State under the Restoration, the marquis, seeking to return to political life, had for some time been preparing his candidacy for the Chamber of Deputies. In the winter he made numerous distributions of firewood and, in the General Council, always vehemently demanded roads for his district. During the hot weather he had had a mouth abscess which Charles had cured as if by a miracle by opening it with a lancet. His steward, sent to Tostes to pay for the operation, told him that evening that he had seen superb cherries in the doctor's garden. Now cherry trees grew poorly at La Vaubyessard; Monsieur le Marquis asked Bovary for a few cuttings, made a point of thanking him personally, saw Emma, discovered that she had a pretty waist and had not in the least a peasant woman's manner, so that at the château it was not felt to be overstepping the limits of condescension nor, on the other hand, committing a social blunder to invite the young couple to visit.

One Wednesday at three o'clock, Monsieur and Madame Bovary, seated in their dogcart, set out for La Vaubyessard, with a large trunk strapped on behind and a hatbox fitted in behind the apron. In addition Charles had a cardboard box between his knees.

They arrived at nightfall, just as the park lanterns were beginning to be lighted, to show carriages the way.

8

*T*HE château, of modern construction in the Italian style, with two wings
to the front and three entrances, stretched across the end
of a vast sweep of lawn where several cows were grazing, among
clumps of great wide-spaced trees, while borders of shrubs, rhodo-
dendrons, syringas and hydrangeas curved their clusters of uneven
foliage along the windings of the graveled drive. A river flowed beneath a bridge; through the mist one glimpsed thatched cottages
scattered on a prairie bordered by two gentle wooded slopes, and
beyond, in two parallel lines among clustered trees, stood the coach-
houses and stables, relics preserved when the old château had been
torn down.

Charles' dogcart stopped before the center door; servants appeared; the marquis came forward and, offering his arm to the doctor's wife, led her into the vestibule.

It was paved with marble slabs, it was very high-ceilinged and
the sound of footsteps and voices reëchoed there as in a church. Opposite, a straight flight of stairs went up, and at the left a gallery
overlooking the garden led to the billiard room from which one
heard, upon entering the door, the click of ivory balls. As she was
crossing this room to reach the drawing-room, Emma saw about the
table grave-faced men, their chins resting on high cravats, all of
them wearing decorations and smiling silently as they made strokes
with their cues.

The marquis opened the drawing-room door; one of the ladies rose
(it was the marquise herself), came to meet Emma and had her sit
down beside her on a love seat, where she began to talk in a friendly
manner as if she had known her for a long time. She was a woman
of about forty, with fine shoulders, an arched nose, a drawling voice
and wearing, that evening, a simple lace fichu which fell to a point

in back. A fair-haired young woman sat beside her in a high-backed chair; and several gentlemen with small flowers in their buttonholes were standing about the hearth talking with the ladies.

At seven o'clock dinner was served. The men, being more numerous, sat at the first table in the vestibule, and the ladies at the second, in the dining room, with the marquis and marquise.

Entering, Emma felt herself enveloped by a warm aroma compounded of the scent of flowers and fine linens, the smell of meat and the odor of truffles. The tapers in the candelabra reflected elongated flames in silver covers; cut crystal, lightly misted with vapor, sent back muted rays; bowls of flowers stood in line the whole length of the table and, on the broad-bordered plates, the napkins, folded into bishops' bonnets, each held in the hollow between its folds a small oval roll. The red claws of lobsters overhung the edges of platters; large fruits were heaped on beds of moss in openwork baskets; quail wore their feathers, steam rose; and, in knee breeches, silk stockings, white cravat and ruffle, grave as a judge, the butler, passing platters of carved meat between the shoulders of the guests, with a flick of his spoon served each with the piece he selected. On the great porcelain stove with brass rods, a statue of a woman muffled to the chin in draperies stared motionless over the room full of people.

Meanwhile, at the upper end of the table, alone among all these women, bent over his full plate, his napkin tied around his neck like a child's, an old man was eating, drops of gravy falling from his lips. He had bloodshot eyes and wore a small queue twisted up with a black ribbon. He was the marquis' father-in-law, the old Duc de Laverdière, former favorite of the Comte d'Artois in the days of the hunting parties at Vaudreuil, at the Marquis de Conflans' estate, and he had been, they said, Marie Antoinette's lover, between de Coigny and de Lauzan. He had led a life wild with debauch, full of duels, wagers, abducted women, had squandered his fortune and dismayed his family. A servant, standing behind his chair, spoke aloud into his ear the names of the dishes he pointed at, stammering; and Emma's eyes kept returning incessantly, of their own accord, to that old man with his pendulous lips, as if to something extraordinary and august. He had lived at Court, and slept in the beds of queens!

Iced champagne was poured. Emma shivered over every inch of her skin upon feeling that cold in her mouth. She had never seen

43

pomegranates nor eaten bananas. Even the powdered sugar looked whiter and finer to her than it did elsewhere.

Afterwards the ladies retired to their rooms to make ready for the ball.

Emma dressed with the meticulous attention of an actress before her debut. She arranged her hair as the hairdresser suggested, and slipped into her barège gown, laid out on the bed. Charles' breeches were too tight in the waist.

"The foot-straps are going to bother me when I dance," he said.

"Dance?" Emma said.

"Yes!"

"You're out of your mind! They'll make fun of you. Stay in your place. Besides, it's more suitable for a doctor," she added.

Charles fell silent. He was pacing up and down, waiting for Emma to finish dressing.

He saw her from behind, in the mirror, between two candles. Her black eyes seemed blacker. The bands of her hair, gently puffed out over her ears, shone with blue lights; a rose in her chignon quivered on its mobile stem, with artificial dewdrops at the tips of its leaves. Her gown was pale saffron, trimmed with three clusters of miniature roses mingled with leaves.

Charles went to kiss her on the shoulder.

"Let me alone," she said. "You're mussing me."

They heard a violin flourish and the sounds of a horn. She went downstairs, restraining an impulse to run.

The quadrilles had begun. Guests were arriving. People pushed against one another. She sat down near the door on a bench.

When the dance was over, the floor was left free for groups of men who stood about, talking, and for liveried servants carrying large trays. Along the line of seated women, painted fans fluttered, bouquets half concealed smiles upon faces and gold-stoppered vials were toyed with by hands whose white gloves outlined the form of the fingernails and squeezed the flesh at the wrist. Ornaments and lace, diamond brooches, medallion bracelets, gleamed on bosoms, whispered on bare arms. Hair was dressed flat across foreheads, twisted into a knot in back, and was crowned with garlands of forget-me-nots, jasmine, pomegranate blossoms, feathery grasses or bluets, in clusters or in sprays. Peaceful in their places, mothers with intent faces wore red turbans.

Emma's heart beat a little faster when, her partner holding her finger tips, she went to take her place in line and waited for the stroke of the bow to start the dance. But soon emotion vanished; and, swaying to the rhythm of the orchestra, she moved forward with delicate motions of the head. A smile rose to her lips at certain graceful passages from the violin, which sometimes played alone while the other instruments were silent; the clear sound of gold coins could be heard as they were flung down on baize tables at one side; then all would take up the melody again, the cornet giving forth a sonorous note. Feet stepped in the measure, skirts billowed and rustled, hands joined and parted; the same eyes, lowering before you, returned to gaze into yours.

A few of the men, perhaps fifteen, ranging from twenty-five to forty years of age, scattered among the dancers or standing talking at doorways, were distinguished from the rest by a family look, whatever the differences in their ages, dress or features.

Their suits, better made, seemed to be of a richer material, and their hair, drawn back in curls at the temples, given luster by finer pomades. They had the complexion of wealth, that white complexion which enhances the translucency of porcelains, the sheen of satin, the finish of beautiful furniture, and which keeps up its health by means of a discreet diet of exquisite foods. Their necks turned in comfort above low cravats; their long side-whiskers fell to their turned-back collars; they wiped their lips with handkerchiefs embroidered with large monograms, from which drifted a pleasant fragrance. Those who were beginning to age had a youthful air, while there was an element of maturity upon the faces of the younger ones. In their indifferent glances was the serenity of passions daily gratified; and through their agreeable manners penetrated that particular brutality communicated by domination in fairly unexacting matters where force is employed and in which vanity takes pleasure: the handling of blooded horses and the society of abandoned women.

The air in the ballroom was heavy; the lamps were growing dim. The throng flowed into the billiard room. A servant climbed upon a chair and broke two windows; at the sound of glass splintering, Emma turned her head and saw in the garden, against the panes, the faces of peasants who were watching. Then the memory of Les Bertaux returned to her. She saw again the farm, the marshy pond, her father in shirt sleeves beneath the apple tree, and she saw herself, as she had once been, skimming the cream from the earthen pans of milk in the dairy with her finger. But in the vivid brilliance

45

of the present hour her past life, so clear until that time, faded away altogether, and she almost doubted having experienced it. She was here; then, surrounding the ball, there was only shadow, spread out over all the rest. At that moment she was eating a maraschino ice in a silver-gilt cup which she held in her left hand, and she half closed her eyes, the spoon between her teeth.

A lady near her dropped her fan. A dancer passed.

"Would you be so kind, Monsieur," the lady said, "as to pick up my fan? It's behind this couch."

The gentleman bent and, as he was stretching out his arm, Emma saw the young lady's hand throw something white, folded into a triangle, into his hat. The gentleman, recovering the fan, offered it respectfully to the lady; she thanked him with a nod and began to sniff at her bouquet.

After supper, at which were served many Spanish wines and Rhine wines, bisque soups and soups made with milk of almonds, Trafalgar puddings and all sorts of cold meats in aspic which quivered on the platters, the carriages began to leave, one after another. Pulling aside a corner of the muslin curtain, one saw the light of their lanterns slipping through the dark. The benches were deserted; a few card players still remained; the musicians cooled their fingers with the tips of their tongues; Charles was half asleep, his back propped against a door.

At three o'clock in the morning the cotillion began. Emma did not know how to waltz. Everybody waltzed, Mademoiselle d'Andervilliers herself, and the marquise; only the guests at the château were left, about a dozen persons.

Nevertheless, one of the waltzers who was familiarly called "Viscount," and whose very open waistcoat seemed to be molded on his chest, came a second time to ask Madame Bovary to dance, assuring her that he would guide her and that she would acquit herself admirably.

They began slowly, then went more quickly. They whirled: everything whirled about them, the lamps, the furniture, the paneled walls, the floor, like a disc on a pivot. As they passed close to doors, Emma's gown was blown against his breeches at the bottom; their legs wove in and out together; he lowered his eyes to her, she raised hers to him; languor overcame her, she stopped. They began again; and with a more rapid step the viscount, drawing her away, disappeared with her into the gallery, to the end of it where, breathless, she all but fell and for a moment rested her head against his chest. And then, still whirling, but more gently, he took her back to her seat; she leaned back against the wall and laid her hand over her eyes.

When she reopened them, a lady seated on a tabouret in the middle of the salon had three waltzing partners on their knees before her. She chose the viscount, and the violins began again.

People watched them. They passed and returned, her body immobile, the chin lowered, and he always in the same pose, back arched, elbow curved, lips thrust out. She knew how to waltz, that woman! They continued for a long time, and tired out all the others.

There were a few minutes more of talk and then, after the good nights, or rather good mornings, the guests went to bed.

Charles pulled himself upstairs by the banister, his knees "were giving way under him." He had spent five hours in a row standing at the tables, watching games of whist without understanding anything about it. He therefore gave a deep sigh of satisfaction when he had pulled off his boots.

Emma pulled a shawl around her shoulders, opened the window and leaned on the sill.

The night was black. A few drops of rain were falling. She breathed in the damp air that refreshed her eyelids. The music of the dance still rang in her ears, and she made an effort to keep herself awake, to prolong the illusion of this luxurious life which she must soon abandon.

Dawn broke. She gazed long at the windows of the château, trying to guess which were the rooms of all those she had noticed the evening before.

She would have liked to know their lives, enter into them, become part of them.

But she was shivering with cold. She undressed and crept between the sheets, huddling against Charles, who was sleeping.

There were many people at breakfast. The meal lasted ten minutes; no liquids were served, which astonished the doctor. Afterwards Mademoiselle d'Andervilliers gathered up bits of brioche in a basket, to take them to the swans in the pools, and they went to walk in the warm conservatory where exotic plants, bristling with spines, rose tier upon tier in pyramids beneath hanging vases which, like overcrowded serpents' nests, let fall over their rims long twining green cords. The orangery, which lay at the end, led under cover to the outbuildings of the château. The marquis, to entertain the young lady, took her to see the stables. Above basket-shaped mangers, porcelain plaques bore the names of the horses. Each animal stirred in its stall when one passed close to it, clucking with the tongue. The floor of the harness room gleamed to the eye like the parquet of a drawing-room. Carriage harness hung in the center on two turning columns, and bits, whips, stirrups, curb chains lined the walls.

Charles, meanwhile, went to ask a servant to have his dogcart harnessed. It was brought to the doorstep and, all the luggage having been stowed within, the Bovarys spoke their farewells to the marquis and marquise and set out for Tostes.

Emma, silent, watched the wheels turn. Charles, perched on the extreme edge of the seat, drove with his two arms wide apart and the little horse ambled along between the shafts which were too wide for it. The limp reins slapped its rump, becoming damp with lather, and the box tied on behind the dogcart gave great rhythmic thumps against the body.

They were on the heights of Thibourville when suddenly a group of horsemen passed them, laughing, with cigars in their mouths. Emma thought that she recognized the viscount; she turned and saw against the horizon only the motion of heads rising and falling according to the uneven cadence of the trot or the gallop.

About a mile farther on, they had to stop to mend with string the harness, which had parted.

But Charles, giving it a last glance, saw something on the ground between the horse's legs; he picked up a cigar case embroidered all over in green silk and emblazoned in the middle like a carriage door.

"There are even two cigars in it," he said. "They'll be for tonight, after dinner."

"So you smoke?" she asked.

"Sometimes, when the opportunity comes my way."

He put his find in his pocket and whipped up the nag.

When they arrived at home, dinner was not ready. Madame flew into a rage. Nastasie answered insolently.

"You may leave!" Emma said. "We can do without you. You're discharged."

There was onion soup for dinner, and a bit of veal cooked with sorrel. Charles, seated across from Emma, said, rubbing his hands cheerfully:

"It's a pleasure to be home again!"

48

They heard Nastasie crying. He was rather fond of the poor girl. In other days she had kept him company through many evenings, in the idleness of his widowerhood. She had been his first patient, his earliest acquaintance in this part of the country.

"Have you sent her away for good?" he asked at last.

"Yes. Who's to stop me?" she answered.

They warmed themselves in the kitchen while their bedroom was being prepared. Charles began to smoke. He thrust his lips forward as he smoked, spat constantly and recoiled at each mouthful of smoke.

"You're going to make yourself sick," she said contemptuously.

He put down his cigar and hurried to drink a glass of cold water at the pump. Emma, catching up the cigar case, hastily pushed it to the back of the cupboard.

The next day was a long day. She walked in her garden, going and coming on the same paths, pausing before the borders, before the fruit trees, before the plaster curé, contemplating with amazement all these things out of the past which were so familiar to her. How far away the ball seemed already! What was it that had set day before yesterday morning at such a distance from the evening of today? Her trip to Vaubyessard had made a chasm in her life, like those great gullies which a storm, in a single night, sometimes scoops out of a mountainside. Still, she resigned herself: she laid reverently away in the wardrobe her lovely gown, and even her satin slippers whose soles had been yellowed by the slippery wax of the dance floor. Her heart was like them: at the touch of wealth it had taken on something that would not be wiped away.

So the memory of the ball became an obsession with Emma. Every Wednesday she reflected as she awoke: "Ah, one week ago . . . two weeks ago . . . three weeks ago, I was there!" And little by little, features became confused in her memory; she forgot the melodies of the quadrilles; she no longer saw so distinctly the rooms, the servants' liveries; some of the details slipped away but regret remained.

9

$\mathcal{O}$FTEN, when Charles had gone
out, she would go to the cupboard and take
the green silk cigar case from among the folded linens
where she had left it.

She would gaze at it, open it, and even sniff the fragrance of its
lining, tobacco mingled with verbena. To whom did it belong? To
the viscount. Perhaps it was a gift from his mistress. It had been
embroidered on some rosewood frame, a delicate little implement
kept hidden from all eyes, which had provided occupation for many
hours, and over which the soft curls of the pensive needlewoman
had hung. A breath of love had woven into the mesh of the canvas;
each stroke of the needle had stitched a wish or a memory to it,
and all those interwoven silk threads were but the continuity of the
same silent passion. And then one morning the viscount had taken
it away with him. Of what had they talked, while he leaned against
the wide-topped chimney piece, between the vases of flowers and
the Pompadour clocks? She was in Tostes. He was in Paris, by now;
he was there! What was it like, this Paris? That magnificent name!
She repeated it to herself half aloud, for the pleasure of it; it resounded in her ears like a great cathedral bell; it flamed before her
eyes even on the labels of her pomade jars.

At night, when the fishmongers in their carts passed under her
windows singing *La Marjolaine*, she would awaken; and, listening
to the noise of iron-sheathed wheels which, going out into the country, swiftly died away:

"They will be there tomorrow," she would think.

And she followed them in imagination, climbing and descending
hillsides, passing through villages, trundling along the highroad in
the clear starlight. At the end of an indeterminate distance there always came a confused spot where her dream expired. Her eyes be-

coming weary, at length she would close her eyelids, and see in the shadows jets of gas flame writhing in the wind, and the footboards of carriages maneuvering in great confusion before the entrance of some theater.

She immersed herself in *La Corbeille*, a woman's journal, and in *Le Sylphe des Salons*. Omitting nothing, she consumed all the descriptions of first nights, race meetings and evening parties, became absorbed in the first appearance of a chanteuse, the opening of a shop. She knew the latest fashions, the address of good tailors, the days for the Bois or the Opera. In Eugène Suë she studied descriptions of furniture; she read Balzac and George Sand, seeking in them some vicarious assuagement of her personal yearnings. She even brought her book to the table, and turned the pages while Charles talked to her over the meal. The memory of the viscount always recurred during her reading. She established similarities between him and the fictional characters. But the circle of which he was the center expanded little by little about him, and the aureole he wore, becoming separate from his face, spread farther out to illuminate other dreams.

So Paris, vaster than the ocean, was reflected to Emma's eyes in an atmosphere of silver-gilt. The multitudinous life which seethed in that tumult was nevertheless divided into parts, classed by distinct pictures. Emma discerned only two or three of them, which concealed all the others from her and represented, in themselves alone, the whole of humanity. The denizens of the ambassadorial world walked over gleaming floors, in salons paneled with mirrors, about oval tables covered with gold-fringed green velvet cloths. There were gowns with trains, deep mysteries, anguish masked beneath smiles. Next came the social sphere of duchesses: in it one was pale; one rose at four o'clock; the women—poor angels!—wore Brussels lace at the hem of their petticoats, and the men, their mental capacities misconstrued beneath a surface of futility, killed their horses in the course of their search for pleasure, went to Baden for the summer season and at length, nearing forty, married heiresses. In the private rooms of restaurants where one went for midnight suppers, the motley host of literary folk and actresses laughed in the candlelight. Prodigal as kings they were, full of idyllic ambitions and of fantastic dreams. This was an existence on a plane above the others, between earth and heaven, beset by storms, with an element of the sublime. As for the rest of the world, it was lost, without any precise position, and as if nonexistent. Besides, the closer things were to her, the more she turned from them in her thoughts. Everything immediately surrounding her, dull countryside, imbecile common folk, mediocrity of life, seemed to her an exception in the world, a particular set of circumstances in which she found herself caught, while beyond stretched, as far as the eye could reach, the vast territory of delights and passion. She confused, in her longing, the sensual appeals of luxury with the joys of the heart, elegance of manners with delicacy of sentiment. Did love not require, like tropical plants, especially prepared soil, a particular temperature? Memories by moonlight, long embraces, tears flowing over the hands one must forsake, all the fevers of the flesh and the languors of tenderness were, therefore, inseparable from the balconies of great châteaux where all was leisure, from a silk-curtained boudoir with a thick carpet, vases full of flowers, a bed raised upon a dais, from the sparkle of precious stones and the braid of liveries.

The stable boy from the post-house who came every morning to groom the mare would walk down the corridor in his heavy wooden shoes; there were holes in his blouse, his feet were bare in his sabots. There was the groom in knee breeches with whom she must be content! When his work was finished, he did not come again all day, for Charles, upon his return, put the horse in the stable himself, unsaddled and slipped the halter on, while the maid brought a bundle of straw and tossed it as best she could into the manger.

To replace Nastasie, who at last departed from Tostes, shedding rivers of tears, Emma took into service a young girl of fourteen, an orphan, with a sweet face. She forbade her to wear dust-caps, taught her to address people in the third person, to bring a glass of water on a tray, to knock on doors before entering, and, with lessons in ironing, starching, dressing her mistress, tried to make a ladies' maid of her. The new maid obeyed without a murmur in order not to be discharged; and as Madame, out of habit, left the key in the sideboard, every evening Félicité helped herself to a small store of sugar which she ate all alone, in her bed, after having said her prayer.

In the afternoon, sometimes, she went to chatter with the post-boys across the street. Madame kept to her room, upstairs.

She wore a very low-necked dressing gown that revealed, between the edges of its shawl collar, a pleated shift with three gold buttons. Her belt was a braided silk rope with heavy tassels, and her small garnet-red slippers had large clusters of ribbon on the insteps. She had bought herself a blotting-case, some stationery, a pen and envelopes, although she had no one to write to; she would dust her whatnot shelves, gaze at herself in the mirror, take up a book, then, dreaming between the lines, let it fall upon her knees. She wanted to travel or to return to her convent. She wished at once to die and to live in Paris.

Charles, in snow and rain, rode about the back roads. He ate omelettes at farmhouse tables, thrust his arm into damp beds, received the tepid gush from a blood-letting in his face, listened to death rattles, examined basins, turned back a great deal of dirty linen; but every evening he found a leaping fire, a set table, comfortable furniture and a charming wife, fastidiously dressed and so fragrant that he could not even tell whence the scent came, or whether it was not her skin that perfumed her shift.

She enchanted him with a quantity of delicate details; now it was a new way of fashioning paper ruffles for the candlesticks, a flounce she had changed on her dress, or the extraordinary name of some quite simple dish which the maid had spoiled but which Charles swallowed to the last morsel with pleasure. In Rouen she saw ladies wearing clusters of charms on their watches; she bought some charms. She wanted two large blue glass vases on her mantelpiece and, some time later, an ivory workbox with a silver thimble. The less Charles understood these elegances, the more he yielded to their seduction. They added something to his sensual pleasure and to the charm of his home. They were like a gold dust sprinkled all along the little pathway of his life.

He was healthy, he had a kind expression; his reputation was quite established. The countryfolk thought highly of him because he was not haughty. He caressed their children, never set foot in the tavern and, further, inspired confidence by his sense of responsibility. He was particularly successful in cases of catarrh and in chest ailments. In extreme dread of killing his patients, Charles actually ordered nothing but sedative potions, an occasional emetic, a footbath or leeches. It was not that surgery frightened him; he bled people freely, like horses, and for tooth extractions he had "the devil of a grip."

At length, in order to keep abreast of his profession, he took a subscription to *La Ruche Médicale*, a new publication of which he had received the prospectus. He read a little of it after his dinner, but the warmth of the room, in conjunction with his digestive processes, sent him to sleep at the end of five minutes; and he would sit there, his chin on his two hands and his hair flowing down like a horse's mane to the base of the lamp. Emma would look at him, shrugging her shoulders. If only she had for a husband at least one of those men of taciturn enthusiasms who work over their books at night and at last, at sixty, when the age of rheumatism sets in, wear a cross upon their black, ill-made suits. She would have liked the name of Bovary, which was hers, to be illustrious, to see it displayed in bookshops, repeated in newspapers, known by all of France. But Charles had no ambition! A doctor from Yvetot with whom he had recently been in consultation had humiliated him somewhat, right at the patient's bedside, in front of the assembled relatives. When Charles, that evening, told her about the episode, Emma flew into a great temper against the consultant. Charles was touched. He kissed her forehead, with tears in his eyes. But she was enraged with shame, she wanted to strike him, she went into the hall to open the window, and breathed deeply of the cool air to quiet herself.

"What a sorry man, what a sorry man!" she muttered softly, biting her lips.

She felt constantly more exasperated with him. With age he was developing coarse habits; during dessert he whittled the corks of empty bottles; after eating he sucked his teeth; in swallowing his soup he made a disagreeable noise with each mouthful and, as he was beginning to grow stout, his eyes, small to begin with, seemed to be pushed up toward his temples by the puffiness of his cheeks.

Sometimes Emma tucked the red edges of his knitted vest back under his waistcoat, readjusted his cravat, or tossed aside the stained gloves he was about to put on; and this was not, as he thought, for his sake; it was for her own, prompted by transferred egotism, nervous irritation. Sometimes, too, she talked to him about things she had read, such as passages from a novel, a new play or an anecdote of the social world told in a news sheet; for after all Charles was a person, an ear always open, approval always ready. She confided many things to her wolfhound! She would have confided in the logs on the hearth, the pendulum of the clock.

In the depths of her soul, meanwhile, she was waiting for an event. Like sailors in distress, she cast despairing eyes about the solitude of her life, searching the horizon mists for some distant white sail. She did not know what the circumstance might be, what wind would drive it to her, toward what shores it would take her, whether it would be a long-boat or a three-masted ship, laden with anguish or filled to the gunwales with delights. But each morning, upon waking, she hoped that day would bring it, and she listened to every sound, sprang up with a start, was astonished that it did not come; then, at sunset, more sorrowful every day, she began to yearn for the morrow.

Spring came again. She had spells of being unable to breathe during the first warm days when the pear trees blossomed.

At the beginning of July she counted on her fingers the weeks that still must pass before October, thinking that perhaps the Marquis d'Andervilliers would give another ball at Vaubyessard. But the whole month of September slipped by without either letters or visits.

After the vexation of this disappointment, her heart remained empty once more, and the procession of days all alike began again.

So they were going to follow one another, like this, in line, always identical, innumerable, bringing nothing! Other existences, dull as they might be, offered at least the chance of an event. Often one adventure might lead to endless variations, and the scene changed. But, for her, nothing happened; it was God's will! The future was an unrelieved black corridor, with the door at the end closed fast.

She abandoned her music. Why play? Who would listen? Since she would never be able to sit in a short-sleeved velvet gown, at an Erard piano, on a concert stage, striking the ivory keys with her agile fingers, and feeling a murmur of ecstasy rise up around her like wind, it was not worth the trouble to undergo the tedium of studying. She left her sketching blocks in the cupboard, and her tapestry frame. What was the use? What was the use? Sewing irritated her.

"I've read everything," she would say.

And she went on, heating the fire tongs to red, or watching the rain fall.

How sorrowful she was, on Sunday, when the bells rang for Vespers! She would listen in lethargic concentration to the broken notes of the bell tolling one by one. A stray cat on the rooftops would arch its back to the pallid rays of sunshine. The wind on the highway would lift eddies of dust. In the distance, sometimes, a dog would howl: and the bell, with measured stroke, would continue its monotonous tolling which died away out over the countryside.

Meanwhile the congregation would be leaving the church. The women in polished wooden shoes, the farmers in new blouses, the little children bounding ahead of them, bareheaded, would all return to their homes. And until nightfall, five or six men, always the same ones, would stay to play tavern-bush in front of the wide door of the inn.

The winter was cold. Every morning the windowpanes were thick with frost and the light, falling dull-white through them, as through ground glass, sometimes did not vary all day long. The lamps had to be lighted at four o'clock in the afternoon.

On fine days she went out to the garden. The dew would have left silvery lace on the cabbage plants, with long bright threads stretching from one to another. No birds were to be heard, everything seemed asleep, the fruit trees heaped with straw and the grapevine like a big sick serpent below the coping of the wall upon which, coming closer, one saw wood lice crawling on their multiple legs. Among the evergreens, near the hedge, the curé in his three-cornered hat read his breviary; he had lost his right foot, and the plaster, scaling away in the bitter cold, had left white scabs on his face.

Then she would go back to the house, close the door, heap coal on the fire and, half fainting in the heat of the hearth, feel the heavier weight of boredom that settled over her. She might have gone down to talk with the maid, but reticence restrained her.

Every day at the same hour the schoolmaster, in his black silk cap, opened the shutters of his house, and the gamekeeper passed, wearing his saber over his blouse. Evening and morning, the horses from the post-house went down the street three by three to be watered at the pond. From time to time the door of the tavern tinkled its bell and, when there was any wind, one heard the two brass bowls that served as a sign for the barber's shop creak on their rods. For decoration the shop had an ancient print showing hair styles pasted to one window, and a wax bust of a woman with yellow hair. He too, the barber, lamented his halted trade, his lost future, and, dreaming of a shop in some great city, like Rouen, for example, on the quay, near the theaters, he spent his time walking up and down, all day long, between the town hall and the church, gloomy, waiting for customers. When Madame Bovary raised her eyes she saw him always there, like a sentry on duty, with his Greek cap over his ear, and his stuff vest.

Sometimes, in the afternoon, a man's head appeared beyond the living-room windows, a swarthy face with black sideburns, which smiled a wide gentle smile with white teeth. At once a waltz would begin and, on top of the hand-organ, in a tiny drawing-room, dancers no taller than a finger, women in pink turbans, Tyrolians in short jackets, monkeys in black coats, gentlemen in knee breeches, would circle, circle among armchairs, couches, tables, reflected in bits of mirror bound at the edges with strips of gold paper. The man turned the handle, glancing right and left and up at the windows. From time to time, squirting a long jet of brown saliva against the post, he would raise his knee under the instrument whose thick strap tired his shoulder; and, listless and dragging or joyous and quick, the music came tinkling from the box, through a rose taffeta curtain behind an elaborate brass scroll-work. They were the melodies that were being played in other places, at theaters, that were being sung in salons, to which people danced in the evening under gleaming cut glass chandeliers, echoes of the great world that reached out to Emma. Endless sarabandes rolled in her head and, like a dancing girl over a flowered carpet, her thoughts leaped with the notes, swinging from dream to dream, from sorrow to sorrow. When the man had received a few coins in his cap, he would pull an old blue wool cover over his organ, raise it to his back and move on with a heavy step. She would watch him go.

But it was at meal times, above all, that she was unable any longer to endure her life, in that small downstairs sitting room, with the smoking stove, the creaking door, the sweating walls, the damp stone floor; it seemed to her that all the bitterness of existence was served on her plate and, along with the steam from the boiled beef, it penetrated to the farthest recesses of her spirit, like other nauseous aromas. Charles sat long over his meals; she would crack a few nuts or else, leaning on her elbow, amuse herself by drawing lines on the oilcloth with the tip of her knife.

Now she neglected everything about the house, and the elder Madame Bovary, when she came to spend a part of Lent in Tostes, was vastly astonished at the change. Once so fastidious and refined, she would now literally go for whole days without dressing, she wore gray stockings and used candles for light. She kept repeating that they had to economize since they were not rich, adding that she was perfectly content, perfectly happy, that Tostes was very pleasing to her, and other novel remarks which closed the mother-in-law's mouth. For the rest, Emma seemed no more disposed to follow her advice; on one occasion, Madame Bovary having seen fit to observe that employers ought to supervise their servants' religion, Emma had answered with so angry an eye and so chilly a smile that the good woman meddled no further.

Emma was becoming difficult, capricious. She would order special dishes for herself and not touch them, one day she would drink nothing but pure milk, and the following day cups of tea by the dozen. Often she would stubbornly insist upon not going out of the house; then she would be stifling, open the windows, put on a thin dress. When she had been thoroughly disagreeable to her servant, she would give her presents or send her to visit neighbors, just as she would sometimes fling all the silver coins in her purse to the poor girl, although she was really not in the least tender-hearted nor easily accessible to others' emotions, like most people born of countryfolk, who always retain upon their spirits something of the callousness of the paternal hands.

Toward the end of February, old Rouault himself, in memory of his cure, brought his son-in-law a superb goose, and stayed three days in Tostes. Charles being occupied with his patients, Emma kept him company. He smoked in the bedroom, spat on the andirons, talked about farming, calves, cows, fowl and the municipal council; with the result that she closed the door, when he had left, with a feeling of satisfaction that surprised even her. In addition she never concealed her contempt for anything or anybody; and she sometimes undertook to express extraordinary opinions, criticizing what others praised and praising perverse or immoral things: which made her husband's eyes widen.

Was this misery to last forever? Would she never emerge from it? She was just as good as all the women who led happy lives! At Vaubyessard she had seen duchesses with thicker waists and more common manners, and she cursed God's injustice; she would rest her head against the walls and weep; she coveted tumultuous living, nights of masquerade, insolent pleasures with all the passions she had not experienced, and which they must give.

She grew pale and had palpitations of the heart. Charles administered valerian and camphor baths. Everything that was tried seemed to irritate her further.

On certain days she chattered with febrile exuberance; these exaltations were abruptly succeeded by torpor in which she sat without speaking, without moving. Then the thing that roused her was sprinkling eau de cologne on her arms.

As she was constantly complaining of Tostes, Charles assumed that the cause of her illness was very likely some local influence and, arrested by this idea, he thought seriously of setting up in practice elsewhere.

From that time on, she drank vinegar to make herself lose weight, contracted a small dry cough and completely lost her appetite.

It cost Charles some pain to abandon Tostes after four years there, and just when he was "beginning to make a go of it." Still, if it had to be! He took her to Rouen to consult his former teacher. It was a nervous affliction; she should have a change of air.

Having turned this way and that, Charles heard that in the Neufchâtel district there was a good-sized town named Yonville-l'Abbaye whose physician, a Polish refugee, had just decamped the previous week. He wrote to the local pharmacist to find out what the population was, how far away the nearest doctor lived, what his predecessor's annual income had been, and so forth; and, the replies being satisfactory, he resolved to move in the spring if Emma's health was not improved.

One day while tidying out a drawer in anticipation of their departure, she pricked her fingers on something. It was the wire of her bridal bouquet. The orange blossoms were yellow with dust, and the satin ribbons with their silver piping were fraying at the edges. She flung it into the fire. It flamed up more quickly than dry straw. Then it was like a red shrub upon the embers, and was slowly consumed. She watched it burn. The small pasteboard berries exploded, the iron wires writhed, the silver braid melted; and the shriveled paper corollas, hovering above the hearthstone like black butterflies, at length drifted up the chimney.

When they left Tostes, in March, Madame Bovary was pregnant.

PART TWO

1

$\mathscr{Y}$ONVILLE-L'ABBAYE — so named
because of an ancient abbey of the Capuchin
order whose ruins no longer even exist—is a town about
twenty-five miles from Rouen, between the Abbeville and Beauvois
roads, at the bottom of a valley watered by the Rieule, a small river
that flows into the Andelle.

Here one is on the borders of Normandy, Picardy and Île-de-
France, a bastard country where the language is without typical accent as the landscape is without character. It is here that the worst
Neufchâtel cheeses of the whole district are made and, on the other
hand, farming is costly because a great deal of manure is needed to
fatten this friable soil, full of sand and pebbles.

Yonville-l'Abbaye, however, has remained stationary. Rather than
improving upon methods of cultivation, the people there persist in
grazing cattle, small as the return is, and the lazy town, withdrawing
from the plain, has naturally continued to grow toward the river.
One sees it from a distance, crouched along the bank, like a cow-
herd napping at the water's edge.

A roadway planted with young aspens leads straight to the first
houses of the region. They are inclosed within hedges, in the middle
of yards full of scattered buildings, wine presses, wagon sheds and
boileries standing about under bushy trees bearing ladders, poles or
scythes propped against their branches. Thatched roofs, like fur caps
pulled low over the eyes, overhang about a third of the low windows
whose broad curved panes are decorated with a knob in the middle
like the bottom of a bottle. An occasional scrawny pear tree clings
to a plaster wall crossed by diagonal black timbers, and the ground-
floor doors have small swinging barriers to protect them against
young chickens who come to the threshold to peck at crumbs of dry
bread moistened with cider. As one proceeds, the yards become nar-

rower, the houses draw closer together, the hedges disappear; a bundle of ferns swings from the end of a broom handle below a window; there is a blacksmith's forge and then a wheelwright, with two or three new carts outside, partly blocking the road. Then, through a wicket gate, appears a white house beyond a circle of lawn graced by a statue of Cupid, its finger at its lips; two cast-iron jars stand at either side of the doorstep; scutcheons gleam on the door; this is the lawyer's house, and the finest in the district.

The church is on the other side of the street, twenty yards farther on, at the entrance to the square. The small cemetery that surrounds it, within a breast-high wall, is so well filled with graves that the older stones, sunk flat in the earth, form a continuous paving upon which the grass, of its own accord, has drawn regular green squares.

The markets—that is, a tile roof supported by a score of posts— take up, in themselves, about half of Yonville's public square. The town hall, constructed "from designs by an architect from Paris," is a sort of Greek temple which stands on the corner, beside the pharmacist's house. On the ground floor it has three Ionic pillars and, on the first floor, a semicircular balcony, while the tympan that tops it is occupied by a Gallic cock with one foot planted on the Charter and holding in the other the scales of justice.

But what most draws the eye is Monsieur Homais' pharmacy, op- posite the *Lion d'Or* inn. In the evening, particularly, when his oil lamp is lighted and the red and green glass jars that embellish his show window cast their two clear colors out over the ground, then, through them as if through Bengal-lights, the shadow of the phar- macist bending over his desk can be seen. His house is placarded from top to bottom with inscriptions in English script, in round hand, in print: "Waters of Vichy, Seltz and Barège, depuratives, Raspail remedy, Arabian racahout, Darcet pastilles, Regnault oint- ment, bandages, baths, health chocolates, etc." And the sign, which takes up the whole width of the shop, says in letters of gold: *Homais, Pharmacist*. Then, at the rear of the shop, behind the great sealed scales upon the counter, the word *Laboratory* is displayed above a glass door which, halfway up from the floor, repeats once more the name *Homais* in gold letters on a black background.

After that, there is nothing more to be seen in Yonville. The street (the only one), a rifle-shot in length and flanked by several shops, stops short at the turn of the road. If one leaves it on the right side and follows the foot of the Saint-Jean hills, one soon reaches the cemetery.

During the cholera epidemic, to enlarge the cemetery, a section of the wall was knocked down and three acres of adjoining land were purchased; but all this new portion is almost uninhabited, the graves continuing, as before, to crowd toward the gate. The guard, who is also gravedigger and beadle of the church (thus deriving a double benefit from the parish's corpses), has availed himself of the vacant territory to plant potatoes. From year to year, however, his little field shrinks and, when an epidemic occurs, he does not know whether he should rejoice over the deaths or mourn over the graves.

"You live on the dead, Lestiboudois!" the priest said to him at length, one day.

This grim remark made him reflect; it stopped him for some time; but today he has again taken up the cultivation of his tubers, and even maintains with composure that they grow naturally.

On the evening the Bovarys were to arrive in Yonville, the widow Lefrançois, the mistress of the inn, was so extremely busy that she was perspiring in great drops as she stirred her stew pots. The following day was market day in the town. Meat must be cut up in advance, chickens cleaned, soup and coffee prepared. In addition, she had her boarders' meals, the doctor's, his wife's and his maid's to attend to; the billiard room resounded with shouts of laughter; three millers in the small sitting room were calling for someone to bring them brandy; the wood was flaming, the roast was crackling and, on the long kitchen table, among quarters of raw mutton, were piled stacks of plates that quivered to the vibrations of the block on which spinach was being chopped. From the back yard they heard the outcry of fowls that the servant was chasing to cut off their heads.

A man in green leather house slippers, somewhat scarred by small-pox and wearing a velvet cap with a gold tassel, was warming his back at the hearth. His face expressed nothing but self-satisfaction, and his air was as unruffled as that of the goldfinch hanging above his head in a wicker cage: it was the pharmacist.

"Artémise!" the hostess cried. "Split some wood, fill the pitchers, bring some brandy, hurry! If I had at least some idea of what dessert to offer the people you're expecting! Heavenly days, the furniture-movers are starting up their racket in the billiard room again! And what about their van, left right in front of the door? The *Hirondelle* is likely to ram into it when it gets here! Call Polyte to put it away! . . . To think that since this morning they've made about fifteen stops, Monsieur Homais, and drunk eight pots of cider! . . . Why, they're going to tear the table cover for me," she went on, eying them from a distance, her basting spoon in her hand.

"It would be no great loss," Monsieur Homais answered. "You could buy another."

"Another billiard table!" the widow exclaimed.

"Since that one's no good any longer, Madame Lefrançois, I repeat, you're doing yourself an injury. You're doing yourself a great injury! And besides, good players nowadays want narrow pockets and heavy cues. They don't play the way they used to any more; everything's changed! Look at Tellier . . ."

The hostess reddened with vexation.

The pharmacist added:

"There's no use talking; his billiard table is nicer than yours; and if it occurred to him, for example, to set up a patriotic pool for Poland or for the flood victims of Lyon . . ."

"It's not scoundrels like him who frighten us!" the hostess interrupted, shrugging her plump shoulders. "Get along with you, Monsieur Homais; as long as the *Lion d'Or* stands, people will come to it. We're not so badly off. Whereas one of these mornings you'll see the Café Français closed, with a fine notice stuck up on the shutters . . . Change my billiard table," she continued, muttering to herself, "when it's so convenient for sorting my laundry, and during the hunting season I've had as many as six guests sleeping on it! . . . But that slowpoke Hivert hasn't come yet!"

"Are you waiting for him for your guests' dinner?" the pharmacist asked.

"Waiting for him? And Monsieur Binet! On the stroke of six you'll see him walk in, for he hasn't an equal on earth for promptness. He always has to have the same seat in the dining room! You'd kill him sooner than get him to eat dinner anywhere else! And fussy as he is, and so difficult about his cider! He's not like Monsieur Léon; that one sometimes comes in at seven, or even seven-thirty; he simply doesn't notice what he's eating. What a nice young man! Never one word louder than another."

"That's because there's a great deal of difference, you see, between someone who's had an education and a retired gunner turned tax-collector."

Six o'clock struck. Binet came in.

66

He was dressed in a blue greatcoat, hanging straight down all around his lean body, and his leather cap, with earlaps tied up with strings on the top of his head, revealed under its raised visor a bald forehead ridged by constant wearing of the cap. He wore a black cloth waistcoat, a horsehair cravat, gray breeches and, in all seasons, well-polished boots which had two parallel swellings caused by bunions on his great toes. Not one hair escaped beyond the line of his blond fringe of whiskers which, following the contours of his lower jaw, framed his long sallow face, with its small eyes and arched nose, like the edging around a flower bed. Excelling at all card games, a good hunter and possessed of an elegant handwriting, he had in his home a lathe on which he took pleasure in turning napkin rings with which he cluttered his house, with the jealousy of an artist and the egotism of a common man.

He made his way toward the small public room: but first it was necessary to eject the three millers from it; and all during the time it took to lay his place at table, Binet remained silent in his seat beside the stove; then he closed the door and removed his cap, as usual.

"If he wears his tongue out, it won't be with polite speeches," the pharmacist said, as soon as he was alone with the hostess.

"He never talks any more than that," she said. "Last week two young traveling salesmen came here, young fellows full of high spirits who spent the evening telling such a lot of funny stories, I laughed till I cried; well, he sat there like a dead fish, not saying a word."

"Yes," the pharmacist said. "No imagination, no wit, nothing of what makes a man a social light."

"Still, they say he has means," the hostess objected.

"Means!" Monsieur Homais replied. "He! Means? In his line of work it's possible," he added in a calmer tone.

And he went on:

"Oh, I understand how a merchant who has a considerable trade, how a lawyer, a doctor, a pharmacist might become so absorbed that they turn queer or even morbid; there are cases of that in history! But at least it's because they have something on their minds. Look at me, for example, how many times it's happened that I've been looking all over my desk for my pen, to write a label, and found that I had stuck it over my ear!"

Meanwhile, Madame Lefrançois went to the door to see if the

Hirondelle was not arriving. She shivered. A man dressed in black came abruptly into the kitchen. One could make out, by the last glimmer of twilight, that he had a ruddy face and an athletic body.

"What can I do for you, Monsieur le Curé?" the mistress of the inn asked, lighting one of the brass candlesticks which were ranged in line on the mantelpiece. "Will you have something to drink? A drop of cassis, a glass of wine?"

The clergyman declined most courteously. He had come in search of his umbrella, which he had forgotten the other day at the Ernemont convent; and, after having requested Madame Lefrançois to have it sent over to the presbytery during the evening, he left to go to the church, where the Angelus was ringing.

When the pharmacist no longer heard the sound of his steps in the square, he found the priest's conduct of a moment ago highly improper. That refusal to accept a bit of refreshment seemed to him one of the most revolting hypocrisies; all priests were given to tippling when no one was watching, and were trying to bring back the times of the tithe.

The hostess came to her curé's defense:

"Anyway, he could break four of you across his knee. Last year he helped our folk bring the hay in; he carried as many as six bundles of it at a time, he's that strong!"

"Fine!" the pharmacist said. "So you send your daughters to confess to gay fellows with a constitution like that! If I were the government, I'd have the priests bled once a month. Yes, Madame Lefrançois, every month an ample phlebotomy, in the interests of order and of morals."

"Oh, hush, Monsieur Homais! You're godless, you have no religion."

The pharmacist answered:

"I have a religion, my own religion, and I even have more religion than all of them, with their mummery and hocus-pocus. I adore God! I believe in the Supreme Being, in a Creator, whatever He is, it doesn't matter to me, who has placed us here below to fulfil our duties as citizens and as fathers; but I don't need to go to church to kiss silver plates and empty my pocket to fatten a lot of humbugs who are better fed than we are! For one can honor Him just as well in the woods, in a field, or even by contemplating the vault of the heavens, as the ancients did. My personal God is the God of Socrates, of Franklin, Voltaire and Béranger. I'm for the *Profession of Faith of the Savoyard Vicar* and the immortal principles of '89! So I don't admit any old codger of a God who walks in his garden with a cane in his hand, lodges his friends in the bellies of whales, dies with a groan and comes to life at the end of three days: absurdities in themselves and, furthermore, completely opposed to all physical laws; which proves, by the way, that the priests have always been sunk in a mire of ignorance in which they force the populace to wallow with them."

He fell silent, looking about him for an audience, for in his enthusiasm the pharmacist had momentarily had the illusion of being in the midst of the municipal council. But the mistress of the inn was no longer listening; she was concentrating on a distant sound of wheels. The noise of a carriage was heard, mingled with the clatter of weary hoofs striking the ground, and the *Hirondelle*, at last, stopped before the door.

Several of Yonville's citizens appeared in the square; they were all talking at once, asking for news, explanations and parcels: Hivert did not know which to answer. An accident had delayed him; Madame Bovary's wolfhound had run away across country. They had whistled for it a good fifteen minutes. Hivert had even turned back for half a mile, thinking to catch sight of it at any minute; but in the end they had had to go on. Emma had cried, had lost her temper; she had blamed Charles for the misfortune. Monsieur Lheureux, the cloth merchant, who had been with them in the coach, had tried to console her with numerous examples of lost dogs recognizing their masters after many long years. He had heard of one, he said, who had returned to Paris from Constantinople. Another had gone more than a hundred miles in a straight line and swum across four rivers; and his own father had owned a poodle who, after twelve years of absence, had suddenly jumped up on him one evening in the street, as he was going to dinner in town.

2

ℰMMA was first to get down,
then Félicité, Monsieur Lheureux, a nurse,
and they were obliged to awaken Charles in his corner,
where he had fallen into a deep sleep as soon as night had come.

Homais introduced himself; he offered his compliments to Madame, his respects to Monsieur, said that he was charmed to have been able to be of service to them, and added with a cordial air that he had ventured to invite himself to dine with them, his wife being absent in any case.

Madame Bovary, when she came into the kitchen, moved toward the fireplace. With the tips of two fingers she picked up her gown at the knee and, having thus raised it to her ankles, she held out to the flames, above the leg of mutton turning on the spit, her foot in its black boot. The firelight fell full upon her, its harsh brilliance picking out the weave of her dress, the regular pores of her white skin and even the eyelids, which she closed over her eyes from time to time. A great red glow flickered over her, responsive to the breath of the wind which came in at the half-open door.

From the other side of the hearth a fair-haired young man watched her silently.

As he was extremely bored in Yonville, where he acted as clerk for Lawyer Guillaumin, Monsieur Léon Dupuis (for this was he, the *Lion d'Or's* second regular guest) frequently put back his dinner hour in the hope that some traveler would come to the inn with whom he could talk during the evening. On days when his chores were finished, for lack of anything else he could think of to do, he had to arrive at the exact hour and endure from soup to cheese the unrelieved society of Binet. So it was with joy that he accepted the hostess' suggestion that he dine with the new arrivals, and they moved to the large room where Madame Lefrançois, out of ostentation, had had the four places laid.

Homais asked permission to keep on his Greek cap, for fear of coryza.

Then, turning toward the lady beside him:

"Madame must be a bit tired? One is so appallingly jounced about in our *Hirondelle!*"

"That's true," Emma answered. "But moving always amuses me. I love changes of scene."

"It's so tiresome, living shut up in one place," the clerk sighed.

"If you were like me," Charles said, "always having to be on horseback . . ."

"Why, there's nothing pleasanter, it seems to me," Léon said, addressing Madame Bovary. "When one can do it," he added.

"Besides," the apothecary said, "the practice of medicine isn't particularly difficult in our district, for the state of our roads permits the use of a carriage, and in general people pay quite well, the farmers being well off. In the medical line, aside from ordinary cases of enteritis, bronchitis, bilious attacks and so forth, we have occasional intermittent fevers at harvest time, but on the whole nothing much of a serious nature, nothing particularly noteworthy, except for a good deal of scrofula which undoubtedly comes of the deplorable hygienic conditions of our peasants' homes. Oh, you'll find plenty of prejudices to combat, Monsieur Bovary; plenty of stubbornness over habits which all the efforts of your science will come in conflict with every day; for people here still resort to novenas, relics, the priest, rather than going naturally to the doctor or the pharmacist. Still the climate, strictly speaking, isn't bad, and we even number a few nonagenarians in the community. The thermometer (I've made observations of it) goes down to four degrees in winter, and in the hot season goes up to twenty-five or thirty degrees Centigrade at most, which gives us a maximum of twenty-four Réaumur, or to put it another way, fifty-four Fahrenheit (an English measurement), no more!—and as a matter of fact, we're sheltered from the north winds by the Argueil forest on the one hand; from the west winds by the Saint-Jean hills on the other; and yet this heat, which because of the water vapor given off by the river and the presence of a considerable number of cattle on the plains, which exhale, as you know, a great deal of ammonia, that is to say nitrogen, hydrogen and oxygen (no, just nitrogen and hydrogen), and which, sucking up the moisture of the earth, blending all these different emanations, uniting them in one bundle, so to speak, and combining itself with the electricity in the atmosphere, when there is any, could in the long run give rise to unhealthy miasmas, as in tropical countries—this heat, as I say, is nicely tempered on the side from which it comes, or rather the side from which it would come, that is to say the south, by the southeast winds which, having cooled themselves by blowing over the Seine, sometimes come to us all of a sudden like breezes from Russia!"

"Have you at least some nice walks in the vicinity?" Madame Bovary continued, talking to the young man.

"Oh, very few!" he answered. "There's a place called the Pasture on the top of the hill, on the edge of the forest. I go there sometimes on Sundays, and I stay there with a book, watching the sunset."

"I think there's nothing lovelier than a sunset," she said, "but especially at the seashore."

"Oh, I adore the sea," Monsieur Léon said.

"And then doesn't it seem to you," Madame Bovary returned, "that the mind sails more freely over that endless expanse, contemplation of which uplifts the spirit and brings thoughts of the infinite, the ideal?"

"It's the same in mountainous country," Léon said. "I have a cousin who traveled in Switzerland last year and who was telling me that you can't imagine the romance of the lakes, the charm of the waterfalls, the gigantic effect of the glaciers. You see incredibly tall pine trees, cottages hung on cliffs above torrents, and a thousand feet below you, whole valleys when the clouds part a little. Spectacles like those must fill you with rapture, make you feel like praying, make you ecstatic! So I'm no longer surprised by that famous musician who, in order to stir up his imagination more, used to go and play the piano in front of some very impressive scene."

"Are you musical?" she asked.

"No, but I'm very fond of music."

"Don't listen to him, Madame Bovary," Homais interrupted, leaning over his plate. "It's sheer modesty. Why come now, my dear fellow, the other day in your room you were singing 'L'Ange Gardien' to perfection. I heard you from my laboratory; you got it off like a professional."

Léon, indeed, lived in the pharmacist's house, where he had a small room on the second story, overlooking the square. He flushed at this compliment from his landlord, who had already turned back to the doctor and was enumerating for him, one after the other, the leading citizens of Yonville. He told anecdotes, gave information. Nobody knew exactly the extent of the lawyer's fortune, and "there was the Tuvache family who made a great deal of trouble."

Emma said:

"And what music do you prefer?"

"Oh, German music, the sort that makes one dream."

"Are you familiar with the Italiens?"

"Not yet, but I shall hear them next year when I go to live in Paris to finish my law courses."

"As I had the honor of informing your husband," the pharmacist said, "in connection with that poor fellow Yanoda who ran away: thanks to the foolish things he did, you will find yourselves possessed of one of Yonville's most comfortable houses. One particularly convenient thing about it, for a doctor, is a door opening on the lane, which permits people to come and go without being seen. Besides, it's furnished with every housekeeping facility: laundry room, kitchen with pantry, family sitting room, orchard and so forth. He was the sort of chap who never counts the cost. He had an arbor built at the end of the garden, beside the water, just to drink beer in, in summer time, and if Madame likes gardening she'll be able to . . ."

"My wife never bothers with it," Charles said. "Although exercise is recommended for her, she prefers to stay in her room and read."

"Like me," Léon observed. "As a matter of fact, what is better than to sit by the fire with a book while the wind shakes the window-panes and the lamp flames up . . . ?"

"Isn't it true?" she said, fixing her great black eyes, wide open, upon him.

"One thinks of nothing," he continued, "the hours go by. Motionless, you walk through the lands you seem to see, and your thought, interweaving with the fiction, lingers over details or follows the outlines of adventures. It becomes involved with the characters; it seems that it is your heart that beats underneath their costumes."

"That's right! That's right!" she said.

"Has it ever happened to you," Léon went on, "that you encounter in a book a vague idea you once had, some cloudy image that returns from a distance, and a sort of complete analysis of your most formless emotion?"

"I have experienced that," she replied.

"That's why I am especially fond of the poets," he said. "I find verse more delicate than prose, and that it makes a much stronger appeal to the emotions."

"Still, it becomes wearisome in time," Emma returned. "Right now I am just the opposite, I adore stories that come one after the other, in the same breath, and frighten one. I detest ordinary heroes and temperate emotions, as they appear in nature."

"Actually, it seems to me," the clerk said, "that those works which do not stir the heart miss the true aim of Art. It is so pleasant, among the disenchantments of life, to be able to escape in thought to noble characters, pure affections and pictures of happiness. As for me, living here, far from the world, that is my only diversion; but Yonville offers so few resources!"

"Like Tostes, no doubt," Emma said. "So I was always a subscriber to lending libraries."

"If Madame will do me the honor of making use of it," the pharmacist said, having just heard the last words, "I will place at her disposal my own library composed of the best authors: Voltaire, Rousseau, Delille, Walter Scott, *L'Echo des Feuilletons,* and so forth; and in addition I receive various periodicals every day, such as the *Fanal de Rouen,* since I have the privilege of being their correspondent for the districts of Buchy, Forges, Neufchâtel, Yonville and the outlying regions."

They sat at table for two and a half hours; for Artémise, the servant, carelessly dragging her list slippers over the stone floor, kept bringing dishes one after the other, forgot everything, understood nothing, and constantly left the door to the billiard room ajar so that it banged the wall with the tip of its latch.

Unconsciously, while talking, Léon had set his foot on one of the rungs of the chair in which Madame Bovary was sitting. She was wearing a little blue silk tie which gathered a pleated batiste collar into a ruff; and, according to the motions of her head, the lower part of her face was hidden in the material or emerged from it with a charming effect. It was thus, sitting side by side, while Charles and the pharmacist chatted together, that they entered into one of those vague conversations in which a chance phrase continually brings one back to the fixed center of shared sympathy. Parisian theaters, titles of novels, new quadrilles, and the world of which they knew nothing,

74

Tostes where she had lived, Yonville where they were, they examined them all, discussed them all until the end of dinner.

When the coffee was served, Félicité went to prepare the bedroom in the new house, and the guests soon broke up the meeting. Madame Lefrançois was asleep beside the ashes of the fire, while the stable boy, a lantern in his hand, was waiting for Monsieur and Madame Bovary, to lead them to their house. His red hair was tangled with wisps of straw, and he limped on his left leg. When he had picked up the curé's umbrella in his other hand, they started off.

The town slept.

The pillars of the market cast long shadows. The earth was all gray, as on a summer night.

But, the physician's house being but fifty yards from the inn, they had almost at once to wish one another good night, and the company parted.

Emma, the moment she stepped into the entrance hall, felt the chill of plaster fall over her shoulders like damp cloth. The walls were new, and the wooden steps creaked. In the bedroom, on the second floor, a pallid light came in at uncurtained windows. One caught a glimpse of treetops and, beyond, the prairie, half submerged in the fog which curled like smoke in the moonlight along the course of the river. In the center of the room, jumbled together, were dresser drawers, bottles, curtain rods, gilded sticks, with mattresses on chairs and wash basins on the floor—the two men who had brought the furniture having negligently left everything there.

It was the fourth time that she had gone to bed in a strange place. The first had been the day of her entrance into the convent, the second that of her arrival in Tostes, the third at La Vaubyessard, the fourth here; and each one had seemed like the inauguration of a new phase in her life. She did not believe that things could turn out to be the same in different places, and since that portion of life already lived had been unpleasant, undoubtedly what remained to be consumed would be better.

3

*T*HE next morning, upon waking,
she caught sight of the clerk in the square. She
was in her dressing-gown. He raised his head and made
a gesture of greeting. She gave a hasty nod and closed the window
again.

Léon looked forward all day to six o'clock in the evening, but,
entering the inn, he found only Monsieur Binet at table.

That dinner the evening before had been an outstanding event for
him; up to then he had never talked for two hours in a row with a
lady. How was it, then, that he had been able to express to her, and
in such language, a quantity of things that he could not have said
so well before? He was timid, normally, and maintained that reserve
which partakes equally of modesty and dissimulation. In Yonville
he was said to have "nice" manners. He listened to older men's rea-
sonings and did not seem at all excited over politics, a remarkable
attribute for a young man. Then, too, he had certain talents, he
painted in water colors, knew how to read music and, of his own
free will, devoted himself to literature after dinner, when he was not
playing cards. Monsieur Homais respected him for his education;
Madame Homais was fond of him for his obliging nature, for he
frequently accompanied the Homais children to the garden, urchins
who were always dirty, extremely poorly brought up and somewhat
lymphatic like their mother. To take care of them they had, in addition to the maid, Justin, the pharmacy student, a distant relation of
Monsieur Homais who had been taken into the house out of charity
and who served at the same time as a servant.

The apothecary proved to be the best of neighbors. He gave Madame Bovary advice about the tradespeople, had his own cider dealer
make a special trip, tasted the beverage himself and supervised the
careful storing of the cask in the cellar; he showed her, too, how to

76

go about securing a supply of butter at a low price, and made arrangements with Lestiboudois, the sacristan, who, aside from sacerdotal and mortuary functions, cared for the principal gardens of Yonville by the hour or by the year, according to the owners' wishes.

It was not merely a need for outside interests that impelled the pharmacist to so much obsequious cordiality; he had a plan beneath it all.

He had contravened Article One of the law of Ventose 19th, year XI of the French Republic, which forbids any individual not possessed of a diploma to practice medicine; with the result that, following certain clandestine denunciations, Homais had been summoned to Rouen, to the presence of the public prosecutor in his private office. The magistrate had received him standing, ermine at his shoulders and his cap on his head. It was in the morning, before court. The stout boots of policemen were heard in the corridor, and a distant sound of heavy bolts being shot. The pharmacist's ears sang in a way that made him think he was about to have an apoplectic stroke; he seemed to see dungeon cells, his family in tears, the pharmacy sold, all the vials scattered far and wide; and he was obliged to go into a café for a glass of rum and seltzer to restore his spirits.

Gradually the memory of that admonition faded, and he continued, as he had done before, to give consultations and anodynes in his back room. But the mayor had a grudge against him, some of his colleagues were jealous, he must go in fear of everyone; by plying Monsieur Bovary with courtesies he hoped to win his gratitude and deter him from speaking out, later, if he should notice anything. So every morning Homais took him the newspaper and often, in the afternoon, left the pharmacy for a moment to go and have a chat with the physician.

Charles was gloomy: patients failed to come. He sat for long hours without speaking, went to sleep in his office or watched his wife sew. For distraction, he worked about his house like a hired man, and he even tried to paint the storehouse with a bit of color the housepainters had left behind. But he was obsessed with financial matters. He had spent so much for repairs in Tostes, for Madame's clothes and for moving that the whole marriage settlement, more than three thousand écus, had melted away in two years. Then too, how many things had been damaged or lost in transit from Tostes to Yonville, to say nothing of the plaster curé which, falling out of the cart at one particularly bad bump, had shattered into a thousand fragments on the street of Quincampoix!

A happier source of concern came to divert him when he learned of his wife's pregnancy. In proportion as her time drew nearer he cared for her more and more tenderly. This was another bond of the flesh being established, and rather like the extended sentiment of a more complex union. When, from a distance, he saw her languid steps, and her waist turning indolently above uncorseted hips; when, face to face with her, he watched her, utterly relaxed, assuming attitudes of exhaustion as she sat in her armchair, then his happiness could not be contained; he would rise, kiss her, run his hands over her face, call her little mother, try to get her to dance and, half laughing, half crying, pour out upon her all sorts of caressing pleasantries that came into his mind. The idea of having fathered a child filled him with delight. Now nothing was lacking. He knew the whole course of human existence, and he sat down to it serenely, his two elbows on the table.

Emma, at first, felt a vast astonishment, then she was anxious to be delivered in order to find out what it was like to be a mother. But, unable to spend as much money as she wanted or to have a bassinet with pink silk draperies and an embroidered hood, she lost all interest in the layette and, in an access of bitterness, ordered it all at once from a village seamstress without selecting or discussing anything. Thus she took no pleasure in those preparations by means of which a mother's tenderness is aroused in advance, and her affection, from the start, was perhaps somewhat attenuated by it.

However, since Charles kept talking about the baby at every meal, presently she began to think about it in a more consecutive manner.

She hoped for a son; he would be strong and dark, and would be named Georges; and this idea of having a male as her child was like a hope of revenge for all her past impotence. A man, at least, is free; he can explore passions and continents, overcome obstacles, nibble at the most distant pleasures. But a woman is continually restrained. Inert and flexible at once, she is confronted with the fragilities of the flesh and the restrictions of the law. Her will, like the veil of her hat caught back with a cord, flutters in every wind; there is always some desire urging her on, some convention restraining her.

She went into labor one Sunday about six o'clock, at sunrise.

"It's a girl!" Charles said.

She turned her head away and lost consciousness.

Almost immediately Madame Homais hastened over to embrace her, and Madame Lefrançois of the *Lion d'Or* as well. The pharmacist, a discreet man, merely called congratulations through the half-open door for the time being. He asked to see the baby and pronounced her well formed.

During her convalescence Emma concentrated largely upon finding a name for her daughter. First she reviewed all those with Italian endings, such as Clara, Louisa, Amanda, Atala; she rather liked Galsuinde and was even fonder of Yseult or Léocadie. Charles wanted the child to be named for his mother; Emma rebelled. They scanned the calendar from end to end and asked the advice of others.

"Monsieur Léon," the pharmacist said, "was astonished, when I talked to him the other day, to hear that you're not choosing Madeleine, which is so fashionable just now."

But the elder Madame Bovary protested vehemently against this sinner's name. Monsieur Homais' personal preference was for those which recalled some great man, an illustrious feat or a generous conception, and it was according to this system that he had christened his four children. Thus Napoléon represented glory, and Franklin liberty; Irma was perhaps a concession to romanticism, but Athalie expressed homage for the most immortal masterpiece of the French stage. For his philosophical convictions did not interfere with his artistic appreciation; he would have liked to crown Racine with his own hands and at the same time argue with him for a full quarter of an hour.

At length Emma remembered that at La Vaubyessard she had heard the marquise call one young woman Berthe; from that time on, this was the chosen name and, as old Rouault was unable to come, Monsieur Homais was asked to be godfather. The evening of the ceremony there was a great dinner; the curé was there; excitement ran high. Over the liqueurs, Monsieur Homais recited *Le Dieu des Bonnes Gens*, Monsieur Léon sang a barcarole and the elder Madame Bovary, who was the godmother, a ballad of the days of the Empire; presently Monsieur Bovary senior insisted that the baby be brought down, and began to baptize her with a glass of champagne which he poured on her head. The curé wanted to leave: the ladies pleaded with him; Homais interceded, and they were able to get the clergyman to sit down again.

Monsieur Bovary remained a month longer in Yonville, whose inhabitants he dazzled with a superb policeman's cap trimmed in silver braid which he wore in the morning to smoke his pipe in the square. Having also the habit of drinking a great deal of brandy, he frequently sent the servant to the *Lion d'Or* to buy him a bottle which was charged to his son's account; and he used up his daughter-in-law's entire supply of eau de cologne, scenting his handkerchiefs.

She was not in the least displeased to have his company. He had traveled about the world: he would speak of Berlin, Vienna, Strasbourg, of his days as an officer, of mistresses he had had, of great breakfasts he had attended; then, too, he was so friendly, and sometimes, on the stairs or in the garden, he would clasp her around the waist, crying:

"Charles, watch out!"

Then the elder Madame Bovary became alarmed for her son's happiness and, fearing that her husband might eventually have an immoral influence upon the young woman's ideas, hastened to urge their departure. Perhaps she had more serious worries. Monsieur Bovary was a man who respected nothing.

One day Emma was suddenly assailed by a desire to see her little girl, who had been put out to nurse with the carpenter's wife, and set out for Rollet's home, which lay at the far end of the village, at the foot of the hill, between the highroad and the prairies. A heavy wind was blowing. Emma felt weak, walking; the gravel of the sidewalk hurt her; she was undecided whether she should not return home or go into some house to sit down.

At this moment Monsieur Léon came out of a near-by door with a bundle of papers under his arm. He came to greet her, and stood in the shade of the awning which jutted out in front of Lheureux' shop. Madame Bovary said that she was on her way to see her baby, but that she was beginning to feel tired.

"So . . ." Léon said, not venturing to pursue the subject.

"Are you going somewhere on business?" she asked.

And, upon the clerk's reply, she begged him to accompany her. By evening, this was known all over Yonville, and Madame Tuvache, the mayor's wife, declared in her servant's presence that "Madame Bovary was putting herself in a compromising position."

Both of them walked slowly, side by side, she leaning upon his arm and he shortening his stride to hers; before them a cloud of flies hovered, buzzing in the hot air.

They recognized the house by an ancient walnut tree which shaded it. Low and roofed with brown tiles, it had a string of onions hung outside under the storeroom window. A few sticks, propped upright against the bramble fence, inclosed a square of lettuce plants, several rows of lavender and some sweet peas climbing upon poles. Dirty water trickled here and there over the soil, and all about were hung a number of nameless rags, woolen stockings, an Indian-red camisole and a wide sheet of thick canvas spread out along the hedge. At the sound of the gate, the nurse appeared, holding on her arm a baby who was nursing at her breast. By the other hand she dragged a wretched puny youngster, his face covered with scrofula, the son of a Rouen hosier, whom his parents, too busy with their trade, left in the country.

"Come in," she said. "Your little girl is asleep over there."

The ground-floor room, the only one in the house, had a wide uncurtained bed at one end, against the wall, while the kneading trough stood beside the window, one pane of which had been patched with blue paper. Emma's baby was sleeping in a wicker cradle that stood on the ground. She picked her up, with the blanket that was wrapped around her, and began to sing softly, swaying her body.

Léon prowled about the room; it seemed strange to him to see this lovely woman in her nankeen gown in the midst of all that poverty. Madame Bovary flushed; he turned away, thinking that perhaps his gaze had been somewhat impertinent. Then she put down the baby, who had just spit up on her collar. The nurse came at once to wipe it off, assuring her that it would not show.

"She does it to me all the time," she said, "and I spend most of my time washing her! So if you'd be so kind as to tell Camus the grocer to let me have a bit of soap when I need it? It would even be more convenient for you; I wouldn't have to bother you."

"Very well, very well!" Emma said. "Good-by, Mère Rollet."

And she went out, wiping her feet at the threshold.

The good woman accompanied her to the end of the yard, talking all the while of the trouble she had getting up at night.

"I'm so worn out sometimes that I fall asleep in my chair; so the least you could do would be to give me a nice pound of ground coffee that would last me a month and I could drink it with milk in the morning."

After having suffered the woman's thanks, Madame Bovary left;

and she was some little way down the path when, at the sound of wooden shoes, she turned her head: it was the nurse.

"What is it?"

The peasant woman, drawing her to one side behind an elm tree, then began to speak of her husband who, with his work and the six francs a year which the captain . . .

"Get to the point faster," Emma said.

"Well," the nurse went on, sighing between each two words, "I'm afraid he may get his feelings hurt, seeing me drink coffee all alone; you know, men . . ."

"But you will have some," Emma said, "I am going to give you some! . . . You're making a nuisance of yourself."

"My poor dear lady, the trouble is that he gets terrible cramps in his chest as a result of his wounds. He says that even cider disagrees with him."

"Will you hurry, Mère Rollet!"

"So," she went on, dropping a curtsy, "if it wouldn't be asking too much . . ." she curtsied again, "whenever you will be so good . . ." and her eyes pleaded . . . "a little pitcher of brandy," she said at last, "and I'll rub your baby's legs with it, they're limp as a tongue."

Rid of the nurse, Emma took Monsieur Léon's arm once more. She walked quickly for a while; then she slowed her pace, and her glance, which she had been directing straight ahead, fell upon the shoulder of the young man, whose coat had a black velvet collar. His chestnut hair hung down over it, flat and neatly combed. She noticed his fingernails, which were longer than was usual in Yonville. Keeping them in order was one of the clerk's chief occupations; and for this purpose he kept a particular penknife in his desk drawer.

They were speaking of a troupe of Spanish dancers who were expected soon in the Rouen theater.

"Are you going?" she asked.

"If I can," he replied.

Had they nothing else to say to one another? Still, their eyes were brimming with more serious talk; and while they forced themselves to find commonplace phrases, they felt an identical languor overcoming both of them; it was like a murmur from the soul, deep, uninterrupted, which rose above that of their voices. Overcome with astonishment at this pleasant new sensation, they did not think to mention it to one another or to seek its cause. Future delights, like

82

tropical coastlines, project upon the immensity which precedes them their native lassitudes, a scented breeze, and one drowses in that intoxication without even troubling to search for the horizon which cannot yet be seen.

At one spot the earth had given way beneath the trampling of cattle; they had to walk upon great green stones evenly spaced in the mud. Frequently she would pause for a moment to see where to set her foot; and, balancing on the unsteady rock, her elbows thrust out, bending forward at the waist, her eye irresolute, she would laugh over her fear of falling into the puddles of water.

When they had reached the front of her garden, Madame Bovary pushed open the little gate, ran up the steps and disappeared.

Léon returned to his office. His employer was out; he glanced at the briefs, then trimmed a pen point, at last took his hat and left.

He went to the Pasture, at the top of the Argueil hill, at the edge of the forest; he lay down on the ground under the pine trees and looked at the sky through his fingers.

"How bored I am!" he said to himself. "How bored I am!"

He felt that he was to be pitied, living in this village with Homais for his friend and Monsieur Guillaumin for his employer. This latter gentleman, utterly absorbed in business matters, wearing eyeglasses with gold temple-pieces and red whiskers over a white cravat, had no appreciation of the finer aspects of the intellect, although he affected a rigid, English manner that had dazzled the clerk in earlier days. As for the pharmacist's wife, she was the epitome of the good Norman wife, gentle as a sheep, cherishing her children, her father, her mother, her cousins, weeping for the ills of others, letting everything go about her house and detesting corsets—but so slow-moving, so dull to listen to, so common in appearance and so limited in conversation that, although she was thirty and he twenty, although they slept in adjoining rooms and he spoke to her every day, it had never occurred to him that she might be regarded as a woman, nor that she possessed any attributes of her sex beyond the dress.

And other than these, who was there? Binet, a few merchants, two or three tavern-keepers, the priest, and finally Monsieur Tuvache, the mayor, with his two sons, wealthy, surly, obtuse folk, cultivating their land themselves, visiting back and forth within their own family, religious besides and utterly unendurable as companions.

But against the common background of all these human faces,

Emma's stood out, isolated and yet even more distant, for he sensed vague chasms between her and himself.

In the beginning he had gone to her home several times, accompanying the pharmacist. Charles had certainly not seemed extremely anxious to receive them; and Léon did not know what course to take between the fear of being overforward and the desire for an intimacy which he considered almost impossible.

4

A<small>FTER</small> the first frosts, Emma
forsook her bedroom for the sitting room, a
long apartment with a low ceiling in which a gnarled
coral plant stood on the chimney-piece, spreading its branches
against the mirror. Sitting in her armchair beside the window, she
would watch the village folk go by on the sidewalk.

Léon, twice a day, went from his work to the *Lion d'Or;* from a
distance Emma would hear him coming; she would lean forward,
listening; and the young man would move past beyond the curtain,
always dressed in the same fashion and without turning his head.
But at twilight when, with her chin in her hand, she had abandoned
her unfinished needlework upon her lap, she often shivered at the
sudden appearance of that shadow slipping by. She would stand up
and order the maid to lay the table.

Monsieur Homais would arrive during dinner. Greek cap in hand,
he would enter on silent feet in order not to disturb anyone, and
always repeating the same phrase: "Good evening, everybody!"
Then, when he had taken his place beside the table, between hus-
band and wife, he would ask the doctor for news of his patients, and
Charles would consult with him about the probability of payment.
At eight o'clock Justin would come to find him to close the pharmacy.
Then Monsieur Homais would eye him banteringly, particularly if
Félicité was in the room, having noticed that his pupil was develop-
ing a fondness for the physician's house.

"This fine fellow of mine," he would say, "is beginning to have
ideas. Devil take me if I don't think he's in love with your maid!"

But a more serious fault, and one with which he was constantly
reproaching him, was Justin's habit of listening to conversations. On
Sunday, for example, it was impossible to get him to leave the
drawing-room, to which Madame Homais had summoned him to

fetch the children who were falling asleep in their chairs, pulling the oversized slip covers out of shape with their backs.

There were not a great many people who came to these evening parties at the pharmacist's, his backbiting and his political opinions having alienated various respectable persons from him, one after the other. The clerk never failed to be there. The moment he heard the bell he would hasten to Madame Bovary, take her shawl, and place the large felt slippers she wore over her shoes when there was snow to one side, under the pharmacy counter.

To begin with, there would be a few games of trente-et-un; later Monsieur Homais would play écarté with Emma; Léon, standing behind her, would give her advice. With his hands on the back of her chair, he would gaze at the teeth of her comb biting into her chignon. At every motion she made in playing her cards, her dress slipped up on her right shoulder. From her upswept hair a deep tan color crept down over her back and, gradually paling, was lost in the shadow. Below, her gown fell to her chair at either side, in soft puffs full of folds, and hung down to the floor. When Léon, occasionally, felt the sole of his boot come down upon it, he started as if he had stepped upon a person.

When the card games were finished, the apothecary and the physician would play dominos, and Emma, changing places, would lean her elbows on the table and glance through the *Illustration*. She brought her own fashion magazine. Léon would sit beside her; together they looked at the pictures and waited for one another at the end of each page. Often she asked him to read poetry to her; Léon recited it in a drawling voice which he was careful to let die away over love passages. But the sound of the dominos disturbed her; Monsieur Homais was a good player, he beat Charles hands down. Then, having finished three hundred-point games, they would both stretch out before the hearth and lose no time falling asleep. The fire would die among its ashes; the teapot would be empty; Léon would go on reading, Emma listened, mechanically turning the lamp-shade upon which were painted pierrots in carriages, and tight-rope walkers with their balancing poles. Léon would stop, making a gesture toward his sleeping audience; then they would talk in low voices, and the conversation between them would seem the more delightful for not being overheard.

So there grew up between them a sort of communion, a constant

86

interchange of books and romantic verse; Monsieur Bovary, rarely a jealous man, was not alarmed by it.

For his birthday he received a fine phrenological skull, all marked off into numbered squares down to the thorax, and painted blue. This was a token of respect from the clerk. He made many others, even going so far as to run errands for him in Rouen; and, a certain novelist's book having made fashionable a craze for cactus plants, Léon bought several for Madame and brought them home on his lap in the *Hirondelle*, pricking his fingers all the way on their tough spines.

She had a shelf with a railing hung outside her window to hold her potted plants. The clerk, too, had his hanging garden; they caught glimpses of one another, tending their flowers at their windows.

Among the village windows there was one that was even more frequently tenanted, for on Sunday, from morning to night, and every afternoon in clear weather, Monsieur Binet's lean profile was to be seen in an attic dormer, bending above his lathe whose monotonous snarling could be heard as far as the *Lion d'Or*.

One evening, returning to his room, Léon found a velvet table cover with flowers and leaves embroidered in wool against its pale background. He called Madame Homais, Monsieur Homais, Justin, the children, the cook; he mentioned it to his employer; everyone wished to know the meaning of this table cover; why was the physician's wife making gifts to the clerk? It seemed very queer, and the general opinion was that she must be his mistress.

He led people to believe it, he talked so constantly about her charms and her intelligence, to such an extent that one time Binet answered him brutally:

"What does it matter to me, since I don't associate with her!"

He tortured himself, trying to invent some way of *making his declaration;* and, forever vacillating between fear of offending her and shame at being so pusillanimous, he would weep with discouragement and desire. Then he would come to rigorous decisions; he would write letters which he tore up, set time limits for himself which he kept postponing. Frequently he set out in the determination of daring all; but this resolution promptly forsook him in Emma's presence, and when Charles, happening in, invited him for a drive in the dogcart, to go and call on some patient in the neighborhood, he would accept at once, bow to Madame and depart. Her husband, after all, was something of hers, was he not?

As for Emma, she did not examine herself to find out if she loved him. Love, she believed, should strike suddenly, with thunder claps and fulgurations—a tornado out of the heavens which hurls itself upon life, turns it upside down, snatches away volition like leaves and sweeps the whole heart off to the abyss. She did not know that, on the terraces of houses, the rain makes lakes when the gutters are choked, and she might thus have remained in her security had she not suddenly discovered a fissure in the wall.

5

$\mathscr{I}$T was one Sunday in February, an afternoon when it was snowing. They had all set out, Monsieur and Madame Bovary, Homais and Monsieur Léon, to see a textile mill that was being built in the valley, a mile and a half from Yonville. The apothecary had brought Napoléon and Athalie with him to give them some exercise, and Justin accompanied them carrying umbrellas on his shoulder.

Homais talked. He explained to the party the future importance of this establishment, calculated the strength of the flooring, the thickness of the walls, and greatly regretted not having a measuring stick, such as the one Monsieur Binet possessed, for his own personal use.

Emma, on his arm, leaned a little against his shoulder and gazed at the sun's disc shedding its dazzling pale radiance afar in the mist; but she turned her head: Charles was there. He had his cap pulled down over his eyebrows, and his two thick lips were quivering, which added an element of stupidity to his expression; even his back, his placid back was irritating to see, and she found displayed there on his greatcoat all the dullness of his personality.

While she was contemplating him, savoring thus in her irritation a sort of depraved gratification, Léon took a step forward. The cold which blanched his skin seemed to invest his face with a gentler languor; between his cravat and his neck, the collar of his shirt, somewhat loose, revealed the flesh beneath; the tip of an ear showed through locks of hair, and his great blue eyes, lifted to the clouds, seemed to Emma more limpid and more beautiful than those mountain lakes in which the sky reflects.

"Little beast!" the apothecary shouted suddenly.

And he ran toward his son, who had just leaped into a pile of lime to paint his shoes white. At the scoldings heaped upon him,

Napoléon began to howl, while Justin wiped off his shoes with a twist of hay. But he had needed a knife; Charles offered his.

"So!" she thought. "He carries a knife in his pocket, like a peasant." Frost was settling, and they turned back toward Yonville.

That evening Madame Bovary did not go to her neighbors', and when Charles had left, as soon as she felt herself to be alone, the comparison recommenced in the clarity of an almost immediate sensation and with that lengthening of perspective which memory gives to objects. Staring from her bed into the bright fire, she saw Léon again as he had been out there, standing upright, flicking his switch with one hand and with the other holding Athalie who was peacefully sucking a bit of ice. She found him charming; she could not tear her mind away from him; she recalled his other attitudes on other days, phrases he had said, the sound of his voice, his whole person; and she kept repeating, thrusting out her lips as if for a kiss: "Yes, charming, charming! . . . Is he in love?" she wondered. "Then with whom? . . . Why, me!"

Then the eternal lamentation began: "Oh, if heaven had only willed it! Why wasn't it so? But what's to prevent . . . ?"

When Charles returned, at midnight, she pretended to wake up and, as he made a certain amount of noise undressing, she complained of a headache; then she asked carelessly what had happened during the evening.

"Monsieur Léon went up to his room early," he said.

She was unable to restrain a smile, and she fell asleep with her spirit full of a new enchantment.

The next day at nightfall she received a visit from Monsieur Lheureux, the linen-draper. He was a very clever man, this shopkeeper.

A Gascon by birth, but turned Norman, he combined his southern fluency with the cunning of Caux. His plump face, soft and beardless, looked as if it had been dyed in a thin solution of licorice, and his white hair accentuated even further the intensity of the sharp glitter in his small black eyes. No one knew what he had been before: a peddler, some said, a banker in Routot according to others. What is certain is that he did in his head calculations complex enough to appall Binet himself. Polite to the point of obsequiousness, he always held himself slightly bent forward at the waist, in the attitude of one who is bowing or issuing an invitation.

Having left his hat with its crêpe band at the door, he placed a green pasteboard box upon the table and began by regretting, with many courteous expressions, that he had gone until now without making Madame's acquaintance. A poor shop like his was not the sort to appeal to an *elegant woman;* he emphasized the words. Nevertheless, she had only to make her wishes known, and he would undertake to supply whatever she wanted, whether in notions or linens, millinery or novelties; for he went to town four times a month regularly. He had connections with the best houses. One could mention his name at the *Trois Frères,* the *Barbe d'Or* or the *Grand Sauvage;* all these gentlemen knew him as well as the inside of their own pockets! So today he had come to show Madame, in passing, various articles which he happened to have on hand, thanks to most unusual circumstances. And he drew from a box a half-dozen embroidered collars.

Madame Bovary examined them.

"I don't need anything," she said.

Then Monsieur Lheureux delicately displayed three Algerian scarves, several packets of English needles, a pair of woven straw slippers and, finally, four coconut eggcups hand-carved by convicts. Then, with his two hands flat on the table, his neck stretched out, bending from the waist, open-mouthed, he followed Emma's glance, which wandered uncertainly among his merchandise. From time to time, as if to flick off a bit of dust, he snapped a fingernail against the silk of the scarves, unfolded to their full length; and they would rustle with a soft sound, making the gold spangles in their fabric shimmer like little stars in the greenish glow of twilight.

"How much are they?"

"Practically nothing," he said. "Practically nothing; but there's no hurry; whenever it's convenient. We aren't like money lenders!"

She reflected for a few moments and, in the end, again thanked Monsieur Lheureux, who replied undisturbed:

"Very well, we'll come to an understanding later on; I always get along with the ladies, that is except my own!"

Emma smiled.

"This is just to let you know," he said with a good-natured air, after his joke, "that it's not money that worries me . . . I would give you some, if need be."

She made a gesture of surprise.

"Oh," he said quickly and in a low voice, "I wouldn't have to go far to find it for you; you may count on that."

And all the while he repacked his box, he commented upon the doctor's practice.

"I suppose it's the weather that causes these illnesses?" he said, glancing at the window with a frowning face. "I don't feel absolutely right, myself; one of these days I'll have to come and consult Monsieur about a pain in my back. Well, good-by, Madame Bovary; your humble servant, at your service!"

And he closed the door very gently behind him.

Emma had her dinner served in her room, beside the fire, on a tray; she sat long over the meal; everything seemed good to her.

"How wise I was!" she said to herself, thinking of the scarves.

She heard steps on the stairs: it was Léon. She rose and snatched from the top of the dresser the first of a pile of dust cloths to be hemmed. She seemed very much occupied when he appeared.

The conversation languished, Madame Bovary abandoning it from moment to moment, while he himself remained as if utterly bewildered. Seated on a low chair by the hearth, he turned the ivory needle-case in his fingers; she plied her needle or, occasionally, ran her fingernail along the creases in the cloth. She did not speak; he fell silent, enchanted by her silence as he would have been by her words.

"Poor boy!" she thought.

"How have I offended her?" he wondered.

At length, however, Léon said that he would have to go to Rouen one day soon, on an errand connected with his studies.

"Your music subscription has run out, shall I renew it?"

"No," she answered.

"Why?"

"Because . . ."

And, pursing her lips, she drew a long needleful of gray thread slowly through the cloth.

That task annoyed Léon. Emma's finger tips seemed to be getting roughened by it; a gallant phrase came into his head, but he did not risk saying it.

"You're giving it up, then?" he asked.

"What?" she said sharply. "Music? Oh, Lord, yes! Haven't I my house to keep, my husband to look out for, a thousand things, duties that have to come first!"

She glanced at the clock. Charles was late. Then she posed as the anxious wife. Two or three times she repeated:

"He's so good!"

The clerk was fond of Monsieur Bovary. But these evidences of tenderness toward him startled him in a disagreeable fashion; nevertheless he took up his praises, he knew how to get along with everyone, he said, and especially the pharmacist.

"Ah, there's a fine man," Emma said.

"Absolutely," the clerk said.

He began to talk about Madame Homais, whose extremely careless attire usually set them laughing.

"What does that matter?" Emma interrupted. "A good mother doesn't bother about her clothes."

Then she relapsed into silence.

It was the same in the days that followed; her speech, her manner, everything about her changed. She was seen taking her housekeeping seriously, going regularly to church and treating her servant more strictly.

She took Berthe back from the nurse. Félicité would bring her in when visitors came, and Madame Bovary would take the child's clothes off to show her legs and arms. She affected to adore children; this one was her consolation, her joy, her obsession, and she accompanied her caresses with lyrical extravagances which, to anyone but the citizens of Yonville, would have recalled Sachette in *Notre-Dame de Paris.*

When Charles came in he would find his slippers set to warm by the embers. Now his waistcoats were never without linings, or his shirts without buttons, and he even had the pleasure of contemplating all his nightcaps arranged in neat piles in the wardrobe. She no longer sulked, as she used to do, over taking walks in the garden; whatever he suggested was always agreed to, even though she might not understand the whims to which she yielded without a murmur; and when Léon saw him beside the fire after dinner, his hands clasped across his paunch, his feet on the andirons, his cheek flushed with digestion, his eyes moist with happiness, with the child creeping about on the carpet and that woman with her slender waist who came to kiss his forehead, leaning over the back of his chair:

"What madness!" he thought. "And how am I to get to her?"

At such times she seemed to him so virtuous and inaccessible that all hope, even the vaguest, forsook him.

But by this renunciation he placed her in an extraordinary situation. She was absolved, for him, of the sensual qualities from which he had nothing to gain; and in his heart she rose higher and higher, withdrawing in the magnificent manner of a newly deified soul taking flight. It was one of those pure emotions which do not interfere with the process of living, which one cultivates for their rarity, and the loss of which is a greater affliction than the possession is cause for rejoicing.

Emma lost weight, her cheeks paled, her face lengthened. With the black bands of her hair, her great eyes, her straight nose, her step light as a bird's and her now almost continuous silence, did she not seem to be moving through life, scarcely touching it, and bearing upon her brow the obscure mark of some sublime predestination? She was so melancholy and so calm, at once so gentle and so remote, that in her presence one felt overcome by a glacial charm, as one shudders in churches under the touch of flower-scents mingled with the chill of marble. Even the others were not proof against this fascination. The pharmacist said:

"She's a woman of great possibilities who wouldn't be out of place in a sub-prefecture."

The middle-class women admired her thrift, the patients her courtesy, the poor her charity.

But she was full of hungers, rage and hate. That gown with its straight folds concealed a heart in turmoil, and those reticent lips did not tell of its torments. She was in love with Léon, and she desired solitude in order to be able more conveniently to delight in her image of him. The sight of his person interfered with the satisfying quality of this communion. Emma quivered to the sound of his step; then, in his presence, the emotion collapsed and there remained only a vast astonishment which fell away into sorrow.

Léon was not aware, when he left her house in despair, that she sprang from her chair behind him, to see him in the street. She worried over his comings and goings, she examined his face; she invented a whole long story as a pretext for visiting his room. The pharmacist's wife seemed very fortunate to her because she slept under the same roof; and her thoughts kept alighting upon that house like the pigeons from the *Lion d'Or*, who came there to dip their pink feet and white wings in the rain gutters. But the more Emma became aware of her love, the more she suppressed it, so that it might not become apparent and in order to diminish it. She would have liked Léon to suspect it; and she would imagine circumstances, catastrophes which would have facilitated his doing so. What restrained her, no doubt, was indolence or fright, and modesty as well. She thought that she had repulsed him too far, that there was no longer time, that all was lost. Then pride, the joy of saying to herself, "I am virtuous," and of watching herself in the mirror while she assumed attitudes of resignation consoled her a little for the sacrifice she believed that she was making.

Then the appetites of the flesh, hunger for money and the melancholy of passion all were blended into a single torment; and, rather than shaking her thoughts free of it, she concentrated upon it the more, arousing herself with the pain of it and seeking new sources for it in all things.

The exasperating thing to her was that Charles had not the air of suspecting her anguish. His conviction that he was making her happy seemed a witless insult, and his sense of security a further ingratitude. For whose sake, then, was she being virtuous? Wasn't it for him, the obstacle to all felicity, the cause of all misery, and in a way the sharp-pronged buckle of the strap that was lashed about her?

So she expended upon him alone the multiple hatreds that rose out of her frustrations, and each effort to lessen them served only to augment them; for that futile exertion added itself to the other sources of despair and contributed even further to her estrangement from him. Her own natural gentleness gave her spasms of rebellion. Domestic mediocrity drove her to lustful fantasies, marital tenderness to adulterous desires. She would have liked Charles to beat her so that she might more justly detest him, and be revenged. She was alarmed sometimes by the appalling conjectures that arose in her mind; and she must go on smiling, listening to herself repeat that she was happy, pretend to be happy, let him believe that she was!

She had moments of disgust, however, at this hypocrisy. Temptations assailed her: to run away with Léon, somewhere, far away, to try to find a new destiny; but at once there would open in her mind a vague chasm, full of obscurity.

"Besides, he doesn't love me any more," she would think. "What's to become of me? What help can I hope for, what consolation, what relief?"

She would lie crushed, panting, inert, sobbing in a whisper and with tears running down her face.

"Why not tell Monsieur about it?" the servant asked her when she came into the room during these spasms.

"It's nerves," Emma said. "You're not to mention it to him, you would upset him."

"Ah yes," Félicité said. "You're just like Guérine, old Guérin the Pollet fisherman's daughter, whom I knew in Dieppe before I came to you. She was so sad, so sad that to see her standing on her own doorstep had the same effect on you as a funeral crêpe hung on the door. It seems her trouble was a sort of fog she had in her head, and the doctors couldn't do anything for her, or the priest either. When it came over her too bad, she'd go down all alone to the seashore, and lots of times the customs officer, making his rounds, used to find her stretched out flat on her face on the sand, crying. Then after her marriage that went away, they say."

"But in my case," Emma said, "it was after marriage that it came."

6

$\mathcal{O}$NE evening when the window
was open and when, seated on the sill, she
had been watching Lestiboudois, the beadle, as he was
trimming the shrubbery, she suddenly heard the Angelus ring out.

To its repeated sounds, the young woman's thoughts wandered among old memories of her youth and the convent. Nostalgia swept over her: she felt soft and utterly forlorn as a bit of down from a bird's breast tumbling in a tempest; and it was unconsciously that she turned her steps toward the church, intent upon some act of devotion, no matter what, so long as she might bend her soul to it, and all of existence melt away.

On the square she met Lestiboudois returning; for, in order not to cut his day short, he preferred to interrupt his tasks, then resume them, with the result that he rang the Angelus whenever he found it convenient. Besides, the bells, when rung earlier, informed the children of catechism time. Some of them who had arrived were already playing marbles on the gravestones in the cemetery. Others, astride the wall, were waving their legs, clipping off with their wooden shoes the great dusty nettles that grew between the low parapet and the last graves.

"Where is the priest?" Madame Bovary asked a young boy who was amusing himself by shaking the turnstile in its overlarge hole.

"He's coming," he answered.

And indeed, the presbytery door creaked, Abbé Bournisien appeared; the children scrambled pellmell into the church.

"Those ragamuffins!" the clergyman murmured. "Always the same!"

And, picking up a tattered catechism which he had just stumbled over:

"They've no respect for anything!"

97

But as soon as he caught sight of Madame Bovary:

"Excuse me," he said, "I didn't recognize you."

He thrust the catechism into his pocket and paused, swinging the heavy key to the sacristy between two fingers.

"How are you?" he added.

"Not well at all," Emma replied. "I'm suffering."

"Well, so am I," the clergyman said. "It's amazing how these first hot days wear you out, isn't it? But after all, what can you expect? We are born to suffer, as Saint Paul said. But what does Monsieur Bovary have to say about it?"

"Him!" she said with a contemptuous gesture.

"What!" the good man said, dumfounded. "Hasn't he prescribed anything for you?"

"Oh," Emma said, "earthly remedies are not what I need."

But the priest kept glancing into the church, where all the children, on their knees, were pushing at one another with their shoulders and tumbling over one another.

She fixed pleading eyes on the priest.

"You . . ." she said. "You ease all torments."

"Ah, don't speak to me about it, Madame Bovary! This very morning I had to go to Bas-Diauville for a cow that had the bloat; they thought it was an evil spell. All their cows, I don't know how . . . But pardon me! Longuemarre and Boudet! Confound it, will you stop!"

And he darted abruptly into the church.

The boys were crowding about the great pulpit, climbing over the precentor's seat, opening the missal; others, on cat-feet, were about to venture into the confessional. But the curé, erupting among them, scattered a hail of cuffs over them all. Catching them by the jacket collar, he lifted them off the floor and flung them down on their knees on the stone floor of the choir, forcefully, as if he were trying to plant them there.

"There!" he said when he had returned to Emma, shaking out his big calico handkerchief, one corner of which he held between his teeth. "The farmers are certainly to be pitied."

"There are many others," she replied.

"Surely! The laborers in cities, for example."

"They aren't the ones . . ."

"Excuse me! I've known poor mothers of families there, virtuous women, I assure you, genuine saints, who even lacked bread."

98

"But those women," Emma said, and the corners of her mouth twisted as she spoke, "those women, Monsieur le Curé, who have bread and have not . . ."

"A fire in winter," the priest said.

"Oh, what does that matter!"

"How's that? What does it matter? It seems to me that when one is warm, well fed . . . for after all . . ."

"Oh, God! Oh, God!" she sighed.

"You feel ill?" he said, moving toward her with a look of uneasiness. "The digestion, very likely. You had better go home, Madame Bovary, and drink a cup of tea; that will fortify you, or even a glass of cool water with sugar in it."

"Why?"

She seemed to have the air of one who rouses from deep meditation.

"Why, you were rubbing your forehead. I thought you felt a fainting spell coming on."

Then, recollecting:

"But you were asking me something. What was it, now? I don't remember."

"I? Nothing . . . nothing . . ." Emma said.

And her gaze, which she had been casting about her, came slowly down to rest upon the old man in the cassock. They stared at one another, face to face, without speaking.

"In that case, Madame Bovary," he said at length, "excuse me, but duty comes first, you know; I'll have to hurry with those rascals of mine."

And he entered the church, genuflecting in the doorway.

Emma saw him move out of sight between the double row of pews, walking with heavy steps, his head tilted slightly toward one shoulder and his hands hanging half-open at his sides.

Then she turned on her heels, all in one piece, like a statue on a pivot, and set out toward her house. But the curé's thick voice and the shrill voices of the children still came to her ears and continued on behind her:

"Are you a Christian?"

"Yes, I am a Christian."

"What is a Christian?"

"One who, having been baptized . . . baptized . . . baptized."

She went upstairs, clinging to the banister and, when she had reached her room, let herself fall into a chair.

The pallid light at the windowpanes faded slowly, wavering. Pieces of furniture in their places seemed to have become more immobile, and to lose themselves in shadow as in a twilight ocean. The hearth was dark, the clock ticked on and on, and Emma wondered vaguely at this tranquillity of things while there was such turmoil within herself. But there was little Berthe, between the table and the window, staggering on her knitted bootees and trying to reach her mother to clutch the ends of her apron strings.

"Let me alone," Emma said, pushing her away with her hand.

Presently the little girl returned, standing even closer against her mother's knees; and, leaning her arms across them, she raised her great blue eyes to Emma, while a thread of clear saliva dribbled from her lip onto the silk of the apron.

"Let me alone!" the young woman repeated, thoroughly irritated.

Her expression frightened the child, who began to cry.

"Oh, will you let me alone!" she said, thrusting her aside with her elbow.

Berthe tottered over to fall against the foot of the wardrobe, encountering the brass drawer-pull; she cut her cheek on it, blood flowed. Madame Bovary sprang to pick her up, broke the bell-pull, called the servant at the top of her voice and was about to burst into imprecations against herself when Charles appeared. It was dinner time; he came in.

"Look, my dear," Emma said to him in a calm voice. "The baby's just hurt herself, playing on the floor."

Charles reassured her, the injury was not serious, and went to get some diachylum.

Madame Bovary did not go downstairs; she wanted to stay alone and watch over her child. Then, watching her sleep, what remained of her uneasiness was dissipated by degrees, and she came to the conclusion that she had been very silly and very kind to have become so distressed just now over so minor a matter. Berthe, indeed, was no longer sobbing. Her breathing now barely stirred the cotton coverlet. Big tears stood at the corners of her half-closed eyelids, which revealed between the lashes pale sunken pupils; the bandage, stuck to her cheek, pulled the stretched skin up at an angle.

"It's a strange thing, how ugly that child is!" Emma thought.

At eleven o'clock when Charles returned from the pharmacy,

where he had gone after dinner to return the remains of the diachylum, he found his wife standing beside the cradle.

"Now, I've told you that it's nothing," he said, kissing her forehead. "Don't upset yourself, poor darling, you'll make yourself sick."

He had stayed late at the apothecary's. "I have something to say to you," he had whispered to the clerk, who walked downstairs ahead of him.

"Can it be that he suspects something?" Léon wondered. His heart thudded and he became lost in conjecture.

At last Charles, having closed the door, requested him to find out, himself, in Rouen what the price might be of a good daguerreotype; it was a sentimental surprise he was preparing for his wife, a delicate attention, his portrait in a black suit. But he wanted first "to know what to expect"; this commission should not inconvenience Monsieur Léon, since he went to the city almost every week.

With what object? Homais suspected some sort of "wild oats," a love affair. But he was mistaken; Léon was not pursuing any lady-love. He was more melancholy than ever, and Madame Lefrançois was made well aware of it by the quantity of food he left on his plate these days. To find out more about it, she questioned the tax-collector; Binet replied in a haughty tone that he was not "in the pay of the police."

His companion, nevertheless, seemed to him to be behaving very oddly; for often Léon would throw himself back in his chair, flinging out his arms and complaining in vague terms of his existence.

"It's because you don't take enough recreation," the tax-collector said.

"What sort?"

"Well, if I were you, I'd get a lathe."

"But I don't know how to turn on a lathe," the clerk said.

"Oh, that's so!" the other said, caressing his jaw with an air of mingled disdain and satisfaction.

Léon was weary of loving without result; then, too, he was beginning to feel that sense of discouragement caused by the constant repetition of the same life when no interest directs it and no hope sustains it. He was so bored with Yonville and the people of Yonville that the sight of certain persons, certain houses, irritated him beyond endurance. At length he wrote his mother a long detailed letter in which he explained his reasons for going immediately to live in Paris. She gave her consent.

He did not hurry. Every day for an entire month Hivert transported for him from Yonville to Rouen, from Rouen to Yonville, trunks, suitcases, parcels; and when Léon had replenished his wardrobe, had his three armchairs reupholstered, bought a supply of silk handkerchiefs, made, in a word, more preparations than for a trip around the world, he postponed his departure from week to week until he received a second maternal letter urging him to leave, since he so desired, before the vacations, in order to take his examination.

When the moment for the final embraces came, Madame Homais wept; Justin sobbed; Homais, as a strong man, concealed his emotion; he insisted upon carrying his friend's greatcoat, himself, to the gate of the lawyer, who was taking Léon to Rouen in his carriage. Léon had just time to say good-by to Monsieur Bovary.

When he had reached the top of the staircase he paused, so breathless did he feel. At his entrance Madame Bovary sprang up quickly.

"It's me again!" Léon said.

"I was sure of it!"

She bit her lips and a tide of blood flooded up under her skin which flushed deep pink from the roots of her hair to the edge of her collar. She remained standing, one shoulder leaning against the woodwork.

"Monsieur isn't at home?" he asked.

"He is out."

She repeated: "He is out."

There was a silence, then. They looked at one another; and their thoughts, mingling in an identical torment, were as if locked in an intimate embrace, like two pulsing bosoms.

"I'd like to kiss Berthe good-by," Léon said.

Emma went down a few stairs and called Félicité.

He cast an all-embracing glance about him, which lingered over the walls, the shelves, the hearth as if to penetrate every object and carry it away with him.

But she returned, and the servant brought Berthe, who was waving a toy windmill upside down on the end of a string.

Léon kissed her neck several times.

"Good-by, poor child, good-by dear little girl! Good-by!"

He restored her to her mother.

"Take her away," she said to Félicité.

They were left alone.

Madame Bovary, her back turned, had her face pressed to a windowpane; Léon was holding his cap in his hand and kept striking it gently against his thigh.

"It's going to rain," Emma said.

"I have an overcoat," he said.

"Ah!"

She turned away again, her chin lowered and her forehead advanced. The light glimmered over it as over marble, to the curve of the eyebrows, without revealing what Emma was watching on the horizon nor what she was thinking within herself.

"Well then, good-by!" he sighed.

She raised her head with an abrupt motion:

"Yes, good-by . . . Go now."

They moved toward one another: he held out his hand, she hesitated.

"In the English fashion, then," she said, forcing herself to laugh, and giving him her hand.

Léon felt it between his fingers, and the very substance of all his being seemed to him to be distilled into that moist palm.

Then he opened his hand; their eyes met once more, and he was gone.

When he reached the market he paused and hid behind a pillar to gaze one last time at that white house with its four green shutters. He thought he saw a shadow behind the window in the bedroom; but the curtain, coming loose from its fastening as if of itself, slowly moved in long oblique folds which suddenly straightened out altogether, and then it hung straight, more motionless than a plaster wall. Léon began to run.

7

𝒯ʜᴇ next day was a dismal one
for Emma. Everything seemed to her to be
swathed in a black miasma that drifted confusedly across
the surfaces of objects, and sorrow rushed into her spirit with soft
moaning sounds, like the winter wind in a deserted castle. It was
the sort of reverie one indulges in upon what will never come again,
the lassitude that overcomes one after each task accomplished, that
pain, in fact, which the interruption of any accustomed procedure
causes one, the abrupt cessation of a prolonged vibration.

As upon her return from La Vaubyessard with the quadrilles still
eddying through her head, she was assailed by a dreary melancholy,
a numb despair. Léon reappeared, taller, more handsome, more polished, more indistinct; although he was parted from her he had not
left her, he was here, and the walls of the house seemed to retain
his shadow. She could not tear her eyes away from this carpet where
he had walked, these empty chairs in which he had sat.

The river still flowed past, and idly pushed its little waves along
the slippery bank. They had walked there many times, to that same
murmur of ripples, over moss-covered stones. What good days of sunlight they had had! What good afternoons, alone in the shadows at
the end of the garden! He used to read aloud, sitting bareheaded
on a rustic wooden bench; the cool prairie wind would flutter the
pages of the book and the honeysuckle blossoms of the arbor . . .
Ah, he was gone, the one charm of her life, the one possible hope
of felicity! Why had she not grasped that happiness when it was
offered? Why not have held him back with both hands, on her
knees, when he wished to go? And she cursed herself for not having
given her love to Léon; she was thirsty for his lips. A desire seized
her to run to him, fling herself into his arms, say to him: "I am here;
I am yours!" But Emma became embarrassed in advance over the

difficulties of such an enterprise, and her desires, aggravated by regret, became only the more ardent.

From that time on this memory of Léon was a sort of focal point for her boredom; and the most distant memories as well as the most immediate events, what she had experienced and what she had imagined, her frustrated desires for physical gratification, her projects for happiness which crackled like dead branches in the wind, her sterile virtue, her fallen hopes, her marriage bed, she gathered up all, accepted all, made all serve to warm her sorrow.

Nevertheless, the flames died down, whether because her inner resources became exhausted or because too much fuel had been heaped upon them. Little by little love was extinguished by absence, regret smothered by habit; and that fiery glow which had washed her pale skies with purple sank away into shadow and was gradually obliterated. In the lethargic state of her consciousness, she even mistook repugnance toward her husband for a yearning for a lover, the scaldings of hatred for the rekindling of tenderness; but as the hurricane continued to blow and as passion was consumed to ashes, and as no help came, no sunlight broke through, on all sides lay black night, and she remained lost in a terrible cold which spread all through her.

Then the bad days of Tostes began again. She considered herself far more wretched now, for she was experiencing grief in the certainty that there would be no end to it.

A woman who had imposed such great sacrifices upon herself could surely take comfort from indulging whims. She bought herself a Gothic prie-dieu, in one month she spent fourteen francs for lemons to whiten her fingernails; she wrote to Rouen to order blue cashmere for a dress; she selected the most beautiful of the scarves in Lheureux' shop; she would tie it about her waist over her dressing-gown and, with the blinds closed and a book in her hand, she would lie stretched out on a couch in this costume.

She frequently changed the fashion in which she dressed her hair: she did it in Chinese style, in soft curls, in neat braids; she parted it on the side and turned the ends under like a man's.

She took a notion to learn Italian: she bought dictionaries, a grammar, a supply of white paper. She tried serious reading, history and philosophy. Sometimes at night Charles awoke with a start, thinking that someone had come to fetch him for a patient:

"I'm coming!" he would mumble.

And it would be the sound of a match Emma was striking in order to relight the lamp. But it was with her reading as with her pieces of needlework which, half-finished, cluttered her chest of drawers; she would take them up, abandon them, go on to others.

She had moments of unrestraint when she could easily have been incited to recklessness. One day she maintained, in opposition to her husband, that she could drink a full half-tumbler of brandy and, as Charles was foolish enough to defy her to do it, she swallowed the brandy to the last drop.

In spite of her giddy airs (as the women of Yonville described them), Emma still did not seem happy, and habitually wore at the corners of her mouth that immobile contraction which creases the faces of elderly spinsters and of those disappointed in their ambitions. She was utterly pale, white as linen; the skin of her nose was drawn toward the nostrils, her eyes gazed at one with a vague expression. Having discovered three gray hairs at her temples, she spoke of how she was growing old.

Often fainting spells overcame her. One day she even spat blood, and as Charles hastened to her, showing his concern:

"Oh, nonsense!" she said. "What's the difference?"

Charles went to take refuge in his office; and he wept, seated in his desk chair beneath the phrenological chart, with his elbows on the table.

Then he wrote to his mother, asking her to come, and they had long conferences together about Emma.

What was the solution? What was to be done, since she refused any treatment?

"Do you know what your wife needs?" the elder Madame Bovary said. "Forced occupation, manual labor! If she were forced to earn her own living, like so many others, she wouldn't have these vapors, which come of a lot of notions she's got into her head, and of the idleness she lives in."

"Still, she keeps busy," Charles said.

"Oh, she keeps busy! Doing what? Reading novels, bad books, works that are against religion and in which the authors make fun of priests with quotations from Voltaire. But all that sort of thing goes a long way, my poor boy, and anyone who has no religion always turns out badly."

So it was decided that Emma was to be prevented from reading any more novels. The undertaking did not seem an easy one. The good woman undertook to see to it herself; she would, when she passed through Rouen, go in person to the circulating library and give notice that Emma was terminating her subscription. Would they not have the right to notify the police, if the library persisted just the same in its faculty as poisoner?

The farewells of the mother-in-law and daughter-in-law were short. During the three weeks they had been left together they had not exchanged four words, aside from inquiries and formal phrases when they met at table or before going to bed.

Madame Bovary left on a Wednesday, which was market day in Yonville.

Emma was leaning on her elbows at her window (she sat there often: in the provinces, the window takes the place of theaters and promenades), and she was amusing herself watching the noisy multitude of rustics when she caught sight of a gentleman dressed in a green velvet coat. He had yellow gloves on his hands, although he was wearing heavy gaiters; and he was making his way toward the doctor's house, followed by a peasant walking with lowered head and a look of being plunged in thought.

"May I see the doctor?" he asked Justin, who was chatting with Félicité on the doorstep.

And, taking him for the servant of the house:

"Tell him that Monsieur Rodolphe Boulanger of La Huchette is here."

It was not out of property vanity that the new arrival had added the explanatory phrase to his name, but in order to introduce himself more accurately. La Huchette, as a matter of fact, was an estate near Yonville, the château of which he had just acquired, along with two farms that he cultivated himself without, however, going to too much trouble.

Charles came into the sitting room. Monsieur Boulanger introduced his man, who wanted to be bled because he felt "ants crawling all over his body."

"That will purge me," he kept insisting in the face of all arguments.

Bovary, therefore, brought a band and a basin and asked Justin to hold it. Then, addressing the already blanched villager:

"Don't be afraid, my good fellow."

"No, no," the other answered. "Go right ahead."

And with a swaggering air he held out his thick arm. At the prick of the lancet the blood spurted and splattered against the mirror.

"Hold the basin closer!" Charles exclaimed.

"Damn!" the peasant said. "You'd swear it was a little fountain running. What red blood I've got! That should be a good sign, isn't it?"

"Sometimes," the physician said, "the patient doesn't feel anything at first, then faintness sets in, more particularly with husky people like this man."

At these words the farmer dropped the small box he was turning between his fingers. A sudden jerk of his shoulders made the back of the chair creak. His hat fell to the floor.

"I was expecting that," Bovary said, applying his finger to the vein.

The basin began to tremble in Justin's hands; his knees wobbled, he turned pale.

"My wife! My wife!" Charles called.

Instantly she ran downstairs.

"Vinegar!" he cried. "Oh, Lord, two at once!"

And in his emotion he was barely able to apply the compress.

"It's nothing," Monsieur Boulanger said with the utmost tranquillity, taking Justin under the arms.

And he seated him on the table, propping his back against the wall.

Madame Bovary began to remove his cravat. He had a knot in the strings of his shirt; she took several minutes, moving her light fingers at the young boy's neck; then she poured a little vinegar on her batiste handkerchief; she dampened his temples with it in little pats and she blew on it, delicately.

The plowman recovered consciousness; but Justin's syncope continued, and his pupils disappeared up under the pale surrounding membranes, like blue flowers in milk.

"We should hide that from him," Charles said.

Madame Bovary took the basin, to put it under the table; in the motion she made as she bent over, her dress (a summer dress with four flounces, yellow, long-waisted, full-skirted) swept out about her on the stone floor of the sitting room; and as Emma, crouching down, wavered a little in stretching out her arms, the puffs of material sank in here and there, with the swaying of her body.

When Justin had left, pulling his clothes back on, they talked a little about faints. Madame Bovary had never experienced one.

"That's extraordinary for a lady!" Monsieur Boulanger said. "On the other hand, there are many very sensitive men. For instance, at a duel once, I saw one of the seconds lose consciousness just from hearing the pistols loaded."

Meanwhile Monsieur Boulanger dismissed his hired man, urging him to set his mind at rest now that his whim had been attended to.

"It brought me the pleasure of making your acquaintance," he added. And he looked at Emma as he spoke.

Then he laid three francs on the corner of the table, bowed casually and went out.

He was soon on the other side of the river (this was his road back to La Huchette): and Emma caught sight of him on the prairie, walking beneath the poplars, slowing his steps from time to time like someone who is meditating.

"She is very attractive!" he was thinking. "She is very attractive, that doctor's wife. Fine teeth, black eyes, a pretty foot and dressed like a Parisian woman. Where the devil does she come from? Where in the world did he find her, that fellow?"

Monsieur Rodolphe Boulanger was thirty-four years old; he was cynical in temperament and keen of intellect, having in addition been much in the company of women and being thoroughly experienced with them. This one had seemed pretty to him; so he mused about her and about her husband.

"I think he is very stupid. She's undoubtedly tired of him. He has dirty fingernails and a three-day beard. While he's trotting about to his patients, she stays home darning socks. And she is bored, she'd like to live in the city, dance the polka every evening! Poor little thing. She's gaping for love like a carp on the kitchen table for water. After three gallant remarks she'd adore you, I'm sure of it! It would be lovely, charming . . . Yes, but how to get rid of her afterwards?"

Then the disadvantages of pleasure, glimpsed in anticipation, made him, by force of contrast, think of his mistress. She was an actress whom he kept, in Rouen; and, when he had lingered over this image with which, even in memory, he was surfeited:

"Ah, Madame Bovary is much prettier," he thought, "and above all, fresher. Virginie is beginning to get decidedly too fat. She's so tiresome about her pleasures. And besides, what a mania for shrimp!"

The countryside was deserted, and Rodolphe heard about him only the rhythmic whisper of grasses brushed by his boots and the distant shrilling of crickets lying close under the oat-stalks; he was reënvisioning Emma in the sitting room, dressed as he had seen her, and he was stripping off her garments.

"Oh, I shall have her!" he cried, smashing a lump of earth in front of him with one blow of his stick.

And at once he fell to studying the strategic aspect of the undertaking. He wondered:

"Where shall we meet? And how? We'll have the brat on our hands all the time, and the maid, the neighbors, the husband, all sorts of annoying problems. Oh, rubbish!" he said. "It's too much of a waste of time."

Then he began again:

"It's because she has eyes that bore into your heart like gimlets. And that pale coloring! . . . I who adore pale women!"

By the top of the Argueil hill he had come to his decision.

"All that's left to do is find opportunities. Well, then, I'll call on them a few times, I'll send them some game, some fowl; I'll have myself bled if necessary; we will become friends, I'll invite them to visit me. . . . Oh, by jove!" he added, "the Agricultural Exposition is coming soon; she will be there, I'll see her. That's the time to begin, and boldly, for that is the surest way."

8

$\mathcal{I}$T came, indeed, that much-
publicized Exposition! Early on the morning
of that solemn occasion all the inhabitants, on their doorsteps, were discussing the preparations; the pediment of the town
hall had been wreathed with garlands of ivy; a tent had been set
up in a meadow for the festivities and, in the center of the square,
in front of the church, a sort of bomb-throwing device was to greet
the arrival of Monsieur le Préfet and the names of the prize-winning
farmers. The National Guard from Buchy (there was none in Yonville) had come to swell the ranks of the firemen, of whom Binet
was the chief. That day he was wearing a collar even higher than
usual; and, belted into his tunic, his torso was so rigid and immobile
that all the vital part of his organism seemed to have descended into
his two legs, which rose in cadence, in one single movement, at a
smart pace. As rivalry flourished between the tax-collector and the
colonel, both were putting their men through their drill, at one side,
to show off their prowess.

Never had there been such a display of pomp! Many of the citizens
had washed down their houses the evening before; tricolored flags
hung at half-open windows; all the taverns were crowded; and, in
that brilliant weather, the starched bonnets, the gold crosses and
colored fichus looked whiter than snow, reflected the clear sunlight
and relieved with occasional splashes of color the somber monotony
of dark coats and blue jackets.

The throng poured into the main street from both ends of the town.
It overflowed out of side streets, paths and houses, and from time
to time one heard doors slam shut behind women in lace gloves,
sallying forth to see the festivities. But the jubilation which bright-
ened every face seemed to depress Madame Lefrançois, hostess of
the inn. Standing on her kitchen steps she kept muttering:

"What nonsense! What nonsense with their canvas shack! Do they think the prefect will be perfectly comfortable, eating his dinner out there in a tent, like a circus clown?"

The apothecary passed. He had on a black coat, nankeen breeches, beaver shoes and, as an extraordinary gesture, a hat—a low-crowned hat.

"Your servant!" he said. "Excuse me, I'm in a hurry."

"Oh, you're going over there?" she said with an air of disdain.

"Yes, I'm going," the apothecary answered, astonished; "am I not one of the advisory committee?"

The widow Lefrançois gazed at him for a few moments, and at length answered, smiling:

"That does make a difference. But what has farming got to do with you? Do you know anything about it?"

"Certainly I know something about it, since I'm a pharmacist, that is to say, a chemist. And chemistry, Madame Lefrançois, having as its object the understanding of the reciprocal and molecular action of all the elements in nature, it follows that agriculture should be included in its domain."

The hostess did not once take her eyes from the door of the Café Français and the pharmacist continued:

"If only God would make chemists of our farmers, or at least if they would listen to the advice of science! I, for instance, have recently written a little opus, a monograph of more than seventy-two pages, entitled: *On Cider, Its Manufacture and Its Effects, followed by a Few New Observations upon the Subject,* which I sent to the Agricultural Society of Rouen; which earned me the honor of being included among its members, in the agriculture division, apple-study section. Well now, if my work had been made available to the public . . ."

But the apothecary paused, Madame Lefrançois seemed so preoccupied.

"Look at them!" she said. "It's impossible to understand. A low tavern like that!"

And, with shrugs of her shoulders that stretched the stitches of her sweater across her bosom she gestured with both hands toward her rival's restaurant, from which the sound of singing was now issuing.

"Furthermore, he won't last long," she added. "Before a week's out, it will all be over."

Homais fell back with amazement. She came down her three steps and, speaking into his ear:

"What, you didn't know that? They're going to attach his property this week. It's Lheureux who's making him sell out. He has ruined him with notes."

"What an appalling catastrophe!" cried the apothecary, who always had fitting expressions for every imaginable set of circumstances.

The hostess then began to tell him the story, which she had through Théodore, Monsieur Guillaumin's servant, and much as she detested Tellier, she censured Lheureux. He was an inveigler, a sneak.

"Oh, look," she said, "there he is, over at the market: he's speaking to Madame Bovary, who is wearing a green hat! She's on Boulanger's arm, too."

"Madame Bovary!" Homais said. "I must hurry over and pay my respects. Perhaps she'd be pleased to have a seat inside the inclosure, under the peristyle."

And, without listening to Madame Lefrançois, who was calling him back to tell him her story at greater length, the pharmacist moved off at a rapid pace, a smile on his face and his legs strutting, distributing many salutations to right and to left and taking up a large amount of space with the ample tails of his black coat, which floated in the breeze behind him.

Rodolphe, having caught sight of him from afar, had taken to a more rapid gait; but Madame Bovary got out of breath; so he slowed and said to her, smiling, in a cynical tone:

"It's just to avoid that coarse man: you know, the apothecary."

She nudged him with her elbow.

"What does that mean?" he wondered. And he studied her out of the corner of his eye as they continued to walk.

Her profile was so placid that one could discover nothing from it. It stood out in the full daylight, within the oval of her hood with its pale ribbons like the leaves of rushes. Her eyes with their long upturned lashes gazed straight ahead of her and, although fully open, they seemed somewhat narrowed by the cheeks, because of the blood that pulsed gently below her delicate skin. A rosy flush crossed the bridge of her nose. She carried her head tipped toward her shoulder, and one could see between her lips the translucent edges of her white teeth.

"Is she making fun of me?" Rodolphe wondered.

This gesture on Emma's part seemed, however, to have been no more than a warning; for Monsieur Lheureux was walking with them, speaking to them from time to time as if in an attempt to enter into conversation.

"A superb day! Everybody is out! The wind is in the east."

And Madame Bovary made him no more answer than did Rodolphe, while at the least motion they made he drew closer, saying, "I beg your pardon?" and raising his hand to his hat.

When they were in front of the marshal's house, rather than following the road as far as the barrier, Rodolphe turned off abruptly into a path, drawing Madame Bovary with him; he called out:

"Good-by, Monsieur Lheureux! We'll see you later."

"How you sent him about his business!" she said, laughing.

"Why let other people force themselves on me?" he returned. "And since I'm fortunate enough to be with you, today . . ."

Emma blushed. He did not finish his sentence. Then he spoke of the fine weather and the pleasure of strolling over grass. A few daisies were in bloom.

"Here are some pretty Easter-flowers," he said, "they make oracles for all country lovers."

He added:

"Shall I pick some? What do you think?"

"Are you in love?" she asked, coughing a little.

"Oh, well, who knows?" Rodolphe answered.

But it was time for the judging, and the farmers, one by one, were filing into a sort of amphitheater formed by a long rope running between sticks. Cattle were there, their noses pointing toward the rope, making an irregular line with their uneven rumps; slothful hogs rooted in the earth with their snouts; calves bawled; sheep bleated. Bare-armed plowmen clung to the bridles of prancing stallions which were whinnying, wide-nostriled, in the direction of the mares. The mares stood quietly, heads and tails drooping, while their foals rested in their shadow or came occasionally to suck.

Meanwhile, between the two rows, gentlemen were walking forward at a ponderous gait, examining each animal, then consulting together in low voices. One of them, who seemed to be the most important, took notes in a notebook as he walked. He was the president of the judging committee: Monsieur Derozerays of La Panville.

The moment he recognized Rodolphe he came forward eagerly and said, smiling amiably:

"How's this, Monsieur Boulanger, you're deserting us?"

Rodolphe protested that he was going to come. But when the president had disappeared:

"My Lord, no," he said, "I'm not going: your company is more to my taste than his."

And, mocking the Exposition all the while, he showed the guard his blue visitor's pass in order to move about more freely, and even paused occasionally before some handsome "specimen" which Madame Bovary did not admire in the least. He noticed this, and then began to make jokes about the Yonville ladies, their costumes; then he made his excuses for the carelessness of his own.

"Besides," he added, "when one lives in the country . . ."

"Everything is a waste of effort," Emma said.

"That's true!" Rodolphe replied. "To think that not one single one of these fine fellows is capable of even appreciating the cut of a suit!"

Then they talked about provincial mediocrity, of the existences stifled by it, illusions lost in it.

"So," Rodolphe said, "I sink deeper and deeper into melancholy . . ."

"You!" she exclaimed with astonishment. "But I thought you were very gay."

"Oh, yes, in appearance, because in the midst of a group I can put a jester's mask on my face; and yet how many times, at sight of a cemetery in the moonlight, I've wondered if I wouldn't be better off going to join those who have nothing to do but sleep . . ."

"Oh? And your friends?" she said. "You don't think about them?"

"My friends? Who are they? Have I any? Who bothers about me?"

And he accompanied these last words with a sort of whistling breath between his lips.

But they were obliged to separate from one another because of a great structure of piled chairs which a man was carrying behind them. Madame Bovary again took Rodolphe's arm; he continued as if speaking to himself:

"Yes, I've missed so much! Always alone. Ah, if I had had an aim in life, if I could have found affection, if I had discovered someone . . . Oh, how I should have poured out all the energy of which I'm capable, I should have overcome everything, broken down everything!"

"Just the same, it seems to me that you're not to be pitied in the least," Emma said.

"Oh, you think so?" Rodolphe said.

"Because after all . . ." she went on, "you are free."

She hesitated. "Rich."

"Don't make fun of me," he said.

And she was swearing that she had not been making fun when a cannon shot resounded; at once everyone pushed pellmell toward the village.

At length, at the end of the square, a big hired coach appeared, drawn by two lean horses which a driver in a white hat lashed by turns with his whip. Binet had just time to shout: "*Aux armes!*" and the colonel to echo him . . . There was a rush toward the stacked arms. And, after a shoulder-arms during which the clank of musket-slings traveling down the line sounded like a copper kettle rolling downstairs, all the firearms were grounded.

Then a man was seen descending from the coach, dressed in a black coat with silver braid, bald in front, wearing a tuft of hair at the back, with a sallow complexion and a most benignant expression. His eyes, very large and heavy-lidded, were half closed to gaze at the throng, as he lifted his pointed nose and made his sunken mouth smile. He recognized the mayor by his sash and informed him that Monsieur le Préfet had been unable to come. He, himself, was a member of the prefectoral council; then he added a few apologies. Tuvache answered with courteous remarks, the other confessed his embarrassment; and they remained so, face to face and their fore-heads almost touching, with the members of the judging committee, the municipal council, the prominent citizens, the National Guard and the crowd all about them.

Meanwhile Rodolphe, with Madame Bovary, had gone up to the first floor of the town hall, into the council chamber, and as it was empty he had declared that this would be a good place for enjoying the spectacle more comfortably. He took three stools from around the oval table beneath the bust of the King, and, having brought them over to the window, they sat down side by side.

There was agitation on the platform, long whispered consultations, conferences. At length Monsieur le Conseiller arose. It was now known that his name was Lieuvain, and his name was repeated from

116

one mouth to another through the crowd. When he had collected a few papers and held them above his eyes in order to see better, he began:

"Gentlemen:

"First permit me (before speaking to you of the object of today's gathering, and this sentiment will, I am sure, be shared by you all), permit me, I say, to render justice to the higher administration, to the government, to the monarch, gentlemen, to our sovereign, to that beloved King to whom no branch of public or private prosperity is indifferent, and who guides the chariot of State among the incessant perils of a stormy sea with a hand at once so firm and so wise, respecting peace as well as war, industry, commerce, agriculture and the arts."

"I ought to move back a little," Rodolphe said.

"Why?" Emma said.

But just then the councilor's voice rose to an extraordinary note; he was declaiming:

"The time is no longer, gentlemen, when civil discord bloodied our public squares, when the householder, the lawyer, even the laborer, falling into a peaceful sleep at night, trembled for fear of being suddenly awakened by the sound of fire alarms, when the most subversive maxims audaciously gnawed at the foundations . . ."

"Because I might be seen from below," Rodolphe said. "Then for the next two weeks I should have to make apologies, and with my bad reputation . . ."

"Oh, you're slandering yourself!" Emma said.

"No, no, it's abominable, I swear it is."

"But, gentlemen," the councilor continued, "if, banishing from my memory these gloomy pictures, I rest my eyes once more upon the present condition of our fair country: what do I see? Everywhere commerce and the arts are flourishing; everywhere new lines of communication, like so many new blood vessels in the body of the State, are establishing new relationships; our great manufacturing centers have resumed their activity; religion, more firmly planted, smiles into all hearts; our ports are full, confidence is reborn, and at last France breathes again! . . ."

"Besides," Rodolphe added, "perhaps there is a reason for it, from the world's point of view."

"How do you mean?" she said.

"Well," he said, "don't you know that there are souls forever in torment? They must have alternate dream and action, the purest passions and the most violent satisfactions, and that way one stumbles into all sorts of whims, of follies."

She gazed at him then as one stares at a traveler who has journeyed through extraordinary lands, and said:

"We haven't even that source of distraction, we poor women!"

"A sorry distraction, for one doesn't find happiness in it."

"But does one ever find it?" she asked.

"Yes, it comes some day," he answered.

"And that is the thing you have understood," the councilor was saying. "You, farmers and country laborers; you, peaceful pioneers of a wholly civilized work; you, men of progress and morality! You have understood, I say, that political storms are truly even more dreadful than atmospheric disturbances . . ."

"It comes some day," Rodolphe repeated, "some day, all of a sudden, when one despairs of it. Then the horizons roll open, it's like a voice crying 'Here it is!' You feel a need to confide your life to that person, to give her everything, sacrifice everything to her! You don't need to explain to one another, you know by intuition. You've seen each other in dreams. [And he gazed at her.] At last, there it is, the treasure you've searched for so long, there, in front of you; it shines, it sparkles. Yet you still doubt, you don't dare believe in it; you go on being dazzled by it, like someone coming out of the shadows into the light."

And as he finished speaking, Rodolphe added pantomime to the words, he passed his hand over his face like a man seized with a dizzy spell! then he let it fall upon Emma's. She drew hers away. But the councilor was still reading:

"And who should be astonished at that, gentlemen? Only he who is blind enough, deep enough (I am not afraid to say it) deep enough in the prejudices of another age . . ." ". . . and to the maintenance of the State, the fruit of respect for law and the fulfillment of duty . . ."

"That again!" Rodolphe said. "Always duty, I'm bored to death with words like that. They're a lot of old imbeciles in flannel vests, and hypocrites in foot-warmers and rosaries who are forever chanting 'Duty, duty!' in our ears. Well, Lord, duty is feeling what is great, cherishing what is beautiful, and not accepting all the conventions of society, along with the ignominies it imposes on us."

"Still . . . still . . ." Madame Bovary objected.

"No, no! Why prate against the passions? Aren't they the only beautiful things on earth, the source of heroism, of enthusiasm, of poetry, music, art, in fact of everything?"

"But surely you have to pay some attention to the world's opinion and obey its moral code," Emma said.

"Ah, but there are two," he answered. "The small, conventional man-made one, the one that's continually changing and that bawls so loudly, stirs up a commotion lower down, close to the earth, like that assembly of imbeciles you see out there. But the other, the eternal one is all about and above, like the countryside that surrounds us and the blue sky that gives us light."

Monsieur Lieuvain had just wiped his mouth with his handkerchief. He went on:

"And who am I, gentlemen, to point out to you here the usefulness of agriculture? For who is it that supplies us with the necessities of life? Who provides our nourishment? Is it not the farmer? The farmer, gentlemen, who, sowing the fruitful furrows of the fields with industrious hands . . ."

Rodolphe had drawn closer to Emma, and he said in a low voice, speaking rapidly:

"Doesn't this conspiracy on the part of the world revolt you? Is there a single sentiment which it does not condemn? The most noble instincts, the purest sympathies are persecuted, slandered, and if two poor souls should finally come together, everything is organized to prevent them from uniting. Still, they try, they beat their wings, they call out to one another. Oh, no matter what happens, sooner or later, in six months, ten years, they will be united, they will love one another, because fate wills it and because they were born for each other."

He had his arms crossed upon his knees and thus, raising his face to Emma, he gazed at her fixedly, from very close. She noticed small gold streaks in his eyes, radiating out all around his black pupils, and she even caught the odor of the pomade that glistened on his hair. Languor overcame her then, she remembered the viscount who had taught her to waltz at La Vaubyessard and whose beard, like this hair, had given off that scent of vanilla and lemon; and, automatically, she half closed her eyelids, the better to breathe it in. But as she made this gesture, leaning back in her chair, she caught sight of the old diligence, the *Hirondelle*, in the distance, far out on the horizon, slowly moving down the slope of the Leux, trailing behind it a long plume of dust. It was in that yellow coach that Léon had so often returned to her; and by that same road that he had gone forever! She seemed to see him opposite her, in his window, then everything became confused, clouds swirled about her; it seemed to her that she was circling again in the waltz, under the blaze of cut glass chandeliers, in the viscount's arms, and that Léon was not far away, that he was going to come . . . and yet she still was breathing the scent of Rodolphe's pomade beside her. So the pleasure of this sensation mingled with her desires of other days and, like grains of sand under a gust of wind, they seethed in the subtle emanations of the perfume which was diffused through her spirit. She widened her nostrils several times, vigorously, to draw in the fragrance of the ivy around the columns. She drew off her gloves and dried her palms; then, with her handkerchief, she fanned her face, while through the pounding of her temples she heard the murmur of the crowd and the voice of the councilor chanting his phrases.

He was saying:

"Continue! Persevere! Listen neither to the suggestions of established routine nor to the overhasty counsels of a reckless empirism! Concentrate above all upon the improvement of soil, upon good feeds, upon the development of equine, bovine, ovine and porcine strains! Let these agricultural expositions be for you like pacific arenas where the victor, as he leaves, will hold out his hand to the vanquished and fraternize with him in the hope of a better success! And you, ancient servants, humble servitors whose painful labors no government up to this day has taken into consideration, come and receive the reward of your mute virtues, and be convinced that the State, henceforth, has its eyes fixed on you, that it is encouraging you, that it is protecting you, that it will render justice to your righteous claims and lighten, so far as is in its power, the burden of your painful sacrifices!"

Monsieur Lieuvain then sat down; Monsieur Derozerays rose, embarking upon another speech. Rodolphe, with Madame Bovary, talked of dreams, presentiments, magnetism. From magnetism Rodolphe gradually arrived at affinities and, while Monsieur le Président was citing Cincinnatus at his plow, Diocletian planting his cabbages and the Chinese emperors inaugurating the year with days of sowing, the young man was explaining to the young woman that those irresistible attractions had their origins in some previous existence.

"Take us," he said, "why did we meet? What chance willed it? The truth is that, across the distance, like two rivers that flow to meet one another, our particular slopes forced us toward each other."

And he grasped her hand; she did not withdraw it.

"Together for good farming!" the president shouted.

Rodolphe pressed her hand, feeling it warm and tremulous as a captive turtledove that wishes to regain its wings; but, whether because she was making an effort to free it or because she was responding to that pressure, her fingers moved; he cried:

"Oh, thank you! You aren't driving me away! You are kind! You understand that I'm yours. Let me see you, let me look at you!"

A breath of wind coming in at the windows rippled the cover on the table, and below, in the square, all the peasant women's wide sunbonnets rose like the wings of agitated white butterflies.

"Use of oleaginous meal-cakes," the president continued.

Rodolphe did not speak. They gazed at each other. An overwhelming desire made their dry lips tremble; and softly, involuntarily, their fingers intertwined.

The ceremony was over; the crowd dispersed; and now that the speeches had been read, everyone returned to his own rank and all was restored to normal: masters berated servants and servants beat the animals, indifferent victors who returned to the stable, green wreaths between their horns.

Meanwhile, the National Guardsmen had mounted to the first floor of the town hall, with brioches strung on their bayonets and the battalion's drum laden with a basket of bottles. Madame Bovary took Rodolphe's arm; he escorted her back to her home; they parted in front of her door; then he went to stroll alone in the meadow while awaiting the hour of the banquet.

The feast was long, noisy, ill-served; people were so closely packed that it was difficult to move one's elbows, and the narrow planks that served as benches all but cracked beneath the weight of the guests. They ate heartily. Everyone was intent upon getting his fair share. Sweat ran down all their foreheads; and a whitish vapor, like the mist over a river on an autumn morning, drifted above the table, between the hanging lanterns. Rodolphe, his back resting against the side-drop of the tent, was thinking so deeply of Emma that he heard nothing. Behind him, servants were piling up soiled plates on the turf; his neighbors spoke to him, he did not answer; his glass was refilled, and silence settled over his thoughts in spite of the swelling tumult. He dreamed over the words she had said and the shape of her lips; her face shone in the insignia on shakos as in a magic mirror; the folds of her gown hung down along the walls and days of love stretched out to infinity in the vista of the future.

He saw her again that evening during the fireworks; but she was with her husband, Madame Homais and the pharmacist, who was working himself up over the danger of stray rockets and kept leaving the group from moment to moment to go and give Binet advice.

Emma, silent, leaned gently against Charles' shoulder, then, raising her chin, she would follow the luminous trail of the rockets across the black sky. Rodolphe watched her by the light of the street lamps which had been lighted.

Gradually they dimmed. The stars came out. A few drops of rain fell. She tied her fichu over her bare head.

Just then the councilor's hired coach drove out of the inn yard. His driver, who was drunk, immediately fell into a doze, and they saw him from a distance, over the hood, between the two lanterns, the mass of his body swinging right and left according to the pitching of the springs.

"Truly," the apothecary said, "drunkenness ought to be attacked with the utmost severity! I should like to see the names of all those who become intoxicated with alcoholic beverages during the week inscribed weekly on a bulletin board by the door of the town hall. Besides, statistically speaking, it would make a sort of legible record to which one could refer as needed . . . But excuse me."

And he hurried off once more toward the captain.

The latter was returning to his house. He was going to have a look at his lathe.

"Perhaps it wouldn't do any harm," Homais told him, "to send one of your men, or go yourself . . ."

"Let me alone," the tax-collector answered. "Everything is all right!"

"Be reassured," the apothecary said, rejoining his friends. "Monsieur Binet has guaranteed to me that precautions were taken. No sparks have fallen. The pumps are full. Let us go and sleep."

"Mercy, I need some sleep!" said Madame Homais, who was yawning frequently. "But never mind, we had a lovely day for our celebration."

Rodolphe repeated in a low voice and with an ardent glance: "Oh, yes, lovely!"

And, having wished one another good night, they turned away.

9

*S*ix weeks slipped by. Rodolphe
did not return. At last, one evening, he appeared. "Better not go again for some time, it would be
a mistake." And at the end of that week he had left on a hunting trip.

After the hunting trip he had thought that it was too late, then he
reasoned:

"But if she loved me at first sight she ought, out of impatience to
see me again, to love me more. So let's go on with it!"

And he came to the conclusion that his calculations had been correct when, upon entering the sitting room, he saw Emma turn pale.

She was alone. Day was fading. The small muslin curtains at the
windows deepened the twilight, and the gilding on the barometer
struck by a ray of sunlight, set flames gleaming in the mirror in the
interstices between the coral branches.

Rodolphe remained standing; Emma barely responded to his first
courteous phrases.

"I have had business to attend to," he said. "I have been ill."

"Seriously?" she cried.

"Well," Rodolphe said, sitting down on a footstool beside her, "no!
. . . It was just that I didn't want to come back."

"Why?"

"Can't you guess?"

He gazed at her again, but in so ardent a manner that she lowered
her head, flushing. He went on:

"Emma . . ."

"Monsieur!" she said, drawing back a little.

"There, you see," he said in a melancholy tone, "I was right not
to want to come back; for that name, that name that fills my soul
and slipped off my tongue, you forbid me to use it! Madame Bo-

vary! . . . Oh, everybody calls you that! . . . Besides, it's not your name, it's another's."

He repeated:

"Another's!"

And he hid his face in his hands.

"Yes, I think of you constantly . . . The memory of you plunges me in despair! Oh, forgive me! I'll go away . . . Good-by! I shall go far away, so far that you will never hear anyone speak of me again . . . and yet . . . today . . . I don't know what force it was that drove me to you again. For one doesn't struggle against heaven, one doesn't resist the smile of the angels! One lets oneself be carried away by what is beautiful, charming, adorable!"

This was the first time that Emma had heard these things said; and her vanity, like one relaxing in a steam bath, stretched languorously and in every part, in the warmth of these words.

"But even if I haven't come," he continued, "even if I haven't been able to see you, at least I have looked often at the things around you. At night, every night, I would get up, come here, stare at your house, the roof shining in the moonlight, the trees in the garden swaying at your window, and a little lamp, a ray of light shining through the windowpanes in the shadow. Ah, you had no idea that a poor wretched creature was there, so near and yet so far . . ."

She turned toward him with a sob.

"Oh, you are good!" she said.

"No, I love you, that's all. You don't doubt it! Tell me you don't. One word, just one word!"

And Rodolphe let himself slip almost imperceptibly from the footstool to the floor; but the sound of wooden shoes came from the kitchen, and the door of the sitting room, he noticed, was not closed.

"Be charitable enough," he went on, rising, "to satisfy a whim of mine."

It was to visit his house; he wanted to get to know her better; and, as Madame Bovary saw no objection, they were both rising when Charles came in.

"Good evening, Doctor," Rodolphe said.

The physician, flattered by this unexpected title, launched into obsequious phrases, and the other profited by the opportunity to recover himself somewhat.

"Madame was speaking to me about her health," he said then.

Charles interrupted him: he, himself, was deeply concerned about it; his wife's depression was recurring. Then Rodolphe asked whether horseback riding might not be good exercise for her.

"Certainly! Excellent, the very thing! . . . There's an idea. You should follow it, my dear."

And, as she protested that she had no horse, Monsieur Rodolphe offered one of his; she declined his offer; he did not insist; then, in order to explain his visit, he told Charles that his plowman, the one who had been bled, was still having dizzy spells.

"I'll drop in and see him," Bovary said.

"No, no, I'll send him to you. We will come, it will be more convenient for you."

"Very well. Thank you."

And, as soon as they were alone:

"Why didn't you accept Monsieur Boulanger's offer, it was so gracious of him?"

She assumed a sulky air, produced a thousand excuses and finally declared that "it might look odd."

"Oh, what do I care about that!" Charles said, whirling about. "Health comes first. You are wrong."

"Well, and how do you expect me to ride, when I have no habit?"

"You must order one!" he said.

The riding habit decided her.

When the costume was ready, Charles wrote to Monsieur Boulanger that his wife had changed her mind, and that he was counting upon his kindness.

The next day, at noon, Rodolphe appeared before Charles' door with two saddle horses. One wore pink pompoms at its ears and a buckskin sidesaddle.

Rodolphe had put on high supple leather boots, thinking that she had undoubtedly never seen any like them; Emma was, indeed, enchanted with his appearance when he came into the hall in his long velvet coat and white woolen breeches. She was ready, she was waiting for him.

Justin slipped out of the pharmacy to see her, and the pharmacist, too, interrupted his work. He gave advice to Monsieur Boulanger.

"An accident happens so quickly! Be careful! Your horses are probably spirited!"

She heard a noise above her head: it was Félicité tapping on the windowpane to amuse little Berthe. The child blew a kiss; her mother answered with a gesture with the handle of her crop.

"Have a nice ride!" Monsieur Homais cried. "Prudence is the chief thing. Prudence!"

And he waved his newspaper, watching them move away.

The moment it felt the earth under its feet, Emma's horse broke into a gallop; Rodolphe galloped beside her. From time to time they exchanged a word. Her face lowered slightly, her hand held high and her arm outstretched, she gave herself up to the rhythm of the motion which rocked her in the saddle.

At the foot of the hill Rodolphe loosened the reins; they set off together as if upon a signal; then, at the top, the horses suddenly halted and her great blue veil sank down again.

It was early October. There was a haze over the land. Trails of mist lay along the horizon, against the curves of hills; others, dissolving, drifted up and were lost to sight. Beside them, on the grass beneath the pine trees, a dusky light was diffused in the mild atmosphere. The earth, rust-red like snuff, deadened the sound of footsteps; and as they walked the horses kicked fallen pine cones ahead of them with the tips of their shoes.

In this fashion Rodolphe and Emma followed the fringe of the woods. She turned away from time to time to avoid his glance, and then she saw nothing but the lines of pine-tree trunks, the uninterrupted procession of which made her feel slightly giddy. The horses snuffled. The leather of the saddles creaked.

Just as they entered the forest the sun came out.

"God is favoring us!" Rodolphe said.

"You think so?" she said.

"Let's go on. Let's go on," he said.

He clicked his tongue. Their mounts moved faster.

Long ferns growing along the edge of the path tangled in Emma's spur. Rodolphe, as he rode, would lean down and pull them off each time. At other times, in order to avoid branches, he would ride close to her, and Emma felt his knee press against her leg. The sky had become blue. The leaves did not stir. There were wide spaces full of heather in bloom; and patches of violets alternated with the interlacing leaves of trees which were gray, tawny or golden according to the variety of foliage. Often they heard in the underbrush a small flutter of wings, or it might be the hoarse unalarmed call of the crows which rose from the oak trees.

They dismounted. Rodolphe tethered the horses. She walked ahead of him over the moss, between the old ruts of the trail.

But her long skirt impeded her, even though she picked it up by the train and carried it, and Rodolphe, walking behind her, saw between that black cloth and the black boot the sheerness of her white stocking which seemed to him a hint of nudity.

She paused. "I'm tired," she said.

"Come, try again," he said. "Courage!"

Then, a hundred yards farther on, she stopped again; and through her veil which fell from her mannish hat obliquely down to her hips, he could discern her face in a blue-tinted transparency, as if she were swimming under azure waves.

"Where are we going?"

He did not answer. She was breathing in short broken gasps. Rodolphe kept glancing about him and gnawing his mustache.

They came upon a wider clearing where trees had been felled. They sat down upon an overturned tree trunk, and Rodolphe began to speak to her of his love.

At first he did not alarm her with his compliments. He was calm, sober, melancholy.

Emma listened, her head lowered, pushing at chips of wood with her toe.

But at the phrase: "Our destinies are now one, aren't they?" "Oh, no!" she replied. "You know very well. It's impossible."

She stood up to go. He caught her wrist. She stopped. Then, having gazed at him for a few moments with ardent moist eyes, she said rapidly:

"Oh, let's not talk about it any more . . . Where are the horses? Let's go back."

He made a gesture of anger and frustration. She kept repeating: "Where are the horses? Where are the horses?"

Then, smiling a strange smile, his pupils staring, his teeth clenched, he advanced upon her, stretching out his arms. She drew back, trembling. She stammered:

"Oh, you're frightening me! You're making me feel ill! Let's go back."

"If it has to be that way," he said, his expression changing.

And he at once resumed his affectionate, respectful, timid manner. She gave him her arm. They turned back. He said:

"What came over you then? Why? I didn't understand. You must have misunderstood. To me you are like a madonna on a pedestal, in a high place, serene and immaculate. But I need you in order to live! I need your eyes, your voice, your thoughts. Be my friend, my sister, my angel!"

And he stretched out his arm and slipped it around her waist. She made a nerveless effort to draw away. He supported her so, as they walked.

But they heard the two horses browsing among the leaves.

"Oh, a little longer!" Rodolphe said. "Let's not go. Stay!"

He drew her farther away, around a small pond where algae made green freckles on the ripples. A few faded water lilies floated motionless among the rushes. At the sound of their footsteps over the grass, frogs hopped away to hide.

"It's not right, it's not right!" she kept saying. "I am insane to listen to you."

"Why? . . . Emma. Emma!"

"Oh, Rodolphe! . . ." the young woman murmured reluctantly, leaning against his shoulder.

The stuff of her skirt clung to the velvet of his coat, she arched her white throat which swelled with a sigh and, half fainting, drowned in tears and hiding her face, with a long shudder she gave herself up.

The shadows of evening were falling; horizontal sunlight, slipping between branches, dazzled her eyes. Here and there, all about her among the leaves or on the ground, luminous spots shivered like humming-bird feathers lost in flight. Silence lay over everything; a sweetness seemed to issue from the trees; she felt her heart begin to beat again and the blood course through her flesh like a stream of milk. Then she heard, far in the distance beyond the woods, upon the other hills, an indistinct and prolonged cry, a voice that lingered on, and she listened to it silently as it blended like music with the last vibrations of her aroused nerves. Rodolphe, a cigar between his teeth, was mending one of the bridles which had broken, with his penknife.

They returned to Yonville, by the same road. They saw again their horses' tracks in the mud, side by side, and the same bushes, the same stones in the grass. Nothing round about them had changed; and yet for her something more momentous had occurred than if the mountains had been moved. Rodolphe leaned over from time to time and took her hand to kiss it.

She was charming on horseback! Sitting straight, with her slender waist, her bent knee against her horse's mane, and her color heightened a little by the fresh air, in the red glow of evening.

Entering Yonville she caracoled in the street.

People watched her from their windows.

Her husband, at dinner, thought that she looked well; but she seemed not to hear when he asked about her ride; and she sat there, with her elbow at the edge of her plate, between the two lighted candles.

"Emma!" he said.

"What?"

"Well, I passed by Monsieur Alexandre's this afternoon; he has an old mare that's still in fine condition, only a little bit broken-kneed, and that I'm sure could be bought for a hundred écus . . ."

He added:

"Thinking it would please you, I spoke for her . . . I bought her . . . Did I do right? Tell me."

She nodded assent; then, a quarter of an hour later:

"Are you going out this evening?" she asked.

"Yes. Why?"

"Oh, no reason, my dear."

And the moment she had got rid of Charles she went up to shut herself in her room.

At first it was like a dizziness; she saw the trees, the paths, the ditches, Rodolphe, and she felt again the pressure of his arms while the leaves quivered and the rushes whispered.

But catching sight of herself in the mirror, she was startled at her own appearance. Never had her eyes been so large, so black or of such depth. Some subtle emanation diffused over her person had transfigured it.

She repeated to herself: "I have a lover! A lover!" reveling in the thought as in a new puberty to which she had attained. So at last she was going to experience those joys of love, that fever of happiness of which she had despaired. She was on the threshold of some miraculous territory where all would be passion, ecstasy, delirium; a blue-tinted immensity surrounded her, pinnacles of emotion glittered in the light of her thoughts, ordinary existence was visible only in the distance, far away, in the shadow, through the spaces intervening between these heights.

Then she recalled the heroines of books she had read, and the lyrical host of those adulterous wives began to sing in her memory with the voices of sisters, enchanting her. She herself seemed to become an actual part of these imaginings and to realize the long reverie of her youth as she took her place among this category of amorous women whom she had so envied. Further, Emma felt the gratification of revenge. Had she not suffered enough! But now she was triumphant, and love, so long repressed, burst forth without reserve, with joyous effervescence. She savored it without remorse, without disquiet, without alarm.

The following day passed in a new delight. They exchanged vows. She told him her sorrows. Rodolphe interrupted her with kisses; and she asked him, gazing at him through half-closed eyelids, to call her again by her name and to repeat that he loved her. This was in the forest, as it had been the day before, in a woodcutter's hut. The walls of it were made of straw and the roof came down so low that one had to stand bent over. They were seated close beside one another on a bed of dry leaves.

From that day on they wrote to each other regularly every evening. Emma took her letter to the end of the garden near the river, leaving it in a fissure of the retaining wall. Rodolphe came there to get it and left another, which she always accused of being too short.

One morning when Charles had gone out before dawn, she was seized with an impulse to see Rodolphe at once. She could reach La Huchette quickly, stay there an hour and be back in Yonville while everyone was still asleep. This idea made her breathless with desire; presently she found herself in the middle of the prairie, walking along swiftly without looking behind her.

Day was beginning to break. From a distance Emma recognized her lover's house with its two swallowtail weather vanes standing out black against the pale dawn light.

Beyond the courtyard of the farm stood a main building which must be the château. She entered it as if the walls had parted of themselves at her approach. A broad straight staircase led up to the hall. Emma turned the handle of a door and suddenly, at the far end of the room, saw a man sleeping. It was Rodolphe.

She cried out.

"You're here! You're here!" he repeated. "How did you manage to come? . . . Oh, your dress is wet!"

"I love you," she answered, throwing her arms around his neck.

That first piece of recklessness having succeeded, now every time

Charles went out early, Emma quickly dressed and tiptoed down the stairs that led to the water's edge.

But when the cattle bridge was raised, she had to follow the walls that ran along the riverside; the bank was slippery; in order not to fall, she clung to clumps of withered wallflowers. Then she picked her way across plowed fields where she kept sinking in, stumbling and miring her thin shoes. Her kerchief, tied over her head, fluttered in the wind over the pasture lands; she was afraid of the bulls, she would begin to run; she would arrive out of breath, her cheeks pink, her whole body exhaling a fresh scent of green growing things, sap and open air. Rodolphe was still sleeping at that hour. It was like a spring morning coming into his room.

The yellow curtains hanging at the windows let a dim golden light fall gently into the room. Emma would grope her way, blinking her eyes, while drops of dew clinging to her braids made a sort of topaz aureole all about her face. Rodolphe, laughing, would pull her to him and press her against his heart.

Later, she would examine the room, open the doors of furniture, comb her hair with his comb and look at herself in his shaving mirror. Often she went so far as to hold in her teeth the stem of a large pipe which lay on the night table among lemons and bits of sugar, beside a pitcher of water.

Their farewells required a full quarter of an hour. Then Emma would cry; she would have liked never to leave Rodolphe. Something stronger than herself kept urging her toward him, to such an extent that one day, seeing her arrive unexpectedly, he frowned like someone who is vexed.

"What is the matter?" she said. "Are you ill? Tell me!"

At length he declared with a serious air that her visits were becoming indiscreet and that she was putting herself in a compromising position.

10

$\mathcal{G}$RADUALLY these fears of Rodolphe's were communicated to her. Love
had overwhelmed her at first; she had thought of nothing
beyond that. But now that it was indispensable to her life she
dreaded losing any part of it, or even allowing it to be touched by
anxiety. Whenever she went back to him now she cast uneasy
glances all about her, watching each form that passed on the horizon and each window in the village from which she might be seen.
She listened to footsteps, cries, the sound of cart wheels; and she
would stop short, paler and more tremulous than the poplar leaves
quivering above her head.

One morning as she was returning in this manner, she suddenly
thought she saw the long barrel of a rifle which seemed to be trained
upon her. It stuck out obliquely from a small thicket half hidden
among the tall grasses on the edge of a ditch. Emma, about to faint
with terror, nevertheless went forward, and a man emerged from
the thicket like those devils on a spring that jump up out of boxes.
He had gaiters buckled up to his knees, his cap pulled down over
his eyes, shaking lips and a red nose. It was Captain Binet, lying in
wait for wild duck.

"You should have spoken from a distance!" he cried. "When you
see a gun you must always call out."

The tax-collector was trying by this means to dissemble the fright
he had just had; for, a prefectoral edict having forbidden duck
shooting except from a boat, Monsieur Binet, despite his respect for
the law, was in the process of breaking it. Thus at every instant he
kept thinking that he heard the game warden approaching. But this
uneasiness interfered with his pleasure and, all alone in his blind, he
had been congratulating himself upon his good fortune and his
cunning.

At sight of Emma he appeared to be relieved of a great weight, and at once, embarking upon conversation:

"It's not warm, there's a nip in the air."

Emma did not answer. He went on:

"And you must have gone out very early?"

"Yes," she said, stammering, "I'm on my way back from the nurse's house where my little girl is."

"Ah, good, good! As for me, I've been here since daybreak, just as you see me; but the weather is so beastly that unless one has the bird right at the end of . . ."

"Good day, Monsieur Binet," she interrupted, turning on her heel.

"Your servant, Madame," he replied dryly.

And he returned to his blind.

Emma regretted having left the tax-collector so abruptly. Doubtless he would draw unfavorable conclusions. The story about the nurse was the worst excuse, everyone in Yonville being perfectly well aware that the little Bovary girl had returned to her parents' home a year before. Besides, no one lived in this neighborhood; the road led only to La Huchette; so Binet must have guessed whence she was coming, and he would not hold his tongue, he would gossip, that was certain! She spent the whole day tormenting her mind with the invention of every imaginable falsehood, and having the image of that imbecile with his game bag constantly before her eyes.

After dinner, Charles, seeing her troubled, insisted upon taking her to the pharmacy by way of diversion; and the first person she saw there was that man again, the tax-collector! He was standing before the counter, full in the light from the red glass jar, and he was saying:

"I want half an ounce of vitriol, please."

"Justin," the apothecary called, "bring the sulphuric acid."

Then, to Emma, who was about to go up to Madame Homais' apartments:

"No, stay here, it's not worth the trouble of going up; she'll be right down. Warm yourself at the stove while you wait . . . excuse me . . . good evening, Doctor" (for the pharmacist took great pleasure in pronouncing that word *doctor*, as if in addressing it to another he caused something of the pomp he found in it to reflect upon himself). ". . . Take care, Justin, don't upset the mortars! Go and fetch some chairs from the little room, instead; you know very well the armchairs in the drawing-room aren't to be disturbed."

And Homais was hastening out from behind the counter to return his armchair to its place when Binet asked him for a half ounce of acid of sugar.

"Acid of sugar?" the pharmacist said disdainfully. "I don't know it, never heard of it! Perhaps you want oxalic acid? It's oxalic, isn't it?"

Binet explained that he needed a corrosive in order to compound a metal polish with which to remove the rust from various hunting equipment. Emma shivered. The pharmacist began:

"Really, the weather is not propitious, because of the humidity."

"There are people, however," the tax-collector said with a sly look, "who manage to put up with it."

She was suffocating. "Give me . . ."

"At this rate he'll never go," she thought.

". . . half an ounce of resin and of turpentine, four ounces of yellow wax and an ounce and a half of charcoal, please, for cleaning the polished leather of my equipment."

The apothecary was beginning to measure off the wax when Madame Homais appeared with Irma in her arms, Napoléon at her side and Athalie following her. She went and sat down on the velvet-covered bench against the window, and the boy squatted on a footstool while his elder sister prowled about the box of jujubes, near her dear papa. He himself was filling funnels and corking bottles, sticking on labels, making up packets. They were silent around him, and only the occasional clatter of weights in the scales was to be heard, along with a few low-voiced words from the pharmacist, instructing his pupil.

"How is your young one?" Madame Homais asked suddenly.

"Silence!" her husband exclaimed, writing figures in his copybook.

"Why didn't you bring her?" she went on in a lower tone.

"Sh!" Emma said, gesturing toward the apothecary.

Monsieur Binet, intent upon checking over the addition, had probably not heard. At last he went out. Then Emma, relieved, sighed deeply.

"How heavily you're breathing!" Madame Homais said.

"Oh, because it's so warm," she answered.

In consequence they decided, the next day, to arrange their meetings; Emma wanted to bribe her servant with a gift; but it would be safer to find some quiet house in Yonville. Rodolphe promised to look for one.

All during the winter, three or four times a week, in the black of night, he came to the garden. Emma had purposely taken away the key to the gate, which Charles believed to have been lost.

To attract her attention, Rodolphe would fling a handful of sand against her blinds. She would spring up; but sometimes she had to wait, for Charles had a passion for chatting beside the fire, and he went on and on.

She would be consumed with impatience; if her eyes had had the power, they would have made him jump out the window. At length she would begin preparing for bed; then she would take up a book and continue to read tranquilly, as if the reading amused her. But Charles, already in bed, would call to her.

"Come, Emma," he would say. "It's time."

"Yes, I'm coming," she would answer.

Meanwhile, as the candles bothered his eyes, he would turn toward the wall and fall asleep. She would slip out, holding her breath, smiling, tremulous, half dressed.

Rodolphe had a great cloak; he would wrap her up in it from head to toe and, with his arm about her waist, would draw her without speaking to the far end of the garden.

It was under the arbor, on that same crumbling wooden bench from which Léon, long before, had gazed at her so ardently during the summer evenings. She never thought of him now.

Stars gleamed through the leafless branches of the jasmine. Behind them they heard the river flowing past and, from time to time, the creaking of dried rushes on the bank. Great pools of shadow spread out here and there in the obscurity, and sometimes, all shivering with a simultaneous motion, they would rise and fall like vast black waves rolling up to break over them. The chill of the night made them cling the more closely together; the sighs from their lips seemed deeper; their eyes, barely visible to one another, seemed larger and, in the midst of the silence, words were softly spoken which fell upon the spirit with crystalline clarity and reëchoed there in multiple vibrations.

When the night was rainy, they went to take refuge in the consulting room, between the cart-shed and the stable. She would light one of the kitchen candles which she had hidden behind the books. Rodolphe made himself perfectly at home there. The sight of the bookcase and the desk, in fact of the whole room, aroused his mirth; and he was unable to refrain from making numerous jokes about Charles, which annoyed Emma. She would have liked to see him more serious, and even more dramatic when the occasion arose, like that time when she had thought she heard the sound of approaching footsteps in the lane. "Someone is coming!" she said.

He blew out the light.

"Have you your pistols?"

"What for?"

"Why . . . to defend yourself," Emma said.

"Against your husband? Ah, the poor fellow!"

And Rodolphe finished his sentence with a gesture that signified: "I'd smash him with one blow of my fist."

She was lost in admiration of his courage, although she sensed in it a sort of indelicacy and frank crudity that shocked her.

Rodolphe reflected deeply over this pistol episode. If she had been speaking seriously, he thought, that was extremely ridiculous, even disagreeable, for he, personally, had no reason to hate that well-meaning fellow Charles, not being what is called consumed with jealousy—and, in this connection, Emma had made him a solemn vow which he also felt to be not in the best taste.

In addition, she was becoming highly sentimental. They had had to exchange miniatures; they had cut locks of one another's hair, and now she was asking for a ring, a genuine wedding ring, as a token of eternal union. She often spoke to him about the bells of evening or "the voices of nature"; then she would talk about her own mother and his. Rodolphe had lost his mother twenty years before. Emma comforted him for it, nevertheless, in affected language such as one might use to a forlorn child, and even went so far as to say to him sometimes, gazing at the moon:

"I'm sure that up there, together, they are smiling on our love."

But she was so pretty! He had possessed so few women of such candor! This love devoid of licentiousness was something new to him, and something which, drawing him out of his easy habits, flattered his pride and his sensuality at the same time. Emma's exaltation, which his good common sense scorned, seemed charming to him in his heart, since she directed it to himself. Later, sure of being loved, he took no more pains, and insensibly his manner changed.

He no longer offered, as he had once done, those words so tender that they made her cry, nor those violent caresses that drove her to frenzy; with the result that their great love in which she lived submerged seemed to dwindle away about her, like the waters of a river being absorbed by its bed, until she saw the slimy bottom. She refused to believe it; she redoubled her tenderness, and Rodolphe concealed his indifference less and less.

She did not know whether she regretted having yielded to him or, on the other hand, if she did not long to adore him all the more. The humiliation of feeling herself to be weak turned to a bitterness that was tempered by physical pleasure. It was not an attachment; it was something like a constant seduction. He dominated her. She was almost afraid of him.

On the surface, however, all was more serene than ever, Rodolphe having succeeded in conducting the affair according to his own fancy; and at the end of six months, when spring came, they found themselves together like two married people placidly keeping alive a domestic flame.

It was the time of year when old Rouault sent his goose in memory of his mended leg. The gift always came accompanied by a letter. Emma cut the string that fastened it to the hamper and read the following lines:

My dear children:
I hope that the present will find you in good health and that this one will be as good as the others; for it seems, if I may say so, a bit more tender and heavier. But the next time I am going to give you a cock, unless you have some preference for hens, and please send me back the basket, along with the other two. I had bad luck with my wagon-shed, the roof of it flew up into the trees one night when the wind was high. The harvest wasn't too wonderful. Really I don't know when I will come to visit you. It's so difficult for me to leave the house now that I'm alone, my poor Emma!

And here there was an interval between the lines, as if the good man had laid down his pen to dream a little.

I learned from a peddler who had a tooth pulled this winter, traveling through your part of the country, that Bovary was still working hard. That doesn't surprise me, and he showed me his tooth; we took a cup of coffee together. I asked him if he had seen you, he told me no, but that he had seen two horses in the stable, from which I assume that business is good. So much the better, my dear children, and may God send you every imaginable blessing.

It grieves me that I have not yet seen my beloved granddaughter Berthe Bovary. I planted a plum tree for her in the garden under your window, and I won't let anybody touch it except to make preserves for her later on, and I'll keep them in the cupboard for her, for when she comes here.

Good-by, my dear children. I embrace you, my daughter, you, too, my son-in-law, and a kiss on both cheeks for the baby.

I am, with affection,

Your loving father,

Théodore Rouault.

She remained for several minutes holding the coarse paper between her fingers. It was a tangle of spelling errors, and Emma searched out the loving thought that prattled through them like a hen half hidden in a thorn hedge. The writing had been blotted with ashes from the hearth, for a little gray dust drifted out of the letter onto her dress, and she almost seemed to see her father bending toward the fireplace to pick up the tongs. How long it had been since she had sat beside him, on the stool in the chimney corner, getting the end of a stick to take fire in the great flame from crackling sea-rushes! . . . What happiness in those days! What freedom, what hope, what abundance of illusions! Nothing of them was left, now. She had expended them on all the adventures of her spirit, throughout all the successive phases, in virginity, in marriage and in love—losing them thus along the course of her life, day after day, like a traveler who leaves something of his wealth at each of the inns along the way.

But what was making her so miserable? Where was the extraordinary catastrophe that had overwhelmed her? And she raised her head, looking about her as if to seek the source of what was making her suffer.

A ray of April sunlight danced on the porcelains of the whatnot; the fire was burning; she felt the softness of the carpet under her slippers; the day was clear, the air mild, and she heard her child laughing aloud.

As a matter of fact, the little girl was then rolling on the lawn in the midst of the grass that was being dried for hay. She was lying flat on her stomach on top of a stack. Her nurse was holding her by the skirt. Lestiboudois was raking near by, and each time he came close to her she would lean over, waving her two arms in the air.

"Bring her to me!" her mother said, running forward to kiss her. "How I love you, my darling! How I love you!"

Then, noticing that her earlobes were a little dirty, she quickly rang for warm water and washed her, changed her underthings, her stockings, her slippers, asked a thousand questions about her health as if upon returning from a journey and at length, kissing her again and weeping a little, she restored her to the hands of the servant who was left highly astonished at this excess of affection.

That evening Rodolphe found her more serious than usual.

"She will get over it," he decided. "It's a whim."

And he missed three consecutive meetings. When he returned, she acted cold and almost scornful.

"Ah, you're wasting your time, my sweet . . ."

And he pretended not to notice her melancholy sighs, nor the handkerchief she was twisting.

It was then that Emma repented!

She even wondered why she had been detesting Charles, and whether it might not have been better to be able to love him. But he showed no great response to these renewals of affection, so that she was left considerably frustrated in her notion for self-sacrifice until the apothecary, just at the right time, happened to offer her an opportunity.

11

$\mathcal{H}_E$ had recently read an article
in praise of a new method for treating club-
foot; and, as he was an upholder of progress, he conceived the patriotic idea that Yonville, in order to "keep abreast,"
ought to perform talipes operations.

"Because," he said to Emma, "what risk is there? Observe" (and
he enumerated the advantages of the attempt on his fingers): "almost certain success, relief and improvement in the appearance
of the patient, a reputation quickly made for the surgeon. Why
shouldn't your husband, for instance, want to help out poor Hippolyte, over at the *Lion d'Or?* Don't forget that he would be sure
to tell all the visitors about his cure, and besides" (Homais lowered
his voice and glanced about him) "what's to prevent me from sending a little note about it to the newspaper? Well, my Lord, an article
goes round . . . it's talked about . . . in the end it's like a snowball!
And who knows? Who knows?"

Indeed, Bovary might be successful; she saw no evidence that he
was not an able man, and what a satisfaction for her to have urged
upon him an undertaking from which his reputation and his fortune
might be made. All she asked was to have something more stable
than love to lean upon.

Charles, importuned by the apothecary and by her, allowed himself to be convinced. He sent to Rouen for Doctor Duval's book, and
every evening, with his head between his hands, he buried himself
in study.

While he was studying equinus, varus and valgus, that is to say
strephocatopody, strephendopody and strephexopody (or, to put it
better: the various malformations of the foot, whether twisted down,
inward or outward), along with strephypopody and strephanopody
(in other words: torsion below and curvature on top), Monsieur

Homais was exhorting the handy-man of the inn, by all manner of arguments, to undergo the operation.

"You'll barely feel it, a slight pain perhaps; it's a mere prick like a minor bleeding, less severe than the removal of certain corns."

Hippolyte, pondering, rolled stupid eyes.

"Besides," the pharmacist went on, "it doesn't make any difference to me. It's for you, out of pure humanity! I should like to see you, my friend, rid of your hideous deformity and that twisting of the lumbar region which, whatever you claim, must hamper you considerably in the performance of your work."

Then Homais described to him how much more cheerful and active he would feel afterwards, and even gave him to understand that he would find himself more attractive to women, and the stable boy began to grin foolishly. Then he attacked his vanity:

"Aren't you a man, for heaven's sake? What would have happened if you had had to serve, to go and fight for your country? . . . Oh, Hippolyte!"

And Homais moved away, declaring that he did not understand that stubbornness, that blindness that denied itself the benefits of science.

The unfortunate fellow yielded, for it was like a conspiracy. Binet, who never meddled in the affairs of others, Madame Lefrançois, Artémise, the neighbors and even the mayor, Monsieur Tuvache, everybody urged him, preached to him, made him ashamed of himself; but what eventually decided him was that "it wouldn't cost anything." Bovary even took it upon himself to provide the equipment for the operation. This generosity had been Emma's idea, and Charles agreed to it, telling himself in his heart that his wife was an angel.

With the pharmacist's advice, then, and after three false starts, he had constructed by the blacksmith, with the aid of the locksmith, a sort of box weighing about eight pounds, in which no amount of iron, wood, sheet-metal, leather, screws and nuts was spared.

Meanwhile, in order to know which tendon to cut for Hippolyte, he had first to determine which type of clubfoot he had.

His foot made an almost straight line with his leg, which did not prevent it from being turned inward, so that it was a talipes equinus combined with a slight varus, or perhaps a slight varus with a pronounced tendency toward the equinus. But with this talipes equinus, literally as large as a horse's hoof with its horny skin, prominent tendons, thick toes on which blackened toenails were like horseshoe nails, the clubfooted boy raced about like a stag from morning to night. One was constantly seeing him in the square, skipping around the wagons, throwing his uneven hip forward at every step. He seemed even more active with that leg than with the other. Through use it had developed something like the moral qualities of patience and energy, and when he was given heavy work to do he rested his weight upon it by preference.

Now, since it was a talipes equinus, it was necessary to cut the Achilles' tendon, leaving it until later to deal with the tibialis anterior muscle to correct the varus: for the physician did not dare risk performing both operations at once, and he was even trembling in advance with the fear of injuring some vital area of which he was unaware.

Certainly neither Ambroise Paré, applying the principle of immediate ligature of an artery for the first time since Celsus, after an interval of fifteen hundred years; nor Dupuytren, about to open an abscess through a thick layer of brain tissue; nor Gensoul, when he performed the first ablation of the maxilla, had so irregular a heartbeat, so tremulous a hand, so tense a state of mind as Monsieur Bovary as he approached Hippolyte, his scalpel in his fingers. And just as in a hospital, there lay on a table at one side a heap of gauze sponges, waxed sutures, many bandages, a pyramid of bandages, all the bandages the apothecary's establishment afforded. It was Monsieur Homais who, early that morning, had organized all these preparations, as much to impress the multitude as to give himself any illusions. Charles thrust his scalpel into the skin; a sharp crack was heard. The tendon was cut, the operation over. Hippolyte could not get over his surprise; he leaned over Bovary's hands to cover them with kisses.

"Come now, calm down," the apothecary said. "You can show your gratitude toward your benefactor later on!"

And he went downstairs to tell the result to five or six curious people who had taken up a position in the courtyard and who imagined that Hippolyte would appear walking straight. Then Charles, having strapped his patient into the mechanical device, returned home where Emma, all anxiety, was waiting for him on the doorstep. She flung herself upon his neck; they sat down at table; he ate a great deal and even insisted upon having a cup of coffee with his dessert, a debauch which he permitted himself only on Sundays, when there were guests.

The evening was delightful, full of talk, of shared dreams. They spoke of their future fortunes, of improvements to be introduced into their household; he saw his reputation expanding, his well-being increasing, his wife loving him forever; and she felt the gratification of being refreshed by a new, saner, more virtuous emotion, of feeling at last some affection for this poor boy who adored her. For a moment the thought of Rodolphe passed through her mind; but her eyes returned to Charles: she even noticed with surprise that his teeth were not at all ugly.

They were in bed when Monsieur Homais, despite the cook's protests, came abruptly into the room holding in his hand a freshly written sheet of paper. It was the announcement he intended for the *Fanal de Rouen*. He had brought it for them to read.

"Read it yourself," Bovary said.

He read:

"Despite the prejudices which still cover part of the face of Europe like a net, the light is nevertheless beginning to penetrate to our countrysides. It was thus that, on Wednesday, our little city of Yonville found itself the stage for a surgical operation which was at the same time an act of philanthropy. Monsieur Bovary, one of our most distinguished practitioners . . ."

"Oh, that's too much! That's too much!" Charles said, choking with emotion.

"Why no, not at all! What do you mean! . . . operated upon a clubfoot . . . I didn't put the scientific term because, you know, in a newspaper . . . perhaps not everybody would understand; the masses must . . ."

"Quite so," Bovary said. "Go on."

"I continue," the pharmacist said. "Monsieur Bovary, one of our most distinguished practitioners, operated upon a clubfooted patient named Hippolyte Tautain, for twenty-five years the stable boy at the *Lion d'Or* hotel, kept by Madame Lefrançois, on the Place d'Armes. The novelty of the undertaking and the interest attached to the subject had attracted such an assembly of people that there was literally a throng at the door of the establishment. In addition, the operation proceeded as if by magic and barely a few drops of blood came up to the skin as if to announce that the rebel tendon had at last yielded to the efforts of skill. The patient (we state it *de visu*) experienced no pain, a strange thing. His condition at present leaves nothing to be desired. Everything leads to the belief that the period of convalescence will be short, and even—who knows?— at the next village festival we may see our good Hippolyte taking part in Bacchic dances, in the midst of a chorus of merry comrades, and thus demonstrating to all eyes, by means of his vigor and his capers, the completeness of his cure. All honor, then, to generous savants! Honor to those indefatigable spirits who consecrate their waking hours to the improvement or the healing of their race! Honor, thrice honor! Is this not an occasion for crying that the blind shall see, the deaf hear, the lame walk? But what fanaticism used to promise its own chosen ones, science now accomplishes for all men. We will keep our readers informed of the successive phases of this remarkable cure."

For all this, five days later, Madame Lefrançois arrived utterly distracted, crying:

"Help! He's dying! . . . I'm going out of my mind!"

Charles dashed to the *Lion d'Or,* and the pharmacist, who caught sight of him passing in the square, without a hat, deserted the pharmacy. He appeared himself, panting, red in the face, uneasy, and asking of all those who were climbing up the stairs:

"So what is the matter with our interesting taliped?"

He was writhing, the taliped, in appalling convulsions, with the result that the mechanical device in which his leg was encased struck against the wall as if to batter it down.

With many precautions to avoid altering the position of the limb, the box was then removed and a frightful spectacle exposed. The shape of the foot was indistinguishable in such a swelling that the entire surface of the skin seemed about to rupture, and it was covered with bruises caused by the famous appliance. Hippolyte had already complained of pain from it; they had paid no attention; they were now forced to admit that he had not been completely mistaken and they left him free for a few hours. But scarcely had the pain of the œdema subsided when the two learned men judged it time to restore the limb to the appliance, squeezing it even more tightly to hasten matters. Then, three days later, Hippolyte being unable to endure it any longer, they removed the apparatus once more, being vastly astonished by the results they discovered. A livid tumefaction extended down the leg, with blisters here and there from which oozed a black exudate. This was taking a serious turn. Hippolyte was beginning to become annoyed about it, and Madame Lefrançois installed him in the small sitting room near the kitchen so that he might at least have some distraction.

But the tax-collector, who dined there every day, complained bitterly at having such surroundings; so Hippolyte was moved to the billiard room.

He lay there, groaning under his coarse blankets, pale, his beard grown long, his eyes hollow and, from time to time, turning his sweating head on the dirty pillow slip, upon which flies kept alighting. Madame Bovary came to see him. She brought him cloths for his poultices, and consoled him, encouraged him. Aside from this, he did not lack company, particularly on market days when the peasants gathered about him, shooting billiard balls, fencing with their cues, smoking, drinking, singing, shouting.

"How do you feel?" they would say, slapping him on the shoulder. "Ah, you're not bragging, by the looks of things! Well, it's your own fault. You should have done this, done that."

And they would tell him stories of people who had all been healed by other remedies than his; then, as a sort of consolation, they would add:

"The trouble is you listen too much. Get up! You're pampering yourself like a king. Oh, never mind, you old rascal! You don't feel well."

Indeed, the gangrene was climbing higher and higher. Bovary was ill over it himself. He came every hour, every moment. Hippolyte would gaze at him with eyes full of terror and babble, sobbing:

"When am I going to be well? . . . Oh, save me! . . . How miserable I am! How miserable I am!"

And the doctor would leave, always prescribing a moderate diet.

"Don't pay any attention to him, my boy," Madame Lefrançois would say. "They've already tortured you good and plenty. You're going to make yourself even weaker. Come on now, eat!"

And she would offer him a rich broth, a mutton chop or a rasher of bacon, and sometimes little glasses of brandy which he had not the energy to raise to his lips.

The inexorable putrefaction kept creeping up from the extremities toward the abdomen. In vain they varied potions and changed poultices, the muscles wasted away more every day, and at length Charles answered with an affirmative nod when Mère Lefrançois asked if she might not, as a last resort, send for Monsieur Canivet of Neufchâtel, who was a celebrity.

A doctor of medicine, fifty years old, enjoying a fine position and with confidence in himself, the consultant did not trouble to suppress a scornful laugh when he saw that leg, gangrenous to the knee. Then, having stated baldly that it must be amputated, he went to the pharmacist's to rail against the asses who had managed to reduce an unfortunate man to such a condition. Shaking Monsieur Homais by the button of his coat he vociferated in the pharmacy.

"That sort of thing is one of those Parisian inventions! Those are the ideas of those gentlemen in the capital! It's like strabism, chloroform and lithotrity, a lot of monstrosities that the government ought to forbid. Straightening clubfeet! Can clubfeet be straightened? It's like trying to make a hunchback straight."

Monsieur Homais suffered, listening to this oration, and he masked his discomfort under a courtier's smile, having need of Monsieur Canivet whose orders sometimes reached Yonville; so he did not come to Bovary's defense, did not even utter one comment, and, abandoning his principles, sacrificed his dignity to the more important considerations of his trade.

This leg amputation by Doctor Canivet was a considerable event in the village. All the inhabitants rose earlier that day, and the main street, although crowded with people, had something lugubrious about it, as if it were a matter of a criminal execution. At the grocer's there were arguments about Hippolyte's illness; the shops sold nothing, and Madame Tuvache, the mayor's wife, did not move from her window, because of her impatience to see the surgeon arrive.

Bovary, meanwhile, did not dare stir from his house. He stayed downstairs in the sitting room, seated beside the lightless hearth, his chin on his chest, hands clasped, eyes staring. What a calamity, he thought, what a disappointment! Yet he had taken every imaginable precaution. Fate had taken a hand in it. No matter; if Hippolyte should die, later, it was he who would have murdered him. And then what excuse could he give, on his rounds, when he was questioned? Perhaps, after all, he had made a mistake somewhere? He searched his mind, found nothing. But the most famous surgeons often made mistakes. That was what people were never willing to believe! They were going to laugh, instead, abuse him! It would spread to Forges, to Neufchâtel, to Rouen, everywhere! Who knew, colleagues might write articles against him! A controversy would result, he would have to answer in the newspapers. Hippolyte might even sue him. He saw himself dishonored, ruined, lost. And his imagination, beset by a multitude of hypotheses, tossed among them like an empty cask swept out to sea and rolling with the waves.

Emma, opposite, watched him; she did not share in his humiliation, she was experiencing another: it was in having deluded herself with the idea that such a man could amount to anything, as if she had not already had sufficient evidence of his mediocrity twenty times over.

Charles was pacing back and forth in her room. His boots clattered on the wooden floor.

"Sit down," she said, "you're making me nervous."

He sat down.

How, then, had she managed (she who was so intelligent) to deceive herself again? Further, what abominable mania led her to destroy her own existence, thus, through continual sacrifices? She remembered all her instinctive desires for luxury, all the privations of her spirit, the meannesses of marriage, of housekeeping, her dreams falling into the mud like wounded swallows, all that she had yearned for, all that she had denied herself, all that she might have had! And why? Why?

In the midst of the silence that lay over the village a piercing scream rent the air. Bovary turned pale as if about to faint. She frowned in a nervous reaction, then continued. It had been for him, all the time, for this creature, for this man who understood nothing, felt nothing! For there he sat, quite calmly, and without even suspecting that the ridicule attached to his name was henceforth going to sully her as well as himself. She had made efforts to love him, and she had repented, weeping, for having given herself to another.

"But perhaps it was a vagus!" Bovary, who was thinking deeply, exclaimed abruptly.

At the unexpected shock of this phrase falling upon her train of thought like a leaden ball into a silver dish, Emma, shuddering, raised her head to discover what he meant; and they stared at one another silently, almost dumfounded at seeing one another, so remote were they in their minds. Charles contemplated her with the troubled look of a drunken man, while listening, motionless, to the last screams of the patient which followed one another in protracted modulations cut short by piercing shrieks, like the distant bellowing of some animal having its throat cut. Emma bit her blanched lips and, rolling between her fingers a nodule of coral which she had broken off, she fixed upon Charles the burning points of her pupils, like two fiery arrows aimed to fly. Everything about him antagonized her now, his face, his dress, the things he did not say, his entire person, his very existence. She repented of her past virtue as if of a crime, and what remained of it crumbled away under the furious blows of her pride. She reveled in all the evil ironies of triumphant adultery. The memory of her lover returned to her with intoxicating charms; she plunged her soul into it, impelled toward that image with new rapture; and Charles seemed to her as divorced from her life, as irrevocably absent, as impossible and annihilated as if he had died and undergone his death agony before her eyes.

There was a sound of footsteps on the sidewalk. Charles looked; and, through the lowered venetian blind, at the corner of the market place, in full sunlight, he saw Doctor Canivet wiping his forehead with his handkerchief. Homais, behind him, was carrying a great red box in his hand, and they were both moving in the direction of the pharmacy.

Then, out of sudden tenderness and discouragement, Charles turned to his wife, saying:

"Kiss me, my dear!"

"Let me alone!" she said, scarlet with anger.

"What is the matter? What is it?" he repeated, amazed. "Calm yourself, get hold of yourself. You know I love you . . . Come, now!"

"Enough!" she cried with a terrible air.

And, running from the room, Emma slammed the door so violently that the barometer leaped from the wall and shattered on the floor.

Charles sank into his armchair, overcome, racking his brains over what might be the matter with her, imagining a nervous ailment, weeping and feeling vaguely about him something malign and incomprehensible.

When Rodolphe came to the garden that evening, he found his mistress waiting for him at the foot of the steps, on the lowest stair. They embraced, and all their bitterness melted like snow in the warmth of that kiss.

12

*T*HEY began to love one another
again. Frequently Emma would even write
him a letter suddenly in the middle of the day; then
she would signal through the window to Justin who, hastily untying
his canvas apron, would speed off to La Huchette: Rodolphe would
come; it was for the purpose of telling him that she was bored, that
her husband was revolting and existence hideous!

"Is there anything I can do about it!" he cried one day, out of
patience.

"Ah, if you would! . . ."

She was sitting on the ground at his feet, her hair hanging loose,
her eyes far away.

"What, then?" Rodolphe said.

She sighed: "We could go and live somewhere else . . . somewhere . . ."

"You really are out of your mind!" he said, laughing. "Is it possible?"

She kept dwelling upon it; he seemed not to understand and
changed the subject. What he did not understand was all this bother
over something so simple as love. She had a motive, a reason, a sort
of auxiliary to her affection.

This fondness, indeed, increased daily in proportion to her aversion for her husband. The more she yielded herself to the one, the
more she detested the other; never had Charles seemed so revolting
to her, had such blunt fingers, so dull a mind, such common manners as after her meetings with Rodolphe, when they were left together. Then, while acting the wife and the virtuous woman, she
would be afire with the thought of that head with its black hair turning in a curl over the tanned brow, of that figure at once so sturdy
and so elegant, of that man, in fact, who possessed so much expe-

rience in judgment, so much passion in desire! It was for him that she filed her fingernails with a sculptor's precision, and that there was never enough cold cream on her skin or patchouli in her handkerchiefs. She loaded herself with bracelets, rings, necklaces. When he was expected she filled her two great blue-glass vases with roses, and arranged her room and her person like a courtesan awaiting a prince. The servant had constantly to be washing linens; and all day long Félicité did not stir from the kitchen, where young Justin, who often kept her company, would sit watching her work.

His elbow on the long board she used for ironing, he would examine avidly all those feminine items spread out around him: dimity petticoats, fichus, collars and pantalettes with drawstring tops, full at the hips and narrowing in at the bottom.

"What is that for?" the boy would ask, passing his hand over crinolines or hooks and eyes.

"Haven't you ever seen anything?" Félicité would answer, laughing. "As if your lady, Madame Homais, didn't wear the same things!"

"Oh, well, yes. Madame Homais!"

And he would add in a meditative tone:

"Is she a woman like Madame?"

But Félicité was becoming impatient over seeing him hover about her this way. She was six years older, and Théodore, Monsieur Guillaumin's servant, was beginning to court her.

"Let me be!" she would say, pushing aside her pot of starch. "Go and steal almonds instead. You're always hanging around women; before you get mixed up in that sort of thing, you naughty little boy, you'd better wait till you have a beard on your chin."

"Now, don't be angry, I'm going to go do her boots for you."

And at once he would reach over to the window ledge for Emma's shoes, all crusted with mud—the mud of the rendezvous—which came away in powder at his touch, and which he watched drift gently upward in a ray of sunlight.

"How scared you are of hurting them!" said the cook, who did not take such pains when she cleaned them herself because the moment the material no longer looked new, Madame gave them to her.

Emma had in her wardrobe a quantity of shoes which she used as carelessly as she pleased, without Charles' allowing himself the least comment.

In the same manner he spent three hundred francs for a wooden leg which she considered it fitting to present to Hippolyte.

151

The lower part of it was finished off with cork and there were joints with springs, a complex mechanism covered with a black pants-leg, which ended in a polished boot. But Hippolyte, not daring to use so fine a leg for every day, begged Madame Bovary to get him another, more suitable one. The physician, of course, again paid the expense of this new acquisition.

After that the stable boy began to work again. One saw him about the village as before, and when Charles heard from a distance the sharp sound of his stick on the pavement, he hurriedly took another path.

It was Monsieur Lheureux, the merchant, who had undertaken to fill these orders; it gave him an opportunity to see Emma frequently. He would talk to her about new merchandise from Paris, about a thousand feminine novelties, seemed extremely obliging and never pressed her for money. Emma gave herself up to that easy way of satisfying all her fancies. Thus, she wanted to give Rodolphe a very handsome whip that was offered in an umbrella shop in Rouen. The following week, Monsieur Lheureux laid it upon her table for her.

But the next day he presented himself at the house with a bill for two hundred and seventy francs, not counting the centimes. Emma was greatly embarrassed: all the drawers of the secretary were empty; more than two weeks' wages were owing Lestiboudois, two quarters' to Félicité, numerous other obligations besides, and Bovary was impatiently awaiting payment from Monsieur Derozerays, who was in the habit of settling his account each year around Saint Peter's Day.

At first she succeeded in putting Lheureux off; then he lost patience: his creditors were after him, he lacked capital and, if he did not recover some of it, he would be obliged to take back from her all the articles she had bought.

"Well, take them back," Emma said.

"Oh, you're joking!" he answered. "The only thing I regret is the whip. Upon my word, I'll ask Monsieur for it."

"No, no!" she said.

"Ah, now I've got you!" Lheureux thought.

And, convinced of his discovery, he left, repeating half aloud and with his slight habitual lisp:

"Very well, we shall see. We shall see!"

She was considering how to extricate herself when the cook, coming in, laid a small roll of blue paper on the mantel; it was from

Monsieur Derozerays. Emma seized it, opened it. There were fifteen napoleons inside. It was the payment of his account. She heard Charles on the stairs; she flung the gold into her drawer and took the key.

Three days later Lheureux appeared again.

"I have an arrangement to suggest to you," he said. "If, instead of paying the amount agreed upon, you would like to take . . ."

"Here it is," she said, dropping four napoleons into his hand.

The merchant was dumfounded. Then, to conceal his disappointment, he launched into excuses and offers of services all of which Emma refused; then she stood for several minutes fingering, in her apron pocket, the two five-franc pieces he had returned to her. She was promising herself that she would economize, in order to pay back later . . .

"Oh, nonsense!" she thought. "He'll never think of it again."

In addition to the crop with the silver-gilt handle, Rodolphe had received a seal with the device: *Amor nel Cor;* also, a scarf for his neck and a cigarette case exactly like the viscount's, which Charles had picked up long before in the road, and which Emma still saved. Yet these gifts humiliated him. He refused several of them; she insisted, and in the end Rodolphe yielded, finding her tyrannical and overforward.

Then, too, she had strange ideas:

"When midnight strikes," she would say, "you must think of me."

And if he admitted having failed to think of her, there were reproaches in plenty, always ending with the inevitable words:

"Do you love me?"

"Why, yes, of course I love you," he would answer.

"Very much?"

"Certainly."

"You've never loved any other, have you?"

"Do you think I came to you a virgin?" he exclaimed, laughing.

Emma wept, and he forced himself to comfort her, enlivening his protestations with jokes.

"Oh, it's just that I love you so!" she would say. "I love you so much that I can't do without you, do you realize that? Sometimes, in my longing to see you again, all the furies of love tear at me. I wonder: 'Where is he? Perhaps he is talking to other women? They smile at him, he moves closer . . .' Oh, no! None of them attracts you, isn't that so? There are more beautiful women, but I know how to love better. I'm your slave and your concubine! You are my king, my idol! You are good, you are handsome, you are intelligent, you are strong!"

He had had to listen to these things so many times that they no longer had any novelty for him. Emma was like all mistresses; and the charm of newness, slipping down little by little like a garment, revealed unclothed the eternal monotony of passion which has always the same forms and the same language. He did not discern, this man so full of the practical, the dissimilarity of emotions beneath the similarity of expressions. Because lustful or mercenary lips had murmured like phrases to him, he believed but little in the candor of hers; they ought to let up a little, he thought, exaggerated turns of speech conceal mediocre affections: as if the fulness of the soul might not sometimes overflow in the emptiest metaphors, since no one, ever, can give the exact measurements of his needs, nor of his conceptions, nor of his suffering, and the human word is like a cracked caldron upon which we beat out melodies fit for making bears dance when we are trying to move the stars to pity.

But, with that critical superiority possessed by one who, in no matter what undertaking, holds himself back, Rodolphe found other pleasures to exploit in this love. He considered all modesty misplaced. He treated her without ceremony. He made of her a pliant and corrupt thing. It was a sort of idiot attachment, full of wonder for him, of sensual pleasure for her, a blissfulness that wrapped her in languor; and her spirit sank into that intoxication and drowned there, a shriveled thing, like the Duke of Clarence in his cask of Malmsey.

Solely from the effect of her amorous habits, Madame Bovary's manner changed. Her glances became bolder, her speech freer; she was even so unconventional as to go out walking with Monsieur Rodolphe, a cigarette in her mouth as if to defy the world; in the end, those who had still doubted doubted no more when they saw her descend from the *Hirondelle* one day, her waist pinched in by a waistcoat, in the masculine manner; and Madame Bovary, Charles' mother, who had come to take refuge with her son after a shocking scene with her husband, was not the least scandalized of the village women. Many other things offended her: to begin with, Charles had paid no attention to her advice about the prohibition of novels; then, the "atmosphere of the house" displeased her; she took the liberty of commenting and there were lost tempers, particularly one time when it was a question of Félicité.

The evening before, Madame Bovary the elder, crossing the corridor, had caught her in the company of a man, a man of about forty, with a dark collar, who, at the sound of her steps, had quickly slipped out of the kitchen. At this Emma began to laugh; but the good woman flew into a rage, declaring that rather than ridiculing standards of behavior, one ought to watch over those of servants.

"What sort of world do you come from?" the daughter-in-law said, with so insolent a look that Madame Bovary asked her if she were not defending her own actions.

"Get out!" the young woman said, springing up.

"Emma! . . . Mother!" Charles cried, to bring them to their senses.

But they had both lost all control in their exasperation. Emma stamped her foot, repeating:

"Oh, what breeding! What a peasant!"

He ran to his mother; she was beside herself; she kept stammering: "She's insolent! Giddy! Worse, perhaps!"

And she insisted upon leaving at once, if the other would not come and apologize to her. Charles returned to his wife and implored her to yield: he fell on his knees; in the end she answered:

"Very well, I'm coming."

Indeed, she did hold out her hand to her mother-in-law with the dignity of a marquise, saying:

"Forgive me, Madame."

Then, going back upstairs to her room, Emma flung herself face down on the bed and cried like a child, her head burrowed into the pillow.

They had agreed, she and Rodolphe, that in the case of an extraordinary occurrence she would attach a small strip of white paper to the window blind, so that if by chance he happened to be in Yonville he would hurry to the little street behind the house. Emma made the signal; she had been waiting for three-quarters of an hour when she suddenly caught sight of Rodolphe at the corner of the market buildings. She was tempted to open the window, to call to him; but he had already disappeared. She relapsed into despair.

Soon, however, it seemed to her that someone was walking back and forth on the sidewalk. It was he, without a doubt; she went downstairs, crossed the courtyard. He was there, outside. She flung herself into his arms.

"Be careful," he said.

"Oh, if you knew!" she said.

And she began to tell him everything, in haste, without coherence, exaggerating the facts, inventing many of them, and interspersing parentheses so lavishly that he understood nothing of what she said.

"Now, now, my poor angel, be brave, it will be all right, be patient."

"But it's been four years now that I've been patient and suffered! . . . A love like ours ought to be avowed before heaven! They're torturing me. I can't stand any more. Take me away!"

She pressed herself against Rodolphe. Her eyes, full of tears, glimmered like flames under water; her throat breathed in short gasps; never had he loved her so much, with the result that he lost his head and said:

"What shall we do? What do you want?"

"Take me away!" she cried. "Take me away! . . . Oh, I beg you!"

And she clung to his mouth as if to snatch from it the unanticipated consent which was breathed out in a kiss.

"But . . ." Rodolphe began.

"Well, what?"

"Your daughter?"

She considered for a few moments, then answered:

"We'll take her with us, I'm afraid."

"What a woman!" he thought, watching her move away.

For she had slipped back into the garden. Someone was calling her.

The elder Madame Bovary, in the days that followed, was vastly astonished at the metamorphosis of her daughter-in-law. In truth, Emma displayed more docility, and even carried deference to the lengths of asking her for a recipe for pickling gherkins. She was living as if submerged in anticipatory savoring of her coming happiness. It was an incessant subject of conversations with Rodolphe. She would lean against his shoulder, she would murmur:

"Ah, when we are in the mail-coach! . . . Do you think about that? Is it possible? It seems to me that the moment I feel the coach set out it will be as if we were going up in a balloon, as if we were starting out for the clouds. Do you realize that I'm counting the days? . . . What about you?"

Never had Madame Bovary been so beautiful as during those days; she had that indefinable beauty which is the result of joy, ardor, success, and which is no more than the harmony of temperament with circumstances. Her desires, her sorrows, the experience of pleasure and her illusions, forever young, had gradually developed her as rich soil, rain, air and sunlight do flowers, and now at last she bloomed in the fulness of her nature. Her eyelids seemed shaped expressly for her long loving glances in which the pupils were lost, while a deep breath widened her narrow nostrils and lifted the soft corner of her lips, lightly shadowed by a trace of black down. One would have said that an artist versed in corruption had arranged the knot of hair low on her neck: it was rolled into a heavy mass, carelessly, after the casual fashion of adultery which daily loosened it. Her voice now took on softer inflections, her figure, too; something subtle and penetrating was exhaled from the very folds of her gown and the arch of her foot. Charles, as in the first days of their marriage, found her enchanting and utterly irresistible.

When he came home in the middle of the night he did not dare to wake her. The porcelain night-lamp sent a circle of tremulous light to the ceiling, and the closed curtains of the little cradle made a sort of white hut swelling up out of the shadow at the side of the bed. Charles would look at them. He would think that he heard his child's light breathing. Ah, how pretty she would be, later on, at fifteen, when, looking like her mother, she would wear wide-brimmed straw hats in the summer time, as she did! From a distance they would be taken for sisters. He imagined her working beside them in the evening, in the lamplight; she would embroider slippers for him; she would take an interest in the housekeeping; she would fill the whole house with her grace and her merriment.

Emma was not sleeping; she pretended to be asleep; and, while he dozed off at her side, she would rouse herself with other dreams.

By four horses going at a gallop, she had been carried away a week before to a new country whence they would never return. They went on, went on, their arms about one another, not speaking. Often, from a mountain height, they suddenly caught sight of some magnificent city with domes, bridges, sailing vessels, groves of lemon trees and white marble cathedrals whose pointed spires were topped with storks' nests. And then, one evening, they reached a fishing village where brown nets were drying in the wind along the shore and beside the cottages. It was here that they settled down to live: they would live in a low flat-roofed house shaded by a palm tree, at the far end of a bay beside the sea. They would sail in a gondola, swing in a hammock; and their life would be easy and ample as their silk garments, warm and starry as the soft nights at which they would gaze.

She had sent for Monsieur Lheureux and told him:

"I shall need a cloak, a big cloak with a long collar, interlined."

"You're going on a trip?" he asked.

"No, but . . . never mind, I'm counting on you, do you understand? And quickly."

He bowed.

"I shall also need a trunk," she went on. "Not too heavy . . . convenient."

"Yes, yes, I understand. About ninety-two centimeters by fifty, the way they're making them now."

"And a suitcase."

"There is definitely," Lheureux thought, "some kind of carrying-on behind all this."

"And here," Madame Bovary said, pulling her watch from her belt, "take this: you can pay yourself out of it."

But the storekeeper cried that she was mistaken; they knew one another; did he doubt her? This was childish! However, she insisted that he at least keep the chain, and Lheureux had already put it into his pocket and was leaving when she called him back.

"You're to leave everything at your shop. As for the cloak—" she seemed to ponder—"no, don't bring that, either; just give me the name of the tailor and tell them to hold it ready for me."

It was the following month that they were to go. She was to leave from Yonville as if for a shopping trip to Rouen. Rodolphe would have reserved seats, secured passports and even written to Paris to engage the whole coach as far as Marseilles where they would buy a carriage and, from there, proceed without stopping, by the Gênes road. She would have taken care to send her luggage to Lheureux' shop, whence it would be taken directly to the *Hirondelle*, so that no one would suspect anything; and, in all this, the question of her child had never come up. Rodolphe avoided speaking of it; perhaps she did not think of it.

He wanted two more weeks ahead of him for settling a few business matters; then, at the end of one week, he demanded two more, then he said that he was ill; later he went on a trip; the month of

August passed and, after all these delays, they agreed to fix irrevocably upon the fourth of September, a Monday.

At length the Saturday, two days before, arrived.

Rodolphe came in the evening, earlier than usual.

"Are you ready?" she asked him.

"Yes."

They strolled all around one of the flower beds, then, and went to sit down near the terrace, on the coping of the wall.

"You are sad," Emma said.

"No. Why?"

And yet he was looking at her oddly, in a tender manner.

"Is it because of going away?" she asked. "Leaving the things you are fond of, your life here? Oh, I understand . . . But as for me, I have nothing in the world, you are everything to me. So I shall be everything to you, I'll be a family, a country to you; I'll take care of you, I'll love you."

"How lovely you are!" he said, clasping her in his arms.

"Truly?" she said with a voluptuous laugh. "Do you love me? Swear it, then."

"Do I love you! Do I love you! I adore you, my love!"

The moon, fully round and crimson, was rising from the earth beyond the prairie. Emma, her eyes half closed, drew deep sighing breaths of the cool wind that was stirring. They did not speak, so lost were they in the flood tide of reverie.

"This beautiful night!" Rodolphe said.

"We will have others," Emma said.

And, as if speaking to herself:

"Yes, it will be good to travel . . . Yet why is my heart sad? Is it dread of the unknown . . . the effect of habits left behind . . . or is it . . . ? No, it's too much happiness. How weak I am, am I not? Forgive me!"

"There is still time!" he cried. "Think it over. You will regret it, perhaps."

"Never!" she said impetuously.

And, moving closer to him:

"What unhappiness can come to me? There is no desert, no precipice, no ocean that I would not cross with you. As we go on together it will be like an embrace, closer and more complete every day. We will have nothing to trouble us, no cares, no obstacle. We will be alone, all to ourselves, forever . . . Say something, answer me."

He had been replying at regular intervals: "Yes . . . Yes . . ." She was stroking his hair with her hands, and she kept repeating in a childish voice, in spite of great tears that rolled down:

"Rodolphe! Rodolphe! . . . Ah, Rodolphe, my darling Rodolphe!"

Twelve o'clock struck.

"Midnight!" she said. "So now it's tomorrow. One more day!"

He rose to go; and, as if this gesture of his had been the signal for their flight, Emma suddenly assumed an air of gaiety.

"You have the passports?"

"Yes."

"You're not forgetting anything?"

"No."

"You're sure?"

"Certainly."

"It's the Hôtel de Provence, isn't it, where you'll be waiting for me . . . at noon!"

He nodded.

"Until tomorrow, then!" Emma said, in one last embrace.

And she watched him go.

He did not turn back. She ran after him and, leaning over toward the water's edge between the bushes:

"Until tomorrow!" she cried.

He was already on the other side of the river, walking rapidly over the prairie.

After a few minutes Rodolphe stopped; and when he saw her with her white dress gradually fade away in the shadows like a ghost, he was overcome by such a palpitation of the heart that he leaned against a tree to keep from falling.

"What a fool I am!" he said, swearing violently. "Never mind, she made a lovely mistress."

And at once Emma's beauty, along with all the pleasures of that love, appeared to him again. At first he softened, then he rebelled against her.

"For after all," he exclaimed, gesticulating, "I can't expatriate myself, be burdened with a child."

He told himself these things to strengthen him further in his purpose.

"And besides, the nuisance, the expense . . . Oh, no, no, a thousand times no! That would have been too stupid!"

13

No more than arrived home,
Rodolphe sat down abruptly at his desk,
beneath the stag's head mounted upon the wall. But
when he had the pen in his fingers he was unable to find words, so
that, leaning on his two elbows, he fell to thinking deeply. Emma
seemed to him to have withdrawn into a distant past, as if the resolution to which he had come had suddenly placed an immense space
between them.

In order to recover something of her, he went to the cupboard at
the head of his bed to get out the old Rheims biscuit-box in which
he habitually kept his letters from women, and from it drifted an
odor of damp rust and withered roses. First he saw a pocket handkerchief covered with small faded stains. It was hers, once she had
had a nosebleed while they were out walking; he no longer remembered it. Next, with all its corners dog-eared, the miniature Emma
had given him; her costume seemed pretentious to him, and her
glance pathetically theatrical; then, through studying this image and
summoning the memory of the model, he found that Emma's features gradually became confused in his recollection, as if the living
face and the painted one, rubbing against one another, had become
mutually obliterated. At length he read some of her letters; they
were full of explanations concerning their journey, short, technical
and hurried as business memoranda. He wanted to look at the long
ones again, those of earlier days; to find them, at the bottom of the
box, Rodolphe pushed all the others aside; and he began to paw
mechanically through that jumbled heap of papers and objects, coming across bouquets, a garter, a black mask, pins and locks of hair—
quantities of hair!—some dark, some fair; there was even some clinging to the clasp of the box, breaking when it was opened.

Thus wandering idly among his keepsakes, he studied the hand-
writings and styles of the letters, as varied as their spelling. They

were tender or merry, facetious, melancholy; there were some that asked for love and others that asked for money. An occasional word recalled a face, a certain gesture, the sound of a voice; sometimes, however, he could remember nothing.

Actually these women, thronging simultaneously into his mind, obstructed one another and dwarfed one another as if subjected to a common leveling process of love which equalized them. So taking a handful of their mixed letters, he amused himself for several minutes letting them cascade from his right hand to his left. At last, bored and drowsy, Rodolphe went to put the box away again in the cupboard, saying to himself: "What nonsense! . . ."

Which summed up his attitude; for pleasures, like students in a school yard, had so trampled his heart that no green thing grew there, and those who passed that way, more heedless than children, did not even leave their names scratched into the wall as they did.

"Come now," he said to himself, "let's get started."

He wrote:

Be brave, Emma, be brave! I cannot bring myself to ruin your life . . .

"After all, that's true," Rodolphe thought. "I am acting in her interest; I am honest."

Have you soberly weighed your decision? Do you realize into what abyss I was dragging you, poor angel? The answer is no, isn't it? You were going along, confiding and reckless, believing in happiness, in the future . . . Ah, unfortunate creatures that we are! Insane!

Rodolphe paused here to seek some valid excuse.

"Suppose I told her that my whole fortune is lost? . . . Oh, no, besides that wouldn't present any obstacle. This would just begin all over again later on. Can women like that be made to listen to reason?"

He pondered, then added:

I shall not forget you, believe me, and I shall always have a deep devotion for you; but one day, sooner or later, this ardor would have cooled, that is the way of human nature! Weariness would have come to us, and who knows but that I might even have suffered the hideous torment of watching your remorse and participating in it myself, since I should have been the cause of it. The mere thought of sorrow coming to you tortures me, Emma. Forget me! Why did I have to meet you?

Why were you so beautiful? Was it my fault? Oh, dear God, no, no! Accuse only fate!

"There's a word that always has an effect," he thought.

Oh, if you had been one of those frivolous-hearted women such as one sees, then certainly, out of vanity, I could have attempted an affair without danger to you. But that wonderful exaltation which is at once your charm and your scourge, prevented you from understanding, adorable woman that you are, the falseness of our future position. I too had not considered it at first, and I was relaxing in the shade of that ideal happiness as in that of the manchineel tree, without foreseeing the consequences.

"Perhaps she is going to think that it's out of avarice I'm giving her up . . . Oh, never mind, so much the worse! I've got to get it over with."

The world is cruel, Emma. Wherever we might have gone, it would have hounded us. You would have had to face indiscreet questions, slander, contempt, perhaps deliberate insult. Insult to you! Oh! . . . And I who wanted to put you on a throne! who will carry the thought of you like a talisman! For I am going to punish myself with exile for all the harm I have done you. I am going away. Where? I do not know, I am mad. Good-by! Always be kind. Keep the memory of the unfortunate soul who was your ruin. Teach my name to your child, that she may repeat it in her prayers.

The two candle flames were trembling. Rodolphe rose to shut the window and, when he had sat down again:

"I believe that's all. Ah, there's still this, for fear she might come trying to start me off again":

I shall be far away when you read these sad lines; for I want to run away as quickly as possible, to avoid the temptation of seeing you again. No weakness! I shall return; and perhaps some day we will talk together quite coolly about our old love affair. Adieu!

And there was a last farewell, divided into two words: *A Dieu!* which he considered to be in excellent taste.

"How am I to sign myself, now?" he wondered. "Your devoted . . . No. Your friend? . . . Yes, that's it."

Your friend.

He reread his letter. It seemed good to him.

"Poor little thing!" he thought with sudden tenderness. "She's going to think me more unfeeling than a stone; there should be a few teardrops on it, but I can't cry; it's not my fault." Then, having poured some water into a glass, Rodolphe dipped his finger into it and let one big drop fall from above, making a pale spot on the ink; after that, as he was about to seal the letter the *Amor nel Cor* seal came to hand.

"It's hardly appropriate under the circumstances . . . Oh, nonsense! What's the difference?"

After which he smoked three pipes and went to bed.

The next day when he arose (at about two o'clock, he had slept late), Rodolphe had a basket of apricots picked. He laid the letter in the bottom, under some vine leaves, and immediately ordered Girard, his manservant, to deliver it tactfully to Madame Bovary. He made use of this means of corresponding with her, sending her fruit or game according to the season.

"If she asks you for news of me," he said, "you're to tell her that I've left on a journey. You must deliver the basket to her, herself, into her own hands . . . Go along, and be careful!"

Girard put on his new blouse, tied his handkerchief over the apricots and set off tranquilly on the road to Yonville, walking with great heavy strides in his big hobnailed clogs.

When he reached her house, Madame Bovary, with Félicité, was arranging a bundle of linen on the kitchen table.

"Here is something our master sent you," the manservant said.

She was overcome by apprehension and, searching in her pocket for some coins, she stared at the peasant with a haggard eye, while he, for his part, gazed at her dumfounded, not understanding why such a gift should so move anyone. He left at last. Félicité remained. Emma could endure no longer; she hurried into the sitting room, as if to leave the apricots there, turned out the basket, snatched away the leaves, found the letter, opened it and, as if there had been a terrible fire behind her, she ran to her room, utterly dismayed.

Charles was there, she saw him; he spoke to her, she heard nothing, and she continued swiftly up the stairs, breathless, bewildered, distracted and still holding that horrible sheet of paper that crackled in her fingers like a strip of sheet metal. On the second floor she paused in front of the storeroom door, which was closed.

Now she tried to calm herself; she remembered the letter; she

164

must finish it, she did not dare. Besides, where? How? Someone would see her.

"Ah, no," she thought, "here I'll be safe."

Emma pushed open the door and went in.

The roof-tiles sent down a thick heat which pressed upon her temples and stifled her; she dragged herself to the closed dormer window, pulled back its bolt, and the dazzling light flooded in.

Opposite, beyond the rooftops, the open country stretched as far as the eye could reach. Below, beneath her, the village square was empty; the pebbles of the sidewalk glittered, the weather vanes on the houses stood motionless; at the corner of the street a kind of snoring sound interspersed with strident modulations came from a lower story. It was Binet working at his lathe.

She leaned against the window embrasure and reread the letter with sneering anger. But the more she fixed her attention upon it, the more confused her ideas became. She was seeing him again, she was waiting for him, she was encircling him with her arms; and palpitations of the heart, which was beating beneath her breast in great strokes like the clapper of a bell, came swiftly one after the other at unequal intervals. She cast her eyes all about her in the hope that the earth might be crumbling to ruin. Why not make an end of it? What was there to hold her back? She was free. And as she leaned forward, she stared at the stones of the street, muttering: "Now! Now!"

The luminous streak that reflected up from below was drawing the weight of her body toward the abyss. It seemed to her that the whirling earth of the square was rising up along the walls, and that the floor was tipping forward like a pitching ship. She stood on the extreme edge, almost hanging, surrounded by vast space. The blue of the sky flooded into her, the wind eddied through her vacant head, she had only to give up, to let herself go; and the snarling of the lathe went on and on like a furious voice which was calling her.

"My wife! My wife!" Charles shouted.

She paused. "Where are you? Come here!"

The thought that she had just escaped death all but made her faint with terror; she closed her eyes; then she shuddered at the touch of a hand on her sleeve: it was Félicité.

"Monsieur is waiting for you, Madame. Dinner is served."

And she must go down, she must sit at the table!

She tried to eat. The bites of food strangled her. Then she unfolded her napkin as if to examine its weave and actually tried to concentrate upon this effort, to count the threads of the material. Suddenly the memory of the letter returned to her. Had she lost it? Where should she look for it? But her spirit was so overcome by lassitude that she could never have invented a pretext for leaving the table. Then, too, she had become cowardly; she was afraid of Charles; he knew everything, that was sure! Indeed, strangely enough, he spoke these words:

"It seems we won't be seeing Monsieur Rodolphe soon."

"Who told you?" she said, trembling.

"Who told me?" he replied, somewhat surprised by her abrupt tone. "It was Girard, I met him just now at the door of the *Café Français*. He has gone on a trip, or is going to go."

She caught her breath.

"What's so surprising? He goes away like that from time to time for diversion, and by Jove I think he's right. When one has a fortune and is a bachelor! . . . Besides, he has a fine time, our friend does. He's quite a fellow! Monsieur Langlois was telling me . . ."

He fell silent, out of propriety, because the servant came.

She replaced in the basket the apricots scattered on the side-table; Charles, not noticing his wife's flush, had her bring them to him, took one and bit it.

"Oh, perfect!" he said. "Here, taste."

And he held out the basket which she gently pushed away.

"Smell them, then: what an aroma!" he said, passing them back and forth under her nose several times.

"I'm choking!" she cried, leaping to her feet.

But, by means of sheer will power this spasm was overcome.

"It's nothing," she said, "it's nothing. It's my nerves. Sit down, eat." For she dreaded being questioned, watched over, never left alone again.

Charles, to obey her, had sat down again and was spitting apricot pits into his hand and then dropping them onto his plate.

Suddenly a blue tilbury drove past in the square at a fast trot. Emma cried out and fell rigid to the floor, backward.

Rodolphe, indeed, had decided after deep reflection to leave for Rouen. Now, as there is no other road from La Huchette to Buchy than the one through Yonville, he had had to drive through the village, and Emma had recognized him by the light of the lanterns which sliced through the twilight like a lightning flash.

The pharmacist, at the tumult that was heard from the house, hurried over. The table, with all the plates upon it, had been over-turned; gravy, meat, knives, the salt cellar and the oil cruet were strewed about the room; Charles was calling for help; Berthe, terrified, was screaming: and Félicité, whose hands were shaking, was unlacing Madame, who was having convulsive spasms all along her body.

"I am going to run and get a bit of aromatic vinegar from my laboratory," the apothecary said.

Then, as she reopened her eyes, inhaling from the vial:

"I was sure of it," he said. "This would wake the dead for you."

"Speak to us!" Charles was saying. "Speak to us. Wake up. It's me, your Charles who loves you. Do you know me? Look, here's your little girl: put your arms around her."

The child stretched out her arms to her mother to put them around her neck. But, turning her head away, Emma said in a broken voice, "No, no . . . nobody."

She lost consciousness again. They carried her to her bed.

She lay there, stretched out, her mouth open, her eyes closed, her hands flat, motionless and white as a wax statue. From her eyes streams of tears crept slowly down to the pillow slip.

Charles stood at the foot of the alcove and the pharmacist, beside him, maintained that thoughtful silence which it is proper to keep on the serious occasions of life.

"Set your mind at rest," he said, touching his elbow, "I think the paroxysm is over."

"Yes, she's relaxing a little now," Charles answered, watching her sleep. "Poor woman . . . poor woman! She's had a relapse!"

Then Homais asked how the accident had occurred. Charles replied that it had come over her all of a sudden while she was eating apricots.

"Extraordinary!" the pharmacist said. "But it may be that apricots have caused syncope. There are natures that are so sensitive to certain odors. It might be a rewarding question to study, as much from the pathological aspect as from the psychological. Priests are aware of the importance of it, they've always mixed aromatics with their ceremonies. It's intended to stupefy your intellect and bring on a state of exaltation, a thing that is easily accomplished, in any case, with persons of the female sex, who are more delicate than others.

Cases have been cited who faint at the smell of burned corn, fresh bread . . ."

"Take care you don't wake her," Bovary said softly.

"And not only are human beings affected by these anomalies," the apothecary continued, "but animals as well. For instance, you are not unfamiliar with the singularly aphrodisiac effect produced by *nepeta cataria*, commonly known as catnip, on the feline race; and, on the other hand, to quote an example I know to be authentic, Bridoux (one of my old classmates, now established in the Rue Malpalu) owns a dog who is seized with convulsions whenever he is confronted with a snuffbox. He even used to conduct the experiment frequently, in the presence of his friends, at his summerhouse in the Bois Guillaume. Can one believe that a simple sternutatory could cause such ravages in the organism of a quadruped? It's extremely curious, isn't it?"

"Yes," said Charles, who was not listening.

"That proves to us," the other went on, smiling with an air of benign complacency, "the innumerable irregularities of the nervous system. As regards Madame, she had always, I confess, seemed to me to be a true sensitive plant. In view of which, my dear friend, I do not recommend any of the so-called remedies which, under pretext of attacking the symptoms, attack the constitution. No, no vain medication. Diet, that's the whole thing! Sedatives, emollients, antacids. Then, too, don't you think it might perhaps help to appeal to the imagination?"

"In what? How?" Bovary said.

"Ah, that's the question! That is definitely the question. As I was reading just the other day in the newspaper, the English put it: *That is the question!*"

But Emma, rousing, cried out: "The letter? The letter?"

They thought her delirious; she was, from midnight on: brain fever had set in.

For forty-three days Charles did not leave her side. He forsook all his patients; he did not go to bed; he was continually taking her pulse, applying mustard plasters, cold compresses. He sent Justin to Neufchâtel to get ice; the ice melted on the way back; he sent him again. He called Monsieur Canivet in consultation; he sent to Rouen for Doctor Larivière, his former professor; he was in despair. The most terrifying thing to him was Emma's prostration; for she did not speak, heard nothing and seemed not even to suffer—as if her body and her soul were resting together after all their disturbances.

Toward the middle of October she was able to sit up in bed with pillows behind her. Charles wept when he saw her eat her first jam-tart. Strength returned to her; she could get up for a few hours during the afternoon and, one day when she felt better, he tried to get her to walk around the garden on his arm. The sand of the paths was all but hidden under dead leaves; she walked, one foot after the other, dragging her slippers and, leaning against Charles' shoulder, she continued to smile.

They walked thus to the end of the garden, by the terrace. She drew herself up slowly, shaded her eyes with her hand to see: she looked out, far out; but on the horizon were only a few great grass-fires smoking on the hills.

"You're going to tire yourself, my dear," Bovary said.

And, urging her gently toward the arbor:

"Sit down on this bench: you will be all right."

"Oh, no, not there! Not there!" she said in a faltering voice.

She lost consciousness, and from that evening on her illness recommenced, with more uncertain symptoms, it is true, and a more complex nature. Now she felt pain at her heart, now in her breast, her head, her limbs; she was attacked by spasms of vomiting in which Charles thought he recognized the first symptoms of cancer.

And on top of all this, the poor fellow had money worries!

14

$\mathscr{F}$IRST, he did not know how he
was to reimburse Monsieur Homais for all the
medications bought from him; and although, as a doctor,
he need not have paid for them, still he was embarrassed over this
obligation. Then the household expenses, now that the cook was in
charge, were shocking; it rained bills in the house; the shopkeepers
were muttering; Monsieur Lheureux in particular kept harassing
him. As a matter of fact, when Emma's illness was at its height,
Lheureux, profiting by the circumstances to increase his bill, had
promptly delivered the cloak, the dressing-case, two trunks instead
of one, a quantity of other things. In vain Charles repeated that he
did not need them, the merchant replied arrogantly that all these
articles had been ordered from him and that he would not take them
back; besides, it would vex Madame during her convalescence;
Monsieur had better think it over; in short, he was determined to
go to court rather than give up his rights and take back his merchandise. Charles immediately ordered them sent back to his shop;
Félicité forgot; he had other concerns on his mind; they did not think
of it again; Monsieur Lheureux returned to the attack and, threatening and whining by turns, maneuvered in such a manner that in
the end Charles signed a six-month's note. But scarcely had he
signed this note when an audacious idea occurred to him: it was
to borrow a thousand francs from Monsieur Lheureux. So, with an
embarrassed air, he asked if there were not some way of obtaining
this sum, adding that it would be for one year and at whatever rate
of interest was required. Lheureux hastened to his shop, brought
back the écus and dictated another note in which Bovary stated that
he was to pay, on the first day of the following September, the sum
of one thousand and seventy francs, which, added to the one hun-

dred and eighty already stipulated, made precisely twelve hundred and fifty.

Charles wondered several times how, during the next year, he was to repay all that money; and he racked his brains, imagined expedients such as appealing to his father or selling something. But his father would turn a deaf ear, and he himself had nothing to sell. Then he found himself in such difficulties that he promptly put out of his mind so disagreeable a subject for meditation. He reproached himself for neglecting Emma because of it; as if, all his thoughts rightfully belonging to his wife, failing to think about her continually would have been robbing her of something.

It was a harsh winter. Madame's convalescence was long. When the weather was fair they pushed her over to the window in her armchair, the window that overlooked the square, for she now had an aversion for the garden, and the blind on that side remained always closed. She wanted the horse sold; what she had once loved was now disagreeable to her. All her ideas seemed limited to caring for herself. She would lie in bed nibbling at small light meals, ring for the servant to inquire about tisanes or to chat with her. Meanwhile the snow on the market roofs cast a motionless white light into the bedroom; later there was the falling rain. And Emma awaited daily, with a kind of anxiety, the inevitable recurrence of the most minute events, which nevertheless meant nothing to her. The most important was the arrival of the *Hirondelle*, in the evening. Then the hostess of the inn would call out and other voices answer while Hippolyte's torch, as he reached up to the luggage carrier for boxes, was like a star in the gloom. At noon Charles came in; later he went out; then she would take a cup of broth and, about five o'clock, at dusk, the children who were returning from school, dragging their wooden shoes along the sidewalk, would all strike the slats of the shutters with their rulers, one after the other.

It was at this hour that Monsieur Bournisien came to visit her. He would ask after her health, bring her news and ply her with religion in a coaxing little talk that was not without charm. The mere sight of his cassock comforted her.

One day when, at the height of her illness, she had believed herself to be dying, she had asked for Communion; and, in proportion as the preparations for the sacrament were made in the room, as the chest of drawers, littered with medicine bottles was arranged as an altar, and Félicité strewed dahlia flowers on the floor, Emma felt some potent force pass over her which relieved her of all her pain, all perception, all emotion. Her flesh, unburdened, no longer had weight, a new life was beginning; it seemed to her that her being, rising up toward God, was about to dissolve in that love like burning incense which is dissipated in smoke. Holy water was sprinkled on the sheets of her bed; the priest lifted the white host from the sacred pyx; and it was swooning with celestial joy that she thrust out her lips to accept the offered body of the Saviour. Her spirit, rigid with pride, at last relaxed in Christian humility; and, savoring the pleasure of being weak, Emma contemplated within herself the destruction of her own will, which was destined to leave a wide doorway open for the incoming of grace. She wanted to become a saint. She bought rosaries, she wore amulets; she longed for an emerald-studded reliquary to keep in her room at the head of her bed, to receive her nightly kiss.

As for the memory of Rodolphe, she had thrust it far down to the bottom of her heart, and there it remained, more solemn and more immobile than a king's mummy in a subterranean vault. From this embalmed passion drifted an emanation which, permeating all things, gave a caressing fragrance to the immaculate atmosphere in which she wished to live. When she knelt at her Gothic prie-dieu, she spoke to God in the same sweet words she had once murmured to her lover in the outpourings of adultery. It was for the purpose of inducing belief; but no sensation of rapture descended to her from heaven; and she would rise, her legs wearied, with a vague consciousness of having been vastly cheated. This quest, she felt, was but an added merit; and in the pride of her piety, Emma compared herself to those great ladies of other days who, sweeping the embroidered trains of their long gowns so majestically, had retreated into solitude, there to shed at Christ's feet all the tears of hearts wounded by life.

Then she dedicated herself to extravagant acts of charity; she sewed garments for the poor; she sent firewood to women in childbirth; and Charles, returning to the house one day, found three beggars in the kitchen, seated around the table eating soup. She sent for her little girl, whom her husband had sent back to the nurse during her illness. She insisted upon teaching her to read; no matter how Berthe wept she did not become irritated. This was the course of resignation she had adopted, a universal indulgence. Her language on all subjects was full of graceful expressions. Madame Bovary senior found nothing to criticize.

In addition to the company of her mother-in-law, who strengthened her somewhat with her rectitude and her sober manners, Emma had other visitors almost every day. There were Madame Langlois, Madame Caron, Madame Dubreuil, Madame Tuvache and regularly, from two to five, the excellent Madame Homais, who had never been willing to believe any of the scandalous rumors which were circulated about her neighbor. The Homais children also came to see her; Justin accompanied them. He would come up to the bedroom with them and stand there, near the door, motionless, not speaking. There were even times when Madame Bovary, forgetting about him, began to dress. She commenced by pulling the comb out of her hair, shaking her head in an abrupt motion; and the first time he saw that cascade of hair which hung down below her knees as its black coils unwound, it was for him, poor boy, like suddenly being admitted to something extraordinary and new, the splendor of which terrified him.

Emma, of course, did not notice his silent intentness nor his timidity. She never suspected that love, vanished from her life, was throbbing there beside her, beneath that coarse cotton shirt, in that adolescent heart laid open to the emanations of her beauty. In addition, she now surrounded everything with such indifference, she used words so affectionate and glances so scornful, manners so contradictory, that there was no longer any distinguishing between selfishness and charity, nor between corruption and virtue. One evening, for example, she flew into a rage with her servant, who had asked to be allowed to go out and was stammering as she searched for a pretext. Suddenly:

"So you're in love with him?" she said.

And, without waiting for an answer from Félicité, who was blushing, she added sorrowfully:

"Go ahead, go to him. Have a good time!"

Early in the spring she had the garden changed all around, from one end to the other, in spite of Bovary's comments; nevertheless he was happy at seeing her manifest any sort of volition. She gave further evidences of it as her recovery progressed. First she found a way of ejecting Mère Rollet, the nurse, who had formed the habit, during her illness, of coming too often to the kitchen with her two charges and her boarder, who had the appetite of a cannibal. Then

173

she shook off the Homais family, dismissed all the other visitors one after another and even frequented the church less assiduously, to the vast approval of the apothecary, who said amiably:

"You were turning into a priest!"

Monsieur Bournisien called every day, as before, after catechism class. He preferred to sit outdoors to take the air "in the bower," as he called the arbor. It was the hour at which Charles usually came home. The men would feel warm; cider would be brought, and they would drink together to Madame's complete recovery.

Binet would be there, or rather a little lower down, at the terrace wall, fishing for crayfish. Bovary would invite him to take a little refreshment, and he was expert at uncorking bottles.

"What you have to do," he would say, casting a satisfied glance about him and out to the far edges of the countryside, "is to hold the bottle straight up and down on the table, so, and after the wires are cut, work the cork up gently, gently, a little at a time, the way they do with seltzer water in restaurants."

But often during his demonstration the cider would spurt out full in their faces, and then the priest, with a gelatinous laugh, never failed to produce his joke:

"Its goodness leaps to the eye!"

Indeed, he was a good fellow, and was not even shocked by the pharmacist, who was advising Charles, one day, to take Madame to the theater in Rouen to hear the celebrated tenor Lagardy, by way of distraction.

This notion of going to the theater rapidly took root in Bovary's mind; for he at once spoke of it to his wife, who at first refused, on the ground of fatigue, the trouble, the expense; but for once in his life Charles did not yield, so convinced was he that this diversion would be beneficial to her. He could see no obstacle to it; his mother had sent three hundred francs upon which he had not counted, there was nothing enormous about his current debts, and the expiration date of his notes to Monsieur Lheureux was so far away that he did not have to think about them. Imagining, in addition, that she was prompted by scruples, Charles insisted the more; with the result that in the end, under pressure, she was persuaded. And the next day at eight o'clock they were packed into the *Hirondelle*.

The apothecary, who had nothing to keep him in Yonville, but considered himself under obligation not to set foot out of it, sighed as he watched them go.

"Well, have a good trip," he said to them, "lucky mortals that you are!"

Then, addressing Emma, who was wearing a blue silk dress with four flounces:

"You look as pretty as a picture. You're going to cut quite a figure in Rouen!"

The diligence stopped at the *Croix Rouge* hotel in the Place Beauvoisine. It was one of those inns such as are found in all provincial suburbs, with large stables and small bedrooms. Charles immediately set about getting seats. He confused the stage boxes with the galleries, the pit with the boxes, demanded explanations, did not understand them, was sent from the box office to the director, returned to the inn, went back to the theater and in this manner strode the whole length of the town several times, from the theater to the boulevard.

Madame bought herself a hat, gloves, a bouquet. Monsieur was greatly afraid of missing the curtain; and, without having had time to swallow a cup of soup, they presented themselves at the doors of the theater, which were still closed.

15

THE crowd stood against the wall,
packed symmetrically in between balustrades.

At the corners of the adjacent streets gigantic posters
repeated in baroque characters: *"Lucia di Lammermore* . . . Lagardy . . . Opera . . . etc."* It was a fine evening; everyone felt the
heat; perspiration started out under curled hair, drawn handkerchiefs all patted at flushed foreheads; and from time to time a mild
wind blowing up from the river softly stirred the edges of canvas
awnings hung over taproom doors.

For fear of appearing ridiculous, Emma insisted on taking a stroll
upon the promenade overlooking the port before going inside, and
Bovary, out of prudence, held the tickets in his hand, in his breeches
pocket, which he kept pressed against his side.

Her heartbeat quickened in the lobby. She smiled involuntarily
with vanity, seeing the crowd which pushed through the other corridor, off to the right, while she walked up the stairs to the dress
circle. She took a child's pleasure in pushing the wide upholstered
doors with her finger; she breathed deeply of the dusty odor of the
corridors and, when she was seated in her box, she arched her back
with the grace of a duchess.

Meanwhile, the orchestra's candles were lighted; the chandelier
was lowered from the ceiling, shedding a sudden gaiety over the
hall with the sparkling of its prisms; then the musicians came in,
one after the other, and there was a prolonged hubbub of bass horns
snoring, violins screeching, cornets hooting, flutes and flageolets
whining. But three knocks were heard on the stage; a roll of drums
began, the brasses added a few chords and the curtain, rising, revealed a country landscape.

She found herself among the readings of her youth, set down in
the midst of Walter Scott. She seemed to hear through the mist the

sound of Scottish bagpipes echoing over the heather. Too, the memory of the novel facilitating her understanding of the libretto, she followed the plot phrase by phrase, while indefinable thoughts which kept returning to her were at once dissipated by gusts of music. She gave herself up to the lulling of melodies and felt herself vibrate throughout her whole being as if the violin bows were being drawn across her nerves. She had not eyes enough for staring at the costumes, the stage settings, the characters, the painted trees that rippled as one walked, and the velvet tam o'shanters, the cloaks, the swords, all these things of the imagination which moved among the harmonies as in the atmosphere of another world.

Edgar Lagardy appeared. He had that splendid pallor which lends something of the majesty of marble to the ardent races of the Midi. His vigorous frame was laced into a brown doublet; a small carved dagger swung on his left thigh, and he cast languishing glances, flashing his white teeth. It was said that a Polish princess, listening to him sing one evening on the shore at Biarritz where he was recalking rowboats, had fallen in love with him. She had ruined herself for him. He had deserted her for other women, and this romantic reputation was of no small service to his artistic renown. The diplomatic troubadour even took great pains always to have a poetic phrase about the fascination of his person and the sensibility of his soul inserted into the notices. A fine voice, an imperturbable composure, more temperament than intelligence and more magniloquence than lyricism combined to enhance that admirable mountebank character, part hairdresser and part toreador.

From the first scene he enraptured the audience. He pressed Lucia in his arms, he left her, he returned, he seemed to be in despair, he indulged in outbursts of anger, then in elegiac warblings of infinite sweetness, and the notes welled from his bare throat, interspersed with sobs and tears. Emma leaned forward to gaze at him, scratching the velvet of the box with her nails. She filled her heart with those melodious lamentations which swelled to the accompaniment of the double-basses like the cries of the shipwrecked in the tumult of a storm. She recognized all the intoxication and anguish of which she had come close to dying. The voice of the singer seemed to her no more than the echo of her own consciousness, and that illusion which cast its spell over her, something out of her own life. But no one on earth had loved her with such a love. *He* had not wept, like Edgar, that last night in the moonlight when they had said to each other: "Tomorrow; tomorrow! . . ." The theater resounded to applause; the entire stretto was begun again; the lovers sang of flowers on their grave, of vows, exile, destiny, hope, and when they sighed the final farewell, Emma gave a sharp cry which was lost in the last chords.

All her impulse toward disparagement fell away beneath the poetry of the rôle which was taking possession of her and, drawn toward the man by the illusion of the character, she tried to imagine his life, that resounding, extraordinary, splendid life which she too could have led if chance had willed it. They would have met, they would have fallen in love! With him she would have traveled from capital to capital through all the kingdoms of Europe, sharing his troubles and his pride, gathering up the flowers that were flung to him, embroidering his costumes with her own hands; then, every evening, from the depths of a box, behind the gold-latticed grille, with parted lips she would have received the outpourings of that spirit which would have sung for her alone; from the stage, while acting his part, he would have looked at her. But now a kind of frenzy gripped her: he was looking at her, that was certain! She wanted to run to his arms, to take refuge in his strength as in the incarnation of love itself, and to say to him, to cry out to him: "Take me, carry me away, let us go! Yours, yours, all my ardors and all my dreams!"

The curtain dropped.

The odor of gas blended with exhaled breath; the breeze from the fans made the atmosphere more stifling. Emma wanted to go out; the throng choked the corridors and she fell back into her chair with palpitations suffocating her. Charles, afraid of seeing her faint, hurried to the refreshment room to get her a glass of orgeat.

He had great difficulty in regaining his seat, for his elbows were jostled at every step because of the glass he was holding in his hands, and he even spilled three-quarters of it over the shoulders of a woman in evening dress who, feeling the cold liquid trickle down her back, screamed like a peacock, as if she were being murdered. Her husband, a mill owner, flew into a rage with the clumsy fellow and, while she was mopping at the spots on her beautiful cherry-colored taffeta gown with his handkerchief, he kept muttering about indemnity, expense and reimbursement in a surly tone. Eventually Charles reached his wife's side, completely out of breath, saying:

"My word, I thought I'd have to stay there! There's a crowd . . . a crowd!"

He added:

"Try to guess whom I met up there? Monsieur Léon!"

"Léon?"

"Himself! He is going to come and pay his respects to you."

And, as he was finishing the words, the former clerk from Yonville entered the box.

He held out his hand with the casual manner of a gentleman: and Madame Bovary automatically laid hers in it, doubtless obeying the attraction of a stronger will. She had not felt it since that spring evening when the rain had fallen on green leaves while they said good-by, standing beside the window. But quickly recalling herself to the proprieties of the situation, with an effort she shook off the torpor of memories and began to stammer swift phrases.

"Ah, good evening . . . What, you're here?"

"Silence!" cried a voice from the pit, for the third act was beginning.

"So you're in Rouen?"

"Yes."

"Since when?"

"Put them out! Put them out!"

Faces were turning toward them; they fell silent.

But from that moment on, she no longer listened; and the chorus of the guests, the scene between Ashton and his servant, the great duo in D major, all took place at a distance for her, as if the instruments had become less sonorous and the characters more remote: she was remembering the card games at the pharmacist's and the walk to the nurse's house, reading in the arbor, quiet talks beside the hearth, all of that pathetic love, so quiet and so long, so discreet, so tender, which she had meanwhile forgotten. Why was it returning, then? What combination of circumstances was restoring it to her life? He stood behind her, his shoulder leaning against the partition; and from time to time she felt herself shiver under the warm breath from his nostrils which stirred her hair.

"Does this amuse you?" he said, bending so close to her that the tip of his mustache brushed her cheek.

She answered carelessly:

"Oh, Lord, no! Not particularly."

179

Then he proposed that they leave the theater to go and have ices somewhere.

"Not yet, let's stay!" Bovary said. "Her hair has come undone: that's a sign it's going to be tragic."

But the mad scene held no interest for Emma, and the soloist's voice sounded exaggerated to her.

"She screams too loudly," she said, turning to Charles, who was listening.

"Yes . . . perhaps . . . a bit," he said, undecided between his own frank pleasure and the respect he paid his wife's opinions.

Then Léon said, sighing: "It's so warm . . ."

"Insupportable, really!"

"Are you uncomfortable?" Bovary asked.

"Yes, I'm stifling: let's leave."

Monsieur Léon delicately laid her long lace shawl over her shoulders, and they all three went to sit on the quay, in the fresh air, in front of the plate-glass window of a café. First they spoke of nothing but her illness, although Emma interrupted Charles from time to time, for fear, she said, of boring Monsieur Léon; then he told them that he had come to spend two years in one of Rouen's leading offices, in order to familiarize himself with legal matters, which were different in Normandy from those dealt with in Paris. He asked after Berthe, the Homais family, Madame Lefrançois; and, as they had nothing further to say to one another in her husband's presence, the conversation soon came to a halt.

People coming out of the theater passed by on the sidewalk, humming or bawling at the tops of their lungs: *O bel ange, ma Lucie!* Then Léon, posing as a dilettante, began to talk music. He had heard Tamburini, Rubini, Persiani, Grisi; and, beside them, Lagardy, despite his great outbursts of sound, was worth nothing.

"Still," Charles interrupted, nibbling his rum sherbet in small bites, "they claim that he is absolutely marvelous in the last act; I'm sorry we left before the end, because it was beginning to interest me."

"After all," the clerk said, "he'll be giving another performance soon."

But Charles replied that they were leaving the next day.

"Unless," he added, turning to his wife, "you'd like to stay on alone, my darling?"

And, changing tactics in view of this unexpected opportunity that was being offered to his aspirations, the young man embarked upon praise of Lagardy in the last act. It was something superb, sublime! Then Charles insisted:

"You can come home Sunday. Come now, make up your mind to do it. If you have the least idea in the world that it helps you, you're wrong to leave."

Meanwhile, the tables about them were emptying; a waiter came discreetly to hover near them; Charles, understanding, pulled out his purse; the clerk caught him by the arm, and even did not forget to leave two silver coins extra, which he rang against the marble.

"I'm really distressed," Bovary murmured, "at the money you . . ."

The other made a negligent gesture, full of cordiality and, taking his hat:

"It's understood, then, tomorrow at six?"

Charles protested again that he could not be absent any longer; but that there was nothing to prevent Emma . . .

"Well . . ." she stammered with a curious smile, "I'm not sure . . ."

"All right, you think it over, we'll see, sleep on it."

Then to Léon, who was walking with them:

"Now that you're here in our part of the world, I hope you'll come sometimes and ask us for a dinner?"

The clerk agreed that he would not fail to do so, having to go to Yonville in any event on a case for his office. And they parted in front of the Passage Saint-Herbland, just as eleven-thirty was striking from the cathedral.

PART THREE

1

*M*ONSIEUR LÉON, while study-
ing his law, had to a certain extent frequented
the *Chaumière*, where he had achieved a very agreeable
measure of success among the grisettes, who considered him to have
a "distinguished air." He was the most proper of students: he wore
his hair neither too long nor too short, did not go through his whole
trimester's allowance on the first day, and kept on good terms with
his professors. As for riotous living, he had always abstained from
it, as much from timidity as from delicacy.

Often, when he sat reading in his room, or, in the evening, beneath the lindens of the Luxembourg, he let his law book fall to
the ground, and the memory of Emma returned to him. But little
by little this emotion had faded, and other emotions accumulated
above it, although it still persisted beneath them; for Léon had not
lost all hope, and there was something like an uncertain promise
that hovered in the future for him, like a golden fruit hanging from
some fantastic tree.

Then, seeing her again after three years of absence, his passion
reawoke. He must, he thought, resolve to try to possess her. Besides,
his timidity had been rubbed off in contact with reckless companions, and he had returned to the provinces contemptuous of all who
did not, with gleaming foot, tread the asphalt of the boulevards.

Faced with a Parisian woman dressed in lace, in the drawing-
room of some illustrious surgeon, a personage with decorations and
carriages, the poor clerk would doubtless have trembled like a child;
but here in Rouen, on the quay, with this country-doctor's wife, he
felt at ease, convinced in advance that he would dazzle her. Self-
assurance depends upon the environment in which it is placed: one
does not use the same manner of speech on the drawing-room floor
as in the servants' quarters, and a wealthy woman seems to have

about her, to defend her virtue, all her bank notes, like a coat of mail, within the lining of her bodice.

Upon taking leave of Monsieur and Madame Bovary, the evening before, Léon had followed them at a distance down the street; then, having seen them stop at the *Croix Rouge,* he had turned on his heel and spent the night devising a plan.

The next day, therefore, at five o'clock, he entered the inn kitchen, his throat tight, his cheeks pale, and armed with that coward's resolution which stops at nothing.

"Monsieur is not here," a servant answered.

This seemed a good omen. He went upstairs.

She was not disturbed at his arrival; on the contrary, she apologized for having forgotten to tell him where they were stopping.

"Oh, I guessed," Léon said.

"How?"

He claimed to have been guided to her by chance, by instinct. She began to smile and at once, to retrieve his blunder, Léon told her that he had spent the morning asking for her in all the hotels in town, one after the other.

"So you decided to stay?" he added.

"Yes," she said, "and I was wrong. One shouldn't become accustomed to impossible pleasures when one has a thousand obligations all about . . ."

"Oh, I can imagine."

"Well, no, because you're not a woman."

But men also had their frustrations, and the conversation began upon a number of philosophical reflections. Emma was eloquent on the poverty of earthly affections and the eternal solitude in which the heart remains wrapped.

For the sake of making an impression, or through ingenuous imitation of the melancholy that evoked his own, the young man declared himself to be constantly very unhappy in his studies. The procedure irked him, other vocations attracted him and his mother never ceased tormenting him, in every letter. They became more and more specific about the sources of their unhappiness, each, as he talked, growing proportionately rather intense in this progressive confidence. But sometimes they hesitated before the complete disclosure of their thoughts, while yet seeking to design phrases that would reveal them. She did not confess her passion for another man; he did not say that he had forgotten her.

Perhaps he no longer recalled his suppers after the ball, with women in carnival costume; and doubtless she did not remember those rendezvous of other days, when she had run through the standing grasses, in the morning, to her lover's château. The noises of the town barely reached them; and the room seemed small, as if made for the purpose of holding their solitude the more closely. Emma, in a dimity peignoir, rested the heavy knot of her hair against the back of an old armchair; the yellow wallpaper made a sort of golden background behind her: and her bare head was reflected in the mirror, with the white part in the center and the tips of her ears showing below its smooth bands.

"But forgive me," she said. "This is wrong of me, I'm boring you with my eternal complaints!"

"No, never. Never!"

"If you knew," she went on, raising to the ceiling her beautiful eyes in which tears stood, "all that I have dreamed!"

"And I! Oh, I have suffered a lot. Often I used to go out, I would walk, drag myself along the quays, trying to lose myself in the noise of the crowd yet unable to shake off the obsession that pursued me. On the boulevard, in an art dealer's shop, there's an Italian etching that represents a Muse. She is draped in a tunic and she is looking at the moon, with forget-me-nots in her unbound hair. Something kept incessantly driving me there; I've stayed there for hours on end."

Then, in a quivering voice:

"She looked a little like you."

Madame Bovary turned her head away, that he might not see upon her lips the irresistible smile she felt rising to them.

"Often," he went on, "I used to write letters to you and then tear them up."

She did not reply. He continued:

"Sometimes I would imagine that chance would bring you here. I thought I recognized you on street corners: and I'd run after all the cabs in which I saw a shawl or a veil like yours blowing in the window . . ."

She seemed determined to let him speak without interrupting him. Crossing her arms and lowering her face, she stared at the rosette on her slipper, and at intervals she made little movements of her toes inside their satin.

Nevertheless, she sighed:

"The most dreary thing of all is dragging out a useless existence as I do, isn't it? If our sorrows could be of use to someone, we could console ourselves in the thought of sacrifice."

He began to praise virtue, duty and silent abnegation, having himself an incredible need of devotion which he was unable to satiate.

"I should like very much to be a nun in a hospital," she said.

"Unfortunately, men haven't any of these holy callings," he answered, "and I don't see any other vocation anywhere . . . except, perhaps, a doctor's . . ."

With a slight shrug of the shoulders, Emma interrupted him to comment sorrowfully upon the illness of which she had failed to die; what a pity, she would not be suffering now! Léon promptly envied the "quiet of the grave," and one evening he had even gone so far as to write his will, requesting to be buried in that handsome velvet-banded coverlet which he had received from her; for it was thus that they would have liked to be, each of them constructing an ideal to which they were now adjusting their past lives. In addition, the spoken word is a roller that always spreads emotions out.

But, at this invention concerning the coverlet:

"Why so?" she asked.

"Why?" He hesitated. "Because I loved you very much."

And, congratulating himself upon having cleared the obstacle, Léon, from the corner of his eye, studied her expression.

It was like the sky when a gust of wind drives away the clouds. The cumulus of sorrowful thoughts which had been darkening them seemed to be withdrawn from her blue eyes; her whole face glowed.

He waited. At length she said:

"I always suspected it . . ."

Then they recalled to one another the small events of that faraway existence, the pleasure and melancholies of which they had just, through a single word, revived. He remembered the clematis arbor, the gowns she had worn, the furniture in her room, her whole house.

"And our poor cactus plants, what became of them?"

"The cold killed them last winter."

"Oh, how I've thought of them, you know? Often I used to see them again, the way they used to be, with the sun falling on the blinds on summer mornings . . . and I would glimpse your two bare arms moving among the flowers."

"Poor dear!" she said, holding out her hand to him.

Léon at once pressed his lips to it. Then, when he had taken a deep breath:

"In those days you were to me a sort of indescribable, incomprehensible force that enslaved my life. One time, for instance, I came to your house; but I suppose you don't remember?"

"Yes, I do," she said. "Go on."

"You were downstairs, in the vestibule, ready to go out, standing on the bottom step; you had on a hat with little blue flowers, too; and without any invitation from you, in spite of myself, I went with you. Yet every minute I was more and more conscious of my blunder, and still I went on walking near you, not daring actually to follow you, and not wanting to leave you. When you would go into a store I would wait in the street and watch you through the window, taking off your gloves and counting out the money on the counter. Afterwards you rang at Madame Tuvache's house, the door opened for you and I was left like an idiot in front of the big heavy door which had fallen closed behind you."

Madame Bovary, listening to him, was startled at being so old; all these things which were reëmerging seemed to her to enlarge her existence; it made what seemed like vast emotional stretches to which she was carried back; and she kept saying from time to time in a low voice and with half-closed eyelids:

"Yes, that's true . . . that's true . . . that's true . . ."

They heard eight o'clock strike from the various clocks of the Beauvoisine quarter, which is full of boarding houses, churches and big abandoned hotels. They were no longer talking; but they felt, as they looked at one another, a ringing in their heads, as if some audible force were radiated mutually by their fixed eyes. They had linked hands; and the past, the future, reminiscences and dreams, all were blended in the charm of this enchantment. Night was thickening over the walls on which still shone, half lost in the shadows, the raw colors of four lithographs representing four scenes from *La Tour de Nesle*, with a legend below in French and in Spanish. Through the window one saw a corner of black sky between pointed roofs.

She rose to light two candles on the chest of drawers, then came to sit down again.

"Well . . . ?" Léon said.

"Well . . . ?" she answered.

And he was wondering how to resume the interrupted conversation when she said:

"Why is it that no one, up to now, has ever expressed such feelings to me?"

The clerk protested that ideal natures were difficult to understand. He had loved her from the very first glance; and he was in despair when he thought of the happiness they would have had if, by the mercy of fate, they had met sooner and joined themselves together in an indissoluble union.

"I have thought of that sometimes," she said.

"What a dream!" Léon murmured.

And, delicately fingering the blue fringe of her long white sash, he added:

"What is there to prevent our beginning all over . . ."

"No. No, my dear," she answered. "I am too old . . . you are too young . . . forget me! Other women will love you . . . you will love them."

"Not as I do you!" he cried.

"Child that you are! Come now, be good. I want you to!"

She outlined the impossibilities of their love for him, and how he must confine himself, as before, to the limits of a merely brotherly affection.

Was it seriously that she spoke thus? Doubtless Emma herself did not know, absorbed in the charms of seduction and the necessity of defending herself against it; and, gazing at the young man with a gentle glance, she repulsed the timid caresses his shaking hand attempted.

"Ah, forgive me!" he said, drawing back.

And Emma was overtaken by a vague alarm in the face of this timidity, more dangerous to her than Rodolphe's boldness when he had advanced upon her, his arms outstretched. Never had any man looked so handsome to her. An exquisite candor was expressed in his demeanor. He lowered his long fine eyelashes which curled back. His soft-skinned cheek was flushed—she thought—with desire of her, and Emma felt an insuperable impulse to lay her lips against it. Then, leaning toward the clock, as if to look at the time:

"Goodness, how late it is!" she said. "How we've been chattering!"

He understood the suggestion and looked for his hat.

"I even forgot the play because of it. Poor Bovary, leaving me behind on purpose for that! Monsieur Lormaux, of the Rue Grand-Pont, was to have taken me with his wife."

And the opportunity was lost, for she was to leave the next day. "Really?" Léon said.

"Yes."

"But I've got to see you again," he said. "I had something to tell you . . ."

"What?"

"Something . . . important, serious. Oh, no, after all, you're not going, it's impossible! If you knew . . . Listen to me . . . Didn't you understand me? Didn't you guess . . . ?"

"Why, you talk very well," Emma said.

"Ah, jokes! No more, enough! Have pity, let me see you again . . . once, just one time."

"Well . . ."

She paused; then, as if upon second thought: "Oh, not here!"

"Wherever you like."

"Will you . . ." She seemed to reflect, then, in a short tone: "Tomorrow, at eleven o'clock, in the cathedral."

"I'll be there!" he cried, seizing her hands, which she pulled away.

And, as they were both standing, he behind her, and Emma lowering her head, he bent forward and pressed his lips long to the nape of her neck.

"Why, you must be mad! Ah, you're mad!" she said with small deep laughter, while the kisses were multiplied.

Then, thrusting his head forward across her shoulder, he seemed to seek her eyes' consent. They fell upon him, full of a frigid dignity.

Léon fell back three steps, to leave. He hesitated on the threshold. Presently he whispered in a quavering voice:

"Tomorrow."

She answered with a nod, and vanished like a bird into the adjoining room.

That evening Emma wrote an interminable letter to the clerk, in which she excused herself from the rendezvous; now all was over, and for the sake of their happiness they should never meet again. But when the letter was sealed, since she did not know Léon's address, she found herself very much embarrassed.

"I shall give it to him myself," she thought. "He will come."

The next morning Léon, humming on the balcony, his window open, polished his dress shoes himself, and with several coats of wax.

He put on white breeches, thin stockings, a green coat, sprinkled his handkerchief with every scent he owned; then, having had his hair curled, uncurled it in order to give it more natural elegance.

"It's still too early!" he thought, glancing at the barber's cuckoo clock, which said nine o'clock.

He read an old fashion paper, went out, smoked a cigar, walked back three blocks, thought that it was time and slowly made his way toward the Notre-Dame cathedral court.

It was a fine summer morning. Pieces of silver-plate gleamed in goldsmiths' shops, and the light that fell obliquely upon the cathedral cast bright reflections on the cracks of the gray stones; a flock of birds eddied about in the blue sky, around the trefoiled bell turrets; the square, clamorous with voices, smelled of the flowers that edged its pavement, roses, jasmine, violets, narcissus and tuberoses, unevenly alternated with patches of moist herbs, of catnip and of chickweed for the birds; the fountain, in the center, was gurgling, and beneath large umbrellas, among cantaloupes heaped up in pyramids, bareheaded vendors were twisting bunches of violets up in paper.

The young man bought one of them. It was the first time he had bought flowers for a woman, and his chest, as he sniffed at them, swelled with pride, as if this homage which he directed toward another were reflected back upon himself.

Still, he was afraid of being overseen; resolutely he entered the church.

At that moment the beadle was standing on the threshold, in the center of the left portal, beneath the *Marianne Dansant,* his feather plume on his head, his rapier at his thigh, his stick in his fist, more majestic than a cardinal and glittering like a sacred pyx.

He strode toward Léon and, with that smile of coaxing benignity which churchmen assume when they question children:

"Monsieur, I presume, is not from hereabouts? Monsieur wishes to see the interesting features of the church?"

"No," the other said.

And first he took a turn about the interior of the church. Then he went to look out over the square. Emma was not here. He went back up to the choir. Never had life seemed so good to him. Soon, now, she was going to come, charming, agitated, glancing behind her for eyes that might be following—and with her flounced dress, her gold lorgnon, her thin slippers, with all sorts of exquisite details which he had not experienced, and in the ineffable allurement of virtue upon the point of yielding. Like a boudoir the church, in its vastness, was prepared for her; the vaults bent down to receive in the shadows the confession of her love: the stained windows gleamed to light her face, and the censers were burning that she might appear like an angel, in perfumed smoke.

Still she did not come. He sat down in a seat and his eyes fell upon a blue window representing boatmen carrying baskets. He looked at it for a long time, attentively, and he counted the scales on the fish and the buttonholes in the doublets while his thoughts wandered in search of Emma.

The beadle, at one side, was inwardly becoming incensed with this individual who took the liberty of admiring the cathedral alone. He seemed to him to be behaving in a monstrous fashion, to be stealing from him in a way, and almost to be committing a sacrilege.

But a whisper of silk over the flagstones, a hat brim, a black shawl . . . It was she! Léon sprang up and hurried to meet her.

Emma was pale. She was walking rapidly.

"Read this!" she said, handing him a paper. "Oh, no!"

And she snatched her hand from him abruptly, to go into the chapel of the Virgin where, kneeling beside a chair, she began to pray.

The young man was irritated by this bigoted caprice; then, nevertheless, he found a certain charm in seeing her thus, in the midst of a rendezvous, lost in prayer like an Andalusian marquise; after this he speedily became bored, for she went on and on.

Emma was praying, or rather forcing herself to pray, in the hope that some sudden resolution would come down to her from heaven; and, in order to summon divine aid, she was filling her eyes with the splendors of the tabernacle, she breathed in the fragrance of full-blown white rocket-flowers and bent her ear to the silence of the church, which only accentuated the tumult of her heart.

She stood up again, and they were about to leave when the beadle walked quickly up to them, saying:

"Madame, I presume, is not from hereabouts? Madame would like to see the interesting features of the church?"

"No!" the clerk cried.

"Why not?" she asked.

For she was clinging with her wavering virtue to the Virgin, the sculptures, the tombs, every opportunity that offered.

Therefore, that they might "take it in order," the beadle led them to the entrance, off the square, where, pointing with his stick to a great circle of black flagstones without inscriptions or carvings:

"This," he said majestically, "is the circumference of the beautiful Amboise bell. It weighed forty thousand pounds. It was without equal in all Europe. The workman who cast it died of joy . . ."

"Let us leave," Léon said.

The fellow started off again; then, returning to the chapel of the Virgin, he flung out his arms in a synthetic gesture of demonstration and, more prideful than a country landowner showing you his fruit trees:

"—this simple stone covers Pierre de Brézé, lord of La Varenne and Brissac, Grand Marshal of Poitou and Governor of Normandy, died in the Battle of Montlhéry, July 16th, 1465."

Léon, biting his lips, stamped his feet.

"And, over to the right, this gentleman all covered with armor, on a prancing horse, is his grandson Louis de Brézé, lord of Breval and Montchauvet, Count de Maulevrier, Baron de Mauny, King's Chamberlain, Knight of the Order, and also Governor of Normandy, died July 23, 1531, a Sunday as the inscription notes; and below, that man preparing to descend into the grave represents exactly the same man. It is not possible to see a more perfect portrayal of the hereafter, is it?"

Madame Bovary took out her lorgnon. Léon, immobile, watched her, no longer even making an effort to say a single word, to make a single gesture, so discouraged did he feel before this dual attitude of idle chatter and indifference.

The eternal guide continued:

"Beside him, this kneeling woman who is weeping is his wife, Diane de Poitiers, Countess of Brézé, Duchess of Valentinois, born in 1499, died in 1566; and at the left, that one with the baby in her arms is the Holy Virgin. Now, turn this way: here are the Amboise tombs. They were both cardinals and archbishops of Rouen. This one was one of King Louis XII's ministers. He did a great deal for the cathedral. In his will it was found that he had left thirty thousand écus to the poor."

And without pausing, talking all the while, he herded them into a chapel crowded with balustrades, moved several of them aside and uncovered a sort of block that might well have been a poorly executed statue.

"Once it decorated Richard the Lionhearted's tomb," he said with a long groan. "It was the Calvinists, Monsieur, who reduced it to this condition. Out of wickedness, they buried it in the earth, under the Bishop's Episcopal seat. Look, here is the door by which he goes to his house, Monseigneur does. Let us move on and see the Gargouille windows."

But Léon abruptly drew a coin from his pocket and grasped Emma by the arm. The beadle remained utterly dumfounded, not understanding this impetuous munificence when there were still so many things left for the stranger to see. So, calling him back:

"Hey, Monsieur! The spire, the spire . . ."

"No, thank you," Léon said.

"Monsieur is making a mistake. It is four hundred and forty feet high, nine less than the Great Pyramid of Egypt. It is all cast iron, it . . ."

Léon fled; for it seemed to him that his love, which for the past two hours had been immobilized in the church like the stones, was now about to be dissipated like smoke through that kind of truncated funnel with its oblong framework, a sort of openwork chimney which perches so grotesquely upon the cathedral, like the extravagant endeavor of some whimsical foundryman.

"Where are we going?" she asked.

Without answering, he continued to stride along at a rapid gait, and Madame Bovary was already dipping her finger in the holy water when they heard behind them a great breathless panting regularly punctuated by the thumping of a cane. Léon turned.

"Monsieur!"

"What?"

And he recognized the beadle, carrying under his arm and balanced against his belly about a score of heavy bound volumes. They were works which "dealt with the cathedral."

"Imbecile!" Léon growled, flinging out of the church.

A street urchin was lounging in the cathedral court.

"Go fetch me a cab."

The boy set off like a bullet along the Rue des Quatre-Vents; then they were left alone for a few minutes, face to face and somewhat embarrassed.

"Oh, Léon! . . . Really . . . I don't know . . . if I should . . ."

She gave a forced smile. Then, with a serious air:

"It's very improper, you know."

195

"In what way?" the clerk answered. "It's done in Paris!"

And this observation, like an irresistible argument, convinced her. Meanwhile, the cab had not arrived. Léon was afraid that she might go back into the church. At last the cab appeared.

"At least go out by the North door!" the beadle, who had remained on the threshold, called to them, "to see the *Resurrection*, the *Last Judgment, Paradise, King David* and the *Reprobates* in the flames of hell."

"Where is Monsieur going?" the cab driver asked.

"Wherever you like," Léon said, urging Emma into the carriage.

And the heavy vehicle started off.

It went down the Rue Grand-Pont, crossed the Place des Arts, the Quai Napoléon, the Pont Neuf and stopped short before the statue of Pierre Corneille.

"Go on!" said a voice which issued from the interior.

The carriage set off again and, from the Carréfour La Fayette, letting itself be carried along by the downward slope, it entered the railway station at the full gallop.

"No, no, straight ahead!" cried the same voice.

The cab emerged from the gates and presently, reaching the drive, trotted leisurely between the great elms. The driver mopped his brow, put his leather cap between his knees and drove the carriage out to the far side of the footpath, to the water's edge, beside the grass.

It followed along the river, on the towpath paved with dry gravel, and, for some time, toward Oyssel, beyond the islands.

But suddenly it shot forward through Quatremares, Sotteville, the Grande-Chaussée, the Rue d'Elbeuf, and came to its third stop before the Jardin des Plantes.

"Go on!" the voice shouted more furiously.

And at once, resuming its course, it passed through Saint-Sever, by the Quai des Curandiers, by the Quai aux Meules, once more across the bridge, through the Place Champ-de-Mars and behind the hospital gardens where old men in black coats stroll in the sunshine along a terrace all green with ivy. It went back up the Boulevard Bouvreuil, ran along the Boulevard Cauchoise, then wandered over the whole of Mont-Riboudet as far as Deville.

It returned; and then, without object or direction, it meandered at random. It was seen at Saint-Pol, at Lescure, at Mont Gargan, at the Rouge-Mare and the Place du Gaillardbois; Rue Maladrerie,

Rue Dinanderie, in front of Saint-Romain, Saint-Vivien, Saint-Maclou, Saint-Nicaise—in front of the Customs House—at the Basse-Vielle-Tour, the Trois Pipes and the Cimitière Monumentale. From time to time the driver, from his perch, flung despairing glances at the taverns. He did not understand what frenzy of locomotion drove these individuals to insist upon not stopping. He tried several times, and at once heard behind him exclamations of rage. So he whipped up his two lathered nags with renewed vigor but without a care for the bumps, lurching this way and that, not caring, demoralized and almost weeping with thirst, fatigue and misery.

And on the quays, in the midst of the carts and barrels, and in the streets, at boundary corners, the townspeople stared open-mouthed before this sight so extraordinary in the provinces, a carriage with drawn blinds which kept continually appearing in this fashion, more tightly closed than a tomb and tossing about like a rowboat.

Once, in the middle of the day, far out in the country, just when the sun beat most strongly against the ancient silver-plated lanterns, a bare hand slipped between the small yellow cloth curtains and flung out scraps of torn paper which were scattered in the wind and settled down farther on, like white butterflies, in a field of red clover all in blossom.

Then, near six o'clock, the carriage stopped in a small street of the Beauvoisine quarter, and a woman stepped out of it who walked with her veil lowered, without turning her head.

2

*A*RRIVING at the inn, Madame
Bovary was astonished not to see the diligence. Hivert, who had waited fifty-three minutes for
her, had at length gone along.

Nothing, on the other hand, obliged her to leave; but she had
given her word that she would return this very evening. Besides,
Charles was expecting her; and already she felt in her heart that languid docility which is, for many women, like the punishment and the
ransom price of adultery combined.

Quickly she packed her bag, paid the bill, took one of the carriages in the courtyard and, hurrying the groom, urging him on,
asking every minute for the time and the number of kilometers put
behind them, succeeded in catching the *Hirondelle* on the outskirts
of Quincampoix.

The moment she was seated in her corner she closed her eyes and
opened them again at the bottom of the slope, where she caught
sight of Félicité, who was standing watch in front of the marshal's
house. Hivert reined in his horses, and the cook, pulling herself up
to the seat, said mysteriously:

"Madame, you must go straight to Monsieur Homais' house. It's
for something urgent."

The village was silent as usual. At the street corners there were
little pink mounds that steamed in the air, for it was preserving
time, and everybody, in Yonville, put up her preserves on the same
day. But in front of the pharmacist's shop a far larger heap was to
be admired, one which surpassed the others with the superiority
which an apothecary's laboratory ought to have over common stoves,
a general necessity over individual fancies.

She went in. The big armchair was overturned, and even the
Fanal de Rouen was lying on the floor, spread out between the two

pestles. She pushed open the door to the passage; and, in the middle of the kitchen, among brown jars full of seeded currants, of grated sugar, sugar in lumps, scales on the table, pots on the fire, she saw all the Homaises, large and small, wearing aprons that came up to their chins and holding forks in their hands. Justin, standing, was hanging his head and the pharmacist was shouting:

"Who told you to go and look in the capharnaüm?"

"What is it? What is the matter?"

"What is the matter?" the apothecary said. "We are making preserves: they are cooking; but they were about to boil over because of cooking up too fast, and I asked for another pot. So he, out of slackness, out of laziness, went and took from the wall where it hung in my laboratory, the key of the capharnaüm!"

This was the pharmacist's name for a closet up under the roof, full of utensils and merchandise for his profession. Often he spent long hours alone there, labeling, decanting, retying; and he considered it in the nature of a true sanctuary, whence presently emerged, compounded by his own hands, all sorts of pills, tablets, tisanes, lotions and potions which went to spread his renown about the surrounding districts. No one in the world set foot there; and he regarded it so highly that he swept it out himself. Indeed, if the pharmacy, open to all comers, was the place where he displayed his pride, the capharnaüm was the refuge in which, egotistically concentrating, Homais delighted in the exercise of his predilections; so Justin's stupidity seemed to him monstrous in its irreverence; and, redder than the currants, he repeated:

"Yes, of the capharnaüm! The key that locks up the acids and the caustic alkalis. To have gone and taken a pot from the stock, a covered pot, and one which I perhaps shall never use! Everything has its importance in the delicate operations of our art. What the devil! You have to make distinctions and not use for practically domestic purposes what is designed for pharmaceutical. It's as if one carved a chicken with a scalpel, as if a magistrate . . ."

"Now, calm yourself!" Madame Homais said.

And Athalie, pulling at his coat:

"Papa, Papa!"

"No, let me alone," the pharmacist cried. "Do you know the risk you were running, you, Justin? Didn't you see anything in the corner, at the left, on the third shelf?"

"I—don't know," the boy stammered.

"Oh, so you don't know. Well, I know! You saw a bottle, blue glass, sealed with yellow wax, that contained a white powder, and on which I had even written: *Dangerous*. And do you know what was in it? Arsenic! And you go and touch that, take a pot that's right beside it!"

"Beside it!" Madame Homais shrieked, clasping her hands. "Beside arsenic? You might have poisoned us all!"

And the children began to scream as if already they felt atrocious pains in their entrails.

But Emma, turning toward Madame Homais:

"You sent for me . . ."

"Oh, dear God!" the good woman interrupted with a saddened expression. "How can I tell you? . . . It's bad news."

She did not finish. The apothecary was thundering:

"Empty it, clean it out, take it back, hurry up!" And, shaking Justin by the collar of his blouse, he caused a book to fall from his pocket.

The boy bent down; Homais was quicker and, having picked up the volume, he stared at it, his eyes squinting, his jaw dropped.

"*Marital . . . Love*," he said, separating the two words slowly. "Ah, very good, very good! Very nice! And pictures! . . . Oh, this is too much!"

Madame Homais stepped forward.

"No, don't touch it!"

The children wanted to see the pictures.

"Leave the room!" he said imperiously. And they left.

First he walked up and down in great strides, keeping the book open in his fingers, rolling his eyes, strangling, tumid, apoplectic. Then he went straight to his pupil and, planting himself in front of him, with his arms folded:

"So you have all the vices, have you, young scoundrel? Take care, you're on a down-grade! It didn't occur to you that this, this vile book, might have fallen into my children's hands, cast a spark into their brains, sullied Athalie's purity, corrupted Napoléon! He is already formed like a man. Are you at least quite sure they haven't read it? Can you guarantee to me . . ."

"But after all, Monsieur," Emma said, "you had something to tell me?"

"That's right, Madame . . . Your father-in-law is dead."

Indeed, Monsieur Bovary senior had died two days before, suddenly, of an attack of apoplexy, upon rising from the table; and out of an excess of solicitude for Emma's sensibility, Charles had requested Monsieur Homais to break this horrible news to her carefully.

He had meditated his speech, he had rounded it, polished it, made it rhythmic; it was a masterpiece of prudence and transition, of fine style and delicacy; but anger had triumphed over rhetoric.

Emma, giving up hope of learning any details, then left the pharmacy; for Monsieur Homais had resumed the course of his vituperations. He was becoming calmer, however, and now was grumbling in a paternal tone while fanning himself with his Greek cap.

"It's not that I disapprove entirely of the work. The author was a doctor. There are certain scientific aspects to it that it's not bad for a man to be familiar with and, I might venture to say, that a man must know. But later on, later on! At least wait until you're a man yourself and until your constitution is fully developed."

At Emma's knock, Charles, who was waiting for her, came forward with his arms outstretched and said to her with tears in his voice: "Oh, my darling . . ."

And he bent down gently to kiss her. But at the touch of his lips the memory of the other seized her, and she passed her hand over her face, shuddering.

At the same time she replied: "Yes, I know . . . I know . . ."

He showed her the letter in which his mother told of the occurrence, without the slightest sentimental hypocrisy. Her one regret was that her husband had not received the succor of religion, having died in Doudeville, in the street, on the threshold of a café, after a patriotic dinner with some retired officers.

Emma handed back the letter; then, at dinner, prompted by tact, she affected some repugnance. But, as he urged her, she began resolutely to eat, while Charles, opposite her, remained frozen in crushed attitude.

From time to time, raising his head, he sent her a long look full of distress. Once he sighed:

"I should have liked to see him once more."

She was silent. Presently, realizing that she must say something: "How old was your father?"

"Fifty-eight!"

"Ah!"

And that was all.

A quarter of an hour later, he added:

"What about my poor mother? What's to become of her, now?"

She made a gesture of ignorance.

Seeing her so taciturn, Charles supposed her to be grief-stricken, and he forced himself not to speak further, in order not to aggravate that grief which moved him. However, shaking off his own:

"Did you have a good time yesterday?" he asked.

"Yes."

When the cloth had been removed, Bovary did not rise. Nor did Emma; and the longer she contemplated it, the more the monotony of this spectacle gradually banished all pity from her heart. To her he seemed paltry, weak, a cipher, in fact, a sorry figure of a man in every way. How to get rid of him? What an interminable evening! Something stupefying as opium smoke was numbing her.

They heard from the vestibule the sharp sound of wood on the floorboards. It was Hippolyte bringing Madame's luggage.

In order to set it down he painfully described a quarter circle with his wooden leg.

"He doesn't even think about it any longer!" she said to herself, watching the poor devil whose thick red hair was drenched with sweat.

Bovary was fumbling in his purse for a copper; and, without seeming to recognize all the humiliation there was for him in the mere presence of that man who stood there like the personified reproach of his incurable disability:

"Well, you have a pretty bouquet!" he said, noticing Léon's violets on the mantelpiece.

"Yes," she said indifferently. "It's a bunch of flowers I bought awhile ago . . . from a beggar."

Charles picked up the violets and, cooling his tear-reddened eyes upon them, delicately sniffed at them. She quickly took them from his hand and went to put them in a glass of water.

The next day, Madame Bovary, the mother, arrived. She and her son wept a great deal. Emma, upon pretext of orders to give, withdrew.

The following day they had to consult together about matters concerning the bereavement. They went, with their work-boxes, to sit at the water's edge, in the arbor.

Charles thought about his father, and was astonished at feeling so much affection for that man whom he had believed he liked only moderately, up to the present. The elder Madame Bovary thought of her husband. The worst days out of the past seemed enviable to her now. Everything was submerged in the instinctive regret of so long a habit; and from time to time, as she plied her needle, a large tear would creep down the length of her nose and hang there for a moment.

Emma thought that barely forty-eight hours before, they had been together, remote from the world, plunged in intoxication, and without eyes enough for gazing at one another. She tried to recapture the most minute details of that vanished day. But the presence of her mother-in-law and husband kept frustrating her. She would have liked to hear nothing, see nothing, in order not to interfere with the recollection of love which kept getting lost, no matter what she did, in these external sensations.

Suddenly they saw Monsieur Lheureux, the shopkeeper, coming through the gate.

He had come to offer his services "in connection with the tragic occurrence." Emma answered that she felt she could do without them. The merchant did not consider himself rebuffed.

"My profound apologies," he said. "I should like a word in private."

Then, in a low voice:

"It's about that matter . . . you know?"

Charles became crimson to the ears.

"Ah, yes . . . certainly." And, in his confusion, turning to his wife: "Couldn't you be the one, my dear . . . ?"

She seemed to understand, for she rose, and Charles said to his mother, "It's nothing, some household detail most likely."

He was extremely unwilling that she should know the story of the note, dreading her comments.

As soon as they were alone, Monsieur Lheureux began, in rather bald terms, to congratulate Emma upon the inheritance, then to speak of indifferent matters, of espaliered fruit trees, the harvest and his own health, which was always "so-so, not good not bad." As a matter of fact, he worked like five hundred devils, although no matter what people said, he didn't make enough to buy butter for his bread.

Emma let him talk. She had been so monstrously bored for the past two days!

"And here you are, quite recovered?" he continued. "My word,

I saw your poor husband in a fine state! He's a great fellow, even though we did have some difficulties between us."

She asked what difficulties, for Charles had concealed the dispute over the merchandise from her.

"Why, you know very well!" Lheureux said. "It was over those things you wanted, the traveling cases."

He had pulled his hat low over his eyes and, with his hands behind his back, smiling and lisping, was staring her in the face in an unbearable manner. Did he suspect anything? She was left bewildered, assailed by all sorts of apprehensions. In the end, however, he resumed:

"We patched things up, and I was coming to suggest another arrangement to him."

It was to renew the note signed by Bovary; Monsieur, after all, might act as he saw fit; he should not torment himself, particularly now that he was about to have a host of anxieties.

"And it would even be better for him to pass the obligation along to somebody else, to you for instance; that could easily be done, with a power of attorney, and then we would have little dealings between the two of us . . ."

She did not understand. He fell silent. Then, proceeding to business, Lheureux declared that Madame could not do without buying one thing from him. He was going to send her a length of black barège, twelve yards, to make a dress.

"What you have on is good enough for the house. You need another for calling. I saw that, myself, at first glance, when I came. I have an American's eye."

He did not send the material; he brought it. Then he returned for the measurements; he came back upon other pretexts, endeavoring each time to make himself obliging, helpful—"enfeoffing himself," as Homais would have said—and always insinuating into Emma's ears a few bits of advice about powers of attorney. He did not mention the note. She did not think of it; early in her convalescence Charles had indeed told her something about it; but so many anxieties had been troubling her mind that she no longer remembered it. Besides, she was careful not to open any discussion of money matters; the elder Madame Bovary was surprised by this, and attributed the change of nature to the religious leanings she had acquired while she was ill.

But as soon as the other woman had left, Emma lost no time in astonishing Bovary by her practical common sense. He was to make inquiries, verify the mortgages, find out whether an auction or a liquidation sale was to take place.

She quoted technical terms at random, uttered the potent words: order, the future, foresight, and constantly exaggerated the difficulties of inheritance: to such an extent that one day she showed him a blanket authorization to "direct and administer his affairs, make all loans, sign and endorse all notes, pay all sums, etc." She had profited by Monsieur Lheureux' lessons.

Charles, innocently, asked where this paper came from.

"From Monsieur Guillaumin." And, with the greatest composure in the world, she added: "I haven't too much confidence in him. Lawyers have such a bad reputation. Perhaps we ought to consult . . . We don't know anybody except . . . Oh, nobody!"

"Outside of Léon," said Charles, who was meditating.

But it was difficult to come to an understanding by means of correspondence. She offered, therefore, to make the trip. He thanked her, but refused. She insisted. A fencing-match of courtesies ensued. At length she cried in a tone of pretended mutiny:

"No, I insist, I am going!"

"How good you are!" he said, kissing her brow.

The next day she set out in the *Hirondelle* to go to Rouen and consult Monsieur Léon; and she stayed there three days.

3

$\mathcal{T}$HEY were three full, exquisite,
shining days, a true honeymoon. They stayed
at the *Hotel de Boulogne,* overlooking the port. And
there they lived, blinds drawn, doors closed, with flowers on the
floor and iced sweet drinks brought to them from morning on.

At evening they engaged a covered boat and went to dine on an
island.

It was the hour when one hears, along the docks, the calkers' mallets against the hulls of ships. Tar-smoke drifted up among the trees,
and on the surface of the river one saw large oily circles rising and
falling unevenly under the purple light of the sun, like floating
plaques of Florentine bronze.

They would move downstream in the midst of moored craft whose
long oblique cables brushed lightly against the top of the boat.

The sounds of the city gradually died away, the rattle of carts,
the tumult of voices, the barking of dogs on the bridges of the ships.
She would untie her hat, and they would land on their island.

They sat in the low-ceilinged room of a tavern which had black
nets hung at its door. They ate fried smelts, cream and cherries.
They lay down in the grass; they embraced, alone among the poplars; and they wished that they might live forever, like two Robinsons, in this small spot which seemed to them, in their bliss, the
most magnificent on earth. It was not the first time they had seen
trees, blue skies, grass, that they had heard water flowing and the
breeze whispering in leaves; but doubtless they had never admired
these things, as if nature had not existed before, or had only begun
to be beautiful since the gratifying of their desires.

At nightfall they would go back. The boat would skirt the islands.
They would recline in the bottom, both hidden in shadow, saying
nothing. The square oars creaked in their iron locks; and the sound

stood out against the silence like the ticking of a metronome, while the hawser which dragged astern never ceased its small gentle slapping at the water.

Once the moon came out; then they did not fail to turn phrases, finding that fixed star melancholy and full of poetry; she even began to sing:

"One night, dost thou remember? we were sailing . . ."

Her voice, harmonious and thin, was lost over the waves; and the wind picked up quavers which Léon heard pass like a flutter of wings about him.

She was sitting opposite him, leaning against the bulkhead where the moonlight fell through one of the open shutters. Her black dress, its folds fanning out, made her taller, thinner. She had her head thrown back, her hands clasped, her eyes raised to the sky. Now and then the shadow of the willows hid her altogether, then she would suddenly appear again, like a vision in the moonlight.

In spite of everything, they had to separate! The farewells were sorrowful. He was to send his letters in care of Mère Rollet; and she gave such precise directions regarding the double envelope that he vastly admired her amorous guile.

"Then you assure me that everything is in order?" she said in a last kiss.

"Yes, certainly!" But why in the world, he wondered afterwards, returning home alone through the streets, did she set such store by this power of attorney?

4

ʙEFORE long Léon was assuming an attitude of superiority toward his friends, forgoing their company and completely neglecting his briefs.

He waited for his letters; he read them over and over. He wrote to her. He called up her image with all the force of his desire and his memories. Rather than diminishing through absence, this desire to see her again increased, to such an extent that one Saturday morning he slipped away from his office.

When, from the top of the rise, he caught sight of the church spire in the valley with its steel pennant turning in the wind, he felt that delight mingled with triumphant vanity and egotistical tenderness which millionaires must feel when they return to visit their native villages.

He prowled about her house. A light was burning in the kitchen. He waited for her shadow behind the curtains. Nothing appeared.

Madame Lefrançois, seeing him, made loud outcries, and thought him "taller and thinner," whereas Artémise, on the contrary, found him "bigger and browner."

He dined in the small room, as before, but alone, without the tax-collector; for Binet, weary of waiting for the *Hirondelle*, had unconditionally advanced his meal time an hour, and now dined precisely at five, still claiming that most of the time "the old rattle-trap was late."

Léon came to a decision; he went to knock at the physician's door. Madame was in her room, from which she did not come down until a quarter of an hour later. Monsieur seemed delighted to see him again; but he did not stir from the house that evening nor all the following day.

He saw her alone, in the evening, very late, in the little street behind the garden—in the little street, just as it had been with the other! It was storming, and they talked under an umbrella, by lightning flashes.

Their separation was becoming intolerable.

"Death would be better," Emma said.

She twisted herself over his arm, weeping.

"Good-by, good-by . . . When shall I see you again?"

They turned back to embrace once more; and it was then that she promised him to find soon, by some means, a permanent pretext for seeing him freely—at least once a week, Emma thought likely. She was brimming with optimism in any case. Some money was about to come to her.

Thus she bought for her room a pair of wide-striped yellow curtains, the cheapness of which Monsieur Lheureux had vaunted to her; she dreamed of a carpet, and Lheureux, declaring that "it wasn't like drinking the sea dry," politely undertook to provide her with one. She could no longer do without his services. Twenty times a day she sent for him, and he would drop everything immediately, without a murmur. Further, no one understood why Mère Rollet lunched at her house every day, and even paid her special visits.

It was about this time—that is, toward the beginning of winter— that she seemed to be seized by a great musical enthusiasm.

One evening while Charles was listening, she began the same piece four times over, each time expressing vexation with herself, while he, without noticing any difference, cried:

"Bravo! . . . Very good! . . . Go along with you, you're wrong!"

"Oh, no, it's terrible! My fingers are rusty."

The next day he begged her to "play something for him again."

"Very well. Just to please you."

And Charles admitted that she had fallen off somewhat. She mistook the key, she stumbled; then, stopping short:

"Ah, that's enough! I'd have to take lessons, but . . ." She bit her lips and added: "Twenty francs a lesson, that's too dear."

"Yes, it is, a little . . ." Charles said, chuckling foolishly. "However, it seems to me you might be able to do it for less; there are artists without reputations who are often better than the famous teachers."

"Name one," Emma said.

The next day when he came home he gave her a sly glance, and at length could not resist saying:

"How stubborn you are sometimes! I was in Barfeuchères today. Well, Madame Liégard assured me that her three daughters, who are at La Miséricorde, were taking lessons averaging about fifty sous apiece, and from a famous teacher besides!"

She shrugged her shoulders and no longer opened her piano. But when she passed it (if Bovary happened to be there), she would sigh, "Oh, my poor piano!"

And when callers came she did not fail to mention the fact that she had given up music and now could not go back to it, for financial reasons. They pitied her, then. It was a shame! She had such a nice talent. They even spoke to Bovary about it. They shamed him, particularly the pharmacist:

"You're making a mistake. Natural talents should never be allowed to lie fallow. Besides, consider, my dear friend, that by urging Madame to study, you will economize later on your child's musical education! In my opinion, mothers ought to teach their children themselves. That's one of Rousseau's theories, still a bit new, perhaps, but it will triumph in the end I feel sure, like maternal breast-feeding and vaccination."

So Charles returned once more to this question of the piano. Emma answered bitterly that it would be more worth while to sell it. To see the departure of that poor piano which had caused him so much prideful satisfaction was for Bovary like the indefinable suicide of a part of herself.

"If you'd like to . . ." he would say, from time to time, "one lesson, that wouldn't be so ruinous, after all."

"But lessons," she would answer, "are profitable only if kept up."

And that was how she went about securing her husband's permission to go to the city once a week to visit her lover. At the end of a month she was even considered to have made considerable progress.

5

$\mathcal{I}$т was Thursday. She would
rise and dress silently, in order not to awaken
Charles, who would have made comments upon her
getting ready too early. Then she would walk up and down; she
would stand at the windows and look out at the square. The dawn
light crept in among the pillars of the market place, and the pharmacist's house, with its shutters closed, flaunted the bold letters of
its sign in the pale light of daybreak.

When the clock pointed to a quarter past seven she would go over
to the *Lion d'Or*, where Artémise, yawning, would come to open the
door. She would blow up for Madame the embers buried under the
ashes. Emma would wait alone in the kitchen. From time to time
she would step out. Hivert would be hitching up without haste,
and, in addition, listening to Madame Lefrançois who, thrusting her
nightcapped head out through a small window, was charging him
with errands enough and giving him explanations enough to turn
the wits of any other man.

Emma would stamp the soles of her shoes against the courtyard
pavement.

At last, when he had eaten his soup, put on his cloak, lighted his
pipe and taken his whip in his fist, he would take his place tranquilly upon the driver's seat.

The *Hirondelle* set off at a leisurely trot and, for about two miles,
kept stopping here and there to take on passengers who stood waiting for it at the side of the road, before courtyard gates. Those who
had given notice the day before kept it waiting; some were even
still in bed in their houses; Hivert would call, shout, curse, then he
would clamber down from his seat and go to beat loudly on the
doors. The wind whistled in through the tattered curtains.

Meanwhile, the four passenger seats filled up; the carriage rolled

211

along, the rows of apple trees passed one after the other; and the road, between its two long ditches filled with yellow water, ran constantly ahead, narrowing toward the horizon.

Emma knew it from end to end; she knew that after a pasture came a sign-post, then an elm tree, a barn or road-worker's hut; sometimes, in order to surprise herself, she would even close her eyes. But she never lost the clear consciousness of the distance still to be covered.

Eventually brick houses began to appear, the ground rumbled beneath the wheels, the *Hirondelle* rolled between gardens in which, through wickets, one saw statues, trailing myrtle, sculptured yews or a seesaw. Then, in the twinkling of an eye, the city came into view.

To her, something dizzying emanated from these massed existences, and her heart swelled amply with it, as if the hundred and twenty thousand souls which throbbed there had all at once sent forth the vapors of the passions she attributed to them. Her love expanded in the presence of the city, and was filled with tumult by the vague humming that rose from it.

They paused at the gate; Emma would unbuckle her overshoes, put on fresh gloves, adjust her shawl and, twenty yards farther on, she would descend from the *Hirondelle*.

By this time the city was waking. Clerks in Greek caps were polishing the show windows of shops, and women carrying baskets on their hips called out piercingly at intervals on street corners. She walked with her eyes on the ground, brushing close to the walls and smiling with delight beneath her lowered black veil.

For fear of being seen, she did not ordinarily take the shortest way. She hurried through dark side streets, and emerged bathed in perspiration near the lower end of the Rue Nationale, by the fountain which stands there. This is the quarter given over to the theater, to taverns and girls. Often a cart passed close to her, bearing some quivering stage-set. Aproned waiters sprinkled sand over flagstones, between green shrubs. One smelled absinthe, cigars and oysters.

She would turn down a street; she would recognize him by the curly hair escaping from under his hat.

Léon would continue to walk along the sidewalk. She would follow him to the hotel; he would go upstairs, open a door, enter . . . what an embrace!

Then, after the kisses, words poured out. They told one another

the sorrows of the week, the presentiments, the anxieties over letters; but now all was forgotten, and they gazed at one another face
to face, with sensuous laughter and tender endearments.

The bed was a large mahogany bed shaped like a boat. The red
silk curtains which hung down from the ceiling curved close to the
broad headboard; and nothing in the world was so beautiful as her
dark head and her white skin standing out against that crimson color
when, in a gesture of modesty, she drew her bare arms together,
hiding her face in her hands.

The warm room with its discreet carpet, its whimsical ornaments
and its tranquil light seemed expressly suited to the intimacies of
passion. The curtain rods ended in arrowheads, the brass clothes
hooks and the large balls of the andirons gleamed suddenly, if the
sunlight shone in. On the mantelpiece, between the candlesticks,
there were two of those great pink shells in which one hears the
sound of the sea when one holds them against the ear.

How they loved this good room full of gaiety in spite of its somewhat faded splendor! They always found the furniture in its accustomed places, and sometimes hairpins which she had forgotten, the
Thursday before, under the base of the clock. They lunched before
the fire, on a small side table inlaid with rosewood. Emma carved,
serving morsels onto his plate while going through all sorts of playful tricks; and she would laugh with a deep-toned voluptuous laugh
when the froth of the champagne overflowed the slender glass onto
the rings on her fingers. They were so utterly lost in possession of
each other that they believed themselves to be in their own home,
there to live until death, like two married people eternally young.
They said our room, our carpet, our armchairs, she even said "my
slippers"—a gift from Léon, a fancy she had taken. They were rose
satin slippers, edged with swansdown. When she sat on his lap her
leg, too short to reach the floor, hung in the air; and the delicate
slipper, which had no back, clung to her bare foot only by the toes.

He was savoring for the first time the inexpressible delicacy of
feminine daintinesses. Never had he encountered that grace of
speech, that conservativeness in dress, those postures of a languid
dove. He admired the exaltation of her soul and the lace of her skirt.
Furthermore, was she not a woman of the world, and a married
woman—a true mistress, in fact?

Through the variety of her moods, mystic or gay by turns, talk-
ative, taciturn, passionate, indifferent, she went on rousing in him

a thousand desires, summoning instincts or reminiscences. She was the lover in every novel, the heroine of every drama, the vague *she* of every poem. Often, gazing at her, it seemed to him that his soul, going out to her, shattered like a wave upon the contours of her head and flowed down, drawn into the whiteness of her bosom.

He would crouch on the floor in front of her; and, his elbows on her knees, would stare at her with a smile, his brow held up to her.

She would lean toward him and murmur, as if stifled with emotion:

"Oh, don't stir, don't speak! Look at me. Something comes from your eyes that is so sweet, that does me so much good!"

She would call him child:

"Child, do you love me?"

And she never heard his answer, in the impatience of his lips rising to meet her mouth.

On the clock there was a small bronze Cupid who simpered, encircling a gilt wreath with his arms. They laughed over him many times, but when they had to part, everything seemed serious to them. Motionless, facing one another, they repeated:

"Until Thursday! Until Thursday!"

Suddenly she would take his head between her two hands, kiss him quickly on the forehead, crying, "Good-by!" and dart down the stairway.

She would go to a hairdresser in the Rue de la Comédie to have her hair rearranged. Night was falling; the gas was being lighted in the shop.

Then she would go out. She walked back up the streets; she reached the *Croix Rouge;* she put on her overshoes which she had hidden that morning beneath one of the stagecoach seats, and huddled in her seat among the impatient passengers. Some of them got out at the bottom of the slope. She would be left alone in the coach.

Beside the downward road there was a poor devil wandering along with his stick in the midst of all the diligences. An assortment of rags covered his shoulders, and an ancient battered beaver hat, bulging out like a basin, hid his face; but when he pulled it off he revealed, in place of eyelids, two gaping bloodshot sockets. The flesh hung out in red tatters; and from it oozed moisture which dried to a green scurf running down to his nose, the black nostrils of which sniffled convulsively. In speaking to anyone he tipped his head back with an idiot laugh; then his bluish eyeballs, rolling in a continuous motion, turned up toward his temples, at the edges of the open sores. He sang a little song as he followed the carriages:

"Warm sun shining up above
Makes a young girl dream of love."

And throughout the rest of it were birds, sunlight and green leaves. Sometimes he appeared suddenly behind Emma, bareheaded. She would draw back with a cry. Hivert would joke with him. He would urge him to take a booth at the Saint-Romain fair, or else ask him, chuckling, how his sweetheart was.

At home, Charles was waiting for her; the *Hirondelle* was always late on Thursday. At last Madame came! She barely kissed the little girl. Dinner was not ready, no matter! She forgave the cook. The girl seemed to be permitted every liberty, now.

Often her husband, noticing her pallor, asked if she did not feel ill.

"No," Emma would say.

"But you're very strange this evening," he would insist.

"Oh, it's nothing, it's nothing!"

There were even days when, no more than returned home, she would go up to her room; and Justin, who often happened to be there, would move about with silent steps, more skilled at waiting upon her than an excellent lady's maid. He placed matches, the candlestick, a book, laid out her nightdress, turned down the bed.

"Go along," she would say. "That's fine, go on!"

For he would stand there, his hands hanging and his eyes staring, as if caught in the innumerable filaments of a sudden trance.

The following day was frightful, and the ones that came after even more intolerable because of Emma's impatience to recapture her happiness—a fierce desire inflamed by familiar images, which, on the seventh day, would be joyfully released in Léon's caresses. His own ardors were concealed beneath transports of wonder and gratitude. Emma savored this love in a prudent and concentrated manner, nourished it by every artifice of her tenderness and was apprehensive that it might be lost later on.

She often said to him, with melancholy gentleness in her voice:

"Ah, you'll leave me . . . you'll get married! You'll be like the others."

He demanded: "What others?"

"Why, men," she answered.

Then she would add, pushing him away with a sorrowful gesture: "You are all scoundrels."

One day when they were talking philosophically of earthly disillusionments, she was inspired to say (in order to experiment with his jealousy, or perhaps yielding to an insuperable need of outlet) that once, before him, she had loved someone, "not like you!" she went on hurriedly, swearing by her daughter's head that "nothing had happened."

The young man believed her, but nevertheless questioned her to find out what had been the other man's trade.

"He was a ship's captain, my darling."

Was this not the way to forestall any investigation, and at the same time raise herself to a very lofty position by this invented fascination exercised upon a man who must have been valiant by nature and accustomed to respect?

Then the clerk felt the instability of his position; he longed for epaulettes, medals, titles. All that sort of thing should appeal to her; he was aware of her spendthrift habits.

Yet Emma was silent about many of her extravagant desires, such as her yearning for a blue tilbury drawn by an English horse and driven by a groom in high-topped boots, to take her to Rouen. It was Justin who had suggested the fancy to her by begging her to take him into service as a houseman; and although this privation did not diminish the joy of arriving at each rendezvous, it did aggravate the bitterness of the journey home.

Often, when they were speaking of Paris together, she would murmur at last:

"Ah, how lovely it would be if we could live there!"

"Aren't we happy?" the young man would return gently, stroking her hair.

"Yes, of course," she would say. "I'm foolish: kiss me!"

Toward her husband she was more charming than ever, made pistachio creams for him and played waltzes after dinner. He considered himself, therefore, the most fortunate of mortals, and Emma was living without any apprehensions when one evening, abruptly:

"It's Mademoiselle Lempereur who's giving you lessons, isn't it?"

"Yes."

"Well, I saw her just now at Madame Liégard's," Charles went on. "I spoke to her about you: she doesn't know you."

It was like a thunderclap. She answered, however, in a natural manner:

"Oh, I suppose she must have forgotten my name."

"But perhaps in Rouen," the doctor said, "there are several Mes-demoiselles Lempereur who are piano teachers?"

"It's possible."

Then, eagerly: "Why, I even have her receipts, look here!"

And she went to the secretary, rummaged in all the drawers, mixed up papers and in the end so thoroughly lost her head that Charles urged her strongly not to go to so much trouble over those miserable receipts.

"Oh, I'll come across them," she said.

Indeed, the very next Friday, Charles, putting on his boots in the dark closet where his clothes were kept, felt a sheet of paper between the leather and his sock; he took it out and read:

"Received, for three months' lessons plus various supplies, the sum of sixty-five francs. Félice Lempereur, professor of music."

"How the devil did it get into my boots?"

"It must have fallen out of the old cardboard box full of bills that's on the edge of the shelf."

From this moment on, her life was no more than an amalgama-tion of lies in which she wrapped her love as if in veils, to hide it.

It was a necessity, a fixation, a pleasure, to such a point that if she said that she had walked down the right-hand side of a street the day before, it should be assumed that she had taken the left-hand side.

One morning when she had just left, rather lightly dressed as usual, there was a sudden snowfall; and as Charles was looking at the weather through the window, he caught sight of Monsieur Bournisien in Mayor Tuvache's dogcart which was taking him to Rouen. He went downstairs, therefore, to intrust to the clergyman a heavy shawl, in order that he might deliver it to Madame as soon as he reached the *Croix Rouge*. Bournisien had no more than ar-rived at the inn when he asked where the doctor's wife from Yonville was. The innkeeper replied that she rarely came to his establishment. That evening, in consequence, meeting Madame Bovary in the *Hirondelle*, the priest told her about his difficulties, without, however, seeming to attach any importance to it; for he launched into praise of a preacher who was working wonders at the cathedral just then, and whom all the women were flocking to hear.

Nevertheless, although he had not asked for explanations, others, later on, might be less discreet. So she found it expedient to stop in at the *Croix Rouge* every Thursday, so that the good folk from her village who saw her on the stairs would suspect nothing.

One day, however, Monsieur Lheureux met her coming out of the *Hotel de Boulogne* on Léon's arm; and she was frightened, assuming that he would gossip. He was not so stupid.

But three days later he came into her room, closed the door and said:

"I need money."

She declared that she was unable to give him any. Lheureux overflowed with lamentations, and recalled all the kindnesses he had shown.

In fact, of the two notes signed by Charles, Emma had so far paid but one. As for the second, the shopkeeper at her request had consented to replace it with two others, and even these had been renewed on a very long term. Then he drew from his pocket a list of merchandise unpaid for: the curtains, the carpet, material for covering armchairs, several dresses and various toilet articles, the value of which came to the sum of about two thousand francs.

She hung her head; he went on:

"Well, if you haven't cash, you have property."

And he mentioned a wretched hovel situated in Barneville, near Aumale, which brought in very little return. It had once been part of a small farm sold by Monsieur Bovary senior, for Lheureux knew everything, even to the number of acres and the names of the neighbors.

"In your place," he said, "I'd discharge my debts, and I'd still have the rest of the money over."

She brought up the difficulty of finding a buyer; he held out hope of finding one; but she asked how she must go about getting the authority to sell.

"Haven't you the power of attorney?" he answered.

These words came to her like a breath of fresh air.

"Leave the note with me," Emma said.

"Oh, it's not worth troubling about," Lheureux said.

He came back the following week and boasted of having at last, after going to great lengths, unearthed a certain Langlois who had for a long time been coveting the property without stating his price.

"Never mind the price!" she exclaimed.

On the contrary, she must wait, sound the fellow out. The matter was worth the trouble of a journey and, as she could not undertake this journey, he offered to go to the spot and interview Langlois. Upon his return he announced that the buyer offered four thousand francs.

Emma glowed at this news.

"Frankly," he added, "it's a good price."

She received half the sum immediately and, when she went to settle her account, the merchant said to her:

"On my honor, I hate to see you give up so important a sum all at once."

She gazed at the bank notes; and, dreaming of the illimitable number of rendezvous these two thousand francs represented:

"What! How?" she stammered.

"Oh," he said, laughing with a good-natured air, "you put whatever you like toward the bills. Don't I understand household matters?"

And he stared at her intently, while holding in his hand two long papers which he slipped back and forth between his fingers. At length, opening his notecase, he spread out on the table four bills, payable to order, each for one thousand francs.

"Sign this for me," he said, "and keep everything."

She protested, shocked.

"But if I give you what's left over," Monsieur Lheureux replied brazenly, "that's doing you a service, isn't it?"

And, picking up a pen, he wrote at the bottom of the bill: "Received of Madame Bovary four thousand francs."

"What's worrying you, since in six months you'll receive the balance from your sale, and I've set the expiration date of the final note for after that payment?"

Emma was somewhat bewildered by these calculations, and her ears were ringing as if gold pieces, bursting from their sacks, were clinking all about her, on the floor. At last Lheureux explained that he had a bosom friend Vinçart, a banker in Rouen, who would cash these four notes, then he himself would return to Madame the surplus over the actual debt.

But instead of two thousand francs, he brought only eighteen hundred, for his friend Vinçart (of course) had taken out two hundred in payment of expenses and commission.

Then he casually asked for a receipt.

"You understand—in business—sometimes . . . And with the date, please, the date."

Now a new horizon of realizable fancies opened out before Emma. She was prudent enough to put aside a thousand écus with which the first three notes were paid as they expired; but the fourth, by chance, came to the house on a Thursday, and Charles, dumfounded, patiently awaited his wife's return for an explanation.

If she had not told him about this note, it was in order to spare him domestic worries; she sat on his knees, caressed him, cooed, made a lengthy enumeration of all the indispensable items bought on credit.

"Anyway, you'll admit that in view of the quantity, it's not too expensive."

Charles, at his wits' end, soon had recourse to the eternal Lheureux, who swore to arrange matters if Monsieur would sign two notes, one of them for seven hundred francs, payable in three months. In order to be able to do this, Charles wrote a pathetic letter to his mother. Rather than sending her answer, she came herself; and when Emma asked whether he had got anything out of her:

"Yes," he said. "But she insists on seeing the bill."

The next day at dawn Emma hurried to Monsieur Lheureux to beg him to make out another statement which would be for not more than a thousand francs; for, in order to show the one for four thousand, she would have had to confess the sale of the real estate, a negotiation discreetly handled by the merchant and actually not known until later.

In spite of the very low price of each article, Madame Bovary did not fail to find the outlay disproportionate.

"Couldn't you do without a carpet? Why have the armchairs recovered? In my day, we had just one armchair in a house, for the old people—at least that's the way it was in my mother's house, and she was an honest woman, I assure you— Everyone can't be rich! No fortune is proof against waste. I'd blush to pamper myself the way you do, and yet I'm old, I need comforts! . . . And more, more! Clothes, claptrap! What, lining-silk at a hundred francs, when there's jaconet to be had for ten sous, even eight sous, that does perfectly well!"

Emma, leaning back in the love seat, answered as serenely as possible:

"Oh, Madame, enough! Enough!"

The other woman continued to preach, predicting that they would end up in the poorhouse. In any case, it was Bovary's fault. Fortunately he had promised to cancel that power of attorney . . .

"What?"

"Oh, he swore to me that he would," the good woman said.

Emma opened the window, called Charles, and the poor fellow was obliged to admit the promise forced out by his mother.

Emma disappeared, then speedily returned, majestically holding out a thick sheet of paper.

"Thank you," the old woman said.

And she flung the power of attorney on the fire.

Emma began to laugh a strident, shrill, prolonged laugh: she was having a hysterical attack.

"Oh, my God!" Charles cried. "Look, you're wrong, too! You come here making scenes with her . . . !"

His mother, shrugging, insisted that "that was all put on."

But Charles, rebelling for the first time, came to his wife's defense, with the result that Madame Bovary insisted upon leaving. She went the next morning and, upon the threshold, as he was trying to deter her, she answered:

"No, no! You love her better than me, and you're right, that's natural. Aside from that, it's so much the worse for you, you'll see! . . . Keep well!— For it will be some time before I come again, as you say, to make scenes with her."

For all this, Charles remained none the less highly abashed in Emma's presence, as she did not conceal the grudge she bore him for having lacked confidence; it took much pleading before she would consent to resume her power of attorney, and he even went with her to Monsieur Guillaumin's office to have a second one drawn up for her, exactly like the first.

"I understand that," the lawyer said. "A man of science can't be bothered with the practical details of life."

And Charles felt comforted by this soothing observation which gave to his weakness the flattering aspect of a superior preoccupation.

What an outpouring, the following Thursday at the hotel, in their room, with Léon! She laughed, cried, sang, danced, had ices sent up, insisted upon smoking cigarettes, seemed to him to be extravagant but adorable, superb.

He did not know what reaction of her whole being it was that drove her to fling herself more recklessly into the joys of living. She became irritable, greedy and sensual; she walked in the streets with him, her head held high, without fear, she said, of being compromised. Sometimes, however, Emma shuddered at the thought of meeting Rodolphe; for it seemed to her that, although they had parted forever, she was not completely delivered from her subjection.

One evening she did not return to Yonville. Charles lost his head over it, and little Berthe, refusing to go to bed without her mother, sobbed as if to rupture her chest. Justin had set out at random upon the road. Monsieur Homais had left the pharmacy because of it.

At length, at eleven o'clock, unable to endure any longer, Charles hitched up his dogcart, leaped in, whipped up his horse and reached the *Croix Rouge* at close to two in the morning. No one there. He thought that perhaps the clerk had seen her; but where did he live? Charles, fortunately, recalled his employer's address. He hurried to it.

Day was beginning to break. He made out a scutcheon above a door; he knocked. Someone, without opening the door, called out the desired information, adding a number of insulting observations upon those who disturbed people at night.

The house in which the clerk lived had neither bell, knocker nor porter. Charles beat on the shutters with his fist. A policeman happened to pass; at this he took fright and went away.

"I'm mad," he thought. "Probably they asked her to stay for dinner at Monsieur Lormeaux'."

The Lormeaux family no longer lived in Rouen.

"She must have stayed to look after Madame Dubreuil. Oh, Madame Dubreuil died ten months ago! Where is she, then?"

An idea came to him. In a café he asked for the *Annuaire* and quickly looked up the name of Mademoiselle Lempereur, who lived in the Rue de la Renelle-des-Marocuiniers, number 74.

As he was turning into this street, Emma herself appeared at the far end; he fell upon, rather than embraced her, crying:

"What kept you, yesterday?"

"I was taken ill."

"With what? Where? How?"

She brushed her hand across her forehead and answered:

"At Mademoiselle Lempereur's."

"I was sure of it! I was going there."

"Oh, it would be a waste of time," Emma said. "She just went out a little while ago. But from now on, don't worry. I'm not free, you know, if I feel that the least delay upsets you this way."

It was a sort of license she gave herself, not to be troubled in her escapades. She took advantage of it as she pleased, fully. When the desire to see Léon took her, she would go upon any pretext whatever, and as he would not be expecting her that day, she would go to his office in search of him.

This was a great delight, the first few times; but soon he no longer concealed the truth, which was that his employer was complaining bitterly of these interruptions.

"Oh, nonsense! Come along," she said.

And he would slip out.

She wanted him to dress all in black and grow a goatee on his chin, to resemble Louis XII's portraits. She wished to see his room, found it mean; he blushed over it, she paid no attention, then advised him to buy curtains like hers and, when he protested the expense:

"Ah, you set store by your little gold pieces!" she said, laughing.

Each time, Léon was obliged to tell her everything he had done since their last meeting. She demanded poems, poems to her, a "love ode" in her honor; he was never able to find a rhyme for the second line, and in the end he copied a sonnet from a keepsake.

It was less from vanity than from the sole object of pleasing her. He did not argue with her ideas; he accepted all her tastes; he became her mistress rather than she his. She used tender words and kisses that took his soul away. Where, then, had she learned this corruption, almost immaterial in its depth and dissimulation?

6

$\mathcal{D}$URING the trips he made to see
her, Léon had frequently dined at the pharmacist's, and felt himself obliged by courtesy to invite
him in return.

"Gladly!" Monsieur Homais had answered. "In any case, I need
a bit of relaxation, for I'm getting in a rut here. We'll go to the
theater, to a restaurant, we'll do the town!"

"Oh, my dear!" Madame Homais murmured tenderly, alarmed by
the vague perils he was about to court.

"Well, what? You think I'm not ruining my health sufficiently,
living among the constant emanations of the pharmacy? That's a
woman's character for you: they're jealous of science, then they're
opposed to one's taking legitimate recreation. Never mind, count on
me, one of these days I'll show up in Rouen and we'll make the chips
fly, the two of us."

Formerly the apothecary would have been most careful to avoid
using such an expression; but now he was developing a sportive and
Parisian manner which he considered in excellent taste, and like his
neighbor Madame Bovary, he questioned the clerk eagerly about the
customs of the capital, he even spoke slang to impress the . . . common people, saying "shanty," "swell," "high-hat," "Breda-street" and
"I'm off" for "I am going."

Thus, on Thursday, Emma was surprised, in the *Lion d'Or* kitchen,
to meet Monsieur Homais in traveling costume, that is: wrapped in
an old cloak which no one knew him to possess, while in one hand he
carried a suitcase and in the other the foot-warmer from his establishment. He had told no one of his plans, for fear of alarming the
public by his absence.

The thought of seeing again the places in which his youth had
been spent must have inspired him, for all along the way he never

ceased chattering; then, barely arrived, he sprang from the coach to go in search of Léon; and the clerk struggled in vain, Monsieur Homais dragged him off to the great *Normandie* restaurant, which he entered majestically without removing his hat, considering it highly provincial to uncover his head in a public place.

Emma waited three-quarters of an hour for Léon. At length she hurried to his office and, lost in all sorts of conjectures, accusing him of indifference and reproaching herself for her weakness, she spent the afternoon pressed to the windows.

At two o'clock the men were still seated at table, face to face. The great room was emptying; the stovepipe, shaped like a palm tree, spread out its gilded fronds against the white ceiling; and near them, behind the plate glass window, in full sunlight, a small jet of water bubbled in a marble basin in which, among the water cress and asparagus, three torpid lobsters stretched out toward some quail, all piled in a heap, on their backs.

Homais was enjoying himself hugely. Although he was even more intoxicated with luxury than with good cheer, still the Pomard wine had stimulated his wits somewhat, and by the time the rum omelet appeared he was expounding immoral theories about women. What attracted him above all was "smartness." He adored an elegant costume in a well-furnished room, and as far as fleshly charms went, was not averse to a "morsel."

Léon was watching the clock with despair. The apothecary was drinking, eating, talking.

"You must have plenty of privacy in Rouen," he said suddenly. "Anyway, your sweethearts don't live far away."

And, as the other reddened:

"Come now, be frank. Can you deny that in Yonville . . . ?"

The young man stammered.

". . . at Madame Bovary's house, you were courting . . . ?"

"Well, whom?"

"The maid!"

He was not joking; but, vanity prevailing over discretion, Léon protested in spite of himself. Besides, he liked only dark-haired women.

"I agree with you," the pharmacist said. "They have more temperament."

And, leaning to his friend's ear, he outlined the symptoms by which one could tell that a woman had temperament. He even embarked upon an ethnographical digression: German women were vaporish, French women wanton, Italian women passionate.

"And Negresses?" the clerk asked.

"That's an artist's taste," Homais said. "—Waiter! Two demitasses."

"Shall we go?" Léon said at last, becoming impatient.

"Yes."

But before leaving, he insisted upon seeing the proprietor of the establishment and offering him a few compliments.

Then the young man, in order to be alone, declared that he had business to attend to.

"Ah, I shall escort you!" Homais said.

And, while walking down the streets with him, he kept chattering of his wife, his children, their future and his pharmacy, describing the decadence in which it had formerly been and the point of perfection to which he had raised it.

Arrived before the *Hotel de Boulogne,* Léon left him abruptly, dashed upstairs and found his mistress in great emotional agitation.

At the pharmacist's name, she flew into a passion. However, he kept heaping up good excuses; it was not his fault, didn't she know Monsieur Homais? Could she believe that he preferred his company to hers? But she turned away; he held her back; and, sinking to his knees, he encircled her waist with his arms in a languorous pose full of concupiscence and supplication.

She was standing; her great blazing eyes stared at him gravely and in an almost frightening manner. Then tears clouded them, her pink eyelids closed down, she yielded her hands and Léon was raising them to his lips when a servant appeared to inform Monsieur that someone was asking for him.

"You will come back?" she said.

"Yes."

"But when?"

"Right away."

"It's a dodge," the pharmacist said, catching sight of Léon. "I wanted to interrupt that visit, it seemed to be annoying you. Let's go to Bridoux' and have a glass of garus."

Léon swore that he must return to his office. Upon this, the apothecary made jokes about red tape and legal procedure.

"Leave Cujas and Barthole for a bit. What the devil, who's to stop you? Be bold! Let's go to Bridoux'; you can see his dog. It's very curious!"

And as the clerk still resisted:

"Then I'll go with you. I'll read a newspaper while I wait for you, or I'll look through a law book."

Léon, stunned by Emma's fury, Monsieur Homais' chatter and perhaps the weight of the luncheon, remained undecided and as if under the spell of the pharmacist who kept repeating:

"Let's go to Bridoux'. It's only a step from here, in the Rue Malpalu."

So, out of cowardice, out of stupidity, out of that indefinable sentiment which forces us into the most antipathetic actions, he let himself be taken to Bridoux' house; and they found him in his small yard, superintending three boys who were panting as they turned the great wheel of a machine for making seltzer water. Homais gave them advice; he embraced Bridoux; they drank garus. Twenty times Léon tried to get away; but the other caught him back by the arm, saying:

"Right away! I'm coming. We'll go to the *Fanal de Rouen*, to see those gentlemen. I'll introduce you to Thomassin."

He extricated himself, however, and raced back to the hotel. Emma was no longer there.

She had just left, enraged. She detested him now. This breach of his word at their rendezvous seemed an outrage to her, and she sought still other reasons for breaking off with him: he was incapable of heroism, feeble, ordinary, softer than a woman, greedy, besides, and pusillanimous.

Then, becoming calmer, she eventually discovered that she had probably been unjust to him. But vilifying those we love always alienates us from them to a certain extent. Idols should not be touched: the gilding comes off on the hands.

Because of this, they began to talk oftener of things unrelated to their love; and, in the letters Emma sent him, she spoke of flowers, poems, the moon and stars, artless resources of a diminished passion which seeks to revivify itself by means of all external stimuli. She continually promised herself, for her next journey, a profound rapture; afterwards she would admit to herself that she had felt nothing extraordinary. This disappointment was speedily submerged beneath renewed optimism, and Emma would return to him more ardent, more avid. She would undress roughly, tearing at the thin lacing of her bodice, which rustled down around her hips like a gliding adder. She would go on tiptoe in her bare feet to see once more if the door was closed, then, in a single movement, let all her garments fall together; and, pale, speechless, grave, she would flatten herself against his chest with a prolonged shudder.

To Léon, however, there was on that brow drenched with cold drops, on those stammering lips, in those frenzied eyes, in the embrace of those arms, something extreme, indefinable and depressing which seemed to slip between them, subtly, as if to separate them.

He did not dare question her; but, discovering her to be so experienced, he told himself that she must have passed through every ordeal of suffering and pleasure. What had once charmed him now alarmed him a little. In addition, he was in revolt against the absorption of his personality, every day more pronounced. He bore Emma a grudge for this constant victory. He even forced himself not to love her; then, at the click of her boot heels, he felt himself go slack, like drunkards at sight of strong liquor.

She did not fail, it is true, to lavish all sorts of attentions upon him, from delicacies for the table to artful details of dress and languishing glances. She brought roses from Yonville in her bosom and flung them in his face, showed uneasiness over his health, gave him advice about his conduct and, in order to hold him the more surely, hoping that heaven perhaps would take a hand in it, she hung a medal of the Virgin around his neck. Like a virtuous mother, she inquired about his friends. She would say to him:

"Don't see them, don't go out, don't think of anything but us; love me!"

She would have liked to be able to superintend his whole life, and the notion came to her of having him followed in the streets. Near the hotel there was always a kind of vagabond who accosted travelers and who would not refuse . . . But her pride rebelled.

"So much the worse, let him deceive me, what do I care? Am I dependent upon him?"

One day when they had parted early, and as she was returning alone by way of the boulevard, she glimpsed the walls of her convent; then she sat down on a bench in the shadow of the elms. What serenity in those days! How she yearned for those ineffable sentiments of love which she had tried, in imitation of books, to envision for herself.

The first months of her marriage, her rides on horseback in the forest, the waltzing viscount and Lagardy singing all passed once more before her eyes . . . And suddenly Léon appeared to her in the same remoteness as the others.

"Still, I love him!" she said to herself.

It made no difference. She was not happy, had never been. Whence, then, came this insufficiency on the part of life, this instantaneous decay of things upon which she leaned? . . . If somewhere there existed a creature strong and handsome, a valiant nature full at once of ardor and of delicacies, a poet's heart beneath an angel's form, a lyre with brazen strings ringing out elegiac nuptial songs to the heavens, why, by chance, should she not find him? Oh, what an impossibility! In any case, nothing was worth the effort of search; everything lied. Each smile concealed a yawn of boredom, each joy a malediction, every pleasure its own disgust, and the most ardent kisses left upon the lips only an unrealizable longing for a higher gratification.

A metallic rattle was drawn out in the air and four strokes sounded from the convent bell. Four o'clock! And it seemed to her that she had been here, on this bench, for an eternity. But an infinity of passions can be contained in a minute, like a crowd in a small space.

Emma lived utterly immersed in hers, and troubled no more about money than an archduchess.

Once, however, an unpleasant looking man, rubicund and bald, came to her house, stating that he had been sent by Monsieur Vinçart, of Rouen. He withdrew the pins which closed the side pocket of his long green coat, thrust them into his cuff and politely held out a paper.

It was a note for seven hundred francs, with her signature, which Lheureux, over all her protests, had made over to Vinçart's order.

She dispatched her servant to his shop. He was unable to come.

Thereupon the stranger, who had remained standing, casting to right and to left inquisitive glances which his heavy pale eyebrows concealed, asked with an innocent air:

"What answer shall I take Monsieur Vinçart?"

"Well," Emma said, "tell him . . . I haven't got it. It will be next week . . . He'll have to wait . . . yes, next week."

And the fellow left without uttering a word.

But the following day, at noon, she received a protest; and the sight of the stamped document upon which was displayed in several places and in large letters: Maître Hareng, Sheriff of Buchy, so terrified her that she ran with all speed to the cloth merchant.

She found him in his shop, tying up a parcel.

"Your servant!" he said. "At your disposal."

Lheureux none the less went on with his task, aided by a young girl of about thirteen, somewhat humpbacked, who served both as his errand girl and as his cook.

Then, clattering his sabots over the floorboards of the shop, he led Madame upstairs to the first floor and ushered her into a narrow office in which a heavy deal table supported several account books, guarded transversely by a padlocked iron bar. Against the wall, beneath some samples of calico, one glimpsed a safe, but of such dimensions that it must have contained something beyond notes and silver. Monsieur Lheureux, as a matter of fact, acted as a pawn-broker, and it was here that he kept Madame Bovary's gold chain, as well as the earrings of poor Père Tellier who, forced at last to sell, had bought a meager stock of grocer's goods in Quincampoix where he was dying of his catarrh in the midst of candles less yellow than his face.

Lheureux sat down in his ample rush-bottomed armchair, saying: "What's new?"

"Look here." And she showed him the paper.

"Well, what can I do about it?"

Upon this she lost her temper, recalling the promise he had given her not to make her notes over to others; he agreed.

"But I was forced into it myself; the knife was at my throat."

"And what is going to happen now?" she said.

"Oh, it's very simple: a court order, and then seizure . . . and it's all over!"

She restrained herself, in order not to strike him. She asked him gently if there were not some way to appease Monsieur Vinçart.

"Oh, my, yes, appease Vinçart! You don't know him; he's more ruthless than an Arab."

Nevertheless, Monsieur Lheureux must take a hand in the matter.

"Listen, it seems to me that up to now I've been pretty good to you."

And, opening one of his registers: "Look here."

Then, running his finger up the page:

"Let's see . . . let's see . . . August third, two hundred francs . . . June seventeenth, one hundred and fifty . . . March twenty-third, forty-six . . . In April . . ."

He paused, as if fearing to make some blunder.

"To say nothing of the notes signed by Monsieur, one for seven hundred francs, another for three hundred! As for your little instalment payments, the interest, that keeps going on and on, it's getting confusing. I won't have anything more to do with it!"

She wept, she even called him "her kind Monsieur Lheureux." But still he kept coming back to "that dog Vinçart." In any case, he hadn't a penny, nobody was paying him these days, they were robbing him, a poor shopkeeper like himself couldn't make advances.

Emma fell silent; and Monsieur Lheureux, who was nibbling the feather of a quill pen, must have been made uneasy by her silence, for he went on:

"If I had at least some repayment one of these days, I might be able . . ."

"As far as that goes," she said, "as soon as the balance from Barneville comes in . . ."

"What?"

And, upon learning that Langlois had not yet paid, he seemed greatly surprised. Then, in a honeyed voice:

"And we're agreed, you say . . . ?"

"Oh, whatever you like!"

At this, he closed his eyes to reflect, wrote down a few figures and, declaring that he would be in for a great loss, that it was a ticklish business and that he was bleeding himself, he dictated four notes, each for two hundred and fifty francs, their expiration dates spaced a month apart.

"Provided Vinçart will listen to me! Anyway, it's understood, I don't go back on my word, I'm square as a brick."

After this he casually showed her several new articles of merchandise, but not one of them, in his opinion, was worthy of Madame.

"When I think that here is dress goods at seven sous a meter, and guaranteed fast color! And yet they swallow that! We don't mention what it's made of, naturally . . ." Trying, by this confession of sharp dealing with others, to convince her completely of his probity.

Then he called her back to show her three ells of guipure lace which he had come across recently "at an auction."

"Isn't it beautiful!" Lheureux said. "It's used a lot just now, for antimacassars, that's the style."

And, swifter than a juggler, he wrapped the lace in blue paper and put it into Emma's hands.

"At least let me know . . ."

"Oh, no hurry," he said, turning on his heel.

That evening she urged Bovary to write to his mother, to have her send them immediately the entire remainder of the inheritance. The mother-in-law replied that she no longer had anything: the liquidation was terminated, and there was left for them, in addition to Barneville, six hundred livres a year which she would forward to them punctually.

Then Madame sent bills to two or three patients, and soon made ample use of this method, which was successful. She was always careful to add a postscript: "Do not mention this to my husband, you know how proud he is . . . My apologies . . . Yours sincerely . . ." There were several complaints; she intercepted them.

To make money she began to sell her old gloves, her old hats, old scrap iron; and she bargained rapaciously—her peasant blood drove her to make a profit. Then, on her trips to the city, she bought up secondhand trinkets which Monsieur Lheureux, in the absence of anything else, would certainly take from her. She bought herself ostrich feathers, Chinese porcelain and chests; she borrowed from Félicité, from Madame Lefrançois, from the hostess of the *Croix Rouge,* from everyone, no matter where. With the money she eventually received from Barneville she paid off two notes, the remaining fifteen hundred francs melted away. She borrowed again, and so it went on.

Sometimes, it is true, she tried to calculate, but she discovered things so exorbitant that she was unable to believe in them. Then she would begin again, speedily become confused, abandon the whole matter and think no more about it.

The house was very gloomy now. One saw merchants leaving it with furious faces. There were handkerchiefs hanging on the stoves; and little Berthe, to Madame Homais' great horror, wore stockings with holes in them. If Charles timidly risked a comment, she answered brutally that it was not her fault.

Why these spasms of rage? He explained everything by her former nervous illness; and, reproaching himself for having taken her afflictions for faults, he accused himself of selfishness, wanted to run and embrace her.

"Oh, no!" he thought. "I'd annoy her."

And he stayed where he was.

After dinner he would walk alone in the garden; he would take little Berthe on his knees and, spreading out his medical journal, try to teach her to read. The child, who never studied, would promptly open great sorrowful eyes and begin to cry. Then he would comfort her; he would go and get water in the watering can for her to make rivers in the sand, or break off branches of privet to plant trees in the flower beds, which did little damage to the garden, all choked as it was with tall weeds; so many days' wages were owing to Lestiboudois! Then the child would feel cold and ask for her mother.

"Call your nurse," Charles would say. "You know, darling, your mama doesn't want to be disturbed."

Autumn was beginning and already the leaves were falling . . . as they had done two years before, when she had been ill! When would it all end? . . . And he would go on walking, his hands behind his back.

Madame stayed in her room. No one went up there. She remained there all day long, torpid, barely dressed, and from time to time lighting tablets of harem incense which she had bought in Rouen, in an Algerian's shop. In order not to have that sleeping man stretched out beside her at night, she finally managed, by showing her distaste, to relegate him to the second floor; and she would read until morning, extravagant books in which were orgiastic images and scenes of bloodshed. Often terror would grip her, she would cry out. Charles would hasten to her.

"Ah, go away!" she would say.

Or at other times, more ardently afire with that intimate flame which adultery fed, panting, shaken, consumed with desire, she would open her window, breathe in the cold air, shake her heavy hair out to the wind and, gazing at the stars, yearn for some princely love affair. She would think of him, of Léon. At such times she would have given anything for a single one of those clandestine meetings which appeased her.

Those were her days of festivity. She wanted them to be magnificent! And, when he was unable to bear the expense alone, as happened nearly every time, she generously made up the balance. He tried to get her to understand that they would be as comfortable elsewhere, in some more modest hotel; but she found objections.

One day she drew from her handbag six small silver-gilt spoons (they were old Rouault's wedding gift), requesting him to go immediately and take them to the pawnshop for her; and Léon obeyed, although this proceeding was distasteful to him. He was afraid of compromising himself.

Then, thinking it over, he decided that his mistress was acquiring strange habits, and that it would perhaps not be unwise to part from her.

As a matter of fact, someone had sent his mother a long anonymous letter to warn her that he was "ruining himself with a married woman"; and at once the good woman, envisioning the eternal bugbear of all families, the vague pernicious creature, the siren, the monster who dwells fantastically in the depths of love, wrote to Lawyer Dubocage, his employer, who handled the matter perfectly. He kept Léon for three-quarters of an hour, trying to open his eyes, to warn him of the abyss. Such an intrigue might prove injurious to his setting up in practice later on. He begged him to break it off, and if he would not make this sacrifice in his own interest, let him at least do it for Dubocage!

Léon had at length sworn never to see Emma again; and he regretted not having kept his word, considering all the embarrassment and talk that woman could still bring down upon him, not to mention his fellow clerk's jests which were recounted the next morning around the stove. Then, too, he was about to become chief clerk; it was time to be serious. He therefore renounced the flute, exalted sentiments, imagination: for every ordinary man, in the fire of his youth, if only for one day, one minute, has believed himself capable of tremendous passions, of lofty enterprises. The commonest libertine has dreamed of sultanas; every notary bears within himself the relics of a poet.

He was bored, now, when Emma suddenly burst out sobbing against his chest; and his heart, like those persons who can endure only a certain amount of music at one dose, became dull with indifference to the outcries of a love whose delicacy he no longer perceived.

They knew one another too well to feel that wonder of possession which multiplies the joy of it a hundredfold. She was as disgusted with him as he was weary of her. Emma was rediscovering in adultery all the platitudes of marriage.

But how to shake free of it? It was in vain that she felt humiliated by the baseness of such gratification, she clung to it out of habit, or out of corruption; and every day she became the more obstinately set upon it, draining every pleasure by wishing it to be too intense. She reproached Léon for her disappointed hopes, as if he had betrayed her; and she even longed for a catastrophe which would bring

234

about their separation, since she had not the courage to make the decision.

For all this, she continued to write amorous letters to him in pursuance of the conviction that a woman should always write to her lover.

But, while writing, she envisioned another man, a phantom contrived out of her most ardent memories, the most beautiful passages in her books, her most intense desires; and in the end he became so real, so accessible that she quivered, marveling over it, without, however, being able to imagine him clearly, so indistinct did he become, like a god, beneath the abundance of his attributes. He dwelt in the blue-white country where silken ladders swing from balconies, under the breath of flowers, in the radiance of the moon. She felt him near her, he was going to come and sweep her away entirely, in a kiss. Afterwards she would fall back flat, crushed; for these spasms of unreal love exhausted her more than great debauches.

She now felt an incessant and universal numbness. Frequently she even received writs on stamped paper at which she scarcely glanced. She would have liked to live no longer, or to sleep constantly.

On the day of mid-Lent she did not return to Yonville; in the evening she went to the masked ball. She put on velvet breeches and red hose, with a clubbed wig and a cocked hat over one ear. She danced wildly all night, to the frenzied sound of the trombones; a circle formed about her; and in the morning she found herself on the peristyle of the theater among five or six masqueraders, women in stevedore's costume or sailors, some of Léon's friends, who were discussing going to supper.

The cafés in the neighborhood were full. Down by the docks they found one of the most undistinguished restaurants, the proprietor of which opened a small room for them on the fourth floor.

The men whispered in a corner, doubtless consulting about the expense. There was a clerk, two medical students and an errand boy: what society for her! As for the women, Emma quickly realized by the quality of their voices that they must almost all be of the lowest class. Then she was frightened, pushed back her chair and lowered her eyes.

The others began to eat. She did not eat; her forehead was burning, her eyelids prickled and her skin was like ice. Inside her head she still felt the ballroom floor leaping to the rhythmic pulsation of a thousand dancing feet. Then the odor of the punch combined with cigar smoke made her dizzy. She was fainting: they carried her to the window.

Day was beginning to break, and a great splash of crimson was spreading over the pale sky over toward Sainte-Catherine. The livid river shivered in the wind; there was no one on the bridges; the street lamps were dying.

Meanwhile she revived and happened to think of Berthe, who was sleeping back in Yonville, in the maid's room. But a cart full of iron rods passed, casting a deafening metallic vibration against the house walls.

She slipped away abruptly, got rid of her costume, told Léon that he must go back, and at last was left alone at the *Hotel de Boulogne.* Everything, including herself, was insupportable to her. She yearned to go, escaping like a bird, to recover her youth somewhere, far away, in the immaculate spaces.

She went out, she crossed the boulevard, the Place Cauchois and the Faubourg, to an open street which overlooked the gardens. She walked rapidly, the fresh air quieted her: and little by little the faces of the crowd, the masks, the quadrilles, the chandeliers, the supper, those women, all vanished like mists blown away. Then, returning to the *Croix Rouge,* she flung herself on the bed in the small second-story room where there were illustrations from *La Tour de Nesle.* At four o'clock that afternoon Hivert woke her.

When she reached home Félicité showed her a gray paper behind the clock. She read:

"In pursuance of the bond, in formal executory notice of a judgment . . ."

What judgment? The day before, indeed, someone had brought another paper of which she was unaware; so she was dumfounded at these words:

"Order, in the name of the King, law and justice, to Madame Bovary . . ."

Then, skipping several lines, she read:

"Within not more than twenty-four hours." What? "To pay the total sum of eight thousand francs." And, farther down: "To this she shall be constrained by every legal means, and notably by the authorized seizure of her furnishings and effects."

What to do? . . . It was to be within twenty-four hours; tomorrow! Lheureux, she thought, was very likely trying to frighten her again; for she suddenly recognized all his machinations, the aim of his obliging behavior. What reassured her was the exaggeration of the amount.

However, by buying, not paying, borrowing, signing notes, then renewing those notes which grew larger at each renewal, she had eventually prepared for Monsieur Lheureux a capital which he was impatiently awaiting for his speculations.

She presented herself at his shop with a casual air.

"Do you know what has happened? It's a joke, I suppose!"

"No."

"Why so?"

He turned slowly and said to her, folding his arms:

"Did you think, my dear lady, that I was going to be your provider and banker until the end of the world, just for the love of God? I've got to get back what I've laid out. Let's be just!"

She protested the amount of the debt.

"Too bad! The court recognized it. There's a judgment. You were notified. Besides, it isn't me, it's Vinçart."

"Couldn't you . . . ?"

"Oh, no, nothing!"

"But . . . still . . . let's talk it over."

And she ranted; she had known nothing . . . it was a surprise . . .

"Whose fault is that?" Lheureux said, bowing ironically. "While I'm slaving like a black, myself, you're enjoying yourself."

"Ah, no moralizing!"

"It never hurts," he answered.

She was humble, she pleaded with him; and she even laid her lovely hand, white and long, on the merchant's knee.

"Let me alone! Anyone would think you were trying to seduce me."

"You're a scoundrel!" she cried.

"Oh, oh, how you go on!" he returned, laughing.

"I'm going to let people know what you are. I'll tell my husband . . ."

"Very well. Personally, I'll have something to show your husband."

And Lheureux drew from his safe a receipt for eighteen hundred francs which she had given him at the time of Vinçart's cashing her note.

"Do you think," he added, "that he won't understand your theft, the poor dear man?"

She sank back, more stunned than she would have been by a blow from a club. He walked back and forth between the window and the desk, repeating:

"Oh, I'll show him . . . I'll show him . . ."

Then he came close to her again and, in a gentle voice:

"It's not amusing, I know; after all, nobody has died of it, and since it's the only way left for you to return my money . . ."

"But where will I get any?" Emma said, wringing her hands.

"Oh, nonsense! With friends like yours!"

And he stared at her in a manner so knowing and so terrible that she shuddered through and through.

"I promise you," she said, "I'll sign . . ."

"I've had enough of your signatures!"

"I'll sell . . ."

"Come now!" he said, shrugging. "You haven't anything left."

And he shouted through the Judas window that opened into the shop:

"Annette! Don't forget the three remnants of number 14."

The servant appeared; Emma understood and asked, "How much money it would take to put a stop to all legal action."

"It's too late."

"But if I brought you several thousand francs, a quarter of the whole, a third, almost all?"

"No, no, it's useless."

He pushed her gently toward the stairs.

"I implore you, Monsieur Lheureux, a few more days!"

She was sobbing.

"Oh, fine! Tears!"

"You're driving me to despair."

"That doesn't worry me particularly," he said, closing the door.

7

$\mathcal{S}$HE was stoical the next day
when Monsieur Hareng, the sheriff, with two
witnesses, came to her home to make the official in-
ventory for the seizure.

They began in Bovary's office and did not write down the phrenological head, which was considered as an "instrument of his profession"; but they counted the plates in the kitchen, the pots, the chairs,
the candlesticks and, in her room, all the trinkets in the whatnot.
They examined her dresses, the linens, the dressing-room; and her
existence, even to its most intimate recesses, was spread out like a
corpse for autopsy, before the eyes of these three men.

Monsieur Hareng, buttoned into a meager black suit, wearing a
white cravat and badly stretched trouser-straps, kept repeating from
time to time:

"With your permission, Madame? With your permission?"

Frequently he gave vent to exclamations:

"Charming! . . . Very pretty!"

Then he would return to writing, dipping his pen into the horn
inkwell he held in his left hand.

When they had finished with the rooms they went up to the
storeroom.

There she kept a desk in which Rodolphe's letters were locked.
It had to be opened.

"Ah, a correspondence!" Monsieur Hareng said with a discreet
smile. "But allow me! I must be assured that the box contains nothing else."

And he tipped the papers slightly, as if to make the gold coins
fall out from among them. Then indignation seized her, seeing that
coarse hand with fingers soft and red as slugs, resting upon those
pages over which her heart had beaten.

At last they were gone! Félicité returned. She had sent her out to stand guard and intercept Bovary; and they quickly installed the bailiff's deputy in the attic, where he swore to stay.

During the evening, Charles seemed anxious to her. Emma watched him with a glance full of anguish, thinking that she saw accusations in the wrinkles of his face. Then when her eyes fell upon the hearth decorated with Chinese screens, on the wide curtains, on the armchairs, on all those things, in fact, which had alleviated the bitterness of her life, remorse took hold of her, or rather a vast regret which passion, far from assuaging it, served to augment. Charles placidly stirred the fire, his feet on the andirons.

There was one moment when the bailiff's man, doubtless becoming bored in his hiding place, made a little noise.

"Someone's walking upstairs?" Charles said.

"No," she said. "It's a shutter left open, the wind is moving it."

The following day, a Sunday, she left for Rouen in order to visit all the bankers whose names she knew. They were in the country or traveling. She did not become discouraged, and of those whom she was able to see she asked money, protesting that she must have it, that she would pay it back. Some of them laughed in her face; all refused.

At two o'clock she hurried to Léon's room, knocked at his door. It was not opened. At length he appeared.

"What brings you here?"

"It's disturbing you!"

"No . . . but . . ."

And he confessed that the landlady did not like her lodgers to entertain "women."

"I have to talk to you," she said.

At this, he reached for his key. She stopped him.

"Oh, no. The other place. Our room."

And they went to their room in the *Hotel de Boulogne*.

Upon arriving, she drank a large glass of water. She was extremely pale. She said:

"Léon, you're going to do me a favor."

And, shaking him by his two hands which she was squeezing tightly, she added:

"Listen to me, I need eight thousand francs."

"You must be mad!"

"Not yet."

And at once, relating the story of the seizure, she explained her predicament to him; for Charles was ignorant of everything: her mother-in-law detested her, old Rouault could do nothing; but he, Léon, was going to set out to find this indispensable sum . . .

"How do you expect . . . ?"

"How cowardly you're acting!" she cried.

Then he said stupidly:

"You're exaggerating the trouble. Perhaps with a thousand écus or so that fellow of yours will calm down."

A further reason for trying to do something; it was not possible that he should not find three thousand francs. Besides, Léon could pledge himself in her place.

"Go, try, you must! Oh, try, try! I'll love you very much!"

He went out, returned at the end of an hour and said with a solemn face: "I've been to three people . . . uselessly!"

Then they remained sitting face to face at the two sides of the hearth, motionless, not speaking. Emma shrugged her shoulders, tapping her foot. He heard her mutter:

"If I were in your place, I'd certainly find it!"

"Where, then?"

"At your office!"

And she stared at him.

An infernal boldness was radiated from her blazing eyeballs, and the eyelids drew together in a manner lascivious and inciting, so that the young man felt himself weaken under the mute insistence of this woman who was urging him to crime. Then he took fright and, to avoid any elucidation, he struck his forehead, exclaiming:

"Morel ought to return tonight! He won't refuse me, I hope" (this was one of his friends, the son of a very rich wholesale merchant), "and I'll bring it to you tomorrow," he added.

Emma did not appear to receive this hope with as much joy as he had imagined. Did she suspect the lie? He went on, flushing:

"However, if you haven't seen me by three o'clock, don't expect me any longer, my darling. I must go, now. Good-by!"

He pressed her hand, but he felt it utterly inert. Emma had no longer strength for any emotion.

Four o'clock struck; and she rose to start back to Yonville, obedient as an automaton to the impulse of habit.

Everything, both within herself and without, was forsaking her. She felt lost, revolving at random in illimitable depths; and it was almost with joy that she saw, upon reaching the *Croix Rouge,* the good Homais watching a great box of pharmaceutical supplies being loaded on the *Hirondelle.*

"Delighted to see you!" he said, offering Emma his hand to help her into the *Hirondelle.*

When the blind man appeared as usual at the foot of the hill, he exclaimed:

"I can't understand the authorities tolerating such sinful industries! These unfortunates ought to be locked up, forced to take up some trade. Upon my honor, Progress moves at a snail's pace! We're floundering in the utmost barbarism."

And, familiar as he was with the poor devil, he feigned to be seeing him for the first time, then asked him in a paternal tone:

"Have you had that horrible affliction long, my friend? Instead of getting drunk in taverns, you'd do better to follow a diet."

The blind man went on with his song; he seemed, in any case, all but imbecile. At length Homais opened his purse.

"Look here, here's a sou, give me back two farthings: and don't forget my advice, you'll find yourself the better for it."

Hivert took the liberty of voicing some doubt of its efficacity. But the apothecary guaranteed that he would cure him himself with an antiphlogistic ointment he had compounded, and he gave his address:

"Monsieur Homais, near the market, well enough known."

Emma, overcome with disgust, flung him a five-franc piece over her shoulder. It was her whole fortune. It seemed splendid to her to cast it away in this manner.

The sight of familiar objects moving past before her eyes gradually distracted Emma from her present distress. An intolerable fatigue overwhelmed her, and she reached home stupefied, discouraged, almost asleep.

"Whatever is to come, let it come!" she thought.

And yet, who knew? Why, between one moment and the next, should some extraordinary event not occur? Lheureux might even die.

She was awakened at nine o'clock in the morning by a sound of voices in the square. There was a crowd gathered about the market building to read a great notice pasted to one of the posts, and she saw Justin climbing upon a stone block and tearing at the notice. But just then the game warden laid his hand upon the boy's collar.

Monsieur Homais emerged from the pharmacy, and Mère Lefrançois, in the center of the crowd, appeared to be making a
harangue.

"Madame, Madame!" Félicité cried, coming in. "It's a shame!"

And the poor girl, greatly upset, handed her a piece of yellow
paper she had just torn off the door. Emma read at a glance that
all her possessions were up for sale.

At this, they stared at one another in silence. Servant and mistress
had no secrets from one another. Presently Félicité sighed:

"If I were you, Madame, I'd go to Monsieur Guillaumin."

"You think so?"

And this question meant:

"You who know the household through the servant, has the master
ever spoken of me?"

"Yes, go to him, you'll be doing the right thing."

She dressed, put on her black dress and her jet-beaded hood; and,
in order not to be seen (there were always many people in the
square), she made her way around the village, by the path at the
water's edge.

She reached the lawyer's gate completely out of breath; the sky
was overcast and a few flakes of snow were falling.

At the sound of the bell, Théodore, in a red waistcoat, appeared
on the doorstep; he came to open the gate for her almost familiarly,
as if for an acquaintance, and ushered her into the dining room.

A wide porcelain stove was muttering below a cactus which filled
the niche and, in black wooden frames against the imitation-oak
wallpaper, hung Steuben's *Esmerelda* and Schopin's *Potiphar*. The
laid table, two silver chafing dishes, the crystal doorknobs, the floor
and the furniture all gleamed with a meticulous, English cleanliness;
the windows were decorated, in each corner, with colored glasses.

"Here is a dining room such as I should have," Emma thought.

The lawyer came in, clutching his dressing-gown ornamented with
palms against his body with his left arm, while with the other hand
he took off and quickly replaced his brown velvet cap, pretentiously
cocked to the right side, from which fell the ends of three blond
locks of hair that, growing out of the occipital region, surrounded
his bald pate.

After offering her a seat, he sat down to breakfast, apologizing
profusely for the discourtesy.

"Monsieur," she said, "I wanted to ask you . . ."

"What, Madame? I am listening."

She began to explain her predicament.

Monsieur Guillaumin was aware of it, being secretly associated with the dry-goods merchant, from whom he always obtained the capital for the mortgage loans he was requested to make.

He knew, therefore—and better than she—the long tale of all those notes, small at first, bearing various names as endorsements, spaced at long-term intervals and continually renewed until the day when, assembling all the nonpayment protests, the merchant had instructed his friend Vinçart to institute in his own name whatever proceedings were necessary, not wishing to earn the reputation of a shark among his fellow citizens.

She punctuated her story with recriminations against Lheureux, recriminations to which the notary responded from time to time with a noncommittal word. Eating his chop and drinking his tea, he kept ducking his chin into his sky-blue cravat, pierced by two diamond pins attached with a fine gold chain, and smiling a singular smile in a sugary and ambiguous manner. But, noticing that her feet were damp:

"Come closer to the stove . . . higher up, against the porcelain."

She was afraid of dirtying it. The notary went on in a gallant tone:

"Beautiful things don't harm anything."

Then she made an attempt to appeal to his emotions and, becoming emotional herself, she reached the point of telling him about the stringencies of her household, her penny-pinchings, her needs. He understood that: an elegant woman! And, without interrupting his eating, he turned toward her completely, so that he was brushing his knee against her shoe, the sole of which was curling as it steamed upon the stove.

But when she asked him for a thousand écus, he pursed his lips, then observed that he was extremely sorry not to have had the management of her fortune earlier, for he had a hundred very convenient methods, even for a lady, of turning money to account. It would almost certainly have been possible to invest in excellent speculations, either in the Grumesnil peat-bogs or in Le Havre real estate; and he left her consumed with rage at the thought of the fantastic sums she would undoubtedly have made.

"How is it," he went on, "that you didn't come to me?"

"I don't quite know," she said.

"Why, eh? Did I scare you so much? But I'm the one to be pitied.

We scarcely know one another! Just the same, I'm very devoted to you: you won't doubt that any more, I hope?"

He stretched out his hand, took hers, pressed a voracious kiss upon it, then kept it upon his knee; and he played delicately with her fingers while showering her with comforting words.

His flat voice murmured like a flowing stream; a spark glittered in his pupil through the reflection of his glasses, and his hands crept into Emma's sleeve to stroke her arm. She felt across her cheek the exhalations of uneven breathing. This man was embarrassing her horribly.

She sprang to her feet and said: "Monsieur, I'm waiting!"

"For what?" the notary said, suddenly becoming extremely pale.

"That money."

"But . . ." Then yielding to the irruption of a too violent desire: "Very well, yes! . . ."

He was dragging himself toward her on his knees, unmindful of his dressing-gown.

"Please, stay. I love you!"

He clutched her around the waist.

A tide of crimson surged up into Madame Bovary's face. She drew back with a terrible expression, crying:

"You're taking impudent advantage of my trouble, Monsieur! I am to be pitied, not bought."

And she swept out.

The lawyer was left utterly dumfounded, his eyes fixed upon his handsome tapestry slippers. They had been a love-gift. The sight of them at length consoled him. In addition, he reflected that such an affair would have involved him too deeply.

"What a villain, what a vile creature! . . . What beastliness!" she kept repeating to herself as she sped on nervous feet under the aspens along the road. The disappointment of failure accentuated the indignation of her outraged virtue: it seemed to her that Providence was concentrating upon hounding her and, at this thought, vanity coming to bolster up her ego, never had she had so much esteem for herself, so much contempt for others. She was transported by a spirit of belligerence. She would have liked to strike out at men, spit in their faces, beat them all to pulp; and she continued to stride rapidly ahead, pale, quivering, enraged, searching the empty horizon with tear-filled eyes and, after a fashion, reveling in the hatred that was strangling her.

When she came within sight of her house, a lethargy overcame her. She could go no farther; yet she must; besides, where was there to go?

Félicité was waiting for her at the door. "Well?"

"No," Emma said.

And for a quarter of an hour they discussed together the various people in Yonville who might perhaps be willing to help her. But each time Félicité named someone, Emma replied:

"Is it likely! They wouldn't!"

"And Monsieur about to come home!"

"I know . . . Leave me alone."

She had tried everything. Now there was nothing further to do; and so when Charles came in she was going to say to him:

"Go back. That carpet you're walking on isn't ours any more. In your house you do not own one piece of furniture, one pin, one straw, and it is I who have ruined you, poor man!"

Then a great sob would come, then he would weep copiously and in the end, the first shock over, he would forgive.

"Yes," she murmured, setting her teeth, "he will forgive me, he who could never have enough millions to offer me to make me pardon him for having known me . . . never! Never!"

This idea of Bovary's superiority over her infuriated her. Then, too, whether she confessed or did not confess, sooner or later, tomorrow, he would know about the disaster just the same; so she must look forward to that horrible scene and endure the burden of his magnanimity. The desire came to her to go back to Lheureux: what was the use? To write to her father: it was too late; and perhaps now she was regretting not having yielded to the other, when she heard a horse's hooves in the alley. It was he, he was opening the gate, he was whiter than the plaster wall. Plunging down the stairs, she fled out into the square; and the mayor's wife, who was chatting with Lestiboudois in front of the church, saw her go into the tax-collector's house.

She hurried over to tell Madame Caron. These two ladies climbed up into the attic and, concealed by some linens stretched out upon poles, placed themselves conveniently for seeing the whole interior of Binet's house.

He was alone in his attic, absorbed in copying in wood one of those indescribable ivories composed of crescents, of spheres fitted into one another, the whole thing straight as an obelisk and serving no purpose whatever; and he was cutting the last piece, he was within reach of the goal! In the half-light of his workshop the golden dust streamed from his chisel like a trail of sparks beneath the shoes of a galloping horse: the two wheels spun, rumbled; Binet smiled, his chin tucked down, his nostrils distended, and seemed lost in one of those moments of utter happiness which doubtless attend only unimportant endeavors that divert the intelligence with easy difficulties and gratify it by a realization beyond which there is nothing further to aspire to.

"Ah, there she is!" Madame Tuvache said.

But it was impossible, because of the lathe, to hear what she was saying.

At last the ladies thought that they caught the word *francs*, and Madame Tuvache whispered:

"She's pleading with him, to get a delay for her payments."

"It looks that way," the other returned.

They saw her walking back and forth, examining the napkin rings, the candlesticks, the banister knobs hung against the walls, while Binet stroked his beard with satisfaction.

"Could she have come to order something from him?" Madame Tuvache said.

"But he doesn't sell anything!" her companion objected.

The tax-collector seemed to be listening, squinting his eyes as if he did not understand. She continued in a gentle pleading manner. She moved closer; his breast rose and fell rapidly; they were no longer talking.

"Is she making advances to him?" Madame Tuvache said.

Binet was red to his ears. She took his hands.

"Oh, this is too much!"

And undoubtedly she was suggesting something abominable to him; for the tax-collector—he was courageous, after all, he had fought at Bautzen and at Lutzen, taken part in the French campaign and even been "put up for the cross"—suddenly, as if at sight of a serpent, sprang back to quite a little distance, exclaiming:

"What are you thinking of, Madame? . . ."

"Women like that ought to be whipped!" Madame Tuvache said.

"Where has she got to?" Madame Caron said.

For she had disappeared during these words; then, catching sight of her running along the Main Street and turning to the right as if to reach the cemetery, they lost themselves in conjecture.

"Mère Rollet," she said, upon arriving at the nurse's house, "I'm stifling! Unlace me."

She fell across the bed; she was sobbing. Mère Rollet covered her with a petticoat and remained standing beside her. Then, as she did not answer, the good woman moved away, took up her spinning wheel and began to spin flax.

"Oh, stop it!" Emma muttered, thinking that she heard Binet's lathe.

"What is the matter with her?" the nurse wondered. "Why has she come here?"

She had hurried here, driven by a sort of horror which impelled her away from her house.

Lying on her back, motionless and staring, she discerned objects only vaguely, although she applied her attention to them with idiot persistence. She stared at the scaly spots on the wall, at two bits of firewood smoking end to end, at an elongated spider which was crawling in a crevice of the beam above her head. At last she collected her wits. She remembered . . . One day, with Léon . . . Oh, how far away that was! . . . The sun was shining on the river and the clematis breathed out its fragrance . . . Then, swept along by her memories as by a seething torrent, she presently came upon a recollection of the previous day.

"What time is it?" she asked.

Mère Rollet went out, raised the fingers of her right hand in the direction where the sky was brightest and returned without haste, saying:

"Almost three."

"Ah, thank you, thank you!"

For he was going to come. That was certain! He would have found the money. But perhaps he would go to the house, not suspecting that she was here; and she ordered the nurse to hurry there and bring him back.

"Make haste!"

"But my dear lady, I'm going, I'm going!"

Now she was astonished that she had not thought of him immediately; yesterday he had given his word, he would not break it; and already she saw herself at Lheureux' shop, spreading out her three bank notes on his desk. Then she must invent a story for explaining matters to Bovary. What should it be?

Meanwhile, the nurse was taking a long time about returning. But as there was no clock in the cottage, Emma feared that she might be exaggerating the length of the time. She began to walk about the garden, step by step; she strolled the length of the hedge, in the path, and turned back eagerly, hoping that the good woman might have come back by another way. At last, tired of waiting, beset by suspicions which she kept rejecting, no longer knowing whether she had been there for a century or for a minute, she sat down in a corner, closed her eyes and thrust her fingers into her ears. The gate creaked: she leaped up; before she could speak, Mère Rollet had said:

"There's nobody at your house!"

"What?"

"Oh, nobody at all! And Monsieur is crying. He's calling for you. They're looking for you."

Emma made no answer. She was panting, rolling her eyes about her, while the peasant woman, terrified by her expression, instinctively drew back, believing her to be mad. All at once she struck her forehead, cried out, for the memory of Rodolphe, like a great lightning flash in a murky night, had darted across her mind. He was so good, so tactful, so generous! And besides, if he hesitated to do her this favor, she would certainly be able to force him to do it by recalling to him, in one single glance, their lost love. She set off, therefore, toward La Huchette, without realizing that she was hastening to offer herself to the one who had once so deeply offended her, without the least misgiving of this prostitution.

8

$\mathcal{A}$s she walked she wondered:
"What am I going to say? Where shall I begin?" And the farther she advanced, the more she
recognized the bushes, the trees, the rushes on the hillside, the
château beyond. She found herself caught up once more in the sensations of her first love, and her poor repressed heart expanded with
them, hungrily. A mild wind blew in her face; the snow, melting,
was falling drop by drop from the buds onto the grass.

She entered, as before, by the small gate of the park, then reached
the main courtyard, bordered by a double row of thick-leaved lindens. They swayed their long branches, whispering. The hounds in
the kennel all barked, and the tumult of their voices reverberated
without anyone's appearing.

She went up the long straight staircase with its wooden balusters
that led to the passage floored with dusty stone from which opened
several bedrooms in a row, as in monasteries or inns. His was at the
extreme far end, at the left. When she came to lay her fingers upon
the knob her strength abruptly forsook her. She was afraid that he
might not be there, she almost hoped that he would not, and yet
here was her only hope, her last chance of rescue. She stood for a
minute collecting herself and, strengthening her courage with the
recognition of immediate necessity, she went in.

He was sitting by the fire, his feet on the mantel, smoking a pipe.

"Why, it's you!" he said, bluntly.

"Yes, it's I . . . Rodolphe, I'd like to ask your advice."

And, despite all her efforts, it was impossible for her to open her
lips.

"You haven't changed, you're still charming."

"Oh," she returned bitterly, "they're sorry charms, my dear, since
you scorned them."

He embarked, then, upon an explanation of his behavior, excusing himself in imprecise terms, being unable to invent anything better.

She gave herself up to his words, even more to his voice and the sight of him; so that she gave the appearance of believing—or perhaps did believe—in the pretext for their having broken off; it was a secret upon which depended the honor and even the life of a third person.

"No matter," she said, gazing at him sorrowfully. "I suffered a great deal."

He answered in a philosophical tone:

"Life is like that."

"Has it at least been good to you since our parting?" Emma asked.

"Oh, neither good . . . nor bad."

"Perhaps it would have been better never to have parted."

"Yes . . . perhaps."

"You think so?" she said, moving closer.

And she sighed:

"Oh, Rodolphe, if you knew! I loved you so!"

It was then that she took his hand, and they stood for a time with their fingers entwined—like the first day, at the Exposition! Out of an impulse of pride, he struggled against the stirring of his emotions. But, collapsing upon his breast, she said:

"How did you expect me to live without you? One can't break the habit of happiness! I was desperate. I thought I would die! I'll tell you all about it, you will see. And you, you ran away from me . . ."

For during the past three years he had carefully avoided her, out of that natural cowardice which characterizes the strong sex; and Emma continued with graceful gestures of the head, more artful than an amorous cat:

"You love other women, admit it. Oh, I understand them, you see, I excuse them; you must have seduced them the way you seduced me. You're a màn! You have everything it takes to make women love you. But we'll begin all over, won't we? We'll love each other. See, I'm laughing, I'm happy! . . . Say something!"

And she was exquisite to see, with tears trembling in her eyes like raindrops in a blue chalice.

He drew her to his knees, and with the back of his hand he stroked the sleek bands of her hair in which a last ray of sunlight reflected in the clear twilight like a golden arrow. She bent her head to him;

at last he kissed her eyelids, gently, just touching them with his lips.

"Why, you've been crying!" he said. "Why?"

She burst out sobbing. Rodolphe thought that it was the violent release of her love; as she remained silent, he took this silence for a last vestige of modesty, and he cried:

"Oh, forgive me! You are the only one for me. I've been stupid and wicked! I love you, I'll always love you. What is the matter? Tell me!" He dropped to his knees.

"Very well! . . . I am ruined, Rodolphe. You're going to lend me three thousand francs."

"Why . . . but . . ." he said, slowly rising to his feet, while his features assumed a grave expression.

"You know," she went on rapidly, "that my husband invested his whole fortune with a lawyer; he has run away. We've borrowed; the patients aren't paying their bills. Besides, the liquidation isn't finished; we'll have plenty later on. But today, for want of three thousand francs, we're going to be sold up; right now, this very instant; and counting on your friendship, I came to you."

"Ah," thought Rodolphe who had suddenly become very white, "that's why she came!"

Presently he said very quietly:

"I don't have it, dear lady."

He was not lying. Had he had it, he would doubtless have given it, although it is normally distasteful to make such fine gestures: a financial demand being the coldest and most estranging of all the ill winds that beset love.

At first she stood for a few moments staring at him.

"You haven't got it!"

She repeated several times:

"You haven't got it! . . . I should have spared myself this final shame. You've never loved me. You're no better than the others!"

She was betraying herself, she was destroying herself.

Rodolphe interrupted her, declaring that he was "feeling the pinch" himself.

"Ah, I pity you!" Emma said. "Yes, a great deal."

And, fixing her eyes upon an embossed rifle that glittered in the trophy case:

"But when one is poor, one doesn't put money into gunstocks. One doesn't buy a clock inlaid with mother-of-pearl," she added, pointing to the buhl clock, "nor silver handles for one's whips"—she touched

252

them—"nor watch charms. Oh, he wants for nothing! Even a liquor cabinet in his bedroom; for you love yourself, you live nicely, you have a château, farms, woods, you ride to hounds, you take trips to Paris . . . Yes, when it wouldn't take more than this," she cried, snatching his cuff links from the mantelpiece, "than the least of these trifles! One could raise money on them . . . Oh, I don't want them! Keep them."

And she flung the two cuff links away, their gold chains snapping as they struck the wall.

"But as for me, I would have given you everything, I would have sold everything, I would have worked with my hands, I would have gone out begging in the streets, for a smile, for a look, for the sake of hearing you say 'Thank you!' And there you sit placidly in your easy-chair, as if you hadn't already made me suffer enough. If it hadn't been for you, I could have lived happily, do you know that? What made you do it? Was it a bet? Still, you used to love me, you said so . . . And again just now . . . Oh, it would have been better to send me away. My hands are warm with your kisses, and there, on the carpet, is the spot where you swore an eternity of love, at my knees. You made me believe in it: for two years you kept me in the most magnificent, the most wonderful dream . . . Isn't that so? Our plans to go away, you remember? Oh, your letter, your letter! It broke my heart. And then, when I return to him, to this man who is rich, happy, free, to beg for help which anyone in the world would give, pleading and offering him all my love again, he casts me aside, because it would cost him three thousand francs!"

"I haven't got it," Rodolphe returned with that perfect calm which is held like a shield over repressed anger.

She left. The walls were quaking, the ceiling was crumbling in; and she went back down the long path, stumbling over heaps of dead leaves whirled up by the wind. At last she reached the hollow in front of the gate; she broke her fingernails on the fastening, so great was her haste to open it. Then, a hundred yards farther on, breathless, about to fall, she stopped; and, turning back, she saw once more the impassive mansion, with its park, its gardens, its three courtyards, and all the windows of its front face.

She remained plunged in a stupor, having no further consciousness of herself beyond the pulsing of her arteries which she seemed to hear emanating like muffled music that filled the countryside. The soil beneath her feet was more yielding than a wave, and the plowed lands looked to her like vast brown billows rolling in. All that was in her mind, memories, thoughts, came flying out at once, in a single instant, like the thousand fragments of a firework. She saw her father, Lheureux' office, their bedroom at home, another landscape. Madness was taking hold of her, she was frightened and presently succeeded in collecting herself, although in a confused fashion; for she did not remember the cause of her horrible condition, the question of money. She suffered only for her love, and felt her spirit forsake her through the memory of it as the wounded, dying, feel life flow out through the bleeding wound.

Night was falling, crows were flying.

It suddenly seemed to her that flame-colored globules were bursting in the air like exploding bullets falling to earth, and whirling, whirling down to melt into the snow among the branches of the trees. In the center of each of them, Rodolphe's face appeared. They multiplied, they came closer, entered into her; everything vanished. She recognized the lights of houses, glowing afar in the mist.

Now her predicament, like a chasm, opened out before her. She was panting as if her lungs were about to burst. Then, in a frenzy of heroism that rendered her almost joyful, she ran down the hillside, crossed the cattle-bridge, the path, the lane, the market place, and reached the front of the pharmacist's shop.

There was no one there. She was about to go in, but someone might come at the sound of the bell; and, slipping through the gate, holding her breath, feeling along the walls, she made her way to the door of the kitchen where a candle, standing on the stove, was burning. Justin, in shirt sleeves, was carrying out a dish.

"Ah, they're having dinner. Wait a little."

He returned. She tapped on the window. He came out.

"The key! The one for upstairs, where the . . ."

"What!"

And he stared at her, utterly aghast at the pallor of her face, which stood out white against the black background of the night. She seemed extraordinarily beautiful to him, and awe-inspiring as a spirit; without understanding what she wanted, he had a presentiment of something terrible.

But she went on swiftly, in a low voice, in a soft, dissolving voice: "I want it. Give it to me!"

As the partition was thin, one could hear the clatter of forks against plates in the dining room.

She pretended that she wanted to kill the rats that prevented her from sleeping.

"I'd have to let Monsieur know."

"No. Stay here."

Then, with an air of indifference:

"It's not worth the trouble, I'll tell him about it later. Come, light the way for me."

She went into the passage from which opened the laboratory door. Against the wall hung a key labeled *Capharnaüm*.

"Justin!" the apothecary called, becoming impatient.

"Let's go up."

And he followed her.

The key turned in the lock, and she went straight to the third shelf, so accurately did her memory guide her, snatched up the blue jar, pulled out the stopper, thrust her hand in and, bringing it out full of a white powder, she instantly put it to her mouth.

"Stop!" he screamed, flinging himself upon her.

"Be quiet! Someone might come . . ."

He was desperate, he tried to call out.

"Don't say anything about it. Everything will be blamed on your master."

Then she turned away, suddenly at peace, and almost in the serenity of a duty accomplished.

When Charles, overwhelmed by the news of the seizure, had returned home, Emma had just gone out. He cried out, wept, lost consciousness, but she did not come back. Where could she be? He sent Félicité to Homais' house, to Monsieur Tuvache's, to Lheureux', to the *Lion d'Or*, everywhere; and, in moments of respite from his anguish, saw his reputation destroyed, their fortune lost, Berthe's future ruined! By what cause? . . . Not a word! He waited until six o'clock that evening. At last, no longer able to endure it, and imagining that she must have gone to Rouen, he went out on the highroad, walked more than a mile, met no one, waited again and then walked home.

She had returned.

"What has happened? . . . Why? . . . Explain to me . . ."

She sat down at her desk and wrote a letter which she sealed deliberately, adding the date and the hour. Then she said in a solemn tone:

"You're to read that tomorrow; until then, please, do not ask me a single question. No, not one!"

"But . . ."

"Oh, let me alone!"

And she stretched out full length on her bed.

An acrid flavor which she tasted in her mouth aroused her. She caught a glimpse of Charles and closed her eyes again.

She concentrated intently upon herself, to discover if she were not in pain. But no, nothing yet! She heard the ticking of the clock, the crackle of the fire, and Charles' breathing, as he stood beside the bed.

"Ah, death is a small thing!" she thought. "I am going to go to sleep, and it will all be over."

She drank a mouthful of water and turned toward the wall.

That vile taste of ink persisted.

"I'm thirsty . . . Oh, I'm so thirsty!" she sighed.

"What is wrong with you?" Charles asked, holding a glass out to her.

"Nothing . . . Open the window. I'm smothering."

And she was overcome by a spasm of nausea so sudden that she had barely time to snatch her handkerchief from under the pillow.

"Take it away!" she said sharply. "Throw it out."

He questioned her; she did not answer. She lay motionless, for fear that the least movement might make her vomit. Meanwhile she felt an icy chill creeping up from her feet to her heart.

"Ah, this is the beginning," she murmured.

"What did you say?"

She rolled her head in a small gesture full of anguish, opening her jaws again and again as if something very heavy lay upon her tongue. At eight o'clock the vomiting recommenced.

Charles noticed that in the bottom of the basin there was a sort of white granular substance clinging to the porcelain sides.

"That's odd! That's queer," he kept repeating.

But she said in a loud voice:

"No, you're mistaken."

Delicately, then, and almost as a caress, he passed his hand over her abdomen. She gave a shrill scream. He drew back, terrified.

Then she began to moan, feebly at first. A prolonged shudder shook her shoulders, and she became paler than the sheet into which her clenched fingers dug. Her uneven pulse was now all but imperceptible.

256

Drops of perspiration stood on her bluish face, which looked as if it had been congealed in the effluvium of some metallic vapor. Her teeth rattled, her distended eyes wandered vaguely about her, and to all questions she responded only with a shake of the head; she even smiled two or three times. Gradually her moaning became louder. A hollow scream was forced from her; she insisted that she was feeling better and that she would get up very soon. But she was seized with convulsions; she cried out:

"Oh, my God, this is agony!"

He fell to his knees beside her bed.

"Tell me, what have you eaten? For the love of heaven, speak!"

And he gazed at her with eyes in which there was a tenderness such as she had never seen.

"Well, then, there . . . there! . . ." she said in a faint voice.

He sprang to the secretary, forced the lock and read aloud: "No one is to be blamed . . ." He stopped, brushed his hand across his eyes and read again.

"What! Help! Someone come!"

And he was able only to repeat the word: "Poisoned; poisoned!" Félicité ran to Homais, who shouted it out in the square; Madame Lefrançois heard it at the *Lion d'Or;* some folk rose from their beds to tell their neighbors, and all night long the village was awake.

Distraught, babbling, barely able to stand, Charles was circling about the bedroom. He knocked against furniture, tore at his hair, and never had the pharmacist believed that so appalling a spectacle could exist.

He returned to his shop to write to Monsieur Canivet and to Doctor Larivière. He lost his head; he made more than fifteen false starts. Hippolyte set off for Neufchâtel, and Justin prodded Bovary's horse so violently with his heels that he left it in the Bois-Guillaume hills, foundered and three-quarters dead.

Charles tried to consult his medical dictionary; he could not see it, the lines danced before his eyes.

"Calm down!" the apothecary said. "It's just a matter of administering a powerful antidote. What poison is it?"

Charles showed the letter. It was arsenic.

"Well, then," Homais said, "we'll have to make an analysis of it."

For he knew that, in all cases of poisoning, an analysis should be made; and Bovary, who did not understand, replied:

"Oh, make it, make it! Save her . . ."

257

Then, returning to her side, he sank down upon the carpet and remained there, sobbing, his head pressed against the edge of her bed.

"Don't cry," she said to him. "Soon I shan't be tormenting you any more."

"Why? What made you do it?"

"I had to, my dear," she answered.

"Weren't you happy? Is it my fault? But I did everything I could."

"Yes . . . that's true . . . you are good."

And she stroked his hair with her hand, slowly. The sweetness of this sensation added unbearably to his burden of grief; he felt his whole being crumble within him with despair at the thought that he must lose her just when she was evidencing more love for him than ever before; and he could think of nothing; he did not know, he did not dare, the urgency of immediate decision completing his disorder.

She was done, she thought, with all the treacheries, the vilenesses, the desires that had tormented her. She hated no one, now; a twilight of confusion was settling down over her mind, and of all earthly noises Emma no longer heard any but the intermittent lamentation of that poor heart, soft and indistinct, like the last dying echo of a symphony.

"Bring the little girl to me," she said, pushing herself up on one elbow.

"You're not sick any more, are you?" Charles asked.

"No, no!"

The child came, grave and still half asleep in the maid's arms, her bare feet showing beneath her long white nightdress. She stared with astonishment about the room in all its disorder, blinking her eyes, dazzled by the candles that were burning on every piece of furniture. They must have reminded her of New Year's or mid-Lenten mornings when, wakened thus by candlelight, she came early to her mother's bed to receive her gifts, for she began to ask:

"Where is it, Mother?"

And, as no one spoke:

"But I don't see my little slipper!"

Félicité bent over the bed with her, while she still kept looking toward the hearth.

"Did nurse take it?" she asked.

And at this name which carried her back to the memory of her adulteries and her disastrous affairs, Madame Bovary turned her head away as if in disgust at another stronger poison that rose again to her lips. Berthe, meanwhile, remained perched on the bed.

"Oh, how big your eyes are, Mother! How pale you are, how you're sweating!"

Her mother stared at her.

"I'm scared!" the child said, shrinking back.

Emma took her hand to kiss it; she struggled free.

"That's enough, take her away!" cried Charles, who was sobbing in the alcove.

After this the symptoms subsided briefly; she seemed less agitated; and, at each insignificant word, at each rise and fall of her breast, now somewhat quieter, he took fresh hope. When at last Canivet appeared, he flung himself weeping into his arms.

"Ah, it's you! Thank you, you are kind! But everything is improving. See, look at her . . ."

His colleague was not in the slightest degree of this opinion and —as he himself put it—without "beating about the bush," he ordered an emetic in order to empty the stomach entirely.

Immediately she began to vomit blood. Her lips pinched more tightly together. Her limbs were contracted, her body covered with brown spots, and her pulse slipped beneath the fingers like a stretched wire, like a harp string about to snap.

Then she began to scream, horribly. She cursed the poison, heaped invectives upon it, pleaded with it to hurry, and pushed away with her stiffened arms all that Charles, more anguished than she, forced himself to make her drink. He was standing, his handkerchief at his lips, weeping, his throat rattling, strangled by sobs that shook him to his heels; Félicité was scurrying here and there about the room; Homais, immobile, was sighing deeply, and Monsieur Canivet, still retaining his composure, was nevertheless beginning to feel concerned.

"The devil! . . . still, she's purged, and the moment the cause is removed . . ."

"The effect ought to disappear," Homais said. "Obviously."

"Save her!" Bovary exclaimed.

So, without listening to the pharmacist, who was once more venturing the hypothesis: "It may be a therapeutic paroxysm," Canivet was about to administer the antidote again when the crack of a whip was heard; all the windows shivered and a traveling-coach pulled at full speed by three horses mud-spattered to the ears, came sweeping around the corner of the market building. It was Doctor Larivière.

The apparition of a god would not have called forth more emotion. Bovary flung up his hands, Canivet stopped short and Homais removed his Greek cap long before the doctor entered.

He belonged to the great surgical school of idealistic practitioners sprung from Bichat's example in that generation, now vanished, surgeons who, cherishing their art with a fanatical love, practiced it with enthusiasm and wisdom. In his hospital everyone quaked when he became angry, and his students venerated him to such an extent that, when barely established, they forced themselves to imitate him as closely as possible; so that, throughout the neighboring towns, one kept seeing again and again, upon them, his long quilted merino greatcoat and his ample black coat, the unbuttoned cuffs of which partly covered his firm-skinned hands, fine hands which never wore gloves, as if in order to be more prompt in searching out pain. Scorning decorations, titles and academies, dedicated to the poor and sick, liberal, fatherly with the unfortunate and practicing virtue without believing in it, he might almost have earned the reputation of a saint if the keenness of his wit had not made him feared like a demon. His glance, more penetrating than his scalpels, probed straight to your soul and cut out any falsehood among the allegations and reticences. And so he proceeded, full of that simple majesty which is the gift of the consciousness of a great talent, of fortune, and of forty years' hard-working and irreproachable existence.

On the threshold he frowned, seeing Emma's cadaverous face as she lay stretched on her back, her mouth open. Then, while seeming to listen to Canivet, he stroked his upper lip with his forefinger, repeating:

"That's right, that's right."

But he made a slow gesture with his shoulders. Bovary noticed it: they looked at one another; and this man, although so accustomed to the sight of grief, was unable to restrain a tear which fell upon his ruffled shirt-bosom.

He insisted upon taking Canivet into another room. Charles followed him.

"She's very sick, isn't she? What if we applied mustard plasters . . . something! You find something to do for her, you who have saved so many!"

Charles flung his two arms around the other man and gazed at him with a frenzied, pleading look, half collapsed against his chest. "Come now, be brave, my poor fellow! There's nothing further to do."

And Doctor Larivière turned away.

"You're going?"

"I will be back."

He went out, as if to give an order to his coachman, accompanied by Canivet, who was no more anxious than he to have Emma die on his hands.

The pharmacist joined them in the square. He was temperamentally incapable of parting from these celebrated gentlemen. He therefore begged Monsieur Larivière to do him the immense honor of accepting an invitation to breakfast.

Justin was speedily dispatched to get pigeons from the *Lion d'Or*, all the chops there were in the butcher shop, cream from Tuvache, eggs from Lestiboudois, and the apothecary himself helped in the preparations.

He saw fit, after the first bites, to supply some details about the tragedy:

"I insisted, Doctor, upon attempting an analysis, and *primo,* I delicately inserted into a test tube . . ."

"It would have been more to the point," the surgeon said, "to insert your fingers into her throat."

His colleague remained silent, having just received, privately, a strong reprimand on the subject of his emetic, with the result that the good Canivet, so arrogant and verbose in the case of the club-foot, was extremely retiring today; he kept smiling constantly in an approving manner.

At last Monsieur Larivière was about to leave, when Madame Homais asked for a consultation for her husband. He was thickening his blood by falling asleep every evening after dinner.

"Oh, I shouldn't think his *blood* was too thick."

And, smiling a little over this unnoticed emphasis, the doctor opened the door. But the pharmacy was crammed with people, and he had great difficulty in extricating himself from Monsieur Tuvache, who feared a chest ailment for his wife because she made a habit of spitting into the ashes; then from Monsieur Binet who sometimes felt sudden hunger pangs, and from Madame Caron who had itchings; from Lheureux who had dizzy spells; from Madame Lefrançois who had heartburn. At length the three horses dashed away, and the general opinion was that he had not been at all obliging.

Public attention was distracted by the appearance of Monsieur Bournisien, who was passing through the market building with the holy oils.

Homais, as he owed to his principles, compared priests to carrion crows, attracted by the odor of death; the sight of a clergyman was personally distasteful to him, for the cassock made him think of the shroud, and he reviled the one partly because of his horror of the other. Nevertheless, not recoiling in the face of what he called his "mission," he returned to Bovary's house in the company of Canivet, whom Monsieur Larivière, before leaving, had strongly urged to do so.

The room, when they entered, was full of gloomy solemnity. Upon the worktable, covered with a white napkin, were five or six small balls of cotton in a silver dish, beside a large crucifix, between two lighted candles. Emma, her chin sunk upon her breast, had her eyelids stretched abnormally wide; and her poor hands crept over the sheet in that hideous soft gesture of the dying, who seem to try in advance to pull the shroud about them. Pale as a statue, his eyes red as coals, Charles, tearless, stood facing her at the foot of the bed, while the priest, kneeling on one knee, muttered low-voiced words.

She turned her face slowly, and seemed overcome with joy at suddenly seeing the violet stole, possibly rediscovering in the midst of a singular quiescence the lost ecstasy of her first mystical ardors mingled with visions of eternal bliss which were beginning.

The priest rose to take up the crucifix; she stretched her neck then, like one suffering from thirst and, pressing her lips to the body of the Man-God, with her full dying strength she bestowed upon it the most genuine kiss of love she had ever given. Next he recited the *Misereatur* and the *Indulgentiam,* dipped his right thumb in the oil and began the extreme unctions: first upon the eyes which had so coveted all earthly splendors; then upon the nostrils, hungry for warm breezes and voluptuous fragrances; then upon the mouth which had opened for falsehood, which had moaned from vanity and cried out in lust; then upon the hands, which had reveled in soft touches, and last upon the soles of the feet, once so swift when she had run to the gratification of her desires, and which now would walk no longer.

The curé wiped his fingers, flung the bits of oil-soaked cotton into the fire and returned to sit beside the dying woman to tell her that she was now about to join her sufferings to those of Jesus Christ and to abandon herself to divine mercy.

As he ended his exhortations, he tried to put into her hand a holy taper, symbol of the celestial glories with which she would soon be surrounded. Emma, too weak, could not close her fingers, and had it not been for Monsieur Bournisien the taper would have fallen to the floor.

Meanwhile her pallor had lessened, and her face had an expression of serenity, as if the sacrament had healed her.

The priest did not fail to remark upon this, he even went so far as to explain to Bovary that sometimes the Lord prolonged life for certain persons when He considered it expedient for their salvation; and Charles recalled a day when, close to death like this, she had received Communion.

"Perhaps we shouldn't give up hope," he thought.

Indeed, she was looking all about her, slowly, like one rousing from a dream; then, in a distinct voice, she asked for her mirror, and she remained leaning over it for some time, until the moment when great tears clouded her eyes. At this, she let her head fall back, sighing deeply, and sank down upon the pillow.

At once her breast began to rise and fall rapidly. Her tongue protruded out of her mouth to its full length; her eyes, rolling up, dimmed like two lamp globes burning out, so that one might have thought her already dead had it not been for the terrifying acceleration of her ribs, shaken by furious breathing, as if the soul were leaping to get free. Félicité knelt before the crucifix, and the pharmacist himself bent a little at the knees, while Monsieur Canivet gazed vaguely out into the square. Bournisien had resumed praying, his face bowed against the edge of the bed, with his long black cassock trailing out behind him into the room. Charles was at the other side, kneeling, his arms stretched out toward Emma. He had taken her hands and was pressing them, quivering at each beat of her heart as if in reaction to the collapse of a ruin. The louder the rattling breath became, the more the priest speeded his orisons: they mingled with Bovary's stifled sobs, and sometimes all seemed to be submerged in the hollow muttering of Latin syllables that tolled like a passing-bell.

Suddenly a sound of heavy wooden shoes was heard on the sidewalk, and the tapping of a stick; and a voice was raised, a raucous voice which sang:

> "Warm sun shining from above
> Makes a young girl dream of love."

Emma reared up like a galvanized corpse, her hair hanging, her eyeballs fixed, staring.

> "Diligently gathering
> Ears the scythe has mowed to earth,
> My Nanette goes, bending low
> Toward the soil that gave them birth."

"The blind man!" she screamed.

And she began to laugh, a shocking, phrenetic, despairing laugh, seeming to see before her the beggar's hideous face rising up like a horror amid the eternal night.

> "Strong that day the wind did blow.
> Up her petticoat did go!"

A convulsion flung her back upon the mattress. Everyone gathered about her. She was dead.

9

After anyone's death, there is
always a sort of stupefaction that sets in, so
difficult is it to realize this actuality of nothingness and
to resign oneself to belief in it. When he became aware of her im-
mobility, however, Charles flung himself upon her, crying:

"Good-by! Good-by!"

Homais and Canivet dragged him from the room.

"Control yourself!"

"Yes," he said, struggling free, "I will be reasonable, I won't do
any harm. But let me alone. I want to see her, she's my wife!"

And he burst into tears.

"Cry," the pharmacist said, "let nature take its course; it will relieve you."

Charles, become weaker than a child, let himself be taken downstairs, into the sitting room, and soon Monsieur Homais returned to
his own home.

In the square he was accosted by the blind man who, having
dragged himself to Yonville in the hope of the antiphlogistic ointment, was asking each passer-by where the apothecary lived.

"Oh, fine! As if I hadn't other fish to fry! Well, I'm sorry, come
back later."

And he hurried into the pharmacy.

He had to write two letters, compound a sedative for Bovary, invent a story that might serve to conceal the poisoning and write
it up as an article for the *Fanal*, not to mention the customers who
were waiting to get information; and when the folk of Yonville had
all heard his tale of the arsenic she had mistaken for sugar in making a vanilla cream, Homais returned once more to Bovary's house.

He found him alone (Monsieur Canivet had just left), seated in an armchair beside the window, and gazing with an idiot stare at the flagstones of the floor.

"Now you must fix the time for the ceremony," the pharmacist said.

"Why? What ceremony?"

Then, in a stammering and frightened voice:

"Oh, no. Do I have to? No, I want to keep her."

Homais, to keep in countenance, took a pitcher from the whatnot and watered the geraniums.

"Ah, thank you," Charles said. "You're kind."

And he did not finish, smothering under a wave of memories the pharmacist's gesture recalled to him.

At this, to distract him, Homais thought it advisable to say a few words about horticulture; plants required moisture. Charles nodded in sign of agreement.

"Anyway, the fine weather will be here soon, now."

"Ah!" Bovary said.

"Well, well! There's Monsieur Tuvache going by."

Charles repeated like an automaton:

"Monsieur Tuvache going by."

Homais did not dare say anything further about funeral arrangements; it was the priest who succeeded in resigning him to it.

He locked himself in his office, took up a pen and, after sobbing for a time, he wrote:

"I want her buried in her wedding dress, with white shoes, a garland on her head. Her hair is to be spread out over her shoulders; three coffins, one of oak, one of mahogany, one of lead. No one is to talk to me, I shall be strong. She is to be laid on a big piece of green velvet. I want it done that way. Do it."

The gentlemen were vastly astonished by Bovary's romantic notion, and the pharmacist promptly went to say to him:

"This velvet seems a superfluity to me. Besides, the expense . . ."

"Is it any of your business?" Charles shouted. "Let me alone! You didn't love her. Go away!"

The priest took his arm to make him take a walk about the garden. He spoke of the vanity of earthly things. God was very great, very good; one should submit to His decrees without complaint, even thank Him.

Charles burst out in blasphemies. "I curse Him, your God!"

"The spirit of rebellion is still in you," the clergyman sighed.

Bovary was far away. He was walking with great strides along the wall beside the fruit trees, and he was grinding his teeth, casting looks of malediction toward heaven; but not even a single leaf stirred for all that.

A fine rain was falling. In the end, Charles, whose chest was bare, began to shiver; he went back to the house and sat down in the kitchen.

At six o'clock the sound of iron-bound wheels was heard in the square: it was the *Hirondelle* arriving; and he leaned his head against the windowpane, watching all the passengers climb down one after another. Félicité spread a mattress for him in the parlor; he flung himself upon it and fell asleep.

Although a philosopher, Monsieur Homais respected the dead. So, without cherishing any resentment toward Charles, he returned that evening to watch beside the body, bringing with him three books and a pad of paper for taking notes.

Monsieur Bournisien was there, and two tall candles were burning at the head of the bed which had been pulled out of the alcove.

Charles entered and, moving toward the bed, he slowly drew back the curtains.

Emma lay with her head bent toward her right shoulder. The corner of her mouth, which hung open, made a sort of black hole in the lower part of her face, her two thumbs were still bent in upon the palms of her hands; a kind of white dust sprinkled her eyelids, and her eyes were beginning to disappear beneath a viscous film that resembled a thin fabric, as if spiders had spun a web over them. The sheet was hollowed between her breasts and her knees, sloping up from there to the tips of her toes; and it seemed to Charles that immeasurable masses, that an enormous weight was pressing down upon her.

He placed himself opposite her in order to see her better, and he lost himself in this contemplation which was no more painful for being profound.

He kept remembering stories of catalepsy, the miracles of magnetism; and he told himself that by wishing it with the utmost concentration he might perhaps succeed in reviving her. Once he leaned toward her and cried aloud: "Emma, Emma!" His breath, violently expelled, made the candle flames flicker against the wall.

At dawn, Madame Bovary, his mother, arrived; Charles was seized by a fresh outburst of tears as he embraced her. She tried, as the pharmacist had done, to make a few comments upon the expenses of the burial. He flew into so furious a rage that she fell silent, and he even persuaded her to go immediately to the city to buy what was necessary.

Charles remained alone all afternoon; Berthe had been taken to Madame Homais, Félicité kept to her room upstairs, with Madame Lefrançois.

That evening he received visitors. He rose, shook hands, unable to speak, then the newcomer sat down beside the others who made a wide half-circle before the hearth. Heads down and ankles on knees, they jiggled their legs, sighing deeply at intervals; and everyone was immeasurably bored, yet they vied with one another as to who would stay longest.

Upon his arrival, the curé asked how Monsieur was feeling; and, at the apothecary's reply, he said:

"The blow is still too recent, you see."

At this Homais congratulated him upon not being in a position, like other people, to lose a dearly beloved companion; from which evolved an argument on the celibacy of priests.

"For it's not natural," the pharmacist said, "for a man to do without women. There are instances of crimes . . ."

"But for goodness' sake!" the clergyman shouted. "How do you expect a married man to keep the secrets of the confessional, for instance?"

The sound of incessant baying rose and fell, somewhere far away.

"Do you hear a dog howling?" the pharmacist said.

"They claim dogs smell death," the priest answered. "It's like bees: they fly out of the hive when people die." Homais did not correct these superstitions, for he had fallen asleep.

Monsieur Bournisien, being sturdier, continued for some time to move his lips softly; then, very gradually, he dropped his chin, let fall his thick black book and began to snore.

Charles did not wake them, coming in. It was the last time. He had come to say good-by to her.

The watermarks shimmered on the satin gown, white as moonlight. Emma was vanishing beneath it; and it seemed to him that, flowing out beyond herself, she was being lost, dissipated in things that pressed in: in the silence, in the darkness, in the wind that blew past, in the damp fragrances that rose from below.

Then, suddenly, he saw her in the garden at Tostes, on the bench, in front of the thorn hedge, or in Rouen, in the streets, on the threshold of their house, in the courtyard at Les Bertaux. He heard again the laughter of young men making merry, dancing under the apple trees; the room was full of the scent of her hair, and her gown shivered in his arms with a sound of sparks. That was the same, the same one!

He stood long, remembering thus all the vanished delights, her attitudes, her gestures, the quality of her voice. After one moment of despair, another came to him, and another and another, inexhaustibly, like the waves of an incoming tide.

He was seized by a terrible curiosity: slowly, with the tips of his fingers, quaking, he raised her veil. But he gave a cry of horror which waked the other two. They drew him downstairs, into the sitting room.

Later Félicité came to say that he was asking for a lock of hair. "Cut one off," the apothecary said.

And, as she did not dare, he came forward himself, scissors in hand. He was shaking so violently that he pierced the skin of the temples in several places. At last, stiffening himself against emotion, Homais slashed two or three times at random, leaving white patches among that beautiful black hair.

The pharmacist and the curé plunged once more into their occupations, not without falling asleep from time to time, for which they mutually reproached each other at each new awakening. Then Monsieur Bournisien sprinkled the room with holy water and Homais scattered a little chlorine on the floor.

Félicité had taken care to set out for them, on the chest of drawers, a bottle of brandy, a cheese and a large brioche. So at four o'clock in the morning the apothecary, who could stand it no longer, sighed: "My word, I'd take a little sustenance with pleasure!"

The clergyman did not have to be coaxed; he went out to say his Mass, returned; then they ate and clinked glasses, snickering a little without knowing why, stimulated by that sourceless gaiety which lays hold of us after periods of sadness: and, at the last little glass, the priest said to the pharmacist, slapping him on the shoulder: "We'll end up understanding each other!"

Downstairs, in the vestibule, they met the workmen who were arriving. Then, for two hours, Charles was forced to endure the torture of the hammer resounding on the boards. After that she was brought down in an oak coffin, which was encased in the two others; but as the bier was too large, the spaces had to be stuffed with wool from a mattress. At last, when the three caskets had been planed, nailed, soldered, she was placed on view before the door; the house was flung open, and the folk of Yonville began to pour in.

Old Rouault arrived. He fainted in the square upon catching sight of the black pall.

10

HE had not received the phar-
macist's letter until thirty-six hours after the
event; and out of consideration for his sensibility, Monsieur Homais had composed it in such a fashion that it was impossible to know what to believe.

He reached the point of supposing that this was perhaps a practical joke, an act of revenge on someone's part, the notion of a man
in a prankish mood; and besides, if she were dead, one could tell.
He came in sight of the village; they saw him pounding along, leaning flat over his horse, which he was flogging mercilessly and whose
saddle girths were flecked with blood.

When he regained consciousness he fell weeping into Bovary's
arms.

"My daughter! Emma, my child! Explain to me . . ."

And the other answered through sobs:

"I don't know, I don't know. It's a curse!"

The apothecary separated them.

"These horrible details are futile. I'll inform Monsieur of them.
Here are people coming. Dignity, confound it! A philosophical
attitude!"

The poor young man wanted to appear strong, and he repeated
several times: "Yes . . . courage!"

"Well," cried the old man, "I'll have that, by God! I'm going to
go with her to the end."

The bell was tolling. All was ready. They had to start.

And, sitting side by side in a choir stall, they saw the three cantors
pace constantly back and forth, chanting psalms. The bass horn rumbled, full-throated. Monsieur Bournisien, in full panoply, sang in a
shrill voice; he saluted the tabernacle, raised his hands, stretched
out his arms. Lestiboudois moved about the church with his strip of

whalebone; the casket stood near the lectern, between four rows of tapers. Charles had an impulse to stand up and put them out.

They chanted, they knelt, they rose again, there was no end to it! He remembered that once, in the early days, they had attended Mass together, and they had sat on the other side, at the right, against the wall. The bell began again. There was a great scraping of chairs. The pallbearers slipped their three poles under the casket, and they left the church.

Just then Justin appeared on the doorstep of the pharmacy. He went back inside at once, pale, tottering.

The black pall, sown with white teardrops, lifted from time to time, exposing the casket. The weary pallbearers walked more slowly; and she advanced by continuous jerks, like a small boat that pitches at every wave.

They arrived at the cemetery.

The men continued on to the far end, to a spot in the grass where the grave had been dug.

They ranged themselves all around it; and while the priest spoke, the red earth flung out on the edges kept trickling down at the corners, soundlessly, incessantly.

Then, when the four ropes had been adjusted, the casket was pushed over them. He watched it sink down. It kept sinking forever.

At last a bump was heard; the ropes came creaking up. Now Bournisien took the spade held out to him by Lestiboudois; with his left hand, while sprinkling holy water with his right, he vigorously prodded a large shovelful; and the wood of the coffin, struck by the pebbles, made that ghastly sound which seems to us to be the reverberation of eternity.

The priest passed the aspergill to his neighbor. It was Monsieur Homais. He shook it gravely, then handed it to Charles, who sank to his knees in the earth and cast handfuls of it into the grave, crying, "Good-by!" He threw her kisses; he dragged himself toward the grave to be buried there with her.

He was led away; and he soon became quieter, experiencing, perhaps, like everyone else, the vague satisfaction of being done with it.

Old Rouault, returning to the house, began placidly to smoke a pipe; which Homais, in his inner consciousness, considered most unsuitable. In the same spirit he observed that Monsieur Binet had refrained from appearing, that Tuvache "had dodged out" after the Mass, and that Théodore, the notary's servant, was wearing a blue suit, "as if he couldn't have got hold of a black one, since it's customary, damn it!" And, in order to communicate his observations, he kept moving from group to group. Everyone was deploring Emma's death, particularly Lheureux, who had not failed to be present at the burial.

"That poor little woman! What a grief to her husband!"

The apothecary answered:

"If it had not been for me, you know, he would have made a tragic attempt upon his own life."

"Such a good person! And to think that I saw her in my shop only last Saturday."

"I didn't have the time," Homais said, "to prepare a few words which I would have cast upon her grave."

Upon returning to the house, Charles undressed and old Rouault put on his jacket again. It was new, and as he had frequently wiped his eyes on the sleeves during his ride, some of the color had run onto his face; and the traces of tears made trails in the layer of dust that dirtied it.

Charles' mother was with them. They were all silent. At length the old man sighed:

"You remember, my friend, how I came to Tostes one time when you had just lost your first wife. I consoled you then. I found something to say; but now . . ."

Then, with a long groan which lifted his chest:

"Ah, this is the end for me, I tell you! I saw my wife go . . . next my son . . . and now my daughter, today."

He insisted upon returning at once to Les Bertaux, saying that he would be unable to sleep in this house. He even refused to see his granddaughter.

"No, no, it would make me too sad. Only you give her a big kiss for me. Good-by . . . you're a good boy. And besides, I'll never forget this," he said, tapping his thigh. "Never fear! You'll still get your goose."

That evening Charles and his mother, despite their weariness, sat very late talking together. They spoke of days gone by and of the future. She would come to live in Yonville, she would keep house for him; they would never part again. She was artful and caressing, inwardly rejoicing at reclaiming an affection of which she had been deprived for so many years. Midnight struck. The village was silent, as usual, and Charles, wakeful, was still thinking of her.

Rodolphe, who had been hunting all day long to distract himself, slept tranquilly in his château; and Léon, in the city, slept too.

There was one other who, at that hour, was not asleep.

Upon the grave, among the pine trees, a child was weeping, on his knees, and his chest, bursting with sobs, heaved in the shadows under the pressure of a vast sorrow, softer than the moonlight and more unfathomable than the night. Suddenly the gate creaked. It was Lestiboudois; he had come in search of his spade which he had left behind earlier. He recognized Justin scaling the wall, and knew then what the truth was about the malefactor who had been stealing his potatoes.

11

$\mathscr{C}$HARLES had the little girl
brought back the next day. She asked for her
mother. They told her that she was away, that she would
bring back toys. Berthe spoke of her again several times; then, at
length, she no longer thought of her. The child's gaiety overwhelmed
Bovary, and he had to submit to the pharmacist's intolerable consolations.

Soon the financial difficulties began again, Monsieur Lheureux
once more egging on his friend Vinçart, and Charles pledged enormous sums; for he would never consent to allow one least article
which had belonged to *her* to be sold. His mother was exasperated
by this. He became more angry than she. He had changed entirely.
She left the house.

Then everyone began to take advantage. Mademoiselle Lempereur demanded payment for six months' lessons, although Emma
had never taken a single one (despite the receipted bill she had
shown Bovary): it had been an agreement between the two women;
the lending library demanded payment for a three-year subscription; Mère Rollet demanded payment for having delivered a score
of letters; and, as Charles requested an explanation, she had the
delicacy to answer:

"Oh, I don't know anything about it, it was business."

At each debt he paid, Charles thought that this was the end of
them. Others kept coming in, endlessly.

He tried to collect overdue payments for professional visits. He
was shown the letters his wife had sent out. Then he was obliged
to apologize.

Félicité now wore Madame's dresses; not all, for he had kept some
of them, and he would go and lock himself up in her dressing-room
and look at them; she was of almost the same build, often Charles,

seeing her from behind, was gripped by an illusion and cried out: "Oh, stay! Stay!"

But at Pentecost she departed from Yonville, carried off by Théodore, and stealing all that was left of the wardrobe.

It was about this time that Madame Dupuis, widow, had the honor of announcing "the marriage of her son, Monsieur Léon Dupuis, lawyer of Yvetot, to Mademoiselle Léocadie Leboeuf, of Bondeville." Charles, among the congratulations he offered him, wrote this phrase:

"How happy my poor wife would have been!"

One day when, wandering aimlessly about the house, he had gone up to the attic, he felt beneath his slipper a wad of thin paper. He opened it and read: "Be brave, Emma, be brave! I cannot bring myself to ruin your life." It was Rodolphe's letter, fallen to the floor among some boxes, which had remained there and which the draft from the dormer window had blown toward the door. And Charles stood motionless and gaping in that same spot where long before, even paler than he, Emma, in despair, had wished to die. At length he discovered a small *R* at the foot of the second page. Who was it? He remembered Rodolphe's attentions, his sudden disappearance and the air of constraint he had had on the two or three occasions when he had met him since. But the respectful tone of the letter deceived him.

"Perhaps they loved each other platonically," he thought.

In any case, Charles was not one of those who delve to the bottom of things; he shrank from proofs, and his uncertain jealousy was lost in the immensity of his sorrow.

People must have adored her, he thought. Certainly all men had desired her. She seemed the more beautiful to him for that; and because of it he conceived a lasting, furious desire that intensified his despair and had no limit, because it was now incapable of being realized.

To please her, as if she were still alive, he adopted her predilections, her ideas; he bought himself polished boots, he formed the habit of wearing white cravats. He waxed his mustache, he signed demand notes, as she had done. From beyond the grave she was corrupting him.

He was obliged to sell the silverware, piece by piece, then he sold the drawing-room furniture. All the rooms became barren; but the bedroom, her bedroom, remained as before. After his dinner, Charles would go there. He would push the round table in front of the fire, and bring up *her* easy-chair. He would sit down opposite. A candle would be burning in one of the gilded candlesticks. Beside him, Berthe colored pictures.

Now no one came to visit them; for Justin had run away to Rouen where he had become a grocer's boy, and the apothecary's children associated less and less with the little girl. Monsieur Homais was not anxious, considering the difference in their social positions, that the intimacy should be continued.

The blind man, whom he had been unable to cure with his ointment, had returned to the Bois-Guillaume hill, where he related the pharmacist's vain attempt to passengers, to such a point that Homais, when he traveled to the city, hid himself behind the *Hirondelle's* curtains in order to avoid facing him. He reviled him; and, in the interests of his own reputation, wishing to be rid of him at all costs, he directed a hidden attack against him which revealed the depth of his intelligence and the atrociousness of his vanity. For six consecutive months there appeared in the *Fanal de Rouen* short paragraphs to this effect:

"All persons who set forth toward the fertile lands of Picardy will undoubtedly have noticed, upon the Bois-Guillaume rise, a wretched creature afflicted with a horrible facial sore. He importunes you, persecutes you and levies an actual tax upon the passengers. Are we still in the monstrous times of the Middle Ages, when beggars were permitted to spread in our public squares the leprosies and scrofulas they had brought back from the Crusades?"

Or:

"Despite the laws against beggary, the outskirts of our great cities continue to be infested by bands of paupers. One sees some of them who operate individually and who are not, perhaps, the least dangerous. What are our lawmakers thinking of?"

Then Homais invented anecdotes:

"Yesterday, on the Bois-Guillaume rise, a skittish horse . . ." And there followed the tale of an accident caused by the presence of the blind man.

He succeeded in getting him jailed. But he was released. He began again, and Homais too began again. It was a battle. He won the victory; for his enemy was condemned to perpetual seclusion in a poorhouse.

This success emboldened him; and from that time on not a dog was run over in the district, not a barn burned down, not a woman beaten but he at once informed the public of it, always guided by love of progress and hatred of priests. He drew comparisons between primary schools and lay-brothers, to the detriment of the latter, recalled Saint Bartholomew in connection with a grant of one hundred francs made to the church and denounced abuses, launched campaigns. This was his own word. Homais was undermining; he was becoming dangerous.

He was stifling, however, within the narrow confines of journalism, and soon he needed the space of a book, an opus! So he composed *General Statistics of the Yonville District, followed by Climatic Observations*, and statistics impelled him toward philosophy. He became preoccupied with great questions: social problems, moralization on the lower classes, pisciculture, rubber, railroads and the like. He reached the point of blushing at being a middle-class citizen. He affected the "artistic manner," he smoked! He bought himself two elegant Pompadour statuettes to decorate his drawing-room.

Charles and he made a trip together to Rouen to look at tombstones at a monument-maker's, accompanied by an artist, a painter named Vaufrylard, a friend of Bridoux' who constantly made puns. At last, having examined a hundred designs, ordered an estimate and made a second trip to Rouen, Charles decided upon a mausoleum which was to bear upon both of its principal sides "a genie holding an extinguished torch."

One strange thing was that Bovary, while thinking constantly of Emma, was forgetting her; and he was in despair at feeling that image escape from his memory in the midst of the efforts he was making to retain it. Each night, however, he dreamed of her; it was always the same dream: he was moving toward her, but when he came to embrace her she crumbled away to putrescence in his arms.

In spite of the sparing fashion in which Bovary lived, he was far from being able to pay off his old debts. Lheureux refused to renew any of his notes. Seizure became imminent. Then he appealed to his mother, who consented to let him take out a mortgage on her possessions, but added lengthy recriminations against Emma; and she asked, in return for her sacrifice, a shawl which had escaped Félicité's ravages. Charles refused it. They quarreled.

She made the first overtures toward patching it up by suggesting that she take the little girl to live with her and help her about the house. Charles agreed to this. But, at the moment of her departure, all courage forsook him. This time the break was definite, complete.

As his other ties disappeared, he clung more and more closely to the love of his child. Yet she caused him concern, for she coughed sometimes, and had red patches over her cheekbones.

Opposite him, flourishing and merry, paraded the family of the pharmacist, to whose satisfaction they all contributed. Napoléon was assisting him in the laboratory, Athalie was embroidering him a Greek cap, Irma was cutting out circles of paper to cover jelly jars, and Franklin could recite the table of Pythagoras in one breath. He was the happiest of fathers, the most fortunate of men.

An error! A secret ambition was gnawing him: Homais desired the Cross. He was not lacking in claims to it:

First, at the time of the cholera, having been distinguished by a limitless devotion to duty; second, having published, and at my own expense, various works of public benefit, such as . . . (and he recalled his monograph entitled: *Upon Cider, Its Manufacture and Its Effects;* further, some observations on the laniferous plant-louse which had been sent to the Academy; his volume of statistics and even his pharmacist's thesis); not to mention that I am a member of several learned societies (he was a member of one).

"Anyway," he cried, making a pirouette, "if it's only to make me conspicuous at fires!"

Then Homais bowed to Power. He rendered Monsieur le Préfet great services, secretly, in the elections. He sold himself, indeed, prostituted himself. He even addressed to the King a petition in which he appealed to him to "see that justice was done him"; he called him "our good king" and compared him to Henry IV.

And every morning the apothecary flung himself upon the newspaper to discover his nomination in it; it did not materialize. At last, no longer counting upon it, he had a grassplot designed in his garden, representing the star of honor, with two small twisted streamers of grass coming down from the top to imitate the ribbons. He would walk around it, his arms folded, meditating upon the ineptitude of the government and the ingratitude of mankind.

Out of respect, or out of a sort of sensuality which caused him to be deliberate about his investigations, Charles had not yet opened the secret compartment of the rosewood desk which Emma had been accustomed to use. Eventually, one day, he seated himself before it, turned the key and pushed the spring. All of Léon's letters were there. No more doubt, this time! He devoured them down to the last one, fumbled in all the corners, all the furniture, all the drawers, behind the walls, sobbing, crying out, distracted, mad. He discovered a box, smashed it with a blow of his foot. Rodolphe's portrait leaped out at him, full in the face, in the midst of tumbled love letters.

People were astonished at his loss of heart. He no longer went out, received no one, even refused to go and see his patients. It was said, therefore, that he "shut himself up to drink."

Sometimes, however, an inquisitive person would crane over the garden hedge and be shocked at seeing that man with his long beard, covered with filthy garments, wild-eyed, weeping aloud as he walked.

On summer evenings he would take his little girl with him and lead her to the cemetery. They would return after nightfall, when there was no other light in the square than Binet's dormer window.

Still, the gratification of his grief was incomplete, for he had no one about him who shared it; and he paid visits to Mère Lefrançois in order to talk about *her*. But the innkeeper listened with only one ear, having troubles of her own, for Monsieur Lheureux had just established the *Favorites de Commerce,* and Hivert, who enjoyed a great reputation as a runner of errands, was demanding a wage rise and threatening to take service "with the Competitors."

One day when he had gone to the Argeuil market to sell his horse —his last resource—he met Rodolphe.

They paled upon catching sight of one another. Rodolphe, who had merely sent his card, first stammered a few apologies, then became bolder and even carried self-confidence to the length of inviting him to have a bottle of beer at the tavern (it was very warm, it was in the month of August).

Leaning on his elbows opposite him, he chewed his cigar as he talked, and Charles lost himself in reverie, faced with those features that she had loved. He seemed to recapture something of her. It was an amazing thing. He would have liked to be that man.

The other continued to talk farming, cattle, fertilizer, plugging with banal phrases every gap into which an allusion might slip. Charles was not listening to him; Rodolphe became aware of this, and traced the passage of his memories upon the mobility of his features. They were crimsoning little by little, the nostrils fluttered rapidly, the lips were quivering; there was even an instant when Charles, full of a somber rage, fixed his eyes upon Rodolphe, who interrupted himself in a sort of terror. But soon the same gloomy lassitude reappeared upon his face.

"I don't bear you a grudge," he said.

Rodolphe remained silent. And Charles, his head in his two hands, went on in a stifled voice and with the resigned accent of infinite grief:

"No, I don't bear you a grudge any more!"

He even added a great observation, the only one he had ever made:

"It was the fault of destiny!"

Rodolphe, who had directed that particular destiny, thought him very good-natured for a man in his situation, comical even, and a bit vile.

The next day Charles went to sit on the bench in the arbor. Daylight filtered in through the trellis; vine leaves traced their shadows on the sand, the jasmine breathed out its fragrance, the sky was blue, flies were buzzing about the flowering lilies, and Charles was smothered like an adolescent beneath the vague amorous effluvia that swelled his grieving heart.

At seven o'clock little Berthe, who had not seen him all afternoon, came to fetch him for dinner.

He was sitting with his head tipped back against the wall, his eyes closed, his mouth open, and held in his hands a long lock of black hair.

"Come, Papa!" she said.

And, thinking that he wanted to play, she pushed at him gently. He fell to the ground. He was dead.

Thirty-six hours later, at the apothecary's request, Monsieur Canivet came. He opened the body and found nothing.

When everything had been sold, there remained twelve francs seventy-five centimes, which served to pay for Mademoiselle Bovary's journey to her grandmother. The good woman died within the year; old Rouault was paralyzed, it was an aunt who took charge of the girl. She is poor, and sends her to a cotton mill to earn her living.

Since Bovary's death, three doctors have followed one another in Yonville, without being able to succeed, so prompt has Monsieur Homais been to open fire upon them. He is building up a spectacular practice; authority deals kindly with him and public opinion protects him.

He has just received the cross of the Legion of Honor.